IN
HER
SHADOW

ALSO BY MARK EDWARDS

WITH LOUISE VOSS

IN
HER
SHADOW

MARK
EDWARDS

THOMAS & MERCER

Text copyright © 2018 by Mark Edwards
All rights reserved.

Published by Thomas & Mercer, Seattle

www.apub.com

Amazon, the Amazon logo, and Thomas & Mercer are trademarks of Amazon.com, Inc., or its affiliates.

ISBN-13: 9781503948082
ISBN-10: 1503948080

Cover design by Ghost Design

Printed in the United States of America

Jessica had to stop herself from saying, 'Yes, Mrs Rose.' Instead she said, 'I'll talk to Olivia and remind her about the importance of sharing and how we shouldn't call each other names. And I'll also remind her that she needs to do as she's told at school.'

Jessica went to get up, but the teacher cleared her throat.

'There's one more thing.'

Oh God, now what? Jessica sat back down. She glanced over at Olivia, who was still happily listening to Mr Cameron read the Mog book.

'I'm not sure if I should mention it,' Mrs Rose said.

'Well, you have to tell me now.'

The teacher flicked her gaze towards Olivia, just for a second. 'This morning, I asked Olivia to sit with me to practise her numeracy and she completely ignored me. When I asked her again, she looked me in the eye and said, "Izzy doesn't want me to."'

Jessica stared at her.

'I asked her if she was playing a game and she gave me this look, as if I was crazy. Then she said, "Izzy thinks numeracy is boring." I told her that it isn't boring, that it's a lot of fun.'

'*Izzy thinks?*'

Mrs Rose nodded. 'I'm sure it's nothing. We've had a lot of imaginary friends visit the classroom over the years. But I wondered if Izzy was on her mind for any reason?'

Jessica thought about it. 'No. I mean, we talk about Isabel at home. Olivia knows who she is. Was.' She swallowed, then a memory came back to her. 'I think I know what it is. My mum was saying last week how much Olivia reminds her of Isabel. Olivia must have overheard.'

'That must be it,' said Mrs Rose, pushing herself to a standing position. She looked sad and Jessica wondered if she was remembering when Izzy was a little girl. 'Your mum has said the same thing to me, in fact.'

other little girl asked Olivia if she could have a go and Olivia refused. Mr Cameron was supervising them and when he told Olivia that it was someone else's turn, Olivia got very cross.'

'Right.'

'She kicked the bike over and told the other girl she was a poohead.'

Jessica just about managed to suppress a laugh. Mrs Rose, though, wasn't amused.

'The other little girl was very upset.'

'I can imagine. But it sounds like pretty normal four-year-old behaviour,' Jessica said. 'Squabbling over toys. Calling each other silly names. It's not like she punched her and told her to eff off.'

Mrs Rose pursed her lips.

'Sorry. I'll have a word with her,' Jessica said, cringing. 'Tell her it's unacceptable.'

'Hmm. Well, the problem is, this is just the latest in a series of incidents.'

Jessica had been about to haul herself off the tiny chair. Now her attention snapped back to Mrs Rose. 'Really?'

Mrs Rose nodded. 'None of them serious. Just little things. Refusing to share. Not doing what she's asked to do first time.'

'Why did nobody speak to me about this?'

'I assumed your husband would. I had a word with him a couple of weeks ago.'

'Oh.' Jessica felt her cheeks colour. Will hadn't said anything but, rather than admit this, she said, 'Actually, he did mention it. Sorry, I forgot. But . . . maybe you could remind me?'

Mrs Rose gave her a tight smile. 'Just little things. Not listening or cooperating. Being reluctant to put her coat on at the end of the day. Snatching toys from other children.'

'She has only just turned four,' Jessica pointed out.

'I know. And I realise children are expected to do a lot these days. I just wanted you to be aware, so we can all work together.'

Olivia's name.

What had she done?

The classroom assistant, Mr Cameron, a lanky guy who was around Jessica's age, gave Jessica a sympathetic smile that made her worry even more.

'Why don't you take Olivia over to the reading corner?' Mrs Rose suggested when all the other children were gone, and Mr Cameron took Olivia's hand and led her to an area filled with beanbags and books. Jessica watched her daughter settle down with *Mog on Fox Night*, the classroom assistant pointing at the pictures and immediately drawing Olivia into the story.

'She loves books,' Jessica said as Mrs Rose took a seat on a tiny chair that made her look like Alice after she'd consumed the 'Eat Me' cake. Jessica sat down too. Nichola Rose, who was fast approaching retirement, had been a teacher in Beckenham for forty years, most of that time spent here at Foxgrove Primary. She had taught both Jessica and her sister, Isabel, when they were at infant school back in the eighties. And though Mrs Rose looked a lot different these days, facing her across the little table threw Jessica back in time to her own childhood. She had been Jessica Brooks then. Jessica and Isabel Brooks, briefly and excruciatingly famous.

'We had a little bit of an incident with Olivia today,' Mrs Rose said, pulling Jessica – now Jessica Gardner – back to the present.

'What happened?'

'I'm afraid Olivia got into a fight with another girl.'

Jessica thought she must have misheard. 'A *fight*?'

Mrs Rose held up a hand. 'Okay, perhaps "fight" is the wrong word. A quarrel. It was at break time. Olivia was playing on the bikes . . .' She nodded in the direction of the playground. Jessica had seen the bikes – actually, trikes – in question. Small and yellow with no pedals, the children scooted them along the ground. 'We encourage the children to take turns and Olivia had been on one for a while. This

Chapter 1

The moment Jessica reached her daughter's classroom door, Mrs Rose leaned out and said the phrase Jessica dreaded more than any other.

'Can I have a word, please?'

They were only six weeks into the school year – the all-important reception year – and Olivia had turned four at the end of August, making her one of the youngest children in the class. For the first few weeks she had clung to her mother every morning, refused to speak to the teachers, cried when she was picked up and generally made Jessica feel like she was evil for leaving her in this place five days a week. But then Olivia had suddenly settled down, appeared even to enjoy going to school. It had been such a relief.

But the tone of Mrs Rose's voice, the slightly nervous look in her eye, suggested something had changed.

Jessica entered the classroom and waved at Olivia, who was sitting on the carpet with the other kids, wide-eyed and pretty, with all that red hair that she had inherited from Jessica. While she waited for the last few kids to be collected, Jessica looked around at the paintings on the wall, the collage of all the children in the class – Olivia smiling angelically – and the 'behaviour balloons'. Green, yellow and red, like traffic lights. Name labels were attached to the balloons, a great cluster on green, none on red and one on yellow, which signified a warning.

PART ONE

Jessica sometimes forgot that Mrs Rose had known her mum for a long time and that they often chatted at the school gates when Mum picked up Olivia.

'I'll talk to her about her behaviour,' Jessica said as Olivia ran over to her, avoiding Mrs Rose's eye and frowning. It was funny – when Olivia pursed her lips like that, she really did look like the aunt she'd never known. If behaviour balloons had been around in Izzy's day, she'd have spent a lot of time on yellow. Even red, occasionally – unlike Jessica, who would always have remained on green.

But being a handful at primary school hadn't done Izzy any harm, had it? She was the successful sister, the businesswoman, the one Mum was most proud of.

The star who had burned brightly – but all too briefly.

ω

Olivia was silent all the way home, resisting Jessica's efforts to draw her into a conversation. The poor thing was undoubtedly distressed by what had happened at school. But Jessica couldn't stop thinking about what Mrs Rose had said.

Looking at her daughter in the rear-view mirror, Jessica said, in her gentlest voice, 'Why did you say numeracy was boring, sweetheart?'

No response.

'Livvy?'

Olivia shut her eyes and appeared to nod off. Was she faking it? Jessica would have to remember that trick herself next time her own mother started going on about whatever bee was in her bonnet.

She decided not to tell Mum about what Olivia had said. She didn't want to put any crazy ideas into her head. For Mum, almost five years after Izzy's death, the pain was as acute as ever, while for Jessica what had once been a sharp agony had dimmed to a dull ache: a chronic condition that she had learned to live with.

Her thoughts stayed on Mum, remembering a couple of errands she'd promised to run for her, and that led her mind back to the list that lived in her head, the Ever-Expanding To-Do List, all the tedious responsibilities that went along with being a mother, wife and daughter. All the things she had to do for other people, never for herself. Sometimes she fantasised about ripping the list up and replacing it with a single selfish action point: Fuck off to Greece.

It was raining, and she sighed as the windscreen wipers mocked her dreams, squeaking against the glass. Olivia was genuinely asleep now, head lolling forward. Great – she wouldn't be tired at bedtime.

Jessica passed the Crystal Palace training ground and the vast soft-play centre that Olivia loved. Familiar streets, and not just because she was raising a family here. She had grown up in Beckenham and, apart from her years at Manchester University and a short stint in central London, she had always lived here. When they were teenagers, she and Izzy had sworn that the moment they were old enough they would escape this 'boring dump'. They were going to move to New York and live in an apartment just like the one in *Friends*. But here she was, back in Beckenham.

Jessica turned on to the new-build estate where she lived with Will, Olivia and Felix. They'd moved here four years ago, almost as soon as the development was finished. At the time, the prospect of living somewhere brand new, a place with no history or damp patches, was highly appealing. Now, though, as she pulled up on the driveway, her internal critic chided her for living somewhere so characterless. It wasn't what she'd dreamed of all those years ago: a house with a perfectly square garden and a purpose-built utility room.

She lifted Olivia out of the booster seat and laid her over her shoulder, stroking her soft hair and carrying her inside. The house was silent, just as she'd left it, their eight-year-old golden retriever, Caspar, snoozing in his bed in the kitchen. She stood in the hallway and enjoyed it: a moment of peace. Felix was at football practice. Will would collect him after work and, as was traditional for a Thursday, they'd get a take-away from the chip shop on the way home. Jessica laid her zonked-out daughter on the sofa and went through to the kitchen, where she stopped in front of a framed photograph. Her favourite photograph, even though she didn't look great in it. Her auburn hair was messy and she was carrying a few extra pounds. Isabel looked perfect as always, fresh from the salon with her blonde pixie cut and big eyes, looking a lot like Mia Farrow in *Rosemary's Baby*.

In the picture, Jessica and Isabel held champagne flutes aloft. Jessica had only just discovered she was pregnant with Olivia and had rushed round to tell her sister. Izzy's husband, Darpak, was there too and he insisted on opening a bottle of bubbly – one last drink before a long period of abstinence. Izzy was beaming and Jessica remembered how relieved she'd been, seeing that smile. For a couple of months before the photo was taken, Izzy had seemed distracted, troubled by something, but she wouldn't talk about it. She wouldn't even admit anything was wrong. But that day she had been serene and happy. Delighted for her little sister. Her old self again.

Six weeks later, she was dead.

Chapter 2

Jessica was helping clear up after lunch when Felix said, 'Have you told Uncle Darpak what Olivia said?'

She stood up from the dishwasher, wishing she'd told Felix not to mention anything. It was her own fault, she supposed. She and Will shouldn't have talked about it in front of their ten-year-old son. The thing was, he was so sensible and mature – an old head on young shoulders, according to Mum – that she sometimes forgot he was a child.

It was Sunday, and they were at Izzy and Darpak's house. Actually, it was just Darpak's place now, wasn't it? She didn't think she'd ever get used to that, although she was grateful, in what she knew was a selfish way, that he hadn't remarried and moved someone else in. His sister, Nina, was usually here for Sunday lunch and Will had started to refer to it as Darpak and Nina's house. But to Jessica it would always be Isabel's.

The house was, like hers and Will's, modern, built just a decade ago. But that was where the similarity ended. Because The Heights was the kind of house that got featured in property magazines. In fact, it had appeared in one a few months before Izzy died, gleaming between its pages: all those clean white spaces, the twisting staircase, walls of shining glass. Flat surfaces, no clutter. The balcony was pictured too: wrought black iron with art deco flourishes, overlooking the natural-granite patio. Jessica found it hard to look at the patio now, even though the blood had long since been washed away. Mum couldn't even come here, said it was like visiting a haunted house. 'He should sell it,' Mum insisted. 'I don't know how he can bear to live there.'

But Darpak didn't even consider moving out. It had been their home, he said, and he found it comforting, imagining her in its empty spaces, feeling her presence between its walls.

'What did Olivia say?' Darpak asked, closing the dishwasher.

Jessica stalled. 'Where is she? I don't want her to overhear us talking about her.'

Nina came into the room, running a hand through her glossy black hair. Nina was 'dressed down' in a Bella Freud sweater, jeans and sneakers, but that didn't stop her from looking like what she was: a fashion model. Not a supermodel – she wasn't a household name – but she made a good living on catwalks and in magazines. She'd been in a couple of TV commercials too, advertising shampoo. She was twenty-six and although Jessica was only eight years older, she felt like there was a generation's gap between them. Jessica had already had a two-year-old when she was twenty-six, and some days she yearned for the freedom that had disappeared when she was still so young.

'Olivia?' Nina said. 'She's in the snug, watching *Trolls*. It's really good – have you seen it?' She sang a snatch of the movie's theme song and smiled, but the smile vanished when it was met by frowns from Jessica and Will. 'Oh. What's up?'

Jessica crossed the kitchen and pushed the door to, just in case.

'It's nothing. Just something silly Olivia said at school.'

'Come on, you have to tell us now.' Darpak emptied the dregs of a bottle of white into his glass. Since Izzy's death, he only drank alcohol once a week, at Sunday lunchtime, with the roast dinner he and his sister had prepared. They were obsessed with these roasts. Their dad had been Indian, their mum white British, and although they had mostly eaten Indian food at home, every Sunday their mum would prepare an enormous, traditional English dinner. Chicken or lamb, roast potatoes, stuffing, Yorkshire puddings, home-made gravy, runner beans and mashed swede. After their parents died – too young, within months of each other – the Shah siblings kept the tradition alive and, apart from a hiatus following Izzy's death, it continued to this day.

Darpak was great with the kids too. He often had Olivia and Felix over, babysitting when Jessica and Will wanted to go out. He'd babysat only a week ago so they could go to the cinema, and had said they could drop the kids off any evening. 'I like having them here,' he'd said. 'It gets a bit lonely on my own.'

Before Jessica could tell them what Olivia had said, Felix piped up, 'She said Izzy had been talking to her.'

Darpak and Nina gawped at him, then at Jessica, who tried to laugh it off. 'I told you, it's just a silly thing she said.'

'What did Izzy say to her?' Nina asked, pouring herself a glass of wine. 'I mean, what does Olivia say she said?'

Jessica repeated what Mrs Rose had told her.

Darpak frowned and Jessica turned to him. 'You're not upset, are you?'

The frown vanished. 'Why would I be upset? I think it's sweet. And I don't find it hard to believe. Isabel hated doing her accounts. I can easily hear her telling Olivia that numeracy is boring. I mean, it *is* boring, isn't it? Even I think it's boring and I'm an investment manager.'

'I think it's creepy,' announced Felix.

All the adults turned their attention to him. He shuffled on his chair. 'I read this story about this girl who becomes possessed . . .'

'Are you letting him read horror stories?' Nina asked, shocked.

'It's only a comic,' Felix said. 'This girl is murdered and her spirit is restless, roaming the earth along with all these other women. Avenging angels. Then she enters the body of her little sister and gets revenge on the people who killed her. It's really cool, actually. It's Romanian, and the woman who wrote it was actually abducted herself and—'

'Well, luckily, there are no such things as avenging spirits,' Jessica said, cutting him off.

'No such thing as spirits, full stop,' said Will.

Nina put down her glass. 'But Jess, what about everything that happened when you and Izzy—'

Jessica interrupted. She didn't want Felix to hear about that. 'Felix, why don't you go and watch the film with Olivia?'

'Because it's boring. Uncle Darpak, can I play on the PS4?'

'Of course.'

Felix grinned and headed off to the living room and his uncle's sixty-inch TV. Jessica watched him go with a sense of alarm. He would be a teenager before too long. He wouldn't be her little boy any more.

But she didn't have time to dwell on this because, as soon as the door shut, Darpak began to cry. He didn't sob. His shoulders didn't shake. But tears appeared on his cheeks and he swallowed hard, blinking furiously.

'Oh, Darpak,' Jessica said. 'Are you okay?'

Nina did nothing but stare at him, apparently stunned by the sight of her usually stoic big brother crying. Will too seemed typically awkward in the presence of another man's tears.

'I miss her,' Darpak said, and Jessica put her arms around him, hugging him until the tears subsided.

'We all do,' she said.

He found a tissue and blew his nose, smiling sheepishly.

'I do think it's sweet, though, what Olivia said. Hey, I've got a box of Izzy's old jewellery upstairs – costume jewellery, I mean. There are lots of bags too. Purses. Lovely stuff for a little girl to play dressing-up with.'

Jessica wasn't sure. She was about to say so when Will said, 'That sounds great, doesn't it, Jess?'

She looked at her husband. They had been together since she was twenty-three and he was twenty-eight. He was better-looking now than ever, the speckles of grey in his stubble and the crinkles around his eyes adding character to his face. Apart from that, he had hardly changed his appearance. He still kept his hair a little too long, though it was starting to thin at the crown, and wore the same clothes he'd worn when they met: jeans, hoodies, Converse and ironic T-shirts. When she mentioned it, he said everyone in the tech industry dressed like that, that he'd feel uncomfortable in a suit. He wasn't lying. When she visited him in his office near Old Street, she saw dozens of men who looked like Will. On the rare occasion when he did put a suit on, for a wedding or christening, the novelty made her want to rip it off and jump on him.

'I guess,' she said.

'Great. I'll go and fetch it now.' Darpak hurried from the room.

A cry came from somewhere else in the house. Jessica leapt up and found Olivia standing in the doorway of the snug. She was sucking her thumb, something she did only very occasionally these days, when she was anxious.

'What's the matter, angel?'

'It's the Bergens. They're scary. I don't like them.' The Bergens were the bad guys in the film.

Jessica picked her up and hugged her. 'Why don't you come to the kitchen? Uncle Darpak's got a present for you. If you're lucky, maybe he'll give it to you now.'

'And can I have a snack?'

'Are you hungry again?'

Olivia grinned, showing her perfect white teeth. 'Mummy, I'm *always* hungry.'

Nina found a packet of crisps for Olivia, and Jessica let her play with her phone while they waited for Darpak to return. Will was playing with his own phone too, and Jessica had the urge to snatch it from his hand. Why couldn't he stay in the room? She was aware, as she watched him, that her irritation level was rising rapidly. Maybe it wasn't surprising. She was exhausted and worried about Olivia and, on top of that, she was really missing her sister. She could feel it bubbling up, the rage that lived inside her, and she tried to suppress it. But it was no good.

She never used to be like this. She never used to lose her temper. She remembered something Izzy once said to her when they were talking about stress. 'Imagine there's a gauge inside you, measuring your mood from one to ten, with one being utterly chilled out and ten being off-your-rocker furious. The more stressed you are, the higher the needle sits. You should be down at three or four most of the time.'

But these days, Jessica's needle was always hovering around seven. It didn't take much to send it soaring to ten.

Will must have sensed it because he glanced up from his screen and, seeing her face, put the phone away.

'Sorry, just checking the football scores. Are you all right?' he asked, but Darpak re-entered the room before she could answer. His face was slightly damp as if he'd just washed it, cleaning away the tracks of his tears. He set a cardboard box on the table.

'This is for you, Livvy.'

Olivia dropped Jessica's phone and the packet of crisps and peered into the box, her face lit up with wonder. 'Oh, wow.'

'This all used to belong to Auntie Izzy,' Darpak said. 'I want you to have it.'

Olivia squealed with delight and reached into the box, rifling through the old jewellery and purses. She pulled out a necklace with a silver pendant shaped liked a bat.

'Can I put this on now?' she asked.

'Sure.' Darpak put it over Olivia's head. 'It's a little long for you.'

'I love it!' she exclaimed. 'Thanks, Uncle Darpak.'

'You're welcome.'

She kissed his cheek. 'Izzy says thanks too.'

She didn't notice how his face crumpled as she held up the bat pendant.

'This was her favourite,' Olivia said.

They all stared at the necklace. It was a cheap old thing that Izzy had bought at Claire's Accessories years before. Olivia grinned at them, then skipped from the room.

'She's right,' Nina said in a whisper. 'It *was* her favourite.'

Chapter 3

Jessica ushered Olivia into the classroom. Olivia hesitated at first, hiding behind her mum's legs just as she had at the start of term, but eventually went inside. Jessica headed back towards the exit.

She took out her phone as she walked down the path. The Halloween decorations in the classroom had reminded her that she still needed to organise the children's costumes. She was so absorbed in the task of adding items to her phone's To-Do list that she almost missed Mr Cameron, who was preparing to close the school gate.

'Oh, hi, Mr Cameron,' she said.

He smiled at her. He had a red mark on his neck. At first she thought it was a love bite but then she realised he had nicked himself shaving. He smelled strongly of deodorant, a cheap brand like Lynx or Sure. As always, he looked tanned and his hair was gelled into the kind of trendy, spiky style worn by many of the boys at the school, including Felix, even though Mr Cameron must have been in his mid-thirties, maybe two or three years older than Jessica. She had seen some of the other mums eyeing him up, but he wasn't her type. There were rumours that his girlfriend was a hairdresser, hence the fashionable cut.

'Can I have a quick word?' Jessica said, seeing an opportunity. 'About Olivia?'

'Of course,' he said. 'Though I have to be in class in five minutes. And please call me Ryan. It makes me feel ancient when parents call me Mr Cameron.'

'Ryan it is. And please, call me Jessica. Not "Mum". It makes me feel ancient when teachers call me that.'

He smiled. 'Got it.'

She returned the smile. 'I had a word with Olivia about sharing and calling other children names.'

'*Not* calling other children names, I hope.' He laughed, showing her his enviably white teeth. Maybe his girlfriend had got him to bleach them?

'Oh no, I gave her a list of insults to use, all of them much better than "poohead". I think you're going to be very impressed.'

'Can't wait to hear them.'

The stream of parents exiting the school had dried up and Ryan looked meaningfully at the gate. It was time to lock the children in, and the world out, for the day.

ʊ

Sometimes Jessica liked to think back to the days before she was most commonly addressed as 'Mum'. She had gone straight from university into PR. That was how she'd met Will. The agency she worked for had landed the account of the dot-com that employed Will back then, a music download site that hadn't lasted long. She and Will had worked closely together as he was the public face of the company, and she had accompanied him to interviews and photo shoots. The rest, like that company, was history.

Her life had been reasonably glamorous back then, when she was in her early twenties, living in a house-share in Camden. Meeting famous people, talking to journalists, going to parties and openings. And then, a few months into her relationship with Will, she had discovered she was pregnant, at the age of twenty-three. It was a shock, to say the least, but their nascent relationship had survived – thrived, in fact. Will was twenty-eight and already owned his own flat, so she moved in with him. Love and excitement got them through, and they had kept on going.

Now she and Will were married with two children – two-point-four if you included the dog – and the glamorous world of PR was a hazy memory. These days she was a one-woman band, operating from home. She had a few clients: local businesses and a couple of authors for whom she organised events and blog tours, as well as looking after their social media.

Things were quiet at the moment, though. Her authors were between books and her other clients all seemed to be cutting back on 'unnecessary' expenditure. Her best client, a horror novelist, had buggered off to Wales and there was still no sign of his second book. Consequently she had very little work on and not much prospect of drumming up new business before Christmas.

She texted a couple of local friends to see if they wanted to meet for coffee, but Katy was heading to the gym and Maria was on a work deadline. All her other friends had full-time jobs. If Jessica's business didn't pick up, she'd be looking for a job soon too.

She went into Olivia's room to tidy up, but was distracted by the cardboard box that Darpak had given her. Jessica fished inside it and pulled out a pair of earrings and an imitation pearl necklace. Most of this stuff was ancient, from the days before Izzy could afford to buy proper jewellery. She spotted something shining inside the box and took it out. It was a sparkly butterfly brooch and seeing it made Jessica's heart contract. Izzy used to wear it all the time when she was in her early twenties. In fact, she'd worn it a few times in the last years of her life, preferring it over the expensive items Darpak had bought her. That bat necklace too. There was something perverse but charming about Izzy's insistence on teaming such cheap jewellery with the designer clothes she could easily afford.

Jessica was shaken from her thoughts by the sound of the landline ringing downstairs. Only one person ever called using the house phone, so Jessica knew exactly what to say when she picked it up.

'Hi, Mum.'

They exchanged small talk for a few minutes. Mum lived in an apartment on the other side of Beckenham on an estate full of retirees. The way Mum described the goings-on there, it was like a student campus with slightly less sex and statins instead of cannabis. Mum, who was sixty-five, was 'seeing' a seventy-year-old gentleman named Pete who took her dancing at weekends and who still had, as Mum had revealed during a mortifying conversation, plenty of lead in his pencil.

Mum went silent for a moment and Jessica could tell she had something on her mind.

'What is it?' Jessica asked.

'It's probably nothing but . . . one of my magazines had a story last week about a woman who fell off her balcony and almost died. She was in a coma for six months.'

Mum was addicted to real-life magazines like *Take a Break*.

'It wasn't far from here,' she said. 'Tonbridge. When she woke up, she was brain-damaged – terribly sad – but the first thing she did was point at her husband and say "Him". He broke down and confessed to pushing her.'

'Mum . . .'

Her mother went on, slightly breathless. 'Jess, listen. The thing was, until that point, everyone thought she'd fallen. She'd had a couple of drinks, you see, and the balcony railing needed fixing, and if she hadn't come out of the coma, do you know what? The bastard would have got away with it.'

'Mum. This has nothing to do with what happened to Izzy.'

'How do you know that? There were no witnesses, were there? No one saw Isabel fall. Where was Darpak? That's what I want to know.'

Jessica could feel a headache coming on. 'Darpak was at work, Mum. We know this. He had a meeting in the morning and then went to his office. We've been over this before. Izzy had been taking drugs—'

There was a sharp intake of breath at the other end of the line. Mum was still in denial about Isabel's drug use.

'—and she and Darpak were happy. He loved her. He still loves her. Yesterday we were at his, and Izzy's name came up and he started crying.'

'Crocodile tears.'

'Mum! Please. The coroner ruled that it was accidental death. Darpak had nothing to do with it. He loved her as much as we did.'

But she wasn't listening. 'We need to get the police to reopen the case.'

Exasperated, Jessica didn't respond. Sometimes it was better to let silence kill the conversation. But Mum wasn't finished. 'Did you know that forty-four per cent of women are murdered by their partners?'

'You mean forty-four per cent of women who are murdered are killed by their partners.' Jessica wouldn't normally be so pedantic but her exasperation was turning to anger, the needle on the gauge swinging towards the red zone. 'Izzy wasn't murdered. And you've got to stop thinking it and saying it. You used to really like Darpak. You should come to Sunday lunch with us.'

'I can't go to that house. I don't care about his supposed alibi. They all stick together, don't they, those City types?'

Jessica groaned. 'He'd be heartbroken if he heard you talking like this.'

'I thought he was already supposed to be heartbroken.' She paused. 'I just wonder what Izzy would tell us if she came back from the dead, like that woman in Tonbridge. I still can't believe Izzy fell. Someone was there. Somebody pushed her.'

Jessica didn't want to go over this again. She changed the subject. 'Olivia said she wants to come and see you. She wants to give you her Christmas list.'

'What, already?'

'She's been working on it since August. Shall I bring her round tomorrow, after school?'

'That would be lovely.'

'Actually, can I leave her with you for her tea? I need to take Felix to his swimming exam.'

'Of course. You don't need to ask. You know I love having her over.'

'Thanks, Mum. I'll pick her up as soon as I can because we're going trick-or-treating.'

Jessica hung up before Mum could protest about how much she disliked Halloween and other imported traditions. Her heart was still beating hard as she went back into the kitchen. Caspar wandered over and lay at her feet, giving her that 'pet me' look, tail banging against the laminate floor. Stroking him calmed her down, but she couldn't get what Mum had said out of her head.

She had lunch, then spent a couple of hours doing laundry, trying to get to grips with the enormous pile of washing that never seemed to shrink. When she wasn't wondering when her life had become so dull, the conversation with Mum looped inside her head.

It was ridiculous to think that Darpak had pushed Izzy off that balcony. He was besotted with her, the most uxorious person Jessica had ever met. Of course, no one really knows what goes on behind closed doors, but Izzy hadn't given any hints that there were problems in her marriage, and after Izzy's death Darpak had been grief-stricken. He hadn't shown any signs of guilt or unusual behaviour. Almost five years on, he still didn't have a new girlfriend. He'd been on a number of dates but said none of the women could measure up to what he'd lost. And he had an alibi. The idea that his colleagues were protecting him was ridiculous.

Mum was wrong.

Darpak hadn't killed Izzy.

Jessica did understand why Mum found it so hard to believe Izzy had fallen. Jessica had always found it difficult to accept too. She struggled to picture Izzy leaning over that balcony and losing her balance so badly that she fell.

But then the coroner had revealed the results of the autopsy, the drugs that were in her system. Not just cocaine but amphetamines and sleeping pills too. Jessica wasn't surprised that Izzy snorted the occasional line of coke; she knew a lot of middle-class people who indulged occasionally. But sleeping pills? Speed? That revelation had shaken her, and with the shock came guilt. Why hadn't she noticed? What could she have done to help?

And as soon as she found out about the medication, another realisation had hit her. Maybe Isabel hadn't fallen.

Maybe she had jumped.

The police seemed to think that was a possibility too, as had the coroner, but they had been kind to the family, ruling it to have been an accident. This was something Jessica never discussed with Mum, but maybe it was time she did. Anything to put out of her head the idea that Darpak had murdered Izzy.

She realised, with a start, that it was almost school pick-up time. As she left the house she wondered why this was happening now. Isabel had died nearly five years ago. She had thought everyone was getting over it. But suddenly her dead sister was all anyone could talk about.

Chapter 4

'Will, are you ready? We really need to get going.'

He came out of the bedroom holding a fabric bat wing over the lower half of his face. 'Mwa-ha-ha!' he exclaimed, flinging his arm aside to reveal his plastic joke-shop fangs and the trickles of blood he'd drawn beneath his lips. He had covered his face with white foundation and slicked back his hair. Jessica had to admit it rather suited him.

He grabbed hold of her from behind and put his lips to her neck. 'I vant to suck your blood,' he said, putting on a ridiculous Transylvanian accent.

She wriggled from his grasp. 'Didn't Dracula only go for virgins?'

'Zis vampire is not so fussy.' Now he sounded French.

She couldn't help but laugh. 'Come on, the kids are waiting.'

They went downstairs. 'I still think you should have dressed up too,' he said. 'You'd have looked great in that Bride of Dracula costume.'

'The one with the fishnets and the neckline that came down to here?' She pointed between her breasts. 'I think I'm a bit old for that.'

'Don't be daft. You're still the second most attractive woman in Beckenham.'

It was a joke that dated back to one of their first dates.

'And you're still the nineteenth most attractive man.'

'Aw, thanks, sweetheart.' He pulled her into an embrace.

'Mum! Dad! That's disgusting.' Felix was dressed as a character called Slender Man: a black suit, rubber tentacles attached to his back and a white mask that covered his face like a stocking, with just two eye-holes cut out. He looked genuinely creepy. Jessica had tried to persuade him to dress as a more traditional monster but it had to be Slender Man.

Olivia stood beside him. Like her dad, she was dressed as a vampire. A very cute little vampire, with a purple cape, a high collar and streaks of blood on either side of her mouth. The bat necklace from Izzy's box hung around her neck. Jessica had gelled Olivia's hair into a quiff, which Olivia kept touching and threatening to flatten.

'Wait, let me take a photo,' Jessica said, producing her phone and taking a few snaps of her family. Will gurned, Felix held up his tentacles and Olivia stood stock-still, staring at the camera with round eyes. 'Are you excited?' Jessica asked her, adjusting Olivia's collar and handing her a little bucket shaped like a pumpkin. 'Hoping to get lots of sweets?'

'Trick or treat,' Olivia said, putting on her most menacing voice.

They headed out. The clocks had gone back a few nights earlier and it was dark and cold on the street. There were already a number of families and groups of teenagers going from door to door. Halloween was a big deal on the estate because there were so many families with young kids. Anyone who was happy to take part had placed a jack-o'-lantern outside their door. There were a few people who, like Jessica's mum, hated Halloween and the children had been told to avoid those houses.

'Someone told me,' Felix said, 'that last year someone tried to trick-or-treat Mr Ellingham and he gave them an apple that was soaked in rat poison.'

Mr Ellingham was an elderly man who lived in an old house near the estate. He was harmless.

'That's an urban myth,' Will said.

'No, it's true,' Felix insisted. 'Jack told me. He said this kid started foaming at the mouth and then fell to the ground, dead.'

'Felix, that's not—'

'Izzy died,' said Olivia.

Jessica stared at her.

'I wasn't talking about her.' Felix pulled a face. 'You're such an idiot sometimes.'

'Don't call your sister an idiot. And please, let's not argue,' said Will, who either hadn't heard what Olivia said or was choosing to ignore it. Jessica wasn't sure.

They approached the first house, which was festooned with creepy decorations. A woman who Jessica recognised – she had kids at the school – opened the door, holding out a large basket full of Haribo and lollipops. Jessica tried not to think about all the sugar the kids would consume tonight.

'What a scary costume,' the woman said as Olivia helped herself to a lolly and dropped it into her bucket, then turned away, unsmiling. She was taking this whole vampire thing very seriously, Jessica thought.

As they headed back down the path, Felix spotted a couple of his friends from school and stopped to chat. Will waited with him but Jessica was forced to chase after Olivia, who was running towards the road. Olivia knew about stopping, looking and listening, but Jessica's pulse still raced whenever her daughter went near traffic.

She caught up with her and tried to take her hand but Olivia resisted and ran on to the lawn of the next house. This house had no pumpkin on display and all the lights were off. Jessica didn't know who lived there.

'Olivia, come back here,' she called.

Olivia ignored her. Jessica hurried after her, cursing as Olivia ran across the flower beds, trampling a couple of shrubs and heading straight towards the door of the dark house.

'Olivia! Don't you dare!'

But Olivia did dare. She wasn't tall enough to ring the doorbell so she banged on the door with her little fist. It made a surprisingly loud noise.

Jessica reached her and tried to grab her hand, but it was as if Olivia was made of smoke. She evaded Jessica's grip and banged on the door again. Jessica grabbed her and picked her up. Olivia wriggled and yelled, 'Put me down!' Jessica held her more tightly – and Olivia bit her hand.

Jessica stopped, putting Olivia down on the doorstep. She couldn't believe it. The bite hadn't really hurt but it had left a pink, wet mark on the fleshy part of her hand just above her thumb. She took Olivia by the wrist and dragged her away from the house.

'You do not bite, do you hear me? It's very, very naughty.'

Olivia pouted, her eyes shining with the thrill of doing something really bad.

'Say sorry now.'

'No.'

'Right, that's it! No more trick-or-treating. We're going home.'

'What's going on?' It was Will, with Felix just behind him.

'She bit me.'

'What? Livvy, did you bite Mummy? You mustn't bite.'

'I've already told her that. And I've told her we're going home. You and Felix can carry on.'

Olivia gazed up at her dad and began to cry. 'I don't want to go home. I want more sweets.'

Will turned to Jessica. 'I expect she just got carried away with the whole vampire thing. Olivia, why don't you say sorry to Mummy and then we can carry on?'

Olivia stared at the grass. She whispered something.

'Say it louder, sweetheart,' Will said.

'Sorry,' Olivia whispered, a little louder.

'Good. Okay, let's carry on.'

Jessica wasn't entirely happy with Olivia's apology, but she guessed Will was right: it was only because Olivia was dressed as a vampire.

She was about to give Olivia a hug when a light came on in the house and the door was opened by an older woman. Olivia ran back up the path towards the house and Jessica realised she recognised the woman who lived there. Her name was Pat Shelton and she worked at Foxgrove as a dinner lady. She was well past retirement age, in her seventies, but she had been serving school dinners back when Jessica was a child and it seemed she would keep going forever.

Jessica hurried after Olivia, calling out, 'I'm sorry.'

Olivia had already reached the door and was holding her orange bucket up towards the woman. 'Trick or treat.'

Jessica caught up. 'It's Pat, isn't it? I'm sorry, she's a little overexcited.'

Pat smiled. 'It's no bother, sweetie.' She bent down. 'Hello, Olivia. Did you enjoy your dinner at school today?'

'No.'

'Olivia!' Jessica felt herself go bright red. 'I'm so sorry.'

But Pat laughed. 'It's all right. I'm used to it. I didn't like school dinners either, but they're a lot better now than they were in my day.' She addressed Olivia. 'Let's see if I can find something that's more to your liking.'

She retreated into the house and came back with a Mars Bar in a wrinkled wrapper. Even in the half-light, Jessica was sure it had been bought a long time ago. But she allowed Pat to hand it to Olivia, who inspected it dubiously before putting it in the bucket.

'So, are you a vampire?' Pat asked.

'Yes.'

'A very scary little vampire.'

Olivia nodded. 'I'm the not-dead.'

'I think you mean the undead.'

Olivia stared at her. 'The *not*-dead. My auntie is dead.' And she gestured as if pointing to someone standing beside her. 'This is Izzy.'

For the second time, Jessica was speechless, but Pat was nonplussed. 'I see.'

'Do you really see?' Olivia said. 'Mummy can't.'

Jessica snapped out of her trance. 'Come on, Olivia, let's leave Pat alone.'

She took Olivia's hand and led her back down the path, heart hammering, to Will and the impatient Felix. Behind them, Pat closed the door.

'What happened?' Will said. 'You look as if you've seen a ghost. I mean, I know it's Halloween, but . . .'

'Just keep walking,' Jessica hissed.

'What is it? Did that woman say something?'

'It wasn't her.' They had reached the main road now. They stood beneath a street light, shadows stretching towards the gutter. Jessica crouched down and spoke to her daughter, who was busy inspecting the out-of-date Mars Bar. She was only four, overstimulated by Halloween and the candy she'd already eaten. Her imagination, always vivid, was in overdrive. What she'd said, the way she'd gestured to an empty space beside her, meant nothing. But Jessica couldn't stop herself from asking.

'You can't really see Auntie Izzy, can you?'

It was cold in the street. Black sky, half-naked trees, wind that nipped at their flesh. That was why Jessica shivered. Nothing to do with the words that had come from her daughter's lips and the distant, dreamy expression on her pretty face.

'I forgot,' she said.

'What did you forget?'

Olivia's voice dropped to a whisper. 'It's a secret, Mummy. A very big secret.'

ᙍ

Jessica stood in the kitchen, half the wine from her glass already percolating through her bloodstream. She didn't usually drink on a school night but tonight, oh my God, she needed it. Will had poured himself a drink too.

29

'You know that expression about feeling like someone's walking over your grave?' Jessica rubbed her arms, goose bumps rippling beneath her palms. She had stopped kidding herself it was the weather that had chilled her bones.

'Next Halloween, she can dress as something from *My Little Pony*.' Will had scrubbed off his Dracula make-up. 'I suppose we should be pleased she has such a strong imagination.'

Jessica glanced over at Olivia's vampire outfit, which lay in a heap by the washing machine.

'So you think it's nothing to worry about?'

'Yeah. File it under "kids say the funniest things". In this case, funny peculiar not funny ha-ha.'

'Definitely not funny ha-ha.'

She went over to the window, which looked out on to the street. It was late now and all the trick-or-treaters had gone home, but jack-o'-lanterns still burned outside a number of the houses, a pattern of flickering orange dots in the darkness. Usually on Halloween she and Will would end the day with a horror movie. They had one lined up, something about a creepy doll that came to life and wreaked havoc. She didn't think she could face it now.

'I am worried about her, though,' she said. 'First there was the incident at school. Then she was scared when she was watching *Trolls*, which she's seen before and wasn't upset by at all. And then tonight – saying what she said and biting me.'

'Again, I think it was her being in character. Felix did lots of peculiar stuff when he was four. Remember when he decided he was a cat? He miaowed all day and insisted on having a bowl of milk for dinner.'

The memory made her laugh. 'You're right. We have imaginative kids.'

They sat in companionable silence for a few minutes before Jessica finished her wine and said, 'I'm going to bed.'

On the way to the bedroom, she opened Olivia's door and slipped into her room. In the pink glow from the night light Olivia looked so peaceful, her favourite giraffe toy, Stretch, clutched against her cheek. Jessica crept closer, leaning over to gently kiss the sleeping beauty's forehead.

That was strange. Olivia had one arm raised, her fist beside her head on the pillow, and she was clutching something. Carefully, Jessica's prised open her daughter's fingers to see what it was.

It was the bat necklace she'd been wearing with her outfit. The metal had left an imprint on Olivia's palm where she'd been holding it so tightly.

Was Olivia developing an obsession with her dead aunt? If that was the case, the box of costume jewellery that sat in the corner of the room certainly wasn't helping. Jessica closed her daughter's fingers, kissed her, then tiptoed from the room, taking the box with her. She held the bat necklace for a minute, remembering when Izzy bought it from Claire's Accessories. Its silver edges had rubbed away so the bat was edged with black.

She thought about throwing it away, but couldn't bear to. Instead she tossed the necklace in the box and put it on top of her wardrobe, out of Olivia's reach. Olivia might protest in the morning but she would soon forget about it and move on.

Jessica got ready for bed, knowing she would dream about Izzy, wondering if Olivia was doing the same.

Chapter 5

Fireworks bloomed against the night sky, green and red and orange. Darpak was already preparing the next rocket, building up to the big finale, which involved a whizzing Catherine wheel and half a dozen Roman candles. He took his annual Guy Fawkes Night display even more seriously than his Sunday lunches.

Jessica stood by the smoking bonfire in the corner of the vast garden, cradling a cup of hot buttered rum, enjoying the way it soothed her insides. She'd eaten too much of Darpak's generous feast – jacket potatoes and pumpkin soup, a camembert fondue with crusty bread, hot dogs and an array of puddings – and her stomach hurt. Beside her, Nina nibbled at a plate of salad.

'Get ready!' Darpak cried, lighting the rocket and walking away quickly. He looked around. 'Hey, where are the kids? They're missing it.'

'They're on the trampoline,' said Nina.

'What?' He called out their names. 'You're missing all the fun.'

'I think I'm going to join them,' said Will, and he ran off towards the trampoline yelling, 'Here I come!' The children's laughter rang out across the garden.

'He's such a big kid,' laughed Nina.

Jessica didn't respond, prompting Nina to say, 'Are you all right? You seem a little stressed.'

'I'm fine, Nina. I'm tired, that's all, worried about Olivia.'

Jessica had already told Nina and Darpak about Olivia's behaviour on Halloween.

'Anyway, I'm getting bored hearing myself talk about it. Tell me something exciting about the fashion industry. Allow me to live vicariously through you for a minute.'

Nina laughed. 'There's not much to tell.'

'Are you seeing anyone? A hot male model, perhaps?'

'Yeah, Nina,' came a voice from behind them. 'We want to hear all about your love life.'

Jessica turned and smiled at the woman who had spoken: Amber, a friend of Nina's who had been invited along tonight. Amber was a photographer, well known in fashion circles but, like Nina, not a household name. She was in her early thirties and had natural auburn hair, a similar shade to Jessica's but longer, falling just below her shoulders. She had a Welsh accent and that skinny, arty look that Jessica found faintly intimidating. A tattoo peeked out from beneath the right sleeve of her coat: stylised red-and-orange flames that almost reached her knuckles. Jessica hadn't seen the full tattoo but apparently there was a red Welsh dragon on Amber's forearm, breathing the fire that was visible now.

'Come on, Nina,' Amber said, sucking on her e-cigarette. 'Spill.'

Nina glanced over her shoulder, as if she was worried about Darpak overhearing. 'Well, there was this one guy that I met in Milan. An American guy, a model. We spent a very nice weekend together. We rented this little sports car and drove out to Lake Como.'

Jessica groaned. 'Oh God, it sounds so glamorous and exciting. I hate you.'

'It's not as glamorous as it sounds,' Nina protested.

'Hey, if you want to swap, you can look after my kids for a week and *I'll* go driving out to Lake Como with a hot model.'

'I'd gladly do that,' Nina said. 'I love your kids.'

'All right. Deal. Does he like frumpy mums?'

'You're not frumpy!'

Jessica turned to Amber. 'So Nina tells me you two are working on a book together?'

'That's right. It's a kind of photographic diary of Nina's life, showing what it's really like to work in this industry.'

'Sounds interesting.'

'Maybe. I haven't got a publisher attached yet. Also, I heard there's someone else doing something similar.'

'Who?' Nina asked.

'Gavin Lawson.'

Nina groaned. 'Oh God.'

'Who's that?' Jessica asked. The name was familiar.

Amber pulled a face. 'This guy I used to work for. I was his assistant.'

Jessica turned to Nina. 'Gavin Lawson. Is he the one who used to go to Mind+Body?'

'Yeah. For a little while.' Mind+Body had been the name of Izzy's business.

'He's far more famous and successful than me,' said Amber. 'So if he gets his book out first, no one will want mine . . .' She trailed off. 'Anyway, let's not ruin the party by talking about that – or him. I might go and get some more of that rum. Anyone else?'

'I'd better not,' Jessica said. 'I'm driving.'

They watched the fireworks for a minute until Amber came back with her cup of rum.

Darpak shouted over, 'Hey! Where are the kids? They're going to miss the big climax.'

'Sorry!' Jessica called, waving to Will on the trampoline. The whole family gathered round to *ooh* and *aah*.

As the last sparks of colour faded from the sky, Olivia tugged at Jessica's coat. 'Mummy, I need a wee.'

'You know where it is, sweetheart.'

'I want you to take me.'

Will spoke. 'I'll do it. I need to check on Caspar anyway.' They had brought the dog with them and put him in a bedroom at the front of the house, a much better option than leaving him at home with loud bangs going off all around him while he was alone.

Will took Olivia's hand and led her towards the house. Jessica carried on chatting with Darpak, Nina and Amber, complimenting Darpak on the fireworks and the food. 'You've outdone yourself this year. I feel guilty, though. You always host everything. Why don't you come to ours next week and let Will and me cook? Don't tell him I said so but he's actually—'

'Mum!'

It was Felix. He was always interrupting her. At home she had taken to using the shortest sentences possible because it was so hard to get to the end of one without a child demanding her attention. 'He's actually a better cook—'

'*Mum!*'

'Felix, what have I told you about interrupting when I'm talking?'

'But Mum, look!' He pointed up towards the house, at the balcony outside the living room. The balcony from which Isabel had fallen. It was dark so it took a couple of seconds to see what Felix was pointing at.

Then she saw it and her heart plummeted into her stomach.

'Olivia!' she yelled, running towards the house.

Olivia had climbed up on to the balcony's black iron railing and was sitting on it, with her back to them. She was going to fall. Jessica could picture it. She was going to fall and snap her neck, smash her head open on the patio, just like Izzy, and as Jessica sprinted towards the door that led into the kitchen, she saw it all unfold: Jessica and Will kneeling beside their broken daughter, a paramedic shaking his head sadly, the funeral, visiting the tiny grave, a great, black path of despair and grief stretching to the horizon.

She yelled Will's name as she entered the house – where was he? – and took the stairs two at a time. A great wave of energy and strength powered her, and she leapt up the final three steps in one bound.

As she sprinted down the hallway, Will appeared from the bathroom. 'I needed the loo. What's going on?'

She didn't reply, just kept running into the living room. There was Olivia, looking over her shoulder towards the garden. Behind her the lights of South London shone, fireworks from distant displays splashing across the sky. Jessica wanted to dash forward and grab her, but she forced herself to slow down. What if she scared her and made her fall? Feeling like she might vomit, she went through the open door slowly, trying to look relaxed, like a woman approaching a snarling dog.

The balcony was about twelve feet across and ten feet deep. There was a small round table and a single metal chair. Isabel used to sit out here in good weather and drink her first coffee of the day, or a glass of wine on summer evenings. Darpak had told Jessica he barely ever came out here now, that he had even considered getting the whole balcony removed. Oh, how Jessica wished he'd done it.

'Hello, Mummy,' Olivia said, turning to look at her and shifting her bottom on the railing.

Jessica took a step forward, with one arm outstretched. 'Olivia, I need you to stay very still. Don't move, okay? I'm going to lift you down.'

Will had arrived behind her and she heard him say, 'Oh Jesus.'

Olivia swung her legs back and forth, heels bouncing against the metal. 'It's a long way down,' she said, looking over her shoulder again.

Jessica inched closer.

'Hi, Felix!' Olivia lifted one hand to wave at her brother, who was standing below with the adults. Craning her neck, Jessica could see that Darpak had his arms out like he was getting ready to catch Olivia. He looked as stricken as Jessica felt. Nina looked sick too. Everyone did.

'Sweetheart, hold the railing with both hands,' Jessica said with a shaky voice.

Olivia ignored her. 'Felix, hello!'

She waved her hand – and slipped. The upper half of her body jerked backwards towards open air. She let out a high-pitched squeal. Will yelled and somebody gasped.

Jessica was already moving. Powered by the adrenalin that had seen her leap up the stairs, she jumped forward. The next moment would replay in her head in the weeks to come, stopping her from sleeping, opening up the view of the black path she had already foreseen.

As Olivia began to tip backwards, Jessica grabbed her arm. For one terrifying second she thought she was going to slip from her grasp. But Jessica clung on. She clasped Olivia's other arm and lifted her off the railing.

Jessica fell to her knees, arms wrapped tightly around her daughter, whispering, '*OhmyGodohmyGod* . . .'

'Mummy, that hurts.'

She relaxed her grip but refused to let Olivia go. Will crouched beside them. He was talking but there was a high-pitched hum in Jessica's ears, blotting out his words. Still holding Olivia, she got to her feet and carried her into the living room.

'What were you doing?' she demanded, holding Olivia away from her. 'That was so stupid, so dangerous.'

Olivia wriggled from her grasp and crawled on to the sofa. Will locked the door to the balcony then knelt by the sofa, taking hold of Olivia's shoulders.

'You have to promise you'll never do that again,' he said.

Olivia shrugged. Jessica felt sick. She was shaking.

'Mummy and I were scared, Livvy. Do you understand?'

Another shrug and a pout.

Jessica couldn't bear it any more. She shoved Will aside. 'Olivia, you could have *died*.'

Olivia stared at her. Jessica was sure Olivia was going to burst into tears, but instead she smiled.

'Don't be silly, Mummy. You can't fall. You have to be *pushed.*'

ɯ

Darpak handed Jessica a glass of brandy. All this drinking – it had to stop. But not tonight. Definitely not tonight. Darpak had said he'd drive them home and Olivia was asleep in the spare room, having crashed out twenty minutes after the incident. Felix was upstairs, playing a video game, with Caspar stretched out beside him. Nina and Amber, who were both visibly shaken by what had happened, had left.

'It's my fault,' Darpak said. 'I should have locked the door to the balcony. I ought to be more careful.'

Jessica raised the glass to her lips and noticed how much her hand was shaking.

'Are you okay?' Will asked. 'This brandy is making me feel better.'

'Why on earth did she do it?' Darpak asked. 'We're always telling the children to stay away from there.'

Jessica didn't know what to say. Just as on Halloween, her daughter's words had shaken her; shaken her as much as her actions. Darpak hadn't arrived upstairs until a few seconds after Olivia had spoken.

You can't fall. You have to be pushed.

'I don't know,' she replied at last. 'Maybe she thought she'd get a better view of the fireworks from up there.'

Jessica watched Darpak as he went over to the sink and fetched himself a glass of water. She remembered what Mum had said, about forty-four per cent of female murder victims being killed by their partner.

Will was watching her from across the table and it was as if she could feel him trying to read her mind. Was he thinking the same thing?

That Izzy had been pushed?

Could Darpak have . . . ?

No, she admonished herself. *He couldn't.*

He had an alibi. And he loved Izzy. He was besotted with her. He was kind and sweet and if she'd had a brother Jessica would want him to be just like Darpak.

So why, when he came back to the table, did she feel herself inching away from him?

Chapter 6

September 2012

Isabel drifted from one couple to the next, checking on their progress, guiding the men who looked like they needed help, keeping her voice low to match the lighting in the room. One couple, a silver fox in his fifties and his wife, were struggling. He had the air of a man who had been handed a guitar for the first time, with no idea how to make it sing. They were going to need a dozen more sessions at least, but the first problem was simple: they weren't using enough lube. She showed him exactly how much to apply and guided his wrist, showing him where and how to touch his partner.

'Gently,' Isabel breathed.

His wife, who was naked from the waist down but with a silk sheet draped across her lap to cover her modesty, wore a faint look of disappointment. Like so many of the nervous but willing couples who came here, she expected ecstasy too soon. But Blissful Massage, like anything that improved your life, required patience and practice.

And then the wife exhaled. A tiny sigh of pleasure. Her husband, like a kid who had just played his first chord, grinned.

'Like that,' Isabel murmured to the husband, who was looking at her with a kind of bashful wonder.

She stood, leaving them to it. She was perspiring beneath the loose-fitting white cotton clothes she always wore during sessions. She would need to have a word with Nina – her sister-in-law, who was also her assistant here at Mind+Body – about regulating the temperature.

'Okay, everybody,' she said, standing at the centre of the space, a dozen pairs of eyes turning towards her, squinting through the gloom. 'We're going to wrap up in ten minutes so you should be thinking about winding down. Coming back to earth.' A communal chuckle rippled through the room and Isabel felt a shiver of pride. This was her business. She had created it, built it up herself. When she'd told people what she was going to do, her friends had been aghast. Sex therapy? *Really?* But look at this place, filled with happy customers, all of them paying handsomely to learn how to make their sex lives better.

A little later, after most of the couples had filed out into the autumn evening – some of them hurrying home to babysitters, others, she expected, going home to practise what they'd learned tonight – she heard a nervous voice say, 'Isabel?'

A couple, the Brannigans, who had been coming to Mind+Body for three months now, stood by the door wearing a pair of sheepish smiles. The woman, Laura, was holding a bottle.

Her husband, Fergus, a ruddy-cheeked man with gravity-defying hair, shuffled on the spot. 'We, er, just wanted to say thank you. A huge thank you, for what you've done for us.'

They caught each other's eye and Isabel knew exactly what they were going to say.

'It's been years since . . . well, since things were good between us in the bedroom. And now they're bloody great.'

It was funny, Isabel reflected, that even after they'd spent the last hour practising Blissful Massage, the Brannigans and many others like them still felt uncomfortable using the words Isabel had been using over the previous hour: *orgasm* and *yoni* and *clitoris*. Even *sex*.

Laura stepped forward and earnestly grasped Isabel's palm with both hands. 'Thank you. Thank you so much. Last night, for the first time since our youngest was born . . .' She handed Isabel the bottle of red wine, clearly on the verge of tears, and the two of them exited at last, arms around each other.

Isabel smiled. Another pair of satisfied customers.

There was only one couple remaining: Gavin Lawson and his partner, Carmen. He had her pressed up against the wall, kissing her. Isabel rolled her eyes. He was a well-known photographer, the closest thing Isabel had to a celebrity client, lean and muscular with close-cropped hair and a neat little beard. He was around forty and his partner was much younger, around half his age from the look of her. They were always the last to leave; most weeks she had to virtually drag them out.

She cleared her throat and, reluctantly, Gavin tore himself away from his girlfriend.

'Sorry, darling,' he said as they left. 'Got a bit carried away, didn't we?'

His erection was clearly visible in his jeans and Isabel took a step back as he passed, leading Carmen by the hand. Priapic bastard. Isabel was glad it was his last session.

As they left, Jess came in from outside. Gavin wasn't looking where he was going and he bumped into her, almost sending her flying.

'Sorry, darling,' he said, grabbing her arm. 'You all right?'

She extricated her arm from his grip and the dirty look Jess gave him made Isabel smile. Gavin turned and left, apparently unbothered.

'That was Gavin Lawson,' Isabel said. 'The new David Bailey, apparently.'

'Oh, right. I think I've heard of him. Seems like a dick.'

'As usual, dear sister, your judgement is spot on.'

Isabel gestured for Jessica to follow her to the back room and handed her the wine the Brannigans had given her, explaining where it had come from.

'Wow, this is good stuff,' Jess said, inspecting the bottle of Château La Conseillante. At one point in her career Jess had done PR for a wine merchant and she could instantly spot the difference between cheap plonk and the kind of stuff rich people kept in their cellars. 'You going to give this to Darpak?'

'Nah, let's open it. There should be glasses in the kitchen.'

Jess went off to find the glasses and a bottle opener while Isabel changed out of her work clothes into jeans and a sweater. Jess came back with the wine in a pair of plastic tumblers.

'This is all I could find.'

They touched the tumblers together and Isabel took a big swig. 'Mmm. That *is* good.'

'Three-hundred-quid wine. They must be having *really* great sex now.' She paused. 'Maybe I should bring Will to one of your classes.'

'You should!'

Jess pulled a face. 'I was only joking. Firstly, he would never come. Secondly, I really don't want my sister telling my husband what to do with my bits. Or his bits, for that matter.'

'You really shouldn't call them *bits*, Jess.'

'Oh, please. The day I call it my *yoni* is the day hell freezes over.'

Isabel laughed. 'Was there a third reason?'

'Yeah. We don't need your help. We're fine.'

'Fine?'

'Oh God, I shouldn't have said anything to you. I really don't want to talk about it.'

'Okay.'

'It's just . . .' Jess obviously *did* want to talk about it. 'We've fallen into that trap, where it's all about biology. Will says he feels like a mobile sperm farm. It's not very sexy.'

Isabel finished getting changed and zipped up her boots. Her tumbler was empty already and she wanted another. After a session, she felt the way she imagined a rock star must feel when they come off stage.

And while she knew she ought to practise what she preached and spend some time meditating, breathing, it was hard not to succumb to the urge to keep hold of that high. Besides, it would be rude not to enjoy the Brannigans' gift, so she poured herself another glass and topped Jess up while she was at it.

'Let's finish this before we head off,' she said.

'Won't we be late?'

'We've got plenty of time.'

It was Mum's birthday and Isabel had booked a table at the best restaurant in Beckenham, even though she knew Mum would think it was too posh, too 'dear'. There was going to be another celebration at the weekend, with the whole family, but tonight it was just the three of them. Like it used to be.

'If she mentions Larry, please don't indulge her,' Jess said.

'I won't. I promise.'

'We need another topic in reserve so we can quickly change the subject if necessary.'

'Hmm. What about Elsie's toy boy?'

'Ooh, good one.'

'They came to one of my classes,' Isabel said with a grin.

'No way.'

'Yep. They were very sweet, actually. And we get people of all ages coming here, you know. Sexuality doesn't end when you're thirty.'

'I hope not! I'd only have a year left. And you'd already be past it. You wouldn't be able to teach thingy—'

'Blissful Massage.' It annoyed Isabel that Jess could never quite bring herself to say it.

'Yeah, that. Could you teach it if you weren't doing it yourself? You'd have to go back to being a yoga instructor.'

That was what Isabel had done until three years ago, leading yoga classes at community centres with the occasional private session. Yoga had been going through something of a boom in the suburbs and Isabel had made a decent living, but soon there was a glut of yoga teachers. For a long time Isabel had wanted to start her own business – a proper business, not just being a self-employed guru for hire – and Darpak had kept telling her she needed to find an angle. 'Something like hot yoga,' he'd said. 'But not that.'

At the same time, mindfulness had become a big thing. Much of it could be boiled down to a simple core idea, that of living in the moment, focusing on what you were doing instead of constantly worrying about the million other tasks you needed to do, all the crap you had to worry about. Remembering to breathe. Isabel had taken a course in MBCT, mindfulness-based cognitive therapy, and was trying to figure out if she should switch from teaching yoga to mindfulness when a client inadvertently gave her an idea.

This client, a wealthy woman who lived in a beautiful house between Beckenham and Bromley, had hired Isabel to visit her once a week to practise yoga. Then they'd moved on to MBCT, combining the two.

At the end of one session the woman had joked, 'I need to do this when I'm having sex with my husband. Try to stop my mind wandering. You've sorted out my body and brain – do you think you could fix my sex life too?'

A light bulb had pinged in Isabel's head. Later she'd stayed up half the night researching what else was out there. Tantric sex classes. Clitoral stimulation workshops. Yonic massage. As always, the Americans were way ahead in this area. But most of it looked intimidating, some of it pretty 'woo-woo'. Isabel knew there were a lot of unhappy, unsatisfied people out there, and she was struck by a vision: a place where people could go to learn to improve their sex lives, a place aimed at couples, somewhere that wasn't intimidating or sleazy or embarrassing.

'And not aimed at hairy hippies?' Darpak had asked when she told him her idea over a late breakfast. When they'd first got together, Isabel had found an ancient copy of *The Joy of Sex* on his bookcase. She had teased him about it at the time, asking him if he was into 'hairy hippies'.

'No,' she had told him. 'Ordinary people. People like you and me.' She had smiled. 'I'm going to need to learn lots of techniques. You can be my study buddy.'

'What are you thinking?' Jess asked now. 'You look sad.'

'Do I? I was just thinking about how well it's all gone over the last couple of years. How dissatisfied I was before. It's kind of crazy.'

The restaurant was within walking distance. They both knew these streets like they knew their own bodies. Walking past WHSmith, Isabel flashed back to their childhood, running into the shop to look for Stephen King books she hadn't read, an obsession which their mum hated. 'We've had enough horror in our lives,' she said.

They passed a shop selling clothes and accessories for babies and toddlers and Jess turned her face from the window, as if it hurt to look inside at all the tiny dresses and comfort blankets. Isabel saw.

'It will happen,' Isabel said, touching her sister's shoulder. 'You need to be patient, that's all.'

'That's what the doctor said.'

Jess and Will had both been examined. Will's sperm count was fine. There didn't appear to be any reason why pregnancy number two wouldn't happen, but Isabel knew that made it even more frustrating for her sister.

'How am I supposed to solve the problem if I don't know what the problem *is*?' Jess said.

They stopped a few metres from the restaurant. Mum, who was always early, would be waiting inside.

'It will happen,' Isabel repeated. 'Come on, let's try to have fun. It's Mum's birthday.'

'I'm sorry.' Jess forced a smile. 'Is that better?'

'Much.'

But Isabel had stopped paying attention. She had experienced a tingle on the back of her neck, the feeling she was being watched. She peered across the street. There was someone standing in the shadows between two shops. From the height and shape, Isabel was sure it was a man, but she couldn't see his face. She took a step closer, but then a bus went past, slowing to block her view. When it pulled away, the man was gone.

Chapter 7

'Jess, come and look at this.'

Olivia was playing with the collection of toys her grandmother kept in her living room, toys that had been around since Jessica and Izzy were kids. There were a couple of Barbies, an assortment of stacking bricks, an old skipping rope, some plastic trolls and a Fisher-Price medical kit complete with stethoscope, thermometer and a reflex hammer. There was a Girl's World styling head too, like a giant decapitated doll, which still bore marks from where Jessica and Izzy had applied make-up to its unblinking face all those years ago. She was called Marnie, and her hair had been plaited and backcombed and coloured so many times that she now looked like an ageing punk with a serious case of bedhead.

Jessica stood in the doorway next to Mum, who nodded at Olivia. Just over a week had passed since the incident on the balcony and everything had gone back to normal. Olivia seemed happy and there hadn't been any more complaints of bad behaviour from her teachers. Jessica had allowed herself to relax – and now here they were at Mum's house, having popped round after school.

Olivia was kneeling on the floor in the living room, in one of those positions that make adults yearn for the flexibility of their youth, performing a medical check-up on Marnie. First, she stuck a thermometer between Marnie's closed lips.

'Hmm,' Olivia said. 'You have a little bit of fever, Marnie.'

Next, she stuck the plastic otoscope in Marnie's ear and said, 'Yuck. Earwax.'

Mum nudged Jessica. 'It's like looking into the past,' she whispered. 'You and Izzy used to fight over who was going to be the doctor and who was the nurse.'

'She was always the doctor.'

Olivia had now put the stethoscope in her ears and was listening to Marnie's invisible chest.

'Oh. No heartbeat. Looks like that fever killed you dead.'

Mum laughed softly, but Jessica wasn't smiling.

'We'd better have a funeral,' Olivia said, lifting Marnie and carrying her over to the sofa. She laid the doll's head on a cushion and stroked its matted hair then kissed its forehead. 'Sleep tight.'

She pulled the throw off the back of the sofa and covered Marnie with it. Olivia was in her own world, unaware they were watching. She stood back from the sofa and bowed her head, crossing her hands across her chest.

Mum was about to enter the room but Jessica stopped her. She needed to see what would happen next. She could tell from Mum's expression that she too was gazing into the past, transported back to the eighties. Izzy used to do this. She was always holding mock funerals for her toys, including Barbie, who kept perishing in unfortunate ways: drowning in the bath, falling off bunk beds, being murdered by Ken. A blast of nostalgia almost knocked Jessica off her feet. She could smell the house where they grew up, the ever-present scent of Pledge. She could taste the Jammie Dodgers they used to raid from the kitchen cupboard.

And she could feel the chill that always hung in the air in that house.

Olivia still had her head bowed. She closed her eyes and began to sing. Her four-year-old voice was sweet but out of tune. She hissed between lines and the melody strayed all over the place.

But, Jessica realised with shock, she recognised the song. She knew the lines about the sun being gone, but being happy. It was 'Dumb', a song by Nirvana. An album track. She hadn't been able to listen to Nirvana since Izzy died, and hadn't heard this song since they were kids, but the words and melody came rushing back, transporting her to their childhood bedroom. There had been posters of Kurt Cobain all over the walls, and the two sisters had jumped around and played air guitar to the faster tracks as Kurt looked down approvingly. When Izzy was fourteen and Jessica eleven, Jessica had come home one day to find her sister wailing. 'He's dead! Kurt's dead!'

Jessica couldn't hold back any longer. She half-ran into the room and crouched beside her daughter. 'Where did you hear that song?'

Olivia blinked at her like she'd been woken from a dream. 'What song?'

'The one you were singing.' Jessica sang a couple of lines from it, all the lyrics coming back to her.

'I don't know.'

'Come on, Olivia, tell me. Where did you hear it?'

Mum was beside them now. 'Jess, stop it. You're upsetting her.'

But Jessica needed to know. She took hold of her daughter's arms, just firmly enough to hold her in place. 'Olivia. How do you know that song?'

'Leave me alone!' Olivia screamed. She wrenched herself out of Jessica's grip and threw herself to the floor, sobbing.

'Now look what you've done.' Mum lowered herself to the carpet and took the little girl in her arms while Jessica remained frozen to the spot, staring at her daughter, wondering what the hell had just happened.

ꞷ

Jessica sat at the little table in the kitchen with Mum's 'gentleman friend', Pete. Olivia was with her grandmother in the living room, watching *Peppa Pig*. She was fine now, the upset forgotten, tears long dried, but Jessica felt hot with shame for the way she had shouted. Hot, but cold too, a trickle of ice in her belly.

'I simply don't understand where she could have heard that song,' she said.

'What was it again?' Pete asked. He had made them both a cup of tea but Jessica had hardly touched hers. Pete was smartly dressed as ever, in a white shirt and grey trousers, and his bald head gleamed beneath the fluorescent strip light.

'An old Nirvana song, "Dumb".'

'Never heard of it.'

'I'm sure Olivia hasn't heard of it either. Hasn't heard it, full stop.'

He wrinkled his nose. 'Nirvana, eh? One of those grungy bands, weren't they? Wasn't he a drug addict? Pretty sad, if you ask me . . .'

Jessica, who was accustomed to Pete's rants – which always ended with the phrase 'I suppose I'm just stuck in my ways' – tuned out. Pete was fine as long as you didn't get him talking about gay marriage, Brexit, the cost of parking, 'spoiled' children, national service, Muslims, vegetarians, Jeremy Corbyn, women drivers, feminism, tax dodgers or immigration.

Mum came into the kitchen and Jessica looked up at her. 'Are Izzy's old Nirvana CDs still here?'

'No. She took them with her when she left. I've still got all *my* old records, though. We were listening to them last night, weren't we, Pete?'

He nodded. 'Johnny Mathis. Lovely voice. Shame he was a—'

Jessica spoke over him. 'So you haven't been playing Nirvana here?'

'That awful racket? Of course not.'

'Then how does she know that song?'

Mum shrugged. 'Maybe she learned it at school?'

'That seems highly unlikely.'

'Or she heard it on the radio?'

'Olivia never listens to the radio unless she's in the car with me and Will, and they never play album tracks like that. Besides, she knew all the words. It's like she's heard it loads of times.'

'Perhaps Will has been playing it at home?' Pete suggested.

Again, that seemed very unlikely. 'Will hates Nirvana. He's always going on about how great it was when Suede came along and kick-started Britpop.'

'I have no idea what you just said, but I'll take your word for it,' said Mum.

'I expect she heard it on TV or on that video site you let her look at,' said Pete.

'YouTube. I guess that's the most likely explanation. Maybe it was background music on some video she was watching.' She hoped not; the lyrics weren't exactly appropriate for the kind of videos Olivia enjoyed, which were mostly of other children opening surprise eggs or playing with toys.

Mum looked towards the door before turning back to Jessica. 'Or . . .'

'What?' Jessica asked, not wanting to hear the answer.

'It's nothing. Just me being silly.'

But Pete's interest was piqued. 'What is it, Mo?'

Mum sat down. Jessica knew exactly what her mother was going to say. She wanted to stop her, to block the idea from entering the room. She didn't want anyone to give it breath. But the memory of how she'd acted with Olivia, shouting at the poor thing, on the verge of shaking her, made her hold back.

'I told you about Larry, didn't I?' Mum said.

Pete's eyes widened.

'He used to do that. He used to teach Izzy old songs.'

Jessica couldn't keep quiet any longer. 'Mum, stop it. This is not Larry. This is not anything like that. Olivia must have learned that song somewhere else, probably YouTube. And whatever you do, I don't want you to talk to her about Larry. I don't want you filling her head with all that. She's too young.'

She snatched up her bag. Once again she had lost her temper, but there was nothing she could do about it.

'Olivia,' she called. 'We're going.'

Mum stayed in the kitchen and Pete came to the front door to wave them goodbye.

'I wish you girls wouldn't argue,' he said.

Jessica wanted to point out that they weren't girls, but bit her tongue. 'Bye, Pete.'

'Bye, love. See you soon, Livvy.' He waggled his fingers at her.

Olivia, who was holding Jessica's hand, looked up at Pete. 'Get well soon,' she said.

Confusion deepened the lines on his brow. 'But I'm not sick, Livvy.'

'Not yet,' she said, breaking away from Jessica and skipping away down the path.

ത

As Jessica pulled away from Mum's apartment, Olivia strapped into her booster seat in the back, the red mist was still clouding her vision. She'd lived with the story of Larry for so long that it felt like exactly that: a story. But once upon a time she had believed wholeheartedly in Larry's existence. She had been terrified by what had happened when they were children.

Now she was an adult, she knew there had to be a rational explanation for Larry, just as there had to be one for Olivia's knowledge of the Nirvana song and all the other weird stuff she'd done and said recently. Jessica was angry with her mum for mentioning Larry, but she was angry with herself too for not being able to explain any of it.

The streets were dark and quiet, not much traffic on the roads. She didn't feel ready to go home yet, even though it was approaching Olivia's bedtime and Will and Felix, who had been at football practice again, would be wondering where she was. She decided to drive around for a while, heading up Beckenham Road and carrying on towards Crystal Palace Park.

'Mummy, where are we going?'

'Just for a little drive, sweetheart.' She paused. 'Livvy, you know that song you were singing earlier? Can you tell me where you learned it?'

'I don't know. I just singed it.'

Olivia hadn't quite got to grips with irregular past tense verbs yet.

'Are you sure?'

'I don't know!'

Jessica knew the harder she tried to prise the answer out of Olivia, the more she would clam up.

She drove anti-clockwise around the perimeter of the park, the shadowy outlines of trees to her left. The famous dinosaurs, which Olivia loved, though not as much as Felix used to love them, were close by. She planned to drive around the park three times before turning back.

On her second turn around the park, she noticed a car behind her. It was hanging back, keeping a distance of around three car lengths, but she was sure this vehicle had been behind her on her first circuit. She carried on, completing another circuit, expecting the car behind to turn at the lights. But it stayed on her tail.

She was being followed.

She squinted into the rear-view mirror, but it was too dark and the other car was too far back for her to make out the licence plate. The poor light made it difficult to discern the car's colour but it was either blue or dark grey, she thought. And the badge on the car's nose was visible too: an H with a sloping horizontal line. Was that Hyundai or Honda? She couldn't remember. She also wasn't sure why she was worrying so much. It was probably someone else like her, driving around the park trying to clear their head. Or young lads who thought it was funny to tail her and try to freak her out.

'You okay, sweetheart?' she asked Olivia, wanting to hear her daughter's voice.

'I'm thirsty.'

'It's okay. We're going home in a minute.'

Olivia appeared to be thinking of something. 'I want to get out.'

'You just need to wait a little while.'

'No. Now.'

Jessica heard a click and the warning signal on the dashboard beeped.

'Olivia!' She had unfastened her seat belt.

Jessica had no choice but to pull over. Fortunately the kerb to her left was clear. She undid her own seat belt and turned around, reaching to pull Olivia's belt back over her. Olivia grinned at her as if what she had done was hilarious. Jessica bit her tongue, refusing to lose her temper again. She visualised something calming – a condensation-streaked glass of wine, waiting for her at home – while she grappled with the seat belt. It wouldn't click into place.

'Goddammit,' she muttered, trying to hold on to the image of that glass of wine. Finally the belt clicked into place. 'Olivia,' she said. 'You mustn't undo your seat belt. It's very—'

She stopped.

The car that had been following them had pulled up ten metres behind them. She could see a single figure through the windscreen, a silhouette obscured by distance. She could feel their eyes on her.

As Jessica stared through the rear window, they turned on their full beams. The sudden bright light dazzled her, forcing her to throw her arm over her face. When she removed it, yellow spots danced in her vision, and as she watched, the car swung out into a gap in the traffic, reversed then sped off, heading back in the direction they'd come.

'Mummy, what is it? What's the matter?' Olivia was looking out the side window. 'Did you see a ghost, Mummy? Was there a ghost in the park?'

Jessica stared at her. A ghost? Where had that come from? She didn't even want to think about it. Because something very real, something tangible, had just happened. Someone had been following them. And she had no idea who, or why.

Chapter 8

Jessica ended the call as Will came back into the kitchen.

'What did the police say?' he asked.

'Not much. They said if it happens again I should try to get the registration number. But they didn't exactly sound concerned. They said it was probably a couple of boy racers messing around.' She rubbed her arms. 'I still feel cold. Can I have a hug?'

He put his arms around her.

'You're shivering,' he said, pulling her more tightly against him and kissing her hair. He was warm and smelled good and, she thought, if it wasn't for the kids she would take him to bed right now, hide with him beneath the covers. That's what they used to do if either of them had a bad day, back before they had kids. They'd get home from work, open a bottle of wine and go upstairs.

Maybe he was reading her thoughts because she could feel him getting turned on. His hand went to the small of her back and she tried to enjoy the sensation as he pulled her closer, but she was unable to relax. What did Izzy use to call it? A vigilance centre, that was it. Izzy said that women were always alert to danger. It was something she had taught in her workshops. To fully enjoy herself, a woman needed her vigilance centre to be relaxed. And right now, Jessica felt like a hen surrounded by foxes.

She pulled away just as Felix came into the room. He went straight over to the cupboard where biscuits and crisps were kept.

'There's nothing to eat,' he complained, staring into the cupboard, which was stuffed full of unhealthy snacks, many of which Felix had thrown into the trolley on their last visit to the supermarket, when Jessica had been too tired to argue. Too Tired To Argue. If she ever wrote a book about parenting, that would be the title.

'Have an apple,' Will said. 'They're not poisonous, I promise.'

Felix ignored his dad and approached the fridge. Jessica intercepted him and pulled him into her arms.

'Come on, give your poor old mum a cuddle.'

'Do I have to?' He said it with a smile.

'You do if you want any snacks.'

He allowed her to hug him for a few seconds before pulling away. She ruffled his hair and admired his good looks. People were always telling her he was the spitting image of her, though his strawberry-blonde hair was lighter than hers. With his hazel eyes and Cupid's bow lips, she could mostly see Will in him. Will and, from certain angles, Isabel. Auntie Izzy. She would never forget having to tell him, aged five, that she had 'gone to heaven'. He'd had a lot of questions. Were there shops in heaven? Could you take all your things with you? What if you forgot something – could you pop back and get it? Tears pricked her eyes when she remembered how sweet he'd been, worrying that the worst thing about death was the risk of being separated from one's toys.

She wondered if he could actually remember Izzy now or if she only existed through family anecdotes and photos.

'I'd better go and make sure Livvy's cleaned her teeth, and get her to bed,' Will said.

'She's acting weird again,' said Felix as his dad left the kitchen.

'What do you mean?' Jessica asked.

'She was going on about ghosts. She said Nanny's house is haunted. I told her she was talking rubbish. I mean, Nanny doesn't even live in a house. She lives in a flat.' He rolled his eyes. 'I don't think we should have let her go trick-or-treating. She's been acting crazy ever since.' He took a bite of the Babybel he'd found in the fridge. 'Still, I'm glad she didn't fall off that balcony.'

'I'm glad you're glad.'

Will came back into the room, looking pained. 'Olivia won't let me read her bedtime story. She says you need to do it, Jess.'

'But it's your turn.'

Jessica enjoyed reading stories to Olivia, but after the day she'd had she couldn't face the whole routine: *I'm thirsty, I'm hungry, I need a wee, I need seventeen very specific soft toys in bed with me.*

Will spun on his heel. 'All right, I'll try. But don't be surprised if I'm up there for an hour, arguing with her.'

Jessica sighed. 'Fine. I'll do it.'

As soon as she entered Olivia's room and saw the delight on her face – mixed, admittedly, with a smirk of victory – Jessica felt bad about being reluctant to read the bedtime story. One day soon, she knew from experience, Olivia wouldn't want stories any more. She'd want to be on her iPad or, hopefully, she'd prefer to read books herself. Jessica should cherish these moments. That's what everyone told her.

And she did. She really did.

'Come on, then, let's tuck you in.'

Olivia snuggled under the duvet with Stretch the giraffe tucked under her arm. She blinked slowly and, not for the first or even thousandth time, Jessica marvelled at her long lashes, the softness of her cheeks, the beautiful creature she had given birth to.

'What story would you like?'

'*There's a Monster in My Pocket.*'

Jessica suppressed a moan. 'Are you sure? We've had this one lots of times.'

'I want it.'

Olivia went to sit up and Jessica hurriedly said, 'Okay, okay.'

59

It was a story about a little girl who carried a tiny monster around with her. The monster whispered reassurances to the girl when she was frightened, gave her advice, helped her stand up to mean children.

Jessica didn't need to read the book; she knew it by heart.

Halfway through, Olivia – who had already closed her eyes, so Jessica thought she was about to fall asleep – said, 'I'm not afraid of monsters.'

'I know, sweetheart.'

Jessica got two words into the next line when Olivia added, 'Or ghosts.'

Jessica laid the book flat on her lap. 'Ghosts aren't real, Livvy. But if they were, you wouldn't need to be afraid of them.'

'I know.' She still had her eyes closed, a smile on her lips.

Jessica carried on with the story. As she neared the end – when the bullies learn the error of their ways and everyone becomes friends with the monster – Olivia's breathing changed, so Jessica was sure she was asleep. She waited, thinking about the hot bath she was going to have, lots of bubbles, while she listened to her Russell Brand podcast and imagined he was in there with her. She was just about to get up and creep from the room when Olivia spoke.

'Auntie Izzy's a nice ghost.'

'What?'

But Olivia was asleep.

ω

Jessica had a bath, listened to her podcast, drank half a bottle of wine. When she went to bed, Will stayed up to watch the football highlights.

She went to sleep thinking about Larry. When she had told Will the story, a few months into their relationship, when she trusted him enough to share, he had laughed at that name. Larry.

'Where did that come from?' he had asked.

'Larry was the name of one of my mum's uncles. He had a temper when he was a young man, apparently. Was known for throwing things around, smashing crockery and slamming doors. There were darker rumours too, that he hit his wife, smacked the kids "a bit too hard", even by the standards of the time. A bit of a dickhead, by all accounts.'

They had been lying in bed in the middle of the afternoon, curtains thrown open, sunlight on the sheets. Jessica was hopelessly in love, floating through life in a haze of blissed-out desire. But talking about Larry had made her pull the quilt up to her throat, as if there was a presence in the room, watching her, making the temperature drop.

'Shortly after it all started, my mum said our visitor reminded her of Uncle Larry. It stuck. Whenever something happened, Mum would say, "Larry's having another tantrum." Or "Sounds like Larry's on the warpath."'

'Did she think it actually was him?' Will had asked. To his credit, he hadn't immediately tried to explain what the family had gone through, like all Jessica's previous boyfriends had. It was a male disease: attempting to find a solution for everything. But Will simply listened. It was one of the things she most liked about him, along with his twin abilities to make her laugh and come.

'No, Uncle Larry – the real one – was still alive at this point, in a nursing home in Bromley. I'd met him a few times. He seemed to have mellowed in his old age.'

Unlike the new Larry, the invisible one, who got worse, more violent, more tempestuous, with every passing day.

Until the day he stopped.

At first, Jessica had felt as if she were holding her breath, unable to believe that it was really over. But she was a child back then, ten years old, and life moved on, more quickly for her than it did for Izzy, who was three years older. For most of Jessica's teenage years, it was a strange episode in the past, one for which she had no explanation. As the memories became less vivid, so they lost their power to scare her, and when she grew up and went off to college she decided that she no longer wanted to be that girl, that haunted girl. So she didn't tell anyone about Larry, not until she trusted them to keep her secret. Her mysterious secret. But she never fully made up her mind about whether Larry had been real. Mum was convinced that ghosts and spirits existed. Despite appearing to believe in Larry at first, Izzy had later insisted he couldn't be real. And Jessica found herself in the middle, unsure what to believe.

She was still thinking about all of this after her bath when Will crept into the room. She pretended to be asleep and then, shortly after he began to snore softly beside her, she really was.

Until a smashing sound woke her.

She opened her eyes. Had she dreamed it?

Was there somebody in the house?

Her mind flashed back to the car that had followed her around the park. Had they followed her home? Were they downstairs now? An intruder?

A murderer?

Will was still asleep and she nudged him with an elbow, hissing his name. He grunted and she prodded him, saying, 'Will. Wake up. I think there's someone in the house.'

He sat up. 'What?'

'I heard something smash.'

He rubbed his eyes, part of him still submerged in a dream. 'What, like a window?'

'I don't know.' She was whispering. 'I'm going to call the police.'

'But what if—?'

He was interrupted by a series of thudding sounds. And then much worse – a high-pitched scream.

'What the fuck?'

But Jessica was already out of bed, heading towards the bedroom door, shouting her daughter's name.

She hurried along the landing, Will right behind her, and into Olivia's room. The night light was on, casting an orange glow over the room, and Olivia was sitting up in bed, eyes wide, confused and fearful. As soon as she saw her parents she began to cry.

Jessica sat on the little bed and pulled Olivia against her. The little girl trembled in her arms. Her pyjamas were wet and cold with sweat. Jessica shushed her, told her it was okay, taking in the room as she did so, while Will stood there with a look of shocked incomprehension on his unshaven face.

The room was a mess. Olivia's books were scattered across the floor. Cuddly toys lay on the carpet. A *My Little Pony* poster had been torn from the wall and ripped in two. Then Jessica spotted the source of the smashing noise that had woken her. A plate Olivia had been given at her christening, which had sat on a display shelf, appeared to have been thrown against the wall. It lay in a dozen pieces in the corner.

Will stared at Jessica, then at Olivia. He crouched beside the bed. 'What happened, princess?'

Olivia buried her face against Jessica's chest.

'I want to sleep in your bed.'

'That's fine. Let's get you out of these wet PJs, eh? Will . . .' She gestured towards the wardrobe.

He found a fresh pair and, as Jessica helped her out of the damp ones, Olivia looked around at the mess.

'Izzy's naughty, isn't she, Mummy?' she said. 'It's because she's cross about what happened to her.'

Jessica and Will exchanged a look. In the glow of the night light, he appeared as sick as Jessica felt.

'Livvy,' she began, pulling the clean pyjama top over her daughter's head, 'it can't have been Auntie Izzy.'

'But it *was*.'

'Sweetheart, it can't have been.'

Olivia stamped her bare foot. 'It *was* Auntie Izzy. I'm not lying.'

Jessica saw Will's Adam's apple bob before he spoke. 'Why did Auntie Izzy do it, Livvy?'

Olivia didn't hesitate. 'She's cross because of what he did to her.'

'What who did to her?' Jessica asked.

Olivia gave her that look, the one that said *Don't you know anything?*

'The bad man, Mummy.' She picked up her toy giraffe and hugged it, little hands around its long neck. 'The bad man who pushed her.'

Chapter 9

'Is it true?'

Isabel had been waiting for this question for a long time, but hadn't expected a journalist from the local paper, the *Bromley Gazette*, this unassuming woman with stringy blonde hair and spots of pink in her cheeks, to be the one to bring it up. They were here to talk about Isabel's business, not her teenage years.

'Is it true that when you were a kid your house was haunted by a poltergeist?'

Isabel took a long drink of water, gathering her thoughts. They were in a little bistro that had recently opened in the centre of Beckenham. Isabel knew the chef – he and his wife were clients – and part of her wanted to flee to the kitchen to avoid this question. Since setting up Mind+Body, she hadn't mentioned Larry to anyone. She knew how it would look to potential customers, not to mention her bank manager and backers. Her business was a hard enough sell as it was, and it was vital for her to seem credible and down to earth.

But she also knew that denying it would be fruitless. It had been in the news back then, after one of the investigators, that idiot Simon Parker, had talked to the press. Isabel had been thirteen at that point.

Mum had gone along with it, letting a journalist and photographer from a national tabloid come along and take photos and spend a night in the house. Nothing had happened that evening, though the disappointed writer reported 'a chilly atmosphere and an air of menace'. Their cat, Oscar, had 'hissed at an unseen presence' too.

It was just enough for the story to run, containing juicy details of what Isabel and the rest of the family had experienced. Crockery flying across the dining room. Coming home to find a knife embedded in a kitchen cupboard. Mysterious puddles in the bathroom. The terrifying phone calls that, according to Mum, sounded like someone was calling from hell.

There was a photo of the three of them, Mum, Isabel and Jessica, on the sofa, beneath the family portrait with the cracked glass. Oscar was on Isabel's lap in the picture, glaring at the camera.

In the report Simon Parker, the so-called 'Ghostbuster of South London', had said it was quite common for unexplained phenomena to occur in the homes of pubescent girls, as if Isabel's hormones were causing cups to fly from shelves. How she wished she did have that power. She'd have sent a whole set of cups and saucers, complete with teapot, flying at his stupid head.

The next day, Isabel had been the centre of attention at her school. *The freak.*

A clear memory came back to her: she was standing alone by the lockers, wiping her eyes and cursing Mum for inviting the press into their home. She banged her locker shut and swore aloud, using a word she would never normally use, a word beginning with *c*, and then heard a noise behind her. She whirled around, thinking it was a teacher or one of the bullies, but it was some kid in her year. A nerdy-looking boy with a bowl haircut and a bad case of acne.

'I believe you,' he said in a tremulous voice. 'They're all idiots . . . They're not like us.'

That had been the worst moment – realising this spotty kid thought they had something in common. That she was a member of the loser crowd now, and for a while she had given in to it.

But not for long. Soon afterwards she had broken free, doing everything possible to fit in, to be popular and successful, to prove she wasn't a loser.

And look at her now! Although she had no desire to be famous, she wanted success, and because of the nature of her business she was already a kind of local celebrity. Recently she'd been at an event for local entrepreneurs and a guy her age had approached her and told her how he'd always known she'd do well. She didn't recognise him, which made him look hurt, and then someone had whisked her off before she could ask him how she knew him.

The *Bromley Gazette* journalist, whose name was Suzanna Salter, reached into her bag and produced a printout. The two-page spread from the tabloid, dated September 1993.

'It was a lot of nonsense,' Isabel said, hoping her fake laugh was convincing.

'Do you mean your mother made it all up?' Suzanna asked.

'I'm sorry. I don't feel particularly comfortable discussing it.'

'I understand, but I think our readers will be interested.'

'I doubt that, Suzanna. Listen, it was a difficult time, my dad had left us, my mum was in a state. I really don't want to upset her by stirring it all up again. Okay?'

'I guess . . .'

'Good. Now, can we get back to the subject we're supposed to be talking about? It's supposed to be about my business. I thought you were going to ask me about being an entrepreneur, not all this rubbish.'

Chastened, Suzanna nodded. 'You're right. Sorry, Isabel. So . . . when did you come up with the idea for Mind+Body?'

ᛟ

Isabel drove away having promised to give Suzanna and her bloke a free taster session. She wouldn't be the first journalist to visit Mind+Body. They all arrived thinking they were going to get an amusing story about sex in the suburbs but went away with the glow of converts, writing rapturous articles that brought even more clients through the front door. They came from all over London and Kent; she'd even had people coming from Manchester and Birmingham, and there was talk of opening a centre up north, plus another in the capital. It was her vision: Blissful Massage spreading out across the country, joy and calm and satisfaction radiating through the nation. A happier Britain, all because of her.

That was why she did this. The money was simply a bonus.

She drove up to the house and parked beside Darpak's car. She sat in silence, touching up her make-up in the mirror, thinking again about Larry and about Mum, who still believed in him.

She ran over what she'd told Suzanna, hoping she hadn't given the impression she was arrogant. She knew people took an instinctive dislike to those whose lives seemed too perfect. She was only thirty-two and successful, with a handsome husband, a beautiful house, a thriving business and – it was inferred – an incredible love life. She was a guru. A sexpert. How could her love life not be perfect? She saw the way men looked at Darpak, the nudge-nudge wink-wink. She could read their minds. *You lucky bastard.*

Her life was pretty good, she supposed. But that didn't mean she was satisfied. For driven people like her, it could always be better. That was the great tragedy of being ambitious. You were never happy.

'I'm home,' she called after she forced herself to get out of the car and go inside.

There was no response. She went up the stairs and approached the bathroom. The door was shut and she could hear the shower running. For a moment she was tempted to go inside and surprise him, undress and get in with him. Do what people thought they did all the time.

Instead she went into the living room, kicked off her shoes and slumped on the sofa. The whole room was cream and white, flooded with natural light, no mess, no dirt. The view of the garden was lovely, even now the trees were shedding their leaves. She felt a glow of satisfaction, a rare moment when she allowed herself to pause and appreciate what she had. Sure, Darpak's money had paid for this place initially, but now she was his financial equal.

She leaned forward and noticed something. Darpak's phone was on the coffee table.

She knew she shouldn't pick it up. She shouldn't key in the PIN code (his mother's birthday). She definitely shouldn't open his messages. But then she thought how he'd been acting recently. Kind of shifty. Like he felt guilty about something. It had been bothering her for weeks, though he denied anything was wrong.

She looked over her shoulder. The shower was still running. What was he doing in there? Having a wank? That thought made her think, *Sod it.* She opened the Messages app, expecting to find nothing. Messages from his boss, his sister, his mates. Or maybe, deep down, she expected to find something worse. Something that would tilt her world off its axis.

There it was: a text from a number that didn't have a name assigned.

A photo of a naked pair of breasts, taken in a mirror. It was a selfie. A topless selfie.

And a message: To keep you going till next time xxxx.

Chapter 10

Jessica was tempted to keep Olivia off school but Will insisted it was better to act as if everything was normal. She watched Olivia trot into the classroom and head over to her peg, where she hung her backpack before trying to get her coat off. She struggled with the zip and Jessica saw her lower lip wobble before Ryan Cameron noticed and hurried over to help her. He caught Jessica's eye and smiled before leading Olivia over to one of the tables, where a jungle scene had been set out. Mr Cameron crouched beside Olivia and drew her into a game involving a toy elephant at a watering hole made from blue paper. She seemed so happy and relaxed; like a different little girl from the one who had tossed and turned between her parents all night, muttering in her sleep, before refusing to eat breakfast this morning. Getting her into her school clothes had been a struggle too.

'I don't want to go to school,' she had yelled. 'I want to stay here.' There'd been a pause before she added the chilling words, 'With Izzy.'

Will had already gone to work by that point. Felix was sitting on the stairs, sneaking in some bonus time with his iPad. Jessica had slumped on the sofa, clutching Olivia's uniform. 'Everybody has to go to school.'

'Izzy wants to stay here.'

'Izzy isn't . . .' Jessica had stopped herself. What was she going to say? Izzy isn't real? Izzy isn't with us any more? Olivia had waited, head cocked, until Jessica found herself saying, 'Izzy's not a little girl. I mean, she wasn't a little girl.'

'She was once. A very pretty girl. Like me.'

That had made Jessica smile, despite everything. 'You certainly are very pretty. And so was Auntie Izzy.' Perhaps, Jessica had reasoned, if she brought Isabel into the daylight, talked about her in a normal, rational way, Olivia would stop having these weird fantasies about her. 'Do you want to see a photo of her when she was your age?'

But Olivia had suddenly lost interest and decided, two minutes before they were due to leave, that she was starving.

'How has Olivia been this week?' Jessica asked Mrs Rose now.

'Much better, actually. She's been on the green balloon ever since we had our chat.'

'Oh, that's great.' Jessica yawned.

'Keeping you up?'

She bit down on a follow-up yawn. 'We had a bad night, actually. Olivia woke up at two. She might be tired today as well.'

'Oh dear,' Mrs Rose said. She glanced over at Olivia. 'Goodness. You know, sometimes when I look at her it's like being thrown back in time. I was saying this to your mum the other day, when she picked Olivia up. She looks so much like Isabel. Apart from the hair. Actually, she's like a perfect cross between the two of you.'

'I'm surprised you remember us so well,' Jessica said.

'Oh, Isabel was a very memorable child. I mean, you both were. And, of course, I remember all the strange goings-on. You were celebrities, weren't you?'

She meant Larry, obviously. Izzy had already left Foxgrove by then, and Jess would have been in year five, or 'third-year juniors', as it was called back in the day.

'I was very upset to hear about Isabel,' Mrs Rose said. Without warning she grabbed hold of Jessica's hand. Her eyes shone with emotion. 'You mustn't ever forget her, Jessica. She lives on in you. You and Olivia.'

Jessica pulled her hand away, shocked. 'I won't forget her. Of course I won't.'

'Good. Because she was a special person.'

Jessica wasn't sure what to say, or how to react. All the other parents had left already. Olivia was still playing with the jungle creatures.

'She loves animals, doesn't she?' Mrs Rose said, suddenly looking a little awkward. 'She was telling us all about her cat.'

'Her dog, you mean? Caspar?'

The teacher frowned. 'No, she definitely mentioned a cat. Oscar.'

'I think you're getting confused. Oscar was Izzy's cat when we were children.'

'Oh. Really? How strange. I'm sure she said Oscar.' She looked Jessica in the eye. 'I might remember you and Isabel clearly, but I certainly don't remember what your pets were called.'

She closed the door, not quite in Jessica's face.

ϖ

Jessica was halfway home when she realised where Olivia must have heard about Oscar. She hit the button on the steering wheel that opened her phone, scrolled through the numbers and called Mum.

'Quick question,' she said once they'd exchanged greetings. 'Do you remember Izzy's cat, Oscar?'

'Of course I do! Lovely old thing, he was. Izzy was heartbroken when he died. We all were.'

'Have you ever spoken to Olivia about him?'

There was a pause. 'No. Why are you asking?'

'Just . . .'

Jessica found herself doing what she'd sworn she wouldn't do. She told her mum what had happened during the night, along with all the other strange things Olivia had done and said during the last couple of weeks. It came out in a rush, with Mum silent at the other end of the line. Jessica left out only two things: Olivia climbing on the balcony, and the car that had followed them the night before. As she finished talking she felt momentarily lighter, unburdened. But she had a horrible feeling she was going to regret being so open.

The pause this time was so long that Jessica thought her mum had hung up. Then she heard an intake of breath.

'It's happening again,' Mum said. 'This family. We're susceptible to it.'

Jessica went cold inside. This was *not* what she wanted to hear.

'But maybe it's a good thing,' Mum went on. 'If we can communicate with Izzy . . .'

Jessica heard a noise in the background. Pete calling Mum's name. In response Mum shouted, 'All right, I'll be there in a second.' She sighed heavily.

'What's up with Pete?'

'He's sick, that's what. Got it coming out of both ends, and muggins here is having to nursemaid him.'

Jessica really didn't want to picture 'it' coming out of Pete, at either end, but was relieved to have something else to talk about. 'What, is it a stomach bug?'

'He insists it must be food poisoning. They had a Chinese meal at the RAFA last night and he's blaming that.' The RAFA was the Royal Air Force Association Club, which, as a former airman, Pete was a member of. They had a bar where he and his old friends hung out. Mum never went, said it was too boring listening to Pete and his mates rattling on about the old days. 'He's saying he knew he shouldn't have eaten that "foreign muck", but I reckon it's a virus.'

'Oh dear. Poor Pete.'

'Poor me having to look after him! He's not the easiest patient.' She raised her voice. '*All right, I'm coming!* I'd better go. Listen, we need to talk about this thing with Olivia. I'll call you later.'

She hung up, leaving Jessica feeling even more uneasy than before the call. It took her a few seconds to remember why, but then it came back to her: Olivia saying 'Get well soon' to Pete.

ᙡ

Jessica tidied up the mess in Olivia's room, sweeping up the fragments of the christening plate, throwing away the torn poster, putting everything else back in its place. As she worked, she realised how much colder it was in Olivia's room than in the rest of the house. *Because it's haunted*, said a little voice in her head, a voice she pushed away. Of course it wasn't bloody haunted. The radiator, which was only warm at the bottom, needed bleeding. That was all.

She went off in search of a radiator key. There was one around somewhere, but she couldn't find it in the kitchen drawer. Thinking back, she remembered that Will had recently bled the radiator in his office on the top floor. Knowing him, he would have shoved the key in the nearest drawer.

She didn't come up to Will's office very often. The room was quite small and crowded with Will's stuff. There was a turntable on the desk, with shelves containing his favourite vinyl, much of it reissues of albums he'd loved when he was a teenager. Depeche Mode, The Pixies, Kate Bush, Public Enemy. Some of his old records were framed on the wall. Morrissey gazed down from above the desk, beside a picture of Will's current fave, Lana Del Rey.

His collection of Funko Pop! toys – pop culture figures with oversized heads – was lined up on another shelf. He had stacks of graphic novels and old DVDs. Among all this were framed awards for websites he'd worked on, boxes of ancient CD-ROMs and old hard drives, all

74

the files he intended to organise one day. Somewhere there was a folder of emails from the early days of their relationship. He had printed them out because, he said, they were the closest thing he'd ever have to an archive of love letters. Some of them were quite explicit. She prayed the children never found them.

She sat at the desk and rifled through the drawers. They were full of pens, headache tablets, screen cleaner, all sorts of junk. No radiator key. In the second drawer down she found a crumpled pack of cigarettes. They had both given up smoking when she got pregnant with Felix, but she knew Will still smoked the occasional 'social' cigarette. She picked up the almost-full packet and sniffed it, the smell shooting her back in time, and she was tempted to light one for old times' sake. She wondered what Will would do if he came home and found her smoking. Laughing at his imagined reaction, she dropped the packet back in the drawer and slammed it shut.

She didn't want to go downstairs yet, so she prodded the keyboard, bringing the iMac to life.

Will's desktop photo was one of Jessica's favourite pictures: six-year-old Felix holding one-day-old Olivia, gazing with amazement at his new baby sister. Forgetting why she had come to Will's office, she found herself opening the computer's photo library. The albums had been automatically organised by person. The great majority of photos were of her, Will, Felix and Olivia. But there were albums of other family members too, along with Will's closest friends. And an 'Isabel' album.

She opened it and scrolled through. The pictures went back to when she and Will had first got together, when she'd invited him to Beckenham to meet the family. She'd been so nervous that weekend, afraid that he'd think she was suburban and dull. But he thought Mum was hilarious and he said Isabel was lovely, although she'd been in a bad mood that weekend and was quite distant, not making much effort. Perhaps because of that first encounter, Will and Izzy were never close, but they'd developed a cordial relationship, and the four of them – Will and Jessica, Izzy and Darpak – had spent a lot of time together. Most of these photos depicted nights out as a foursome, Christmases spent together, lots of Sunday lunches.

She was about to click back to look at more baby photos when she spotted a subfolder labelled 'Izzy Website'. She opened it and found herself looking at a collection of pictures, some of which were familiar: photos in which Izzy was smiling, looking sleek and groomed but also approachable. These were the pictures that Will had used when he revamped the Mind+Body website. They all had dates attached and Jessica was surprised to remember this had been only a few weeks before Izzy's death.

She sighed, staring at her lost sister, before noticing that there were a number of pictures she hadn't seen before, presumably out-takes from the same photo shoot. In most of these pictures, which had been taken on the balcony – that fucking balcony – Izzy wasn't looking at the camera. She was gazing into space, frowning. Jessica moved her fingers to her own lips, shocked by how unhappy Izzy looked in these pictures. Like someone whose heart had been broken. Beautiful and sad.

This was a side of herself Isabel never showed to the world. In public she was always happy, confident, full of *joie de vivre*. The successful businesswoman and wife. The sadness in Isabel's eyes reminded Jessica of when her sister was fourteen or fifteen, when she went through a dark period, typical teenage angst connected to a cheating boyfriend and tension at home. Jessica was surprised that her sister had allowed Will to photograph her like this, without her mask of contentment.

She was still contemplating the pictures – the radiator key and the chill in Olivia's room completely forgotten – when the doorbell rang.

She hurried downstairs, thinking it was probably a delivery guy with the first of the Christmas presents she'd ordered. Christmas. Whenever she thought about it, a chain of tasks appeared before her like, well, a string of fairy lights, their brightness outshining all the other things on her mind. She would need to hide these presents, buy wrapping paper, then there was all the food to pre-order and the tree and . . .

'Oh.' It wasn't the delivery man. 'Mum. What are you—?'

She stopped. There was someone standing behind her mother on the front step. A man with white hair and a mottled, bulbous nose.

'Jess, you remember Simon Parker, don't you?'

The old man smiled, revealing a perfect set of what could only be dentures.

'Hello, darling,' he said. His voice, the theatrical way he spoke, brought it all back. She knew why he was here and it was only her overriding fear of appearing rude that stopped her slamming the door in his florid face.

Chapter 11

'It's blowing a gale out here,' Mum said. 'Aren't you going to invite us in?'

Anger bubbled up in Jessica's belly – how dare Mum bring Simon Parker here? But before she could work out how to turn them away without causing huge amounts of upset, they were inside, the door shut behind them.

Simon walked a few paces down the hallway, looking around like an estate agent who'd been sent to value a property, hands clasped behind his back. His stomach was bigger than it had been, hair thinner, but he was still wearing a white suit – not the same one, surely – and his blue eyes were as sharp as ever.

'Hmmm,' he said. 'Hmmmm.'

Mum gawped at him like he was about to impart some devastating piece of wisdom. Jessica remembered that credulous, desperate look. It was all coming back to her, the events of 1993, the last time she'd encountered this man. He'd had an assistant then, a middle-aged woman who never spoke but who spent a lot of time staring at Jessica and Izzy with bulging eyes. Jessica was transported back in time to their childhood bedroom.

'Did you see the way she was looking at me?' Izzy asked, peering through the slats of the top bunk at Jessica below.

'*Like she wanted to gobble you up.*' *Jessica put on a troll voice. 'I've got my eye on you, little girl.*'

Izzy clamped her hand over her mouth.

Jessica got up and brushed her fringe over her eyes, which she opened as wide as they'd go. She pretended to be Madam Grimm, as they called her, drifting around the room like a fairy-tale witch, long fingers outstretched, as silent as the object of their fun. Izzy lay on her back on the bunk bed, trying not to giggle. She gazed at the posters: Kurt Cobain on one wall, Snoopy on another.

Jessica stared at her sister, unblinking. 'Mr Parker, Mr Parker. Where shall I put the equipment? What's that? You want me to put it up your bottom?'

Izzy exploded with laughter. 'Stop it!'

Jessica clawed at the bunk bed ladder. 'Oh, Mr Parker. You set my heart aflame and make my knickers tremble. Please let me give you a big, slurpy kiss . . .'

They both shrieked with laughter. It felt so good, after the horrific tension of the last few days.

'I think it's you he wants to kiss,' Jessica said. 'I've seen the way he looks at you.'

'Oh, gross! Don't be disgusting!'

'It's true, though. His eyes follow you around the room.'

Isabel made retching noises and they both started laughing again. When they had calmed down, Jessica said, 'Do you think Mum's okay?'

Izzy shrugged. 'Is she ever okay? She's so highly strung.'

'You can't blame her, though, can you?'

Izzy did an imitation of their mother. 'Do you think it's easy, bringing up the two of you, single-handed?'

'She's not doing it on her own, though, is she? Larry's helping her.'

Izzy sniggered then stopped smiling. Since the newspaper story, both girls had been teased endlessly at school. It was Mum's fault. Izzy had begged her not to contact the Psychical Investigation and Research Association, reminding her that Larry always hid when visitors came anyway, but Mum had made up her mind.

'I wonder what Dad's doing now?' Izzy asked in a soft voice.

Jessica didn't want to think about him. Izzy made him out to be a saint but the man Jessica remembered had been grumpy and distant, making them go to bed straight after dinner. She had actually been relieved when he left and couldn't understand why Izzy was so upset.

Wanting to see her sister laugh again, she went back into Madam Grimm mode, making her eyes bulge and pointing at a spot behind Izzy's head. 'I've found it. The foul intruder. A creature that cannot be from this world.' She formed a cross with her fingers. 'Be gone, strange being. Leave these fair maidens be!'

Izzy whirled round, realised Jessica was talking to a poster of Kurt Cobain, and the two of them dissolved once more into a fit of laughter.

'What are you smirking at?' Mum asked, bringing her out of her daydream.

'Absolutely nothing. What are you doing here?'

'That's not very—'

'Mr Parker. Why are you here? What has she told you?'

He ignored the question and drifted further down the hall, fingers outstretched, seemingly sniffing the air. 'I can feel it,' he said. 'A presence.'

'Oh, for goodness' sake.' Jessica folded her arms, wondering if it would be okay to forcibly eject an eighty-year-old man. 'Where's your assistant?'

'Ingrid Jenkins?' So that had been Madam Grimm's name. 'She moved to Texas and married an oilman.'

Jessica hadn't been expecting that.

Simon Parker was examining a framed photo of Izzy that hung on the wall. A fingertip hovered above the glass. 'She grew up to be even more beautiful, didn't she? I remember seeing her in the newspaper, when she opened her . . . business.' There was a faint crease of distaste.

'I was delighted to see how well she did. And then . . .' A solemn shake of the head. 'Poor you, Mo. And you, Jessica.'

He carried on along the hallway, resuming his air-sniffing. *Grew up to be even more beautiful.* Thinking back to how Simon had let his eyes wander over the thirteen-year-old Isabel's body made Jessica want to vomit.

'What did you tell him?' Jessica hissed.

Mum wanted to follow Simon, but Jessica blocked her path, demanding answers.

'I told him about the unusual occurrences we've been experiencing.'

'We?'

'The family. Everything you told me this morning.'

Jessica slapped her own forehead. 'I *knew* I was going to regret it.'

Mum tutted. 'Don't you see – this was how it started before. Izzy knew things she shouldn't. She said all sorts of peculiar stuff that didn't make sense. And the first time Larry began flinging stuff around, it started in Izzy's room.'

Jessica remembered. Before that the girls had had their own rooms. They only got bunk beds and moved into a single room when Jessica got too scared to sleep alone.

'We need to nip it in the bud, Jessica. Before it gets as bad as it was last time.'

'But—'

Something went crash in the kitchen and Jessica hurried along the hall to find out what was going on. Simon Parker was standing near the cooker, which was in an island in the centre of the room, with Caspar at his feet, the dog wagging his tail furiously. A broken plant pot lay nearby, dirt spread out across the tiles.

'I'm so sorry. Your dog jumped up at me and I knocked into the pot.'

'Are you sure it was you and not a poltergeist?' Jess said.

Mum had followed her into the kitchen. 'There's no need to be like that.'

Jessica dragged Caspar away from Simon, telling him to get on his bed, then retrieved the dustpan and brush from beneath the sink. She needed to get rid of Simon and Mum, but felt compelled to clean up the mess first. She prepared an argument as she swept up the dirt, determined not to shout and rage, but when she looked up they had both left the room.

She abandoned the dustpan and followed them, hearing voices from above. She hurried up the stairs. They were in Olivia's bedroom.

'What the hell are you doing in here?'

'I wanted to show Simon where it happened.'

Jessica pointed at the doorway, the other hand on her hip. 'Get out.'

But Simon didn't move. He was crouching on the carpet, holding a shard from the smashed plate which Jessica must have missed.

'It's cold in this room,' he said. 'Colder than the rest of the house.'

'That's because the radiator needs bleeding.'

He ignored her. 'It's stronger here too. The sense of . . . other.'

Mum put her hand to her mouth, eyes wide. 'Other?'

Simon got to his feet. He was surprisingly limber. 'Yes. I mean, I need my equipment—'

Jessica suppressed a smile.

'—but I've become increasingly sensitive over the years. Even more attuned to the spirit world.'

'Do you think it's Larry?' Mum asked. She sounded scared but kind of excited too, like a woman hearing that her bad-boy ex was back in town. 'Has he returned?'

Simon went over to the bookcase, touching the spines of some of the books Jessica had found on the floor during the night. Jessica wanted to grab hold of him, drag him out, but there were two things stopping her: social niceties, and a twisted desire to find out what he was going to say. Because weird stuff *had* been happening. And she couldn't deny it: there was a large part of her that believed in the paranormal. It was why she couldn't pass a lone magpie without saluting it. That superstitious part of her refused to completely die, no matter how hard she tried to smother it with reason.

'I don't think it's him,' Simon said. 'This presence feels different. Softer. And newer.'

Mum gasped. 'You mean . . .'

'A tender spirit. Like they only crossed over within the last five years.'

'Oh. Isabel.' Mum turned to Jessica. 'That fits, doesn't it? Isabel taught Olivia that song. She's been talking to her.'

She told Olivia she was pushed off the balcony by a bad man. Jessica's heart jolted.

'It could be,' Simon said. 'But if Isabel's spirit is lingering, that suggests—'

'No!' Jessica yelled, trying to hold on to reason. 'That's enough! My daughter is not being visited by the ghost of her dead aunt. This is craziness. And I don't want that old lech in my daughter's bedroom. You need to leave. Now.'

'Old lech?' Mum spluttered. 'What are you talking about?'

Simon tried to touch Jessica's arm and she backed away, pointing towards the door again. 'Go.'

He still didn't move.

'I said, *go!*' This time she did shout. Mum was horrified, and tried to apologise on Jessica's behalf, which made her even more furious.

'Get *out!*'

Simon left the room first, then Mum, and Jessica shooed them towards the stairs and down to the front door.

'I'm not having you coming round here, freaking out my daughter. There has to be a simple explanation for everything that's happened. Olivia made all that mess in her room herself. Maybe she was sleepwalking, who knows? Four-year-olds do that kind of stuff. As for the song, she must have heard it online or on the radio. There's no great mystery here. No need for all this overreaction.'

By the time she had finished she had almost convinced herself.

'Will you not even let me set up some equipment?' Simon asked.

She stepped past him and opened the front door. A blast of cold, refreshing air hit her. 'Goodbye, Simon.'

She held up a hand to indicate that she didn't want Mum to speak. As soon as they were outside she shut the door and slumped against it.

She felt ashamed for having let the irrational voices creep into her head. The idea that Izzy's ghost was visiting them, talking to Olivia, was ludicrous. Again she chided herself for telling Mum what had happened. She should have known she'd get overexcited.

She spoke to the empty air. 'You're not there, are you, Izzy?' She forced herself to laugh, to make light of it. 'Knock once if you are.'

A thump came from the kitchen.

Jessica clutched her chest, then collapsed on the floor, giggling helplessly. It was the dog, that was all, and here he was, trotting along the hallway to lick her face. No ghosts here. No phantoms – just an overweight golden retriever with meaty breath.

She led Caspar back to the kitchen, wishing it wasn't too early for a glass of wine, and her phone rang.

'Is that Mrs Gardner?'

It was a young woman. She didn't recognise the voice. 'Yes.'

'I'm calling from Foxgrove School. It's about Olivia.' The woman had a smooth, officious voice, but she sounded a little nervous. 'Um, would you be able to come and collect her? It's nothing to worry about, but there's been an incident.'

Chapter 12

All the way to school Jessica imagined the worst. The woman had said there was nothing to fret about, but how could a mother not worry? She pictured Olivia falling from a climbing frame and landing on her face. Or riding one of those stupid trikes into a wall. Although if Olivia was really hurt they would have said 'accident' not 'incident', wouldn't they?

Oh God, what had happened? It was almost home time so it must be serious, otherwise they would have waited until then.

She pulled into the school car park a little too fast, narrowly avoiding a shiny four-by-four that looked far too expensive for a teacher. Squeezing her car into the gap beside it, she ran up to the double doors that led to the reception area and pressed the buzzer. She stood there, sweaty and dishevelled, tapping her foot impatiently and pressing the buzzer again before telling herself to calm down. She could imagine the school staff judging her, thinking it was no wonder Olivia was acting up, before getting straight on the phone to social services. Will always laughed at her when she mentioned social services, which, in Jessica's mind, was a great modern bogeyman, a band of contemporary child-catchers who would swoop in with their big net and take your kid away if it had a dirty face or was overweight or underweight or watched too much TV.

It didn't matter that the papers were full of contradictory evidence: all those neglected, abused children who were left to live with their parents after multiple visits from social workers, before ending up dead. With a mixture of horror and fury Jessica recalled that case of the little girl who had been forced to live with her dad despite her grandparents' protests; the dad who had tortured and murdered her. It was a grim reality check: no one was going to take Olivia away. But that didn't mean people wouldn't look at Jessica and judge her. *Bad mother.* That was the very worst label of all.

Finally she was let in and the receptionist asked her to wait. She anxiously chewed her thumbnail until Mrs Rose appeared.

'Ah, Jessica, thanks for coming in.'

'What's happened? Is Olivia all right?'

Mrs Rose led her into a little room beside the school hall and asked her to take a seat on a rickety wooden chair. It wouldn't have surprised Jessica if this very chair had been here when she attended Foxgrove thirty years ago. There was probably chewing gum stuck beneath it that was older than most of the teaching assistants.

'I'm afraid we had a biting incident,' Mrs Rose said, pulling up an equally rickety chair.

Jessica was thrown back to Halloween, when Olivia had bitten her. She put her head in her hands. 'Oh God. I'm so sorry.'

'Oh no – it wasn't Olivia doing the biting. Another child bit *her*.'

'What? Is she okay?' Jessica stood up, emotions torn in two: guilt that she had presumed her daughter was the offender, but, chiefly, concern. 'I want to see her now.'

'Please, Jessica, sit down.'

Reluctantly Jessica did as she was asked, but a torrent of questions rushed forth the moment her bottom touched the chair. 'Is she hurt? Where did they bite her? Did they break the skin?'

'She's fine. The other child bit her on the arm.' She touched a point just below her elbow. 'And no, it didn't break the skin. It's left a bit of a red mark but it's nothing serious.'

Jessica knew Mrs Rose wouldn't tell her who the other child was, so it wasn't worth asking.

'I don't understand. Isn't this something you could have told me when I picked her up? Why did you bring me in early?'

Mrs Rose shifted on her seat. 'It's because, well, the other child says he bit Olivia because she was scaring him.'

Here it came. The ice-cold trickle in her guts. She swallowed. 'Scaring him?'

'Yes.' Mrs Rose fiddled with the collar of her blouse. 'They were all in the playground for afternoon break. It's difficult to get much sense out of a group of four- and five-year-olds, but apparently Olivia wanted to play "ghosts".'

Jessica held her breath.

'It's something she's wanted to play a lot recently, according to the other children. Like I said, it's hard to get a coherent picture, but I think the game consists of one child pretending to die, before coming back to haunt the other children and chase them around until they find out who killed them.'

'Oh my God.'

Mrs Rose smiled wryly. 'It was all tag and kiss chase in your day, wasn't it? Anyway, this boy, the one who bit Olivia, says that she really frightened him because she was playing the ghost and was running after him screaming, "You killed me, you killed me." She grabbed hold of him, so he says, and said she was going to kill him too, and that's when he bit her.'

Jessica didn't know what to say. It was another thing. Another strange, disturbing incident to add to the list.

'Is everything all right at home?' Mrs Rose asked.

'Yes. It's fine.' She hoped Mrs Rose couldn't see through the lie, although the teacher was used to dealing with small children. She was undoubtedly an expert at sniffing out bullshit.

'Hmm. Olivia seems . . . unusually interested in death. Isabel died before Olivia was born, didn't she? Have you had any other, more recent deaths in the family?'

'No.'

'What about pets? Have any of them died?'

Jessica shook her head.

Mrs Rose attempted a reassuring look. 'I'm sure it's nothing to worry about. This is the age when most children start to develop an awareness of death. It's generally more pronounced when they've experienced it directly – a grandparent or other elderly relative, or a pet. But maybe . . . I don't know. Do you talk about what happened to Isabel a lot at home? I know I said you mustn't forget about Isabel but perhaps you shouldn't talk about her so much in front of Olivia.'

'But we don't.'

'Oh. Well, perhaps Olivia really is being visited by a ghost. Like you and Isabel when you were children.'

'*What?*'

Mrs Rose held her hands up. 'I'm only joking, Jessica. Listen, Olivia has a vivid and creative imagination. I expect in a couple of years her English teacher will be getting her to read her stories out to the class. As long as they're not *too* scary. But I'm sure that's all it is. Her imagination.'

'You don't think I need to seek professional help? Take her to a child psychologist?'

'Oh, goodness, no. Like I said, it's her imagination. We certainly don't want to stunt or curb that in any way, do we? But we need to ensure she understands boundaries. That the other children are less comfortable with make-believe than she is.'

Jessica was silent for a minute. The teacher's words made sense, but Mrs Rose didn't know about everything that had been happening at home.

Unusually interested in death. Mrs Rose's words made Jessica shudder. She had no idea what was going on with her daughter, and it made her want to weep with frustration. The only thing she knew for certain was that this interest wasn't because of a real ghost. She knew that one hundred per cent.

Well, ninety-nine per cent.

Ninety per cent.

'Honestly, Jessica, I don't want you to be overly concerned,' Mrs Rose said, breaking the silence. 'But we should both work on ensuring Olivia knows not to frighten her classmates. I think we should get her to channel her imagination in other ways. Like drawing. That would be an excellent outlet for her. I know she's a keen artist already, so let's really try to encourage her.'

The bell rang. Almost immediately there was a shift in the atmosphere inside the school, the sound of doors opening, little feet dashing for freedom. Outside, parents would be gathered around the classrooms like zombies crowding a shopping mall.

'That time already?' said Mrs Rose, standing up. 'I need to get back. If you wait here I'll get someone to bring Olivia up.'

'Okay. Thank you.'

Jessica paced around the room, thoughts overlapping one another, until a member of staff brought Olivia in. Jessica wanted to look at her skin, to see how bad the bite mark was, but Olivia ran straight into her arms, pushing her hot little body against Jessica's and bursting into tears. Jessica held her, stroking her back and shushing her, but the tears didn't stop.

'He . . .' Olivia fought for breath, on the verge of hyperventilating. '. . . bited . . . me . . .'

'It's okay, sweetheart. It's okay.'

'He said . . . I . . . was a . . . monster.'

Jessica lifted Olivia, still sniffling against her shoulder, tears soaking through to Jessica's skin, and carried her through the playground towards the car park. She didn't need to pick Felix up yet because he had football practice after school.

A woman was standing by the fence at the edge of the playground. It was Pat, the dinner lady they had encountered on Halloween. She nodded at the clearly upset Olivia.

'Oh dear. What's the matter?'

'Just an upset at playtime,' Jessica replied.

'Poor mite. Nothing serious, I hope.'

'No, it's fine . . .'

Olivia lifted her head from Jessica's shoulder and stared at Pat.

'Will it hurt?' she said.

'Pardon?' Pat looked from Olivia to Jessica and back again.

Jessica knew Olivia was going to say something terrible. She could feel it. She tried to hurry away, nodding an apology to Pat, but she was too slow. Olivia was still staring at the dinner lady.

'When you die,' she said to her. 'Will it hurt when you die?'

Chapter 13

Jessica left Pat reeling and hurried to the car park. She put Olivia into her car seat and strapped her in.

'Why did you say that?'

Olivia closed her eyes. 'Because she's going to die.'

Jessica was about to say 'Everybody dies', but remembered Mrs Rose talking about Olivia's 'unusual interest in death' and decided it was probably best to change the subject completely. 'We're going to go to the shop and buy you a nice present.'

Olivia swallowed, gazing at Jessica with big, shining eyes. 'What kind of present?'

'How about a big new drawing book and pens?'

Olivia thought about it. 'And a new pony?'

'Maybe.'

Olivia's bottom lip trembled.

'Okay, a new pony.'

The little girl brightened and launched into a commentary about which *My Little Pony* character she most wanted. Applejack or maybe Fluttershy or perhaps even Pinkie Pie. Jessica closed the car door and stood there, taking deep breaths, the bitter November air tasting sweet, even as the wind chilled the damp patch of tears on her shoulder. The act of doing nothing but standing there, eyes closed, breathing, calmed her. Mrs Rose's words, the visit from Mum and Simon Parker, all the worries that had been crowding her mind, drifted away like smoke caught on the breeze.

Inhale. Exhale.

Leaning against the car, she felt her shoulders relax, was aware of her feet on solid ground. She counted to five as she breathed in, then seven as she breathed out.

Inhale. Exhale.

Her mind tried to rebel, to pull back all those escaping worries – Olivia's behaviour, what to do about Mum, the fear that everyone would think she was a bad parent – but she was able to focus on breathing, just as Izzy had taught her. Finally, and she had no idea how long it had taken, she felt calm. Clear-headed and able to drive home. To face the rest of the day.

'Are you all right?'

She opened her eyes, startled. It was Mr Cameron. *Ryan.* Jessica must have been standing there a while because the car park was half-empty and most of the kids had gone from the playground. She guessed dozens of parents must have walked past and looked at her like she was crazy. With her newly clear mind, though, she found she didn't care.

'I thought you'd fallen asleep on your feet,' he said.

She was going to make something up, but the truth came out before she could stop it. 'I was practising my mindfulness exercises. Trying to calm myself down.'

Ryan nodded as if this was perfectly normal. 'Some of the teachers here are into that stuff. It's all the rage these days, isn't it?'

'My sister was an early adopter.'

He smiled. 'Yeah . . . I read an interview with her. The one that was in *The Herald.*' He glanced at Olivia, who was starting to look very bored inside the car. 'I guess you needed to calm down after what happened this afternoon. The biting thing, I mean.'

'Did you see it?' Jessica asked.

'No. I saw her immediately afterwards, but I was on the other side of the playground.'

She fought the temptation to ask him who the culprit was – or the victim, she should probably say, as it sounded like Olivia had scared the poor kid out of his wits.

Instead she said, 'Mrs Rose thinks Olivia has some kind of obsession with death.'

'Is that what she said?' Ryan looked uncomfortable, as if he was on the verge of crossing a professional line.

Jessica was about to tell him what Olivia had just said to Pat, but was too ashamed. 'Have you heard Olivia say anything . . . out of the ordinary? Since that time she claimed to have spoken to her dead aunt, I mean?'

He seemed even less comfortable now. 'I don't know. I guess . . . There was one thing she said. Last week, I think.'

'What was it?'

'She asked me where people go after they die. I told her they go to heaven.'

That was the response she expected. 'Okay.'

'And she said, "But do they sometimes wait around first? Before they go up?"'

'What did you say?'

'I told her no, that good people go straight to heaven. But she didn't seem satisfied. She said, "But what if they need to tell someone something? There aren't any phones in heaven, are there?"'

He searched Jessica's face, apparently checking to see if this would make her smile. Normally it would. But not today.

He went on. 'To be honest, I didn't really know what to say. I think I tried to change the subject.'

'I understand. But—'

'I'm sorry, Jessica, but I need to get going.'

He waved through the window to Olivia, who was now smiling at him. Jessica watched him lope across the car park and climb into a red VW Polo.

'Mummy, are we going to the shop?' Olivia demanded when Jessica opened her door.

'Right away, madam.' She got in and started the engine. Ahead of them, Ryan left the school grounds.

'Good,' Olivia said. A pause. 'Because Izzy wants to come too. Don't you, Izzy?'

She looked at the empty space beside her and Jessica stalled the car.

'Oh, Mummy,' Olivia said. 'Please be careful. Izzy isn't wearing her seat belt.'

Jessica turned around in her seat. She had gone cold inside. 'Can you see her, Olivia? Can you see Izzy next to you?'

Maybe she had spoken too harshly. Maybe it was the look on her face. But Olivia began to cry.

Jessica couldn't get any sense out of her, just more tears. But she was sure the temperature inside the car had dropped, and she found herself rubbing her eyes, almost convinced she could sense a shimmering presence on the back seat.

Chapter 14

October 2012

Isabel's first instinct, when she saw the picture of the naked breasts on Darpak's phone, was to confront him. To shout at him and demand answers. Who was she? How long had it been going on? Did he love her? There was a pre-existing script for people who found out their partner was cheating on them. A script with a set of storylines that could go in one of two directions. Split or stick.

She knew what would happen if she chose to confront him. She could see it. Anger, tears, his shame, the excuses and justification he would no doubt come out with. All that pain. The prospect of it was exhausting.

She heard the bathroom door open, bare feet padding across the floor towards her. He must have sensed her presence. Or maybe he was coming to get his phone, planning to take it back into the bathroom with him so he could ogle those naked breasts, touch himself . . .

A spasm of loathing almost made her throw up. The sensation was so shocking – this was the man she loved – that the red mist in her head cleared for a moment. Maybe there was an innocent explanation. One of his mates messing around. Maybe he was innocent but was being pursued by whoever had sent the photo.

The tart.

She could hear her mum's voice, using that stupid word to describe the woman Dad had run off with. She could still remember overhearing Mum screaming at him when she found out. Could hear their shouts. That was long before the days of cameras on phones, and Izzy didn't know how Mum had discovered his affair. But what she did know was that after that argument he had left. Run off to Ireland.

And Izzy had never seen him again.

Did she want to risk that happening with her and Darpak? Especially as she didn't have proof, yet, that this selfie meant anything. He hadn't shown any other signs that he was having an affair. Maybe she was jumping to conclusions . . . although it was hard not to.

She quickly put the phone back on the table where she'd found it and crossed to the window, pretending she was admiring the view. She hoped he couldn't see how she was trembling.

'Oh. Hi.' He came into the room. He was wearing the white robe she'd bought him for his birthday. His hair was still wet and he needed a shave. 'I didn't know you were back.'

She turned, just as his eyes flicked away from his phone. Was he wondering if she'd looked at it? It was important to act normal, so he didn't suspect anything was wrong.

'I just did that interview with the local paper,' she said.

He picked up his phone and stuck it in the pocket of his robe. 'How did it go?'

She decided not to tell him about the Larry questions. 'Really well, I think.'

He smiled. She had always loved that smile, the one she was sure he showed only her. Now she pictured him smiling at the other woman. Smiling as she took off her clothes in front of him. Where did they do it? Hotel rooms? Her place? In his car? Had he been in the shower because he'd been with his slut today?

She forced herself to stop thinking about it, knowing the disgust would be visible on her face.

'That's great. I'd better get dressed,' he said. 'I've got a meeting at two.'

With the slut? Was that why he'd been in the shower?

She followed him into the bedroom. 'Do you really have to go to this meeting? I thought maybe we could spend the afternoon together.' She sat on the bed and smiled up at him, not sure what she was doing. Was she really suggesting sex when she suspected him of adultery? Testing his desire for her?

'Oh God, Izzy, I'd love to. But I really can't afford to miss this meeting.'

He came over and kissed her. He was still a little damp. The kiss got hotter and he made the groaning noise he always made when he was turned on. But then he pulled away.

'Can we park this till later?'

'I might not be in the mood later.'

'Isabel . . .'

She stood up. 'It's fine. You've put me off now anyway, talking about "parking it".'

She left the bedroom, ignoring his protests.

He came out ten minutes later. She refused to kiss him goodbye. As he was leaving she asked who the meeting was with and he named one of his wealthiest clients. He went out to his car, unlocking it remotely, and the beeping noise reminded her of a text message, which made her picture the topless selfie.

She ran out after him and grabbed hold of him just before he could get in his car.

'Are you all right?' he asked. 'You're acting weird.'

'Do you love me?'

'What? Yes, of course. What's going on?'

'It's just . . . On the radio on the way home there was a phone-in about infidelity. All these woman whose husbands were cheating on them. You wouldn't do that, would you?'

'When I've got *you* at home?' He laughed. 'No way.'

He kissed her and slipped into the driver's seat. His eyes travelled up and down her body. 'Are you really not going to forgive me for asking if we can "park" it?'

'We'll see.'

He drove away and she watched him go. As he turned off the drive on to the road, the tears came. Because everything he'd said and done should have reassured her, except for the way his eyes had shifted when he'd said, 'No way.'

He'd looked away, just for a fraction of a second. She knew him. She knew that look.

He'd been lying.

Chapter 15

A week had passed since the biting incident at school, and nothing strange had happened during those seven days. Jessica had spent much of the week Christmas shopping and catching up with a few bits of work.

Today, Wednesday, Jessica didn't fancy going straight home after picking the kids up from school, so she took them to the local swimming pool. Felix was already a better swimmer than his mum – he'd recently earned his 1500-metre badge – and one of his mates was at the pool, so he swam with his friend while Jessica tried to encourage Olivia to take off her armbands.

'You don't really need them,' she said. 'Come on, I'll be right here next to you.'

'But I'm scared.' Olivia grabbed at her, the plastic armbands rubbing against Jessica's flesh in the water. She thought back longingly to the days when she could go swimming and enjoy herself instead of having a child clinging to her.

'Why are you scared?'

But Olivia wouldn't answer. She wanted to go in the toddlers' splash pool, even though she was too old for it. After attempting to argue, Jessica acquiesced and spent the next twenty minutes sitting in twelve inches of warm water, the upper half of her body freezing while Olivia paraded around happily, her armbands still on.

Afterwards, when she was helping Olivia get dressed, she said, 'Why were you scared of going in the pool?'

'I wasn't.'

'But . . .'

'Auntie Izzy can't swim.'

Once upon a time, Jessica would have considered this a non sequitur. But not now. It was true, for one thing. Izzy had never learned to swim. Though they had both had lessons when they were at primary school and Jessica had quickly taken to it, Izzy had hated it and used every excuse she could think of to get out of it. This was back before Dad left. He would take them to their weekly lesson and Jessica could still remember their arguments in the car afterwards, when she had secretly enjoyed his praise, the positive comparison to her older sister. In the end he'd given in, and Izzy had stopped going to lessons.

The goose bumps returned, even though she was fully dry and dressed now.

'How do you know Izzy couldn't swim?' she asked.

Olivia shrugged.

'Did she tell you?'

She thought Olivia was going to clam up as usual, but then she said, 'Nanny told me.'

At last, something with a simple explanation!

'Nanny?'

A nod. 'She showed me a picture.'

'Of what?'

Jessica ascertained that Mum had shown Olivia some photos of a holiday they'd taken when they were young. It must have been Pontins in Camber Sands, as there were, apparently, pictures of a sandy beach alongside some taken at an indoor swimming pool.

'You were in the water but Auntie Izzy was sitted by the side. She looked unhappy.'

'Yeah. That sounds right.'

Olivia nodded. 'She was frightened.'

Jessica kissed her head. 'Maybe. But there's no need to be afraid of the water, sweetheart.'

'No.'

Jessica continued to dry Olivia and get her dressed. Olivia appeared to be deep in thought and Jessica assumed she was thinking about Izzy and the pictures Mum had shown her. Though who knew what went on inside the head of a four-year-old. She might be thinking about what she was going to have for dinner or wondering if she was going to be on Santa's nice list.

'Mummy,' she said as Jessica finished putting her shoes on.

'Yes, Olivia?'

'What about fire? Should I be frightened of fire?'

Jessica held Olivia lightly by the shoulders. 'Why are you asking that?'

'It's a secret.'

'What?' She tightened her grip. 'What's a secret?'

Olivia wriggled away. 'You're hurting me!'

'Sorry. But you have to tell me – what secret are you talking about?'

Olivia squeezed her lips together until they all but disappeared.

'Olivia! Tell me! Why are you asking about fire?'

The other women in the changing room were staring at them, and Jessica realised she'd raised her voice. An elderly woman in a one-piece swimsuit gave her an admonishing look and Jessica took a deep breath, counting to three.

'Come on,' she said to Olivia. 'Let's go.'

They found Felix and drove home, skirting the park where the grey car had followed them. The road was quiet and a couple of street lights had died, sending them into a pocket of darkness beneath the overhanging trees. A chill passed through Jessica's body and she stared into the rear-view mirror, convinced they were being followed again. But when they hit the main road and the car was filled with light, she was able to persuade herself it had been nothing more than an echo of her earlier fear. No one was following them.

They stopped at the traffic lights beside Jessica's old school, William Peacocke Secondary. She noticed that Olivia had her face pressed to the window, looking out at the dark, squat building.

'That's my and Auntie Izzy's old secondary school,' Jessica said.

It had a bad reputation now, and Felix was going to go to a better school near Penge. She realised as she looked at William Peacocke that she had few happy memories of the place. Mean teachers, even meaner kids. Revolting dinners. Izzy had had a miserable time there too, especially in the months immediately following the newspaper article about Larry. It struck Jessica that she wouldn't be unhappy if the place burned down.

And as she thought this, Olivia whispered something she didn't catch.

The lights turned green and the car behind her sounded its horn. She drove on, hardly able to concentrate on the road.

'What did you say, Olivia?' Jessica asked.

'Nothing,' Olivia replied.

Felix, in the passenger seat beside Jessica, tutted. 'She said, "Fire is scary."' He peered back at his little sister and tutted again. 'Yeah, Olivia, that's right. Fire is scary. She's a psycho, Mum. A weird little psycho.'

But Olivia didn't seem bothered by her brother's insult. She continued to look back at the school, mouthing something under her breath.

ʊ

They continued the drive home in near silence. Jessica stared out of the window at the dark streets, longing for a glass of wine.

She saw the flashing blue light as soon as they entered the estate. An ambulance, parked a little way up the hill, with a small group of people crowded around. Jessica slowed the car to a halt and wound down her window. Felix and Olivia craned their necks to look.

One of the neighbours, Derek, approached the car, at the same time that Jessica realised whose house the ambulance was outside.

'What happened?' she asked.

Derek, a man in his sixties who was tall and dapper, held his hat against his stomach. 'It's Mrs Shelton,' he said. 'Pat. They say she had a fall.'

'Oh my God. Is she all right?'

'I'm afraid not. She banged her head and . . .' He glanced at the children, clearly not wanting to say any more in front of them.

Jessica whispered, 'She's dead?'

He nodded. 'She was a fine lady,' he said.

Jessica wound up the window and Derek drifted back towards the house. It wasn't unusual for an elderly lady who lived alone to fall and hurt herself, Jessica told herself. Not unusual at all.

She looked back at Olivia, whose face was pressed against the window, staring at the flickering light of the ambulance.

She must have felt Jessica looking at her, because she turned towards her mum. 'What happened, Mummy?' she asked. 'Who was that man talking about?'

Felix piped up. 'Mrs Shelton, the dinner lady. She's dead! He said she fell over and banged her head.'

Jessica winced, but couldn't take her eyes off her daughter. Realisation bloomed on her face as blue light bounced across it. In that instant she didn't look like a child, she seemed wise and old, just the latest face on a line that stretched back through history, into the ancient mist.

'Poor lady,' Olivia said. 'I bet it *did* hurt.'

Chapter 16

'Are you sure you've got everything?' Jessica asked for the fifth time, after Will had carried his and Felix's bags out and put them in the car.

'Yes! And they have shops on the Isle of Wight, you know.'

Felix was standing behind Will on the doorstep, impatient to get going. He looked so grown-up with the trendy new haircut he'd got during the week, and Jessica was certain he'd got a couple of inches taller in the past month. She had been so busy worrying about Olivia recently that she'd hardly given her son a thought. Guiltily, she made a vow to change that when he got back from this trip to a football tournament, which he and Will were both looking forward to hugely. A couple of days away from the stresses of home. She wished she were going instead of Will.

She kissed Will on the lips then grabbed Felix and mussed his hair before pulling him into a hug. 'Look after him,' she said.

'Who are you talking to?' Felix asked. 'Dad or me?'

'Both of you.'

Olivia came out and they waved as the car pulled away.

'Right,' she said to Olivia. 'It's just us girls now.'

Olivia beamed, showing off her perfect little teeth. 'All the girls.'

They went inside. The house felt strange. Jessica was so used to her radar tracking two children that when one of them was absent it took a while for her system to adjust. Olivia had already run into the kitchen, declaring that she was hungry. Caspar followed her with his eyes, thumping his tail against his bed. Once, when he was younger, Caspar would have bounded around too, but these days he was content to watch, tongue lolling.

'Okay, what would you like for dinner?'

'An ice lolly.'

'Livvy, you can't have an ice lolly for dinner. How about mac and cheese?'

'A jam sandwich. And a lolly.'

If it didn't contain sugar, Olivia didn't want it. 'Mac and cheese it is.'

While Jessica made Olivia's dinner she reflected on the week just gone. Everything had been quiet on the Olivia front. There had been no nocturnal disturbances. No incidents at school. In fact, both Mrs Rose and Ryan said Olivia had been 'good as gold' all week and there had been no sign of her supposed death fixation. And what Olivia had said to Pat Shelton, only a week before she died, had to be a coincidence. There was no other possible explanation for it. No rational one, anyway.

Olivia and Felix had gone to Mum's for tea on Tuesday and Thursday, because Jessica suddenly had a rush of pre-Christmas work to get done, and Mum hadn't reported any strange occurrences either. Jessica had immediately shut down Mum's attempt to talk about Simon Parker. She was sick of talking and thinking about all of it. Christmas was a month away and Jessica didn't want to think about anything except all the presents she needed to buy, all the preparation that would fill December. Soon, she was sure, Olivia's recent strange behaviour would be nothing more than a small family mystery, something she and Will would laugh about until it was wholly forgotten.

Yesterday evening, when she'd gone to pick the kids up, Olivia had been sitting quietly on the living room floor with her new drawing pad while Mum and Pete watched their favourite quiz show. (One of the contestants was black and another was in a wheelchair, which was, according to Pete, the BBC 'pandering to political correctness'.) Jessica had gone to take a look at what Olivia was drawing but Olivia had snatched the book away, saying it was 'a secret'.

'I think she's doing a picture for your Christmas card,' Pete whispered when Olivia left the room with the pad. He had recovered from his bug and had already regaled Jessica with the grim details. 'I lost two pounds!' he said, patting his belly.

As well as refusing to worry about Olivia's behaviour and so-called death obsession, Jessica had been practising her mindfulness techniques every day, so by the time the weekend approached she was as relaxed as she ever got. Yes, Will was going away, so she worried about him and Felix, but only a little. She was determined that this weekend would be stress-free. Stress-free and fun.

She served the macaroni and cheese and sat with Olivia while she ate.

'Aren't you having dinner too, Mummy?'

'I'm going to eat a bit later.'

Olivia thought about this. 'Are you going to have yucky food?'

'Oh yes. Lots of vegetables. A whole plate full of vegetables.'

Olivia stuck out her tongue. 'Disgusting.'

Jessica tried not to laugh, but it was hard. 'Come on, sweetheart. Eat yours before it goes cold.'

'Yes, Mummy.'

Caspar had hauled himself out of his bed and was lying by Olivia's chair, hoping she would drop a piece of cheesy pasta. He had loved it when Olivia was a baby, food falling to the floor with pleasing regularity. Pickings were slimmer these days.

Olivia glanced down at Caspar then back at Jessica. 'There are three girls and one boy here.'

'Two girls, you mean.'

A look of surprise flitted across Olivia's face before she nodded seriously. 'Oh yes.' Her voice dropped to a whisper. Jessica wasn't one hundred per cent sure, but she thought her daughter said, in her most serious voice, 'It's a secret.'

'What's a secret, sweetheart?' Jessica was ignoring the butterflies in her stomach.

'Nothing, Mummy.'

She threw a strand of macaroni on the floor, which Caspar seized.

'Olivia!'

The little girl gazed at her with those big, innocent eyes. 'It wasn't me.'

'Then who was it?'

But Olivia didn't respond. She got down from her chair and embraced Caspar, pressing her face against his fur. Jessica's first instinct was to tell her to get up or she'd be covered in dog hair, but then she heard a sob.

'Olivia? What's wrong?'

Olivia hugged Caspar harder. He was so gentle and tolerant. He just lay there and took it.

'Sweetheart?' Jessica asked, dropping to her haunches beside them.

Olivia tore herself away from Caspar. A long gold hair clung to her damp cheek. Jessica plucked it away and pulled Olivia into a hug. 'Come on, tell me.'

She waited, sure Olivia was going to tell her it was a secret again. But instead all she said was, 'Can I have an ice lolly now? Please?'

ω

Jessica let Olivia stay up late, snuggling with her on the sofa and putting on *Frozen*. Olivia rarely sat through a whole film, but now she was enrapt. She watched with her eyes on stalks, her expression so comical that Jessica had to sneak a photo, which she texted to Will.

Are you sure she should be watching that? he texted back.

She replied: Why do you say that?

Isn't it a bit scary for a four-year-old? And then there's the sisters thing. Anyway, about to board ferry. Will call when we get there x

Oh God, had she made a mistake letting Olivia watch it? She didn't seem frightened, even when Elsa and Anna's parents were killed early on. But they hadn't yet got to the part when Elsa uses her powers to summon a gigantic snow monster . . . What if it triggered the darker part of Olivia's imagination?

She hit pause.

'Mummy!' Olivia wailed.

'We should finish it tomorrow morning. It's very late. How about I make you a hot chocolate and we watch *Peppa Pig* before bed?'

'*Peppa Pig* is for babies. I want to watch *Frozen*!'

But in the end, the promise of hot chocolate ('With marshmallows!') was enough, and by the time they'd got through four episodes of *Peppa Pig* Olivia's eyelids were drooping. Once in bed, she fell asleep during her second story. Jessica kissed her forehead and tiptoed from the room.

She opened a bottle of red wine and poked through the cupboards, trying to find something that appealed. She rarely ate dinner if Will was out. In the end she grabbed a bag of Kettle Chips and some dip. She went back upstairs and put her fleece pyjamas on before settling on the sofa, with Caspar snoozing on the armchair. She flicked through the channels and scoured Netflix but couldn't find anything to watch, so decided to put on the last thirty minutes of *Frozen*.

She hadn't seen it before. The film came out not long after Olivia was born, when looking after a baby consumed her entire life. And there was another reason, although she'd never acknowledged it. *The sisters thing*, as Will had put it. She knew – because the songs were inescapable – that the movie was about a pair of sisters. For a long time after Izzy's death she had avoided anything that even touched on that topic. In the same way

Mum still couldn't watch certain soap operas, Jessica couldn't face books or films or TV shows that featured female siblings.

She thought she'd got over that, but watching the end of *Frozen* – when the blonde sister, the one with powers, was reunited with the younger, duller sister – Jessica felt that familiar burning behind her eyes. She fought it, laughing at herself, but it was impossible not to see Anna and Elsa as herself and Izzy. Except in this fictional world there was a happy ending. Nobody died.

By the time the film ended she was sobbing, a great torrent of tears bursting through the dam. She hugged Caspar, burying her face in his fur until she managed to get hold of herself.

The final credits rolled and the TV fell quiet. Apart from the sound of Caspar breathing beside her, the house was silent. Before moving here they had lived on a busy road, so the rush of traffic and the loud con-versations of passers-by had formed a constant backdrop to her life. She still hadn't got used to the end-of-the-world atmosphere of the estate.

Crossing to the window, she parted the curtains and peered out into the darkness. A fine, misty rain fell, the sodium-orange street lights failing to pierce the gloom. A cat slunk along a wall in search of shelter but, apart from that and a TV flicker in a house across the street, there was no sign of life. She shivered as she turned away, making sure there was no gap in the curtain. She laughed at herself. This was something she'd picked up from her mother, who said a gap allowed the devil to peek into the room.

Needing to eradicate the silence, Jessica put on a cookery show, just for the background noise, and poured a second glass of wine. She checked her phone, scrolled through Facebook and commented on a cute picture a friend had posted of her little boy. She had been so busy recently that she hadn't seen any of her friends, something she would need to rectify in the run-up to Christmas. She texted Will, asking him if they'd reached the hotel yet. The message displayed as 'read' almost immediately but he didn't respond. This was faintly irritating but she wasn't too bothered, not like in the old days when it would drive her crazy if he didn't answer a text quickly.

Caspar jumped down from the sofa and nudged her leg with his nose.

'Need a wee?' she said, leading him out to the kitchen and opening the back door, letting in a blast of frigid air.

She noticed that a pot plant had been knocked over. Caspar, presumably, when she'd let him out earlier. The rain had stopped temporarily so Jessica went out in her slippers to right it, the security light coming on as she crossed the small patio.

Caspar immediately ran over to the gate and barked. Maybe he'd spotted the cat Jessica had seen earlier. But then he barked again.

Jessica approached the gate, the dog at her feet. He wouldn't stop barking. She shushed him but he ignored her, yapping at something beyond the fence. She knew she could drag him inside but she had a strong urge to see what had excited him.

There was a gap between two of the panels on the fence, which they'd been meaning to fix for ages. Standing on the edge of the lawn, she looked through it. There was a grey car on the other side of the road, with someone sitting in the driver's seat. It was too dark to see them properly, but she was sure the driver was looking at her house.

Caspar let out a volley of barks and the car engine and lights came on. Immediately it pulled away and vanished around the corner. But not before Jessica saw the badge on the back. The H.

It was the same car that had followed her around the park. This time, she definitely wasn't imagining it.

Chapter 17

Jessica went back into the kitchen with Caspar at her heels, and shut and double-locked the door.

The same car.

She stood with her back to the door, hand on her chest, feeling as if her heart was going to burst out of it. She could call the police, but what was the point? *There was a car parked opposite my house that I think might have followed me around the park a couple of weeks ago.* It sounded ridiculous.

But her entire body thrummed with unease. The empty spaces in the house felt haunted. The shadows were dark with menace. Every creak and rustle startled her. The dog seemed tense as well, staring into the hallway outside the kitchen and barking as if there was something, someone, there. She rubbed his ears, wishing they didn't own such a soft dog, that they'd got a vicious Dobermann or German shepherd instead.

She walked around the house with Caspar following, checking the doors and windows were secured and drawing the curtains. All the while she told herself she was worrying about nothing. She had looked up the H badge after the previous incident and confirmed that it was the Hyundai symbol. It was a common make, and grey was an even more popular colour. It had to be some random person, unconnected to the incident by the park, which itself had almost certainly been an idiot messing around.

She found her wine glass. As she raised it to her lips her phone rang, making her jump.

It was Will, telling her about the journey, the choppy ferry, how Felix had gone green and almost thrown up, the cramped room they were staying in. She was going to tell him about the car but stopped herself. He was a hundred miles away and couldn't do anything to help. That made her wonder if the car owner – the word 'stalker' tried to creep into her head but she rejected it – had known Will was going away. Were they watching her because they knew she was alone with Olivia?

By the time she got her thoughts in order Will was saying, 'Okay, I'd better go. Felix needs a good night's sleep for the tournament tomorrow.'

He hung up, leaving her alone. Caspar had flaked out in the kitchen. It was half ten and she was way too wired to sleep. She went back to the sofa with her wine and switched on the TV. The local news was on. It took a moment for her to register what she was seeing. It was a building, ablaze and surrounded by fire engines, great jets of water arcing into the flames. The ticker at the bottom of the screen declared that these were live pictures. She grabbed the remote and turned it up, just as the picture cut back to the news anchor in the studio.

'Scenes there from William Peacocke Secondary in Beckenham, South London. For updates on that story . . .'

Jessica gasped and got up from the sofa.

'How?' Jessica said aloud. 'How is that possible?' She stared at the TV, which had moved on to the next story.

Fire is scary. Olivia had said that, hadn't she, when they'd driven past the school? A chill rippled through her, making her shiver from head to toe. She thought of Pat Shelton, who would never serve another school meal. She remembered how Pete had got sick after Olivia told him to get well soon.

Jessica had gone cold. Because no matter how much she kept telling herself there had to be a rational explanation for all this, the evidence was mounting that there was something inexplicable going on. Something seriously fucking creepy.

She poured herself another glass of wine and threw it back. Then poured another.

She didn't want to think about any of it any more. She wanted to knock herself out.

ʊ

Jessica dreamed she was running through a school playground at dusk. The school looked like William Peacocke but the brickwork was crumbling and ivy crept up its facade, as if the school had stood abandoned for decades. *All the children, all those poor children*, she thought, though her dreaming brain couldn't tell her what had happened to them. All she knew was that she was being chased by someone in a grey car, the vehicle barely visible in the fading light, the driver hidden behind tinted windows. Clutching her chest, she ran, past the climbing frame and goalposts, leaving the tarmac of the playground and entering the field. The car was getting closer, its engine growling, closer and closer until it was on her heels, but somehow she was able to keep just ahead as she hurtled down a slope.

She heard Olivia calling to her from somewhere ahead, hidden by shadows, a desperate cry that squeezed Jessica's heart. She tried to speak, to call her daughter's name, but she had forgotten how to. She kept running, muscles aching, knees and lungs begging her to stop, but she had to keep going, had to find Olivia, had to—

A door slammed.

She woke up.

In those first disorientating seconds she didn't know where she was. Will was not beside her. She wasn't even in bed. No, she was on the sofa and the TV was still on. She must have fallen asleep. Half a glass of wine sat on the coffee table before her, the bottle empty beside it. Her mouth felt as if some small furry creature had set up home on her tongue, and she was shivering. The heating had gone off and the room was so cold she could almost have been outside.

She had a flash of herself running across the playing field in her dream.

The slamming door. Had it been in her head? On TV? Or had it been in real life? Had a noise in the house woken her?

Was there someone in the house?

The stalker. The man in the car.

She pushed herself off the sofa, wincing at the stiffness in her neck, and looked around for something she could use as a weapon. There was a heavy brass candlestick above the fireplace. She picked it up and weighed it in her hand. She looked around for her phone, then remembered she'd left it charging in the kitchen.

She opened the living room door and peered out into the hallway. The light was on, and everything was silent and still. She tried to persuade herself she was worrying about nothing, that the noise had been in her dream. Or maybe it had been the dog. He occasionally barked in the night and had been known to knock things over. Most likely, that's what had happened.

Or it was Olivia.

Olivia, throwing things around in her bedroom again.

The thought propelled her into the hallway. The floorboards were cold through her thin socks. There was no noise coming from upstairs and the kitchen was closer so she decided to check in there first, rather than risk disturbing her sleeping daughter.

She turned on the kitchen light and Caspar looked up at her from his bed, hoisting himself up on his ageing legs and trotting towards her, tail wagging. There was no sign that he was responsible for the noise. After she petted him he lumbered back to his bed.

She grabbed a glass and filled it with water which she gulped down, washing away the furry creature on her tongue. Perhaps the noise had been in her dream after all.

No, whispered a little voice in her head. *It was Olivia.*

She needed to check. Taking the candlestick with her, she left the kitchen and climbed the stairs to the dark middle floor of the house. She flicked on the light, bracing herself, half expecting something to leap out at her. The loose floorboard at the top of the stairs creaked as she trod over it.

Gently, as quietly as she could, she pushed open Olivia's bedroom door and slipped inside.

The first thing she saw in the orange glow of the night light was a couple of small dark shapes on the floor.

Tiny bodies.

She shook herself. They were soft toys, that was all.

But there was something wrong in the room. She couldn't hear her daughter's soft breathing. And the covers were pulled back.

Trying not to panic, she dashed over to Olivia's bed.

It was empty.

Chapter 18

'Olivia!'

Jessica hurtled along the landing, skidding on the carpet, gripped by a blind desperation. First, she checked her and Will's bedroom. She could imagine Olivia crawling into their bed, looking for Mummy and Daddy, and falling asleep. But the bed was empty and undisturbed, the quilt smooth and flat.

She ran into Felix's room. It was a mess, with clothes hanging from drawers and video game cartridges scattered across the carpet. Normally this sight would poke directly at Jessica's inner neat freak but right now she couldn't care less. Olivia was not in the room. That was all that mattered.

It was the car. The grey car. She ran over to Felix's bedroom window and yanked the curtains aside, half expecting to see the car parked outside, or pulling away, Olivia pressing her palms against the window, screaming for help. But the street was empty. Maybe he'd already been and gone, the child abductor, spiriting Olivia away to a dark basement somewhere, an empty warehouse, an abandoned outhouse, the kind of place where children were murdered.

And worse.

She dug her fingernails into her palm. *Get a grip*, she told herself. *Get a fucking grip*. She had locked all the doors and windows. There was no way anyone could have got into the house.

So perhaps Olivia had wandered out. Perhaps she had looked for Jessica in her bed and, using whatever logic four-year-olds use, decided she must have left the house and gone looking for her.

No, that was impossible. The bolts on the front and back doors were too high for Olivia to reach.

Except . . . A foggy memory came back to her: she had let Caspar out for a final wee shortly before she'd fallen asleep. Had she remembered to slide the bolt back into place? She sprinted downstairs and into the kitchen.

The bolt was in place at the top of the door. Olivia had to be in the house.

But where?

Feeling a little less panicked, she looked in the downstairs rooms, then went back up the stairs, calling Olivia's name. There was no response. She looked in the spare room, which was mainly used to store junk, boxes full of stuff that hadn't yet made it into the loft. There was nowhere in this room for a little girl to hide, but one of Olivia's teddy bears lay just inside the door. That was strange. It was unusual too for this door to be open. There was a wooden cabinet just inside the room. Was that the noise Jessica had heard? This door banging into the cabinet as Olivia pushed it open?

She picked up the teddy, which was lying face down, turned it over and almost dropped it. She blinked, thinking she might be hallucinating, but no – this was real.

The teddy bear's eyes had been ripped off, white stuffing spilling from the holes.

Had Caspar done it? He had been known to chew up soft toys and pull bits off them. Not possible. Jessica was sure this bear had been sitting on Olivia's quilt when she put her to bed, and the dog hadn't been upstairs.

Which meant Olivia must have removed the eyes.

Olivia or someone else.

Something else.

She remembered the dark shapes she had seen on Olivia's floor. She had been so fixated on Olivia's absence that she hadn't given them a second thought. But now she needed to see. Fear squeezed her insides but she fought it and went back into Olivia's bedroom. She dropped to her hands and knees and grabbed the closest toy, a brown dog.

Its eyes were missing too, stuffing creeping out of its face.

Lying next to the dog was Olivia's giraffe, Stretch. Her very favourite toy. His eyes had been cut off too. Horrified, Jessica threw it on to the floor, along with the dog and teddy bear. As they landed, she saw a pair of scissors, poking out from beneath the chair. It was a sharp pair of scissors that had gone missing ages ago. What were they doing in Olivia's room?

Jessica stood in the centre of the room, semi-delirious, and closed her eyes. When she opened them she was sure the soft toys had shuffled a couple of inches closer to her, with their sightless faces turned towards her, and in her head she heard the giraffe speak to her in the high-pitched voice Olivia always used for it.

Help us.

Finding it hard to breathe, Jessica threw herself out of the room, hitting the wall and sinking to her haunches. She had her hands in her hair. Olivia had taken a pair of scissors and cut the eyes out of her favourite toys. It was almost impossible to believe. Jessica reached forward and pulled the bedroom door closed, gripped by the belief that they were going to come out after her, grotesque, blind animals, lurching towards her. She could picture them in there now, coming to life, shuffling towards the door.

Help us.

Pushing herself to her feet, she ran back along the landing, towards the master bedroom, away from Olivia's room. And then she heard it: a faint, high-pitched noise. A whimper.

It had come from above. From Will's office.

She hurtled up the stairs, grabbing the banister to swing round into Will's office. She flicked on the light, expecting to see her daughter, but there was no sign of her.

'Olivia?' she said.

Silence.

'Olivia! Where are you?'

A sob came from beneath the desk. Almost fainting with relief, Jessica dropped to her knees and found herself looking at her daughter.

She was under the desk, back pressed against the wall, arms wrapped around her knees, face pressed into a pyjama sleeve. Jessica shuffled forward and put out a hand.

'Sweetheart. Come on out.'

Olivia lifted her face. Her eyes were pink with the echoes of tears. 'I'm frightened.'

Jessica scooted beneath the desk and put her hands on Olivia's shoulders. She didn't want to forcibly pull her out. 'There's nothing to be scared of.'

Olivia still didn't move.

'Come on. Please, Livvy.'

Slowly, glacially, Olivia inched forward. Unable to hold back any longer, Jessica grabbed hold of her shivering daughter and pulled her into an embrace. Olivia was as cold as a body in a morgue. Jessica lifted her up and carried her downstairs to the master bedroom, putting her into the big double bed. She got in beside her and wrapped the quilt around them, holding on to her daughter's skinny little body. Eventually, Olivia stopped shivering.

'Livvy, tell me what happened. Why did you go up to Daddy's office?'

'Because they were watching us.'

'Who were?'

Olivia didn't reply at first. She buried her face against Jessica's chest. When she spoke her voice was muffled. 'My animals.'

Jessica pictured them, eyeless and sad, and shuddered. Again she had an image of the toys coming to life, groping their way along the hallway towards them, whispering *Help us* as they made their sad journey towards the little girl who had hurt them.

'That's why you . . . removed their eyes?'

A little nod. 'I'm sorry. I broked them. I broked Stretch.' Her voice trembled and she began to cry.

'It's okay,' Jessica whispered. 'We can fix them.' She hoped they could, anyway. She could still hardly believe that Olivia had done it. Had *managed* to do it. It must have taken a considerable amount of strength and dexterity. Olivia must have been . . . what?

Possessed.

She shook that thought away immediately, even if there was a grain of truth in it. Something had possessed Olivia. Some need. Some fear. And it had made her strong enough, desperate enough, to dig the scissors into the toys she cherished.

Olivia was on the verge of crying herself to sleep. Normally Jessica would have let her. But tonight, now, she needed to talk to her daughter. To find out what the hell was going on.

'What did you mean, sweetheart? When you said they were watching "us"?'

'Me and Izzy.'

Jessica shuffled backwards so she could see her daughter's face. 'Does Auntie Izzy talk to you?'

A nod. Then Olivia touched the side of her skull.

'She's inside your head?' Olivia flinched away. 'Come on, sweetheart, there's no need to be scared. Please, I need you to talk to me. Do you hear Izzy speaking to you?'

'I'm not allowed to talk about it.'

Jessica sat up straighter. 'What do you mean?'

'It's a secret.'

'What? Did Izzy tell you it's a secret?'

Pursed lips. No response. She was about to clam up completely.

Jessica changed tack. 'Do you think Izzy would talk to me too?'

'No. She only talks to me.'

'Why's that?'

'Because no one is allowed to know.'

'To know that she's talking to you?'

Olivia yawned and her eyes drooped. Oh God, she was falling asleep. Jessica couldn't let her – not just yet. She said, 'Is that why you had to cut out your animals' eyes? Because they saw Izzy?'

A tiny nod. 'Izzy doesn't want anyone else to see her.'

'Is that what she told you?'

Olivia tried to turn away, clearly getting fed up with all these questions.

But Jessica had to keep asking. 'Does Izzy tell you secrets?'

A long pause. 'Yes.'

'What kind of secrets?' Sensing that her daughter was about to shut down, she said, 'You can tell me. Auntie Izzy was my sister. I'm your mum. Can you tell me what kind of secrets they are?'

Silence. Olivia's eyes closed and her chin dipped. She had fallen asleep. Gently, Jessica laid her down, putting her head on the pillow. She sighed. It was exasperating. She lay down, putting her arm around Olivia.

The little girl wasn't fully asleep. She whispered something.

Jessica sat up, unsure of what she'd heard. 'What was that?'

Olivia didn't respond. Her breathing had changed now. She was fast asleep.

Jessica got out of bed. There was no way she was going to be able to get back to sleep now. She went back up to Will's office. She had been hit with an overwhelming need to smoke a cigarette, and she opened the drawer in which she'd found the packet the other day when she was looking for the radiator key.

The pack of cigarettes wasn't there.

Slumping back in Will's desk chair, she felt a flare of anger. He'd taken them with him. He was smoking again. Smoking while he was away with their son. She was tempted to call him right now, wake him up and tell him what had been going on at home, and as she imagined herself ranting at him it came to her: what Olivia had said as she fell asleep.

'*I drawed it.*'

Chapter 19

October 2012

Isabel gazed from the passenger window at the passing houses. She and Nina were on their way to meet a supplier of lubricants to talk about creating a Mind+Body brand of lube. It was potentially very exciting – the idea was that eventually they would have a whole range of products – but Isabel was finding it hard to concentrate.

Her thoughts kept drifting to Darpak. A week had passed since she'd found the selfie. She'd only had one other chance since to look at his phone. There were no more naked pics or mysterious messages, and the original selfie had been deleted, along with the phone number of the woman who'd sent it.

So the evidence of his adultery was gone, and she cursed herself, wishing she'd noted down the phone number or, better still, taken a photo of his screen. Every day she went to confront him but couldn't get the words out. If it had been her marriage alone, she could have faced it, but she was terrified of what it would mean for the business too. Darpak held forty-nine per cent of the shares in the company, an arrangement that had made sense when they set it up because he had provided the start-up capital.

If they split, she would need to buy Darpak out, unless he was willing to give her his shares, and finding the cash to do that, when the value of the company was booming, would be a nightmare. He could make things very difficult for her, and the thought of a long, painful court battle was too much to bear.

She hadn't slept properly since, tormenting herself with doubt and fear, constantly on the verge of shaking him awake and asking him about what she'd seen. Hating herself for not having the courage to do it.

'Are you all right?'

Nina had taken her eyes off the road to stare at her. They were stuck in stationary traffic.

'What? Yes, I'm fine.'

'You look like you're about to cry.'

Isabel turned her face away, towards the other vehicles. A tattooed guy in a white van winked at her. Behind him the golden arches of a McDonald's loomed. 'I'm tired, that's all.'

The traffic inched forward. 'Are you sure that's all it is?'

'Yes.'

But as she said this word, a tear, fat and treacherous, escaped and rolled down her cheek.

'Oh my God. Isabel. What's wrong?'

Suddenly Isabel felt the need to talk to someone. As well as being her assistant, Nina was Darpak's little sister. On one hand, that made her the worst person to talk to. On the other hand, she knew him. Maybe she could offer reassurance. Or give Isabel good advice.

It seemed that her body had already made its mind up, as more tears came. She swore at herself as she wiped them away with the sleeve of her new coat. This wasn't like her. She wasn't weak. She didn't cry like this.

'I think . . . I need a coffee,' Isabel said, half-laughing and half-crying, gesturing towards the McDonald's.

Nina nodded. She sounded the horn and edged her way through the traffic, ignoring the angry gestures of the other drivers, including the man in the white van. Eventually, reluctantly, they let her through. She turned into the McDonald's and drove up to the Drive-Thru window to order two coffees.

'So,' Nina said, pulling into the car park, 'do you want to tell me? It's not tiredness, is it? And if it's not nerves . . .'

Isabel sipped her drink. It burned her tongue.

'Do you promise this is between you and me? No matter what I tell you?'

'You haven't murdered someone, have you?'

'Ha! I've only thought about it . . . But seriously, do you promise?'

'Okay.'

Isabel took a deep breath.

'I think Darpak is cheating on me.' She exhaled. She felt a tiny bit better now the words were out there in the world.

'What? This is a joke, right?'

'No, Nina. It's not a joke. I found a picture on his phone. A woman sent him a photo of her tits with the message *To keep you going till next time.* And four kisses. Let's not forget the four kisses.'

Nina gawped at her. 'What woman?'

'I don't know her name. Stupidly, because I was so shocked, I didn't note down the number. And her face wasn't visible. He's deleted it since.'

'Does he know you saw it?'

'No. I don't think so, anyway.'

'You haven't spoken to him about it? Why not?'

'Because . . . I'm scared. Scared of what it will lead to. Divorce. Loads of messy shit around the business. And what if I give him an ultimatum, me or her, and he chooses her? Maybe if I leave it, pretend I don't know, it will burn itself out.'

Nina had been holding her coffee cup throughout this conversation without taking a sip. 'If he was having an affair, would you want to stay with him?'

'I don't know. I really don't know.' Isabel smiled humourlessly. 'But I'd like to be the one to decide.'

Nina finally took a sip of her coffee. 'I just can't see it. He adores you. It must be a mistake . . . A prank or something, one of his mates messing around. Or some woman who's into him, trying to come on to him. Did you see any messages from him to her?'

'No.'

'Then I bet that's it. Some slut trying to lead him astray.'

Isabel cringed. She hated that word. But she couldn't deny it had gone through her head numerous times recently, adding to her self-loathing, making her hate Darpak because it was his fault she was thinking it.

'The message said *Till next time*. Not *All this could be yours*.'

'I know. But . . . he loves you, Isabel. You're amazing. Beautiful and successful and . . . an expert in the thing men are most interested in.'

'Female pleasure?' Isabel said, deadpan.

That made Nina laugh. 'I meant sex. But I get your point.'

Isabel laughed too. 'The thing is, and I know you don't want to hear about your brother's sex life, the last few months it's like he's completely lost interest. He never comes near me. Don't pull that face – you did make me tell you what was wrong.'

Nina shook her head. 'I find that hard to believe too. That he'd lose interest in you.'

'You've never been married. Most people go through dry patches. If it was only that, I wouldn't be too worried. I admit I haven't been that amorous lately either. Christ, I spend my days teaching other people about sex. Doing it myself is almost like a busman's holiday. Maybe Darpak got sick of me telling him I was tired.'

'That's not an excuse, though.'

'I know it's not! If he's met someone he can't resist, a woman who inspires him and makes him feel love and excitement and passion, that's one thing. If he's gone off looking elsewhere because he wasn't getting enough at home, because his wife didn't understand him . . .' She didn't need to complete the sentence. 'It's made me wonder about our whole relationship. Could a slowdown between the sheets really send him straight off into the arms of another woman? Could it make him stop loving me?'

Nina didn't know the answers. 'What are you going to do?' she asked.

'What do you think I should do?'

'Oh God. If I was married and my husband was cheating on me, I wouldn't be able to hold back. I'd have to confront him. And I wouldn't want to be with him any more, even if it was messy and painful. But I think there's a very good chance he's innocent. None of what you're saying makes sense. He still talks about you as if he worships you.'

'Really?'

'Yes. He was talking to me last week about what to get you for Christmas. I think you should speak to him. Tell him you saw something that made you worry, and see what his reaction is. I think you'll know if he's lying. Imagine how good you'll feel if you realise you've been fretting about nothing.'

'You're right. I have to do it. Rip off the Band-Aid.' She yawned. 'Sorry. I haven't slept properly all week.'

Nina reached over to the back seat for her bag. She took out a little brown bottle of tablets. 'Here, take this.'

'What is it?'

'Zopiclone. The doctor prescribed it earlier this year when I was having trouble sleeping. I stopped after a few days because I didn't like it. Maybe it will help you, though.'

Isabel hesitated, then slipped the little bottle into her own bag. 'Thanks. Maybe I'll just take one tonight. I just need one good night's sleep.'

'Exactly.' Nina gripped her hand. 'You're a strong, amazing woman, Izzy. You're not the type to let a man screw you around.'

'Huh. Maybe.'

'And one more thing. If my brother *is* cheating on you, *I'll* bloody kill him.'

Isabel forced a smile. 'Thanks. Now, come on. We need to go and talk to a man about lube.'

Chapter 20

Jessica was woken by her phone vibrating on the bedside table and was shocked to see it was ten in the morning.

'What's going on?' Will asked as soon as she picked up. 'I've been trying to call you for the past hour.'

She sat up. Olivia was still asleep beside her, the quilt pulled over the bottom half of her face. Angelic.

Memories of everything that had happened during the night rushed in. The eyeless toys. The car outside. *I drawed it.*

'I had a bad night, okay?' she said. 'We were having a lie-in.'

'Oh. Are you both okay?'

'I'll . . . explain later. Can I talk to Felix?'

She had a quick chat with Felix, wishing him luck in the tournament, then went downstairs in search of caffeine.

Wrapped in her dressing gown, she went out into the garden with Caspar, coffee steaming in the cold morning air. She opened the gate and peered out. No sign of the grey Hyundai, not that she'd expected there to be. She went back inside and up to Olivia's room, where she gathered the mutilated toys and put them away in a cupboard. In daylight they looked sad rather than scary. She also doubted her ability to fix them. She could take them to a professional, but it would probably be cheaper to buy replacements.

She woke Olivia and told her to come downstairs. Olivia rubbed her eyes, but sprang to life in that way small children do, as if a switch flicks and they're on, wide awake and ready for the day.

Back in the kitchen she made boiled eggs and soldiers.

'Sweetheart,' she said, as Olivia dipped a soldier into her egg, 'do you remember what we talked about last night?'

A frown. 'No.'

'You said that Izzy told you a secret.'

Olivia stuffed toast into her mouth so she wouldn't have to speak. She looked like a hamster, cheeks bulging.

'You said that you drew the secret.'

Silence. Olivia chewed slowly and swallowed. Perhaps realising that her mum wasn't going to give up, she nodded.

'Where's the drawing, Livvy?'

Olivia threw her head back and huffed like this was the most tedious, stupid question ever. 'It's a *secret*, Mummy.'

But her reticence probably didn't matter. Because halfway through the conversation Jessica remembered something. She was sure she knew where the drawing was.

ω

'This is a surprise,' Mum said, opening the front door to find Jessica and Olivia, both wrapped in their winter gear, Caspar beside them, tail wagging at the sight of one of his favourite people.

'Hello, boy!' Mum bent to ruffle the dog's fur and he pushed his face against her legs.

'Mummy said we could take Caspar for a walk,' Olivia said as they went into the house. It was warm and smelled of fried bacon. 'Me and you and Pete.'

'Oh, did she?'

Jessica smiled and held up her laptop. 'I've got some work to catch up with, Will's on the Isle of Wight and I thought you and Pete might appreciate the exercise.'

'Sounds like a great idea to me,' Pete said, coming out of the kitchen. He had a smear of ketchup on his cheek. 'Although your mother and I expended a lot of energy last night.'

'Dancing!' Mum interjected hurriedly.

Pete winked at Jessica. 'Oh yes. That as well.'

Mum tutted. 'Dreadful news about Pat Shelton, wasn't it? That's why I'm glad I moved into this place.'

'Did you know her?' Jessica asked. It had been all over the local paper the last few days. The police weren't treating it as a suspicious death, just a tragic accident.

'Of course! She used to work at William Peacocke. She was a dinner lady when you and Izzy were there. Oh, goodness – did you hear about the fire last night? It's all happening around here, isn't it? Thank God nobody was in the building.'

Jessica didn't want to think about the fire right now.

'I thought Pat had always been at Foxgrove.'

Mum shook her head. 'No, she was definitely at Peacocke for a while. She probably worked at a few other places too.'

Jessica had forgotten that. As a child, most of the dinner ladies had been interchangeable.

'Poor old thing,' Mum said. 'Pete knew her too.'

'That's right,' he said, searching for his coat. 'She used to come to the RAFA occasionally.'

Jessica wasn't surprised that Mum and Pete had known Pat. Mum knew everyone in Beckenham. Walking down the high street with her was a nightmare; she stopped every two minutes to chat to someone.

'Come on, then,' Mum said, patting the dog. 'Want to go walkies, Caspar?'

As soon as the house was empty Jessica hurried into the living room. Now, where would Mum have put Olivia's new drawing book, the one Olivia wouldn't let her look at the other day? It wasn't in the box of toys or on the coffee table where Mum had a stack of that week's real-life magazines. She went into the kitchen but there was no sign of it there either.

She was sure it wouldn't be in Mum's bedroom, which left the spare room. This was where Olivia and Felix slept on the rare occasions when Mum looked after them for the night. There was another box of toys in here, along with a shelf full of old children's books that used to belong to Jessica and Izzy. Roald Dahl and the Wombles and a few novels they'd read as young teenagers. John Wyndham's *Chocky* and *The Midwich Cuckoos*, plus a creepy book called *The Midnight House*, which they'd read to each other under the covers.

Not spotting the drawing book straight away, Jessica picked up *The Midnight House*. Opening it, she was thrown back in time and across town, to their old house, their childhood bedroom.

They huddled together beneath the covers on the bottom bunk, using the torch Izzy had sneaked out of the downstairs cupboard.

Izzy held the book, reading the final words of a chapter near the end of the book. 'Sally crept up the stairs, her heart pounding beneath her nightdress. She was sure the noise had come from Father's study. But it was impossible! No one had been in the study since Father died . . .'

Jess squealed and put the pillow over her face. 'I don't want to hear any more. It's too scary!'

But Izzy ignored her, pulling the pillow away and reading on. In the book, Sally tried the door to her dead dad's study and, to her amazement, the handle turned and the door opened.

'If it were possible to die of fright, Sally would have expired right there on the spot. But her heart kept on beating, faster and harder than ever, as she took in the state of the room.'

'Please, stop,' Jess begged.

'Drawers had been yanked open, some of them hanging at crooked angles. Papers were scattered everywhere. The paperweight Sally had loved to play with as a small child lay on the floor, a crack snaking across its hard glass surface, like it had been hurled there with enormous force.'

'Oh God, Izzy! Don't!'

'In the middle of the desk stood Father's old typewriter, on which he had written all his Important Letters. A single sheet of paper had been inserted into it and, as Sally crept closer, she saw three words typed there in block capitals.'

Izzy paused.

'What did it say?' Jess half-shouted, trying to grab the book from Izzy, who giggled as she held it out of Jess's reach.

'Patience, sister.'

'Tell me!'

'Okay.' She read on, repeating the previous line. '. . . Sally saw three words typed there in block capitals: DON'T TRUST MOTHER.'

Jessica gasped with horror.

Now, twenty-five years later, Jessica laughed as she snapped the book shut. As far as she remembered, it turned out that Sally's mother had killed her father and intended to kill her too. But Sally's dad's ghost came back and saved her.

She was amazed Mum had let them read that book, what with everything that had been going on . . . No, actually, that wasn't right. They had read that book before all the strange occurrences started. Dad had still been around. Larry hadn't made his first appearance till around six months after they'd read the book.

But before she could think about this any more, and work out if it meant anything, she spotted Olivia's drawing book. It was on one of the spare beds, half-covered by a blanket.

She sat on the bed and paused before opening the book, unsure of what she'd find. *The secret.* She leafed through childish sketches of dogs and houses, flowers and people who were drawn in Olivia's current style: elongated bodies, long stretchy limbs, like daddy-long-legs with faces. In Olivia's pictures everyone was smiling and the sun was always shining. There was no sign here, in these pictures, of Olivia's so-called obsession with death. There wasn't even a flicker of interest in the subject. No pictures of bodies. No blood, no gravestones, no ghosts.

She reached a blank page and stopped. She leafed back, studied the drawings again. If Izzy had told Olivia a secret, it was supremely benign. She stopped and laughed at herself. *Of course* Izzy hadn't told Olivia a secret, because ghosts weren't real. Olivia had imagined her deceased aunt telling her something. That was why Jessica was here. She wanted to know what was going on in Olivia's head, hoping it would give her some clue, an idea of what do about it.

Except . . . except that wasn't entirely true, was it? Because in the dead of night, when Olivia had told her about the secret, Jessica *had* believed. She had been as credulous as she was when she was a little girl, when she saw all those broken plates and smashed picture frames as evidence that their poltergeist was real. In a way, it was easier to believe. Lying in bed, listening to Olivia talk about secrets and explaining why she had cut out her toys' eyes, it was easier to believe a ghost told her to do it. There was no confusion that way. Superstition was simpler than science. Why spend years looking for evidence of how the universe was created when it was right there in the Bible? God did it.

A ghost did it.

Except, according to the evidence here in this sketch pad, Izzy's ghost hadn't told Olivia to do anything. There was nothing to see.

Jessica ran a hand across her forehead. She was so tired. The pain-killers she'd taken had dulled her headache but it was still there, and she found herself reluctant to set the sketch pad aside. Because no matter how hard she tried to rationalise everything, she didn't believe Olivia had been making it up when she said, 'I drawed it.'

She must be missing something.

She turned to the last drawing, turned over to the blank page and kept going. Because if you were going to draw a secret, you'd hide it, wouldn't you? Hide it within the empty pages, where no grown-up would think to look.

She found the drawing halfway through the book.

On the left half was a house. A square with a triangle for a roof, four windows and a door. The kind of house Olivia always drew. But protruding from the upper right-hand side of this house was another, much smaller square.

A balcony.

And beneath the balcony lay a figure. One of Olivia's stretched-out people. It had long yellow hair and eyelashes. There was a scribble of red next to her.

Here it was: the dead body and blood that had been absent from all the other pictures.

Jessica turned the page and found herself looking at an almost identical drawing. Except this one had an extra detail. The scale was wrong; the balcony was bigger, almost a third the size of the house. Olivia had drawn it big so she could add another figure, standing in the box, a curling smile on his face.

A man.

Jessica stared at the drawing. What had Olivia said on Bonfire Night? *You can't fall. You have to be pushed.*

Pushed by a man. *A bad man.*

No matter how much Jessica told herself it was impossible, that Olivia couldn't possibly know anything, the doubt was creeping in. Not just creeping in but swirling, shouting, overriding logic. Olivia knew the truth. Izzy, desperate for justice, had come back and spoken to her niece, told her what had happened. It wasn't just a little girl's imagination – because Olivia knew things she couldn't have imagined. The song and the name of the cat. And not just that. Because it struck Jessica now that, as far as she knew, no one had ever told Olivia that Isabel had died falling from that balcony.

Jessica sat there for a long time, until she heard the others come back. As the front door slammed and Pete called out, 'Cup of tea?', Jessica got up and went into the hall. Olivia had gone into the living room to find her toys. Mum, who was taking off her coat and boots, turned when she heard Jessica behind her.

'What's the matter?' Mum asked. 'You look like you've seen a ghost.'

Silently, Jessica handed Mum the drawing, waited while she took it in.

'I think you were right,' Jessica said, her voice shaking. 'I think someone murdered Izzy.'

Chapter 21

Pete came out of the kitchen carrying two mugs of tea. 'What's going on, Mo?' He glanced down at the drawing in her hand. 'What's that?'

'Pete,' Mum said. She had gone pale. 'Can you go and keep Olivia entertained? Play with her or put *Peppa Pig* on or something.'

'Of course. But—'

'I'll explain later.'

Mum ushered Jessica into the kitchen. Condensation clung to the inside of the window and the smell of bacon still lingered. Jessica had forgotten to eat breakfast, but that wasn't why she felt faint. She sat at the kitchen table and told her mother everything that had happened during the night.

Mum pointed at the male figure in the picture. 'It's got to be Darpak.'

'But he had an alibi.'

'I told you. I bet that was his colleagues protecting him.'

Jessica still couldn't quite believe that. But who else could 'the bad man' be?

'Are you actually coming round to my way of thinking?' Mum asked. 'That it was Darpak?'

'I don't know.'

Mum pursed her lips. 'I bumped into that sister of his the other day. Nina.'

'You didn't tell her you think Darpak killed Izzy?'

'Of course not. We had a nice chat, though. She told me about what happened on Bonfire Night. Why didn't *you* tell me about that?'

'Because I knew you'd worry. Try to persuade me that Olivia wasn't ever allowed to go round to Darpak's again.'

'Well . . .'

Jessica held up a hand. 'Can we focus? I think,' she said, trying to choose her words carefully, 'that if Darpak – or someone else – *did* push Izzy off that balcony, and if she's up there trying to communicate that to us, we owe it to her to investigate. To keep an open mind.'

There. She had said it.

Mum reached across and patted Jessica's hand. 'Good girl.'

'I should go to the police,' Jessica said.

Mum pulled back her hand. 'You can't do that yet. Do you remember what happened when I told them about Larry? They ridiculed me, Jess. Treated me like I was madwoman. A time-waster. If you go to them and say your daughter is being given information by Izzy's spirit, they'll laugh you out of the station.'

'*Anyone* I tell will laugh at me. It'll be like being back at school, after we were in the paper.'

'Exactly. But there's one person who will believe.'

Jessica groaned. 'Not Simon Parker.'

'Yes, Jess. Simon will be able to help us. If we can communicate with Izzy, maybe she can tell us something concrete, show us where to find evidence to take to the police. They won't laugh at us if we have proof.'

'But Simon . . . He's a pervert. You didn't see the way he used to look at Izzy.'

Mum waved a hand. 'That's just what men are like. He didn't actually touch her, did he?'

'No, but . . .'

'Well, then. It doesn't matter. Simon and I grew up in a different time. I'm not saying it was right, of course I'm not, but Izzy had boobs and long legs when she was thirteen. I bet Simon wasn't the only grown man who eyed her up.'

'That's disgusting.'

'Men *are* disgusting. But Simon knows about the spirit world, Jess. He can help us.'

Jessica felt her resistance ebb away. She still didn't like Simon. But maybe Mum was right. Maybe she could put up with him for a day, even if he did give her the creeps.

'Have you told Will about this?' Mum asked.

'God, no.'

'When do he and Felix get home?'

'Tomorrow evening.'

'So we've got about thirty-six hours.' Mum got up and found her phone, an old Nokia which handled nothing but calls and texts. 'Let me ring Simon now.'

She took the phone into the corner of the room. Soon she was murmuring into it, facing away from Jessica and speaking quietly, her words inaudible. Jessica put her head in her hands. The craving for a cigarette came back. She had a horrible feeling that by talking to Mum and allowing her to call Simon she'd voluntarily stepped on to a runaway train. She had no idea where the train would take her but, wherever it was, the journey was going to be bumpy and scary. She had to do something, though, didn't she? And she really believed what she'd said. She owed it to Izzy to find out the truth, to seek justice.

Mum ended the call and turned around.

'He's going to meet us at your house in an hour.'

'An hour?'

'That's right. There's no time to waste, Jessica. I think it's best if Olivia stays here for a while. Pete can look after her.'

139

'I'm not sure . . .'

'He's perfectly capable of babysitting Livvy for a couple of hours. He looks after her all the time when you leave her here and I'm busy.'

'Okay.' Jessica heaved herself up from the table, surprised by how weak her legs felt. 'We'd better get going, then, hadn't we?'

ω

Simon Parker came round shortly after they got back to Jessica's house. He was wearing his white suit again, those sharp blue eyes fixing on Jessica as soon as she opened the door.

'I'm so pleased you changed your mind,' he said as he came in, nodding a greeting to Mum, who was hovering in the hallway and acting like a good Catholic receiving a visit from the Bishop.

'Don't make me regret it,' Jessica murmured.

'What was that?'

'I said, I hope you didn't forget your equipment.'

He held up a black holdall. 'It's all in here. Amazing how everything is so much smaller these days, isn't it? I can carry everything I need in one hand. I'd better start setting up.'

'Wait,' Jessica said. 'Why do we have to do all this? Can't we just ask Olivia what Izzy's spirit has told her?'

Simon exchanged a quick look with Mum, as if this was something they had already discussed. 'Because we have to be as sure as we can be that it is indeed Izzy's spirit.'

'What do you mean?'

'Well, sometimes a malicious spirit will imitate a deceased person.'

Jessica shuddered. 'A malicious spirit?'

'Or mischievous. That's why we have to be careful, and why we can't ask Olivia outright. She says she is being visited by her aunt but I'm afraid we can't take her word for it. This happened in another case of mine. A child was seemingly communicating with a deceased sibling, but it turned out to be . . .' He stopped, clearly troubled by the memory. 'I'm not saying that is the case here but I do think it's better to be cautious.'

Jessica felt even more sick than before. 'So how do we find out?'

'Well, there will be some gut instinct involved. That will have to come from you. But, more importantly, we need to communicate with the spirit, to test it.'

Jessica glanced at Mum, who looked anxious and excited. *Gut instinct*, Jessica thought. She had no idea what her gut was telling her right now.

'Would you like a cup of tea, Simon?' Mum asked.

'That would be lovely, Mo.'

'Milk and no sugar? Because you're sweet enough?'

He grinned. 'You remembered.'

Cringing so hard it made the muscles in her neck hurt, Jessica said, 'Follow me.' She led Simon up the stairs and into Olivia's room, feeling like she was violating the space by allowing him in here, having to remind herself she was doing this for Izzy. She was pleased she had removed the eyeless toys and tidied the room before going out this morning.

Simon set his holdall on the floor and crouched beside it, removing several objects from the bag and laying them carefully on the carpet.

'I can feel something in this room, even without equipment,' he said.

'The cold? I told you before, the radiator doesn't work properly.'

'No, it's more than that. It's like an echo. It's likely that the spirit has attached itself to Olivia—'

'*Her*self.'

'Sorry? Oh yes, of course. If it is Isabel, of course.' He looked up at her. 'I was going to say that the spirit has attached itself or herself to your daughter rather than taking up residence in your house.'

'You mean . . . Olivia might be possessed?' She felt sick.

141

'No, not possessed, exactly. More that the spirit accompanies her. Kind of like an invisible friend.'

Jessica thought back to when Olivia had said Izzy was in the car with them.

'There's no need to be alarmed,' Simon said. He had finished laying out the equipment. 'If it is Isabel, it's probable that Olivia finds her presence comforting. You know when children have imaginary friends? I believe those friends are often spirits.'

'Can I ask you something else?'

'Of course.'

'Have you ever heard of spirits predicting the future? I mean, telling the people they're in contact with about things that haven't happened yet?'

He rubbed his chin. 'Why are you asking that?'

'Just . . . curious.'

'Hmm. Well, it's not unheard of. Many people think that time in the spirit world is fluid, that spirits can move backward and forward in time as if it's an ocean. Some mediums claim to have received prophecies and there are some documented accounts of those prophecies coming true. It's not something I've witnessed personally, though. If you're saying that Olivia—'

'Why don't you show me what we've got there?'

Jessica didn't want to think about this prophecy stuff any more. She wanted to know about the past, not the future.

Simon held up a device that was the shape of an iPhone but bigger and thicker. It had an LED display on the front along with three rows of different-coloured lights. 'This is an EDI. Environment detection instrument. It's a wonderful device. Firstly, it measures the ambient temperature of the room, because if there are cold spots, that can tell us that there's paranormal activity. Secondly, it has an EMF detector. It stands for electro-magnetic field.'

'So what does that do? You'll have to forgive me – I'm sure you talked about all this when we were kids but I can't remember any of the details.'

He smiled. 'I wouldn't expect you to. Spiritual activity causes a shift in EMF, and this measures it, setting off an alarm if there's a sharp change. Finally, there's a geophone, which captures vibrations.'

'I see.'

'I also have another EMF meter which we can place outside the door. Oh, one more thing. I'm going to set up an infrared camera too, so we can see anything moving in the room.'

'A camera? No way.'

Mum arrived with Simon's tea. 'What's going on?' she asked.

'He wants to set up a camera in Olivia's room, presumably so he can watch her while she's asleep. I don't know about you but I find that deeply bloody creepy.'

Simon stood up. 'Jessica, I can assure you I have no interest in watching your little girl. I only want to see if there's movement in the room at night. For example, if objects are moved by the spirit.'

'I'm sorry, but no. That's not happening.'

'Jess, don't be ridiculous,' Mum said.

That made her angry. 'I knew this was a mistake. I think we should call the whole thing off.' She stooped and picked up the EDI, ready to return it to the holdall, but Simon dropped to his haunches and caught her wrist.

'Wait. How about if only you can see the monitor? I'll set it up in your bedroom. Like a baby monitor. I'll wait downstairs and monitor the other equipment.'

'That sounds fair enough, doesn't it, Jess?' Mum said.

'I guess so.'

Simon got back up, wincing. All this standing and crouching clearly wasn't good for his ageing knees. 'I'd better get on and set everything up,' he said.

As Jessica backed out of the room, following Mum, she caught Simon's eye. 'You know my husband will be back tomorrow night? So you only have until then to get a result.'

'Yes, yes, your mother told me. But don't worry, Jessica. Like I said, I can sense a presence here even without my gear. I have a feeling it's not going to take long to make contact. Not long at all.'

Chapter 22

October 2012

'Hey, are you coming?' Darpak called from the living room. They were halfway through the DVD box set of *The Killing*.

Isabel was in the kitchen. She shouted up the stairs. 'In a minute. Do you want a beer?'

'What?'

Who was it who said that marriage is forty years of shouting at each other from different rooms? She couldn't remember. She opened a beer for him anyway, knowing he'd want one, and held the cool bottle against her forehead. She was getting a fever, which made her angry at herself, or whichever bastard had passed on the germs. She didn't have time to be ill.

After pouring herself a very large glass of Sancerre, she took the drinks into the living room and settled down on the sofa beside Darpak. He pressed play, but she couldn't concentrate. The subtitles might as well have been in Japanese for all the sense she could make of them. She ought to go to bed, get some desperately needed sleep, but she couldn't. Not now. She had made a promise to herself. She was going to have it out with Darpak. She was going to ask him about that photo. That woman.

Last night, after the conversation outside McDonald's with Nina, she had come home full of good intentions. But Darpak had been on his way out – some crisis at work – and had vanished before she could open her mouth. By the time he got home she had finished a bottle of wine and passed out on the sofa.

But that was yesterday. Today, she was going to do it.

She took a big slug of wine and Darpak gave her a sideways glance. 'Drinking again?'

'Said the man with the bottle of beer in his hand.'

'Which you handed to me. I didn't ask for it.'

She rolled her eyes. 'So what if I'm drinking? I've had a stressful day.'

'Me too.' His eyes had roamed back to the TV, where the Danish detective was talking to a shifty politician.

Isabel grabbed the remote from the coffee table and switched off the TV.

'What are you doing?' he asked.

She drained her glass, buying herself a few seconds. She placed the empty glass on the coffee table. She could see herself reflected in the floor-to-ceiling window, glowing like a ghost of herself. 'I need to talk to you,' she said.

'What about?' There was no immediate spark of alarm. Nothing more than the vague worried expression he usually wore in such situations, trying to work out if he'd done something wrong. He didn't look guilty, and that almost made her back off straight away.

But it wouldn't be backing off, would it? It would be chickening out.

'I saw something on your phone,' she said, forcing the words out. 'A woman. A naked woman.'

There it was: a flicker of guilt, one that came and went in an instant. He frowned. 'What are you talking about?'

'Remember when I came home and you were in the shower? I was standing near your phone and a message flashed up.' She was only twisting the truth slightly. 'It was a selfie. A woman, topless. And it said *To keep you going till next time.*'

She studied his face as she recounted this. He seemed stunned, confused. She wanted him to laugh, to immediately come up with a rational explanation. *It was a prank. James at the office sent it to me.* Or, *Oh God, it's this woman – she's been pestering me, coming on to me, but nothing has happened.*

Even an instant admission of guilt – *I'm so sorry, it was a one-night stand, it meant nothing* – would have been better than his actual response.

'I have no idea what you're talking about.'

She paused. 'So you're denying receiving that message?'

'Well, I certainly didn't see it.' He shook his head. 'My God, Izzy. This is crazy. Are you sure you didn't dream it?'

'Of course I'm bloody sure! It was right there, on your phone.'

He took his phone out of his pocket and began scrolling through it. 'When was this?'

'It's not there now.'

He looked up.

'I've already checked,' she said. 'You deleted it.'

'Wait. You've been going through my phone?'

'Yes, I did. Don't play the outrage card. I'm the only one with the right to be outraged here. You're having an affair, aren't you?'

He stood up and loomed over her. For the first time in their relationship she found she was afraid of him, suddenly aware of his greater size and strength.

'You probably imagined it when you were drunk,' he said, snatching up her wine glass. 'Hadn't you been out for a boozy lunch with that journalist?'

'What? I had one glass.'

'Are you sure?' His tone switched from angry to soothing. 'I've been really worried about you, Izzy, and the amount you've been drinking.'

She got to her feet and stepped away from him, whirling round to jab a finger in his direction. 'This is bullshit. Fucking hell, you're trying to gaslight me.'

'Gaslight?'

'Don't pretend you don't know what it means. You're trying to make me believe I'm going crazy. Well, it's not going to work. I know what I saw.'

She hadn't imagined the conversation going like this, hadn't foreseen it spiralling out of control. She needed to calm things down.

But before she could speak, Darpak left the room, his palm pressed hard against his forehead, and ran downstairs to the kitchen. She followed and found him pouring whisky into a tumbler. He knocked it back.

'Are you going to talk to me?' she asked.

He looked up at her, eyes burning. His jaw was clenched and she could see the muscles moving, the suppressed frustration and – what was it – rage? Hatred?

He took a step towards her.

Chapter 23

Jessica drove her mother home and picked up Olivia and Caspar, both of whom seemed sad to say goodbye to Pete. He'd made Nutella on toast, Olivia's absolute favourite. Smelling the sweet chocolate-and-hazelnut spread on her daughter's breath as she picked her up jolted Jessica back to childhood. She and Izzy had gone through a phase when they were obsessed with Nutella, eating it morning, noon and night until Mum told them it was too expensive and that she was switching to a supermarket own brand, which both girls declared inedible. Jessica smiled as she recalled herself shouting, 'This is the worst day of my life!'

On the drive home Jessica spied a grey car in her rear mirror and her foot slipped from the clutch as she was changing gears, making the car bump and shudder. But the grey car turned down a side street, and it wasn't a Hyundai anyway.

It was hardly surprising she was jumpy. If Simon Parker was right, she was on the verge of making contact with her dead sister. Of finding out her secret.

She had given up trying to tell herself this was impossible.

ʊ

Back at home Simon had finished setting up the equipment, including the monitor in Jessica's bedroom, which displayed a surprisingly clear colour image of Olivia's room.

Olivia was shocked to find the old man in the white suit in their kitchen, drinking tea.

'Who are you?' she asked, peering out from behind Jessica's legs.

'This is Simon,' Jessica said.

'Are you a magician?' Olivia asked, eyeing his suit.

'I suppose I am a kind of magician.'

Olivia frowned. 'I don't like magic. It's a total rip-off.'

'We hired a magician for Livvy's fourth birthday party,' Jessica explained, wincing at the memory. She hadn't realised Olivia had absorbed Will's scathing review.

Simon was giving Jessica a meaningful look, and she remembered that before taking Mum home she'd agreed that she would ask Olivia to play in her bedroom when they got back. Simon wanted to see if the measurements he had taken in Olivia's room differed when she was in there.

'Olivia, why don't you go and play in your room?'

'Okay.' Sometimes children were surprisingly amenable.

Jessica waited till she heard Olivia's footsteps reach the top of the stairs. 'Anything?' she asked.

Simon was able to check the readings using an app on his phone. He sat at the kitchen table, with the dog at his feet, and studied his screen, brow furrowed with concentration.

'It's too early to tell at the moment. Why don't you try to relax while I keep an eye on this?'

Feeling like a stranger in her own home, Jessica went up to her bedroom and sat on the bed, in front of the little screen with its view of Olivia's bedroom. It reminded her of when Olivia was a newborn and Will had set up a video baby monitor. Jessica had sometimes watched it for hours, fixated on the image of their sleeping daughter. She had been a good baby, much easier than Felix, who had been colicky and fractious. She and Will had congratulated themselves on getting it right with their second child, even though they knew it was all down to luck. Then, when Olivia turned two and transformed into the toddler from hell, they had regretted being so smug about their perfect baby. A horrible thought struck her. Had Olivia been so difficult back then because Izzy was visiting her? Was that the cause of the night terrors that had plagued her for several months a couple of years ago?

How long had Izzy's spirit been around?

There was another question tickling the back of her head, one she couldn't quite formulate. But it boiled down to this: Why was Izzy using Olivia? If she wanted to communicate with the living world, why go through a young child? And why, when she'd died in 2013, had she waited until now? It didn't make sense.

Jessica was about to go downstairs to ask Simon what he thought when she saw something on the monitor.

Olivia was crouching on the floor of her room, rummaging through a little toy box. Every day when Jessica tidied Olivia's room she would organise toys into their categories, *My Little Pony* in one box, *Toy Story* in another. The box Olivia was currently emptying contained all sorts of junk that didn't belong anywhere else. She was clearly looking for something, taking out items and casting them aside, chucking old Happy Meal toys and stray building blocks across the carpet. Jessica could see her face, which went from frustrated to delighted when she found what she was looking for.

It was a necklace. She put it over her head. It was already fastened at the back.

Jessica wasn't able to zoom in, but she could make out the shape of the creature that hung from the chain. She knew what it was.

It was Izzy's old bat necklace, the necklace Jessica had removed from Olivia's room when all this weird shit had first started happening. How the hell had Olivia got it back? The necklace had been in a box on top of the wardrobe here in the master bedroom. There was no way Olivia could have got to that box, even if she'd stood on a chair.

Jessica got up, feeling faint. But before storming into Olivia's room she sent a text to Will.

Did you give Olivia that bat necklace back?

Will replied almost immediately.

Sorry, I have no idea what you're talking about. Are you OK? Xx

She hesitated, then replied: Yes, just checking something. Can you ask Felix if he got it down for her? Make it clear that we won't be angry if he did! X

Jessica waited for what felt like minutes, before the answer came back.

He says no. Why are you asking? Are you talking about Izzy's necklace? Xx

She didn't respond. She threw the phone on the bed and hurried along the hall to Olivia's bedroom, taking deep breaths and reminding herself not to go in all guns blazing. But she forgot her vow the second she entered the room.

'Livvy, show me that necklace.'

Olivia clutched it, eyes wide with alarm.

'Let me see, Olivia.'

Reluctantly the little girl let go of the pendant, giving Jessica a clear view. She had been right. She grabbed the chain and pulled it over Olivia's head, cradling the bat in the palm of her hand. It was weird: she was sure she could feel it vibrating with energy. Isabel's energy.

'I took this away. How did you get it?' she demanded.

Olivia burst into tears.

'Oh, sweetheart, I'm sorry.' She pulled Olivia into a hug, murmuring apologies until she calmed down. Sitting on the floor, with Olivia on her lap, she spoke gently: 'Can you tell me how you got it? I promise I won't be cross.'

Olivia sniffed. 'Auntie Izzy gave it to me. But she told me not to tell you.'

'Another secret?'

'Yes. I'm sorry, Mummy.'

Jessica had no idea what to do or think. There was nothing in the many parenting guides she'd read that told her how to deal with this situation. *My sister's ghost retrieved the necklace I confiscated from my daughter. What should I do?* Jessica felt bubbles of hysteria rising inside her.

It was cold in the room again. She wondered if it showed on Simon's app downstairs, the decrease in the ambient temperature or whatever he had called it.

'Is she here now?' Jessica asked.

'Who?'

'Auntie Izzy.'

Olivia shook her head, then stopped, as if she had something very important to say. Jessica waited, heart thumping so hard she was sure Olivia must be able to feel it.

'Can I have a snack?' Olivia asked.

Jessica squeezed her fists tight, just about managing to keep a lid on the hysteria. 'Of course. Come on, come downstairs. Do you want a jam sandwich? You can eat it in front of the telly.'

She took Olivia's hand and led her from the room. As they reached the top of the staircase, Olivia said, 'I don't want you to be sad, Mummy.'

'I don't want you to be sad either.' She stopped walking and knelt beside her daughter. 'But it's very important that you don't keep any more secrets from me, okay?'

'Okay.' There was a long pause. 'Can I have a jam sandwich *and* a packet of crisps?'

ꕙ

She put the TV on in the living room and left Olivia watching *Peppa Pig*. In the kitchen she took the jam out of the fridge and put it down with a thud in front of Simon, making him jump. He was wearing headphones, which were plugged into his phone.

'So?' she said, grabbing the bread and making a sandwich on autopilot. 'Did you pick anything up?'

'I'm not sure. It's too soon to—'

She cut him off. 'We don't have time to be patient.'

'Because your husband is back—?'

Again, she didn't let him finish. 'Because I *need* to know if it's Izzy talking to Olivia. I can't take any more of this.'

She explained what had happened upstairs, with the necklace.

Simon's mouth opened then closed. 'You're saying . . . the spirit transported a physical item from one room of your house to another?'

'Is that shocking? Larry used to do that kind of thing all the time.'

'Actually, that entity, the one you call Larry, was only able to use its kinetic force to hurl or dislodge objects. There was no control. Nothing this . . . deliberate.' He opened a notebook and scribbled in it. 'This is fascinating.'

She dropped the jam-smeared knife, sending it clattering to the floor. 'I don't give a flying fuck if it's fascinating. I want this dealt with. Now.'

He stared at her, shocked.

'Wait here,' she said. She took the sandwich and pack of Wotsits to Olivia, kissed the top of her head and returned to the kitchen, where Simon was now consulting a thick book that he must have had in his holdall. Caspar was standing at the back door, asking to be let out. Jessica opened the door and noticed how dark it was outside. Evening had arrived without her realising.

Simon licked his finger and turned the page. There was no sense of urgency about him. It was infuriating.

'Well?' she asked. 'What should we do?'

'Jessica, I don't think we should rush this. If it is a malevolent spirit, we risk angering it. If it's your sister, we might scare her off.'

Jessica was beginning to feel like a malevolent spirit herself. 'I remember now, how you were like this when I was a kid. You hung around our house for weeks. And what did that achieve, huh?'

'We made a lot of interesting discoveries.'

She could feel it. Her internal pressure gauge swinging towards red.

'No. All you did was make us feel like lab rats. This is not *interesting*. I don't care about furthering scientific knowledge. All I want is for this to be over, for my family to be free of all this insanity and . . . and for justice to be done. If you can't help with that now, perhaps you should go.'

'Jessica . . .'

'Be quiet. So what do I need to communicate with the spirit? A Ouija board?'

'No! That could be highly dangerous. Why don't you let me do a little more research, and then . . .'

'No, I don't have time.' She leaned over to grab his book. As she did, she noticed how he stared at her chest, his eyes zooming in on her cleavage.

'Oh my God,' she said.

'What?'

'You're still the same. You say you made a lot of interesting discoveries, but the only thing I saw you discovering back then was how much you liked gawping at my sister.'

He stood up. 'That's outrageous!'

'No, it's true. I bet that's why you hung around so long. So you could spend more time perving over a thirteen-year-old girl.'

He put his hands on his hips. 'I'm not going to stand here and listen to this!'

'Good. Because I've had enough. I'm going to deal with this myself.'

He tried to grab the book back but she dropped it in his holdall, picked the bag up and handed it to him. 'I want you to go.'

'What?'

'You can pick up your equipment tomorrow.'

'Jessica, you don't know what you're dealing with.'

'Go!'

She grabbed the holdall back from him and took it with her, striding towards the front door. Simon followed.

'I'll see you tomorrow.' She yanked the door open and chucked his holdall on to the doorstep. Outside, the wind had picked up and leaves chased each other in a circle on the front path. As usual, there was no one around. Jessica quickly glanced left and right, looking for the grey car, but there was no sign of it.

'You're making a dreadful mistake,' Simon said in an angry tone as he left the house, turning on the doorstep to say more.

'Maybe,' she said, shutting the door in his face, not allowing him to speak. 'But it will be my mistake.'

Chapter 24

Jessica sat at Will's computer, navigating to the photo album that contained the pictures of Isabel, thinking that doing so might help her focus. She flicked through, stopping on a photo in which Izzy looked unhappy and distracted; so beautiful, yet so sad. A month after this, Izzy was dead.

What had been going on in her life in those days? Had Jessica let her down during those final weeks? Could she have saved her, protected her? She racked her brain, trying to remember if Izzy had given her any clue, any coded cry for help. Was there something about Darpak's behaviour that should have made Jessica suspicious? Jessica had been pregnant with Olivia and self-absorbed, hardly paying attention to anyone else. Yes, Izzy had been subdued and unhappy over Christmas, but the day Jessica told her she was pregnant she'd seemed much happier. Had she been putting on a brave face? Izzy had never wanted to 'burden' her little sister with her problems.

That was no excuse, though. Jessica should have noticed, should have seen that something was wrong.

Now was the time to make amends for her neglect. And if she managed to make contact with Izzy, it was also her chance to say sorry.

But how was she going to do it? Perhaps she shouldn't have kicked Simon out . . . She frowned. It was too late now, and Jessica also had a feeling, an instinct, that Izzy was far more likely to talk if it was just Jessica and Olivia in the house. Family. No creepy blokes.

She closed her eyes and breathed in deeply, trying to empty her mind of everything. She was sure she could feel something in the room, a shift in the atmosphere. Izzy watching. Waiting. But Jessica didn't feel afraid like she used to when Larry was around. She was frustrated rather than scared. Because she wanted Izzy to talk to her.

'Can you tell me?' she whispered. 'What happened?'

Something cold tickled the back of Jessica's neck. Downstairs, Caspar barked. Up here in the office she could hear the wind chasing its tail around the chimney, and she was sure it grew stronger and louder as she waited.

She opened her eyes, sure she was going to see Izzy before her. But there was nothing.

Closing her eyes again she whispered, 'Please, Izzy. Talk to me. Tell me: did someone push you?'

She waited, straining for a sign, a shift in the atmosphere. Expecting to hear a whisper in her ear. She was sure she could feel something, like a cold breeze caressing her face.

But again, when she looked, there was nothing there.

This was maddening. How could she get Izzy to communicate? A memory came back to her.

A rainy Sunday afternoon in winter. Mum was doing the ironing and there was nothing on TV. They were waiting for the top forty to come on the radio so they could listen to it and tape their favourite songs, something they did every week. Isabel went off and came back with a board game that she'd found under the stairs.

'Come on,' she'd said. 'Let's play Scrabble.'

Jessica groaned. 'Do we have to? It's so boring.'

'No, it's not! You just know I'm going to thrash you.'

There was no way Jessica, the one who was always top of the class at English, could resist that challenge.

They had a set here, didn't they? They must have, although she hadn't played it in years. Where would it be? She went down to the landing and looked up at the loft hatch, then pulled down the ladder and climbed up into the darkness. The light bulb had died, so she had to use the light from her phone to illuminate the piles of old toys and broken gadgets, and the Christmas decorations that would soon need to come down. Up here the wind was really howling. She felt something brush against her face and jumped back, banging her head against the low ceiling and clutching her chest. Something black skittered across the floor.

She was about to give up when she saw it – the Scrabble set poking out from beneath a stack of old books. She pulled it out and went back down the ladder, itching and trying not to imagine spiders in her hair, then knelt on the carpet and opened the box. She looked through the little square plastic tiles. They all seemed to be here.

She took a long, deep breath. Izzy had beaten Jessica at Scrabble that day. In fact, she had won every time, until it got to the point where Jessica refused to play any more. Years later, at a dinner party at the flat Izzy lived in before she married Darpak and they bought their big house, Izzy had brought out the Scrabble and suggested a game for old times' sake. She had won, of course.

'Mummy, what are you doing?' Olivia asked, suddenly appearing at the top of the stairs. 'What's that?'

Jessica smiled up at her. 'Hi, Livvy,' she said. 'Guess what? We're going to play a game.'

ʊ

'It looks boring,' Olivia said as they went into her room, and the echo sent a shiver through Jessica's veins.

'It's not boring, I promise.'

'What do we have to do?' Olivia asked.

'You'll see.' She leaned forward and squeezed her daughter's hand. 'It's going to be fun.'

One by one, Jessica took the little square Scrabble tiles from the box and laid them out in rows, alphabetically, from the nine tiles bearing the letter *A* to the single *Z* piece. There were one hundred tiles in all, and Jessica arranged them in ten rows of ten, so they formed a square in the centre of the room. Olivia watched intently. At school she was learning all these letters now – she could easily recite the alphabet – but was more familiar with the lower-case figures. Every few days Olivia brought home a new book from school along with lists of common words she needed to learn: *a, the, and, because*. Jessica knew from helping her that Olivia would have no problem recognising each of these letters, even in upper case, but she had only turned four a week before starting school three months ago. She would struggle to spell all but the shortest, easiest words. But that was good. This exercise wouldn't work with an older child.

Jessica finished laying out the tiles and got up to close the curtains. The wind was even stronger now, and the tree that stood by the side of the house, its branches winter-bare, swayed out of the darkness to tap against the window. It was hard not to believe that the wind was only swirling around their property, that Izzy was somehow responsible for it. Mum had said the same once when Larry visited during a storm. As hail bounced off the roof and thunder boomed across the sky, Mum had said, 'We've made him angry', as if they had awakened a god.

Ridiculous.

Jessica shut the curtains, then closed the door, and sat down beside the grid of Scrabble tiles. The house was silent apart from the wind, and the room was colder than ever. *The malfunctioning radiator*, said the rational part of her brain. The rest of her was convinced that Izzy was here in the room, as cold in death as she had been warm in life. She wondered what readings Simon's equipment would be giving now.

'Okay,' she said. 'Livvy, here's what we're going to do.'

Olivia's face was pale with worry.

'You know that Mummy isn't able to talk to Auntie Izzy?'

A nod.

'So I'm going to need you to help me. I'm going to ask Auntie Izzy a question, and I want you to listen to her answer. I'm going to ask her to choose letters.' She indicated the Scrabble tiles. 'And you just have to pick out the ones she tells you she's chosen.'

If she asked Olivia simply to say what Izzy told her, there was no way of telling if Olivia was making it up, saying whatever she thought her mummy wanted to hear. But if Olivia was able to spell out words using the Scrabble tiles, words she didn't know how to spell, that would be proof, wouldn't it? Proof that she really was receiving messages from the dead.

'Is Auntie Izzy here now?' Jessica asked.

Olivia hesitated for a drawn-out moment, then whispered, 'I think so.'

Jessica held her breath. Could it be true? Could Izzy really be here in the room? She couldn't see anything. No shimmering presence. No imprint in the air. But it had been the same with Larry. He never showed himself.

'Let's start with something simple,' she said, mainly to herself. She paused because she felt foolish, but forced herself to say, 'Izzy, can you hear me? If you can, I need you to spell out the word. Tell Olivia which letters to pick. Olivia, when Izzy tells you the letters I want you to pick them up and lay them down here, okay?' She touched the carpet in front of the spot where Olivia sat.

'Okay.'

Nothing happened. Olivia stared at the ten-by-ten grid. She appeared to be concentrating hard, but she didn't move her hand.

Jessica said it again: 'Izzy, can you hear me? If you can, tell Olivia which letters to pick.'

Olivia sat cross-legged, gazing at the tiles. She was motionless, silent.

Something tap-tapped against the window: the tree, battered by the wind. The sound made Jessica suck in air, but Olivia showed no sign of having heard it. She continued to stare at the Scrabble tiles.

Her hand moved towards them and Jessica almost gasped, had to force herself to keep quiet. She watched as Olivia's hand hovered over the letters, down in the right corner.

She picked up the *Y* and placed it in front of her. Then she stopped, apparently waiting for more instructions.

When nothing happened, Jessica said, '*Y* for *yes*?' It had to be. But, of course, it meant nothing. *Yes* was one of the words Olivia had learned at school. Or perhaps she had only half-learned it and couldn't remember what came after that first letter.

Jessica put the *Y* back in its place between the other *Y* and the *Z*.

Keeping her voice as calm and gentle as possible, Jessica said, 'Izzy, can you tell me our mum's name?'

Again there was a long, silent stretch of time when nothing happened. At least, it felt like a long time. Later Jessica would wonder if it had only been a few seconds before Olivia moved her hand.

It went straight to the middle of the grid, locating the first *M*. Olivia laid it on the carpet. Then her hand went back and picked up an *O*.

MO.

That was right.

Jessica took a deep breath. She had deliberately chosen a question with a short answer, something simple, to get things moving. But Olivia knew Mum's name, heard Will and Pete use it all the time. And if there was a malevolent or mischievous spirit here, telling Olivia what to do, they probably knew the name too. Jessica needed to ask something else. Something only Jessica and Isabel knew. A question with a short, one-word answer. She wished she'd prepared for this, had had the questions ready when they started. Because what if Izzy disappeared, got bored with this game, while Jessica was hesitating?

She thought of something.

'Izzy, what did we use to call our car when we were children?'

She waited. It was even chillier in the room now. *Ambient temperature: Arctic.* Olivia sat stock-still, staring at the letters. Jessica had never known her daughter to sit still for so long, even when she was exhausted. She appeared to be straining to hear something, as if listening to a voice in an adjacent room. The tree continued to tap and scrape at the window.

Olivia's hand crept out, swaying back and forth above the letters like a cobra preparing to strike. The hand descended and she touched a *C*. That was wrong. Disappointment kicked Jessica in the gut – but Olivia didn't pick that tile up. Her hand moved down two rows.

She picked up an *F* and placed it before her.

Oh Jesus. *F*. That was right.

Jessica could hardly breathe as Olivia's fingers roamed above the letters before she plucked another tile, then another, then one more.

R then *E* then *D*. She placed them in order to spell the four-letter word: *FRED*.

Mum had only had one car when they were growing up, a red Citroën GS that was always breaking down. She'd bought it after Dad drove away in the family car, and kept it right up to the sad day when it finally failed its MOT and was sent to a scrapyard. Jessica and Izzy christened it Fred, just because they thought it was a funny name.

Jessica stared at her daughter. There was no way she could have known that. And it seemed unlikely that any malevolent spirit would know it either. Jessica had never really believed in the evil ghost that Simon had warned her about. But when it came to believing in Izzy's spirit, her last shred of scepticism was blown away, like a leaf stripped from the tree that swayed outside.

Izzy was here.

This was real.

Gasping for breath, terrified and excited and trying desperately to stay in control, she counted to five in her head, stopping herself from babbling and telling Izzy all the things she wanted to say.

Like *I miss you* and *I'm sorry* and *I love you*.

She fought back tears, dug her fingernails into her palm, felt a shuddering breath course through her. At the same time, Olivia wriggled on the spot, as if she was getting restless. Oh God, the spell was going to be broken. Her chance would be lost. Immediately Jessica abandoned her plan to test Olivia and Izzy further. She set aside all the other questions that were begging to be answered. Because there was only question that really mattered, wasn't there?

'Izzy,' she said, voice cracking. A small voice was shouting at her, telling her this was wrong, that she shouldn't be doing this with Olivia. But it was too late. She was unable to stop herself. She needed to know. 'Who pushed you off that balcony? Who killed you?'

She waited, heart thudding so hard she feared it would burst from her chest.

Olivia's hand moved towards the letters – but then stopped.

'I can't,' she said. She turned her face towards Jessica, tears spilling from her eyes.

'Did she tell you the answer?' Jessica whispered.

A tiny nod.

'Then please, Livvy. You need to tell me.'

'But I don't want to.'

'Please.'

She waited. Olivia was rocking back and forth, clearly distressed, and every part of Jessica longed to snatch her up, pull her into a hug. Stop this. But she had to know. *She had to know.*

'Olivia. Who pushed Auntie Izzy?'

Olivia pulled a sleeve across her eyes, wiping away the tears. Jessica inched closer to her. Outside, the wind howled. The tree tapped at the window, faster and faster. Olivia stretched out her arm, her face turned half away from the letters as if she couldn't bear to look at them, as if they burned her retinas.

She picked up a *D*. Placed it on the carpet.

Next, Olivia picked up an *A*.

Jessica watched, strangely calm, accepting what she was seeing. Mum had been right all along. It was Darpak. A man Jessica liked and respected, who was part of their family. She pictured him serving up his traditional Sunday roast, his face alive with joy as he set it down on the table; she saw him setting off fireworks, cuddling Olivia when she had a grazed knee. Kissing Izzy on their wedding day, promising to love and cherish her forever.

She was so lost in her head, so convinced she knew what Olivia was spelling out, that she stopped watching. But she got a jolt when she looked down to see that Olivia had laid down a third letter.

D.

That didn't make sense. Olivia had made a mistake. She almost snatched the letter up, put it back, ready to tell her daughter she was spelling it wrong. But Olivia had already picked up letter four, which she placed beside the first three.

Another *D*.

Jessica watched as Olivia, with tears streaming down her face, picked up the fifth letter and laid it down.

Y.

Jessica stared, unable to take it in.

Who killed Auntie Izzy?

There was the answer, spelled out before her.

DADDY.

PART TWO

Chapter 25

December 2012

The doorbell rang, the chime loud and harsh to Isabel's ears, reverberating through all that white empty space. She put down her wine glass and headed downstairs, holding the banister to steady herself. When they bought this place she had loved the straight lines, the blankness. It was clean, minimal. No dirt, no clutter. Now, though, as her footsteps echoed around her, the atmosphere felt oppressive. Cold. She missed the colour and chaos of the home she'd grown up in. She missed having somewhere to hide. And she missed dealing with the kind of mess that could be swept under the carpet.

'Hey, Will,' she said, letting him in and gesturing for him to follow her to the kitchen. 'Wine?'

'I shouldn't. I'm driving.' But he sounded hesitant.

'One won't hurt, surely? I really need one and I don't want to drink alone.' She didn't tell him she'd already had two glasses, which she'd drunk on her own upstairs. She was confident that she was good at hiding it. Her voice wasn't slurred; she could still walk in a perfectly straight line.

Will accepted a glass of red and took a sip. 'Hey, this is really nice.'

'It should be. It's from the cellar.'

'Whoa. I thought Darpak was saving this stuff till the apocalypse.'

Isabel smiled at him. 'Life's too short to wait for the end of the world.'

She led him up the stairs to the living room, taking the bottle with her. It was worth several hundred quid; she wasn't sure how much exactly. But since that afternoon six weeks ago when she found the selfie, she had been helping herself to the finest pieces in Darpak's precious wine cellar. A bottle a day, sometimes two. She couldn't wait for him to notice.

'Where is Darpak, anyway?' Will asked, sinking into the sofa.

'He's taken a couple of clients out for dinner.'

'Clients you don't like?'

She looked at him. 'Why do you say that?'

'Oh, just your tone of voice. Still, I wouldn't want to go for dinner with Darpak's clients either. All that talk about hedge funds and exchange rates.' He pulled a face.

Isabel would have loved to know how Will saw her. The first time they'd met she'd been rude to him. She'd regretted it instantly but their relationship had never quite recovered. They were civil to each other; they got on well in company, when there was lots going on around them. But if Jess and Will split, Isabel doubted she'd see him again. It wasn't as if there was anything wrong with him. He was a good dad, quite funny, knew a lot about films and books and music, and Jessica loved him. He was good-looking too, although he was a bit of a Peter Pan type, not wanting to grow up. The complete opposite of Darpak.

Had Will ever cheated on Jess? He seemed to adore his wife, almost to the point of annoying uxoriousness. But you could never tell, could you?

Until recently, she had thought Darpak would never cheat on her.

But then, on that terrible night five weeks ago, after she confronted him, he had confessed.

ʊ

He came towards her, fists clenched by his side.

She took a step back, groped for a way to dial down the tension.

'I just want to talk about it. Like adults. Who is she? What . . . what does it mean?'

But he didn't answer. He turned around and stormed from the room.

She waited, counted to three. None of the mindfulness techniques she had practised and taught other people would help her now. On three, she followed him into the living room, where he sat on the sofa, breathing heavily.

'Darpak . . .'

He turned his face to her, slowly. 'Her name's Camilla.'

She stared at him.

'She was an intern at work.'

An intern. That meant she was young. Young and smooth and pert.

'She left last week. The day she sent me that text. That photo.'

He hung his head, unable or unwilling to look at her. All the rage, all the fury that had been aimed inwards, appeared to have melted away.

'You slept with her,' Isabel said, surprised by how calm she sounded.

'Only once.'

She waited.

'It was a work night out. Everyone had too much to drink. Somebody brought cocaine. A group of us went back to Giles's apartment, including Camilla.'

Isabel remembered that night. He'd told her he'd missed the last Tube and crashed at Giles's place. She hadn't thought anything of it at the time. She had trusted him.

'Anyway, that's where it happened,' he said.

'Do they all know? Everyone at work?'

'No! There were only a few of us left, including Giles and this woman from marketing. They went to bed, leaving me and Camilla alone. I could hear Giles and Suzi doing it in the other room, and Camilla looked at me . . .'

Isabel thought she might be sick, but part of her craved details.

'And then what?' she asked.

He stared at an invisible spot on the floor. 'It . . . happened. It was over in a minute. She left. I passed out, drunk. And woke up feeling like the biggest piece of shit on earth. I saw her later at the office and she acted like nothing had occurred. She never mentioned it, neither did I, and I tried to forget about it. Tried to pretend it wasn't real.' He rubbed his face. 'I couldn't believe it when she sent me that photo. I guess she thought it was funny. Maybe she wanted you to see it, to get me into trouble. I don't know.'

She managed to ask, 'You haven't heard from her since?'

'No.'

The living room lights were too bright. Isabel thought she might faint.

'What are you going to do?' he asked, his voice sounding like it was coming from a long way away. She was so cold inside, like her heart had stopped working, stopped pumping, and the blood in her veins was growing old.

'I don't know,' she said, voice cracking.

'Please don't leave me,' he said, getting up, his eyes shining with tears. He tried to grab hold of her and she resisted at first, then let him. He clung to her desperately while she stood there, limp, a conflicted mess of hate and love.

ᗯ

'Shall we get down to it, then?' Will asked, drawing her out of her head. What was he talking about? She must have been more drunk than she realised because it took a few seconds to remember why he was here. He took out his laptop and flipped it open. Her website. He was here to talk to her about the Mind+Body website.

'Okay, so I've knocked up a few ideas,' he said.

Over the next hour he went through the rough mock-ups he'd designed. It was all quite straightforward, with big images, bold text, tasteful palettes. The site would encourage potential clients to request an information pack, after which they would be encouraged to attend a 'taster' class.

'So what do you think?' he asked.

She thought about it. All the way through the tour, something had been bugging her. She refilled her glass and was surprised to see the bottle was nearly empty. She might need to fetch another.

'I like it,' she said.

'But . . .' He was smiling but she could see that he was slightly hurt.

'It's just . . . I think it should be sexier.'

'Sexier?'

'Yeah. My business is about pleasure. It's about couples connecting. The promise we make is that we will supercharge your relationship. It's about orgasms, Will. The site needs to be tastefully sexy.'

'Right.' She saw his Adam's apple bob.

'Does this make you uncomfortable?'

'No. Well, maybe a little. It's a bit weird talking about orgasms with my sister-in-law.'

The look on his face, the way he was squirming, made her feel mischievous. 'You and Jess should come to one of my classes.'

He laughed. 'She told me you'd suggested it.'

'Perhaps you could persuade her. You should come along, and that would help you understand what this website needs to convey.'

He had gone pink, though he was still smiling. 'Jess would never agree to it. She's not . . . she's not like you.' Hurriedly he added, 'I'm not saying she's repressed or anything like that.'

'I know. But she's shy. And she probably thinks it's a load of hippie nonsense, though she's too polite to say that to me. It took me a year to persuade her to practise mindfulness.'

He nodded and took a sip of wine. Isabel had been sitting on an armchair, leaning over to see Will's laptop screen, but now she got up – surprised by how much the wine had gone to her head – and sat beside Will on the sofa.

'I do think it would be useful for you to learn about Blissful Massage,' she said. Their thighs were only an inch apart. He seemed agitated by her nearness, but didn't move away. Again his reaction made her feel wicked. 'Perhaps I could teach you.'

He went a deeper shade of pink.

She began to explain to him exactly what Blissful Massage involved. How it was all about touch, taking time, not rushing things.

'It really frustrates me that Jess won't try it,' she said. 'She has this silly squeamishness about her body.'

'Or maybe our sex life is perfect already,' Will said.

She raised an eyebrow. 'Is it?'

He looked away.

'Okay,' she said. 'Maybe Jess won't ever do it. Maybe you think it's a load of New Age crap too. But I still think it's important for you to understand the fundamentals. Let me show you how it's done.' Seeing his face, she said, 'Don't worry, I'm not going to take my knickers off. Wait here.'

She went off to her study, detouring to the kitchen on the way back, where she grabbed another bottle of wine she had already brought up from Darpak's cellar. She leaned against the counter, opening it, thinking about how Darpak owed her.

After that night in October when Darpak had confessed to his 'mistake' – that was what they were calling it – they had sat up all night talking. A lot of wine had been drunk by both of them while he pleaded for forgiveness. He had been stupid and disrespectful. But surely that wasn't enough for them to give up on their marriage, their partnership? They were good together, and he promised – *he swore* – to be a better husband from now on.

At one point she had wondered how many other couples were having the exact same conversation in homes around the globe at that moment. And in the list of things she was still angry about, that was up there: that he had made her life a cliché.

She had always sworn she wouldn't tolerate infidelity, but she had found herself agreeing to give him another chance. Because they *were* good together. And she didn't want to give up on something she had poured so much life and love and energy into.

That didn't mean she wasn't angry and disappointed and, at least several times a day, filled with hatred. Hatred and suspicion and pure, wounded misery.

So she drank. She drank to numb those emotions.

She drank to get through the night.

Like now. She returned to the living room holding the wine along with an object that made Will's eyes widen.

'I'm sure you know what this is,' she said.

It was an anatomically correct, life-size model of female genitalia. Isabel used it occasionally in class, though it was a poor substitute for the real thing. She sat beside him again, holding the model on her lap.

'Okay,' she said. 'Here's what happens during Blissful Massage. The woman removes her clothes from the waist down. Then she lies back – we tend to use cushions or beanbags to create a comfortable place where

175

the woman can recline. It's important that she's supported and doesn't feel any physical discomfort at all.'

'Makes sense.'

'Okay. First, the couple spend a few minutes talking to each other, using some words of praise. You would tell the woman how beautiful you find her. We can skip that bit and go straight to the main part. You put your thumb here . . .' She demonstrated on the model. 'And then you use your left hand like this.'

It was almost silent in the room. All Isabel could hear was Will's breathing. It was getting heavier.

'And you stroke, using a circular motion, like so.'

She showed him how it was done.

'It's important to communicate,' she said. 'Ask the woman how she's feeling. What's good, what isn't. Try to find the perfect speed and rhythm. If you get it right, your partner could have up to ten orgasms in one session.'

'Wait. *Ten?*'

'Yep.' She laughed. 'Mind-blowing, huh?'

Her finger continued to stroke the plastic clitoris of her model, which Will was watching intently. She wondered if he was picturing himself doing it to Jess.

Or maybe he was imagining that it was her, Isabel.

She felt a little guilty for thinking it. He was enrapt, watching her fingers move on the model as if he was hypnotised. He was visibly sweating. Was he aroused? What would he do now if she touched him? Would he respond?

She mentally slapped herself. He was her sister's husband. And even though she was drunk, even though – she realised with a start – it would give her pleasure to take revenge on Darpak by screwing another man, she would never do that. And she was sure Will wouldn't either.

Ninety per cent sure.

She stopped stroking and stood up, holding the model vagina behind her back.

'So there you go,' she said with a smile. 'What do you think?'

He stared at her. He had that look, the one a man gets when he's turned on and can't think about anything else.

'Will?' she said. 'Are you okay?'

But he just kept staring at her, his breathing audible in the quiet room.

Chapter 26

Once or twice during the night, Jessica felt herself slipping into the merciful oblivion of sleep, submerging for a second or two before she awoke, gasping for air. Remembering. And then she would be wide awake again, but desperate for sleep. Desperate to escape.

Finally, at some point between the witching hour and dawn, she surrendered and sat up. Her pyjamas were soaked through with sweat and the sheets were damp and rucked up. It almost looked like she'd spent a night of passion here with a lover.

She went to the bathroom, stripped off her wet pyjamas and got under the shower, turning the temperature up so the water burned, scrubbing her skin till it was pink. When she couldn't stand the heat of the shower any more, she went back to the bedroom and sat on the bed. Simon's monitor was still on, displaying an infrared image of Olivia's room. Jessica leaned closer, gazing at her daughter. After the seance – she had no idea what else to call it – Olivia had sobbed and clung to her mum as if terrified she had done something awful. Jessica had brought her in here and lain down with her, whispering consoling words, wishing she had someone to do the same for her.

'Olivia, it's really important that you don't tell Daddy about the game we played, okay? It's our little secret.'

'Me, you and Auntie Izzy.'

'Yes. Just us girls.' She forced a smile.

'Okay.'

'And it's extra important that you're not scared of Daddy, even if he might have done something . . . naughty.'

'What about Santa?' Olivia asked.

'Huh?'

'Will he put Daddy on the naughty list?'

Jessica smiled and felt tears fill her eyes. She stroked Olivia's hair. 'I think he might. But you're definitely on the nice list.'

Olivia nodded, apparently satisfied, and Jessica felt relief wash over her. It seemed the whole idea of what her dad might have done to the aunt she'd never met was an abstract one. She wasn't frightened of him in the way she would be if she saw him do something violent.

Of course, Jessica knew there must be stuff going on in that little head that she didn't understand. Children are sponges: they soak up and process experiences even if they profess not to remember them. Jessica had no idea what long-term effect all this would have on Olivia – especially if it turned out that Will was guilty. Maybe it would be a good idea to take her to see a child psychologist at some point in the near future. Until then, Jessica was going to keep an eye on her. Right now, in the immediate aftermath of the seance, Olivia seemed surprisingly unaffected.

It hadn't taken long for Olivia to fall asleep, but at some point – Jessica must have been asleep longer than she realised – Olivia had got up and gone back to her own room.

The little girl lay on her side in bed with a teddy bear pressed against her chin. She looked peaceful, the very opposite of haunted, and Jessica wondered if Izzy had gone now, having imparted the information she needed to share. Or would she stay until Jessica had done something about it?

Done something about it. Like what? What was she supposed to do?

The weird thing – the funny thing? – was that of tonight's two revelations, the idea that Izzy's spirit really had returned and was talking to Olivia was easier to believe than the other. *Will had murdered Izzy?* It was ludicrous. She knew Will. He wasn't capable of murder. He didn't have a violent bone in his body. But then she thought about all those people you'd see on the news, the wives and mothers of murderers, the lovers of men who had been proven to be killers. *I know him*, they would say with blind conviction. *He would never do something like this.*

Was she one of those women now?

Tearing herself away from the monitor, Jessica put on a clean pair of PJs, wrapped herself in her dressing gown and went down to the kitchen to make a cup of tea. Caspar hauled himself out of his bed, excited to see her, and she sat at the table and stroked his ears.

Could Will really have killed Izzy? Why would he have done it? She forced herself to push aside the voice that told her it was impossible and tried to think logically, like a detective. It would be easier, she realised, if she could write it down, so she opened the drawer where the children's art supplies were kept and took out a few sheets of paper and a felt-tip pen.

At the top of the page, she wrote *Why?*

The first possibility was almost too horrific to contemplate but she made herself write it down: *They were having an affair.*

She stared at the words, a bubble of nausea swelling in her stomach. Could two of the people she loved most in the world really have betrayed her like that? It seemed impossible to believe – that both of them would be willing to hurt her in the most devastating way possible – but it was another thing that happened all the time, wasn't it? A staple of agony columns and real-life magazines. *I only did it because she looked like you*, the men would say to their wives.

She thought back to 2012–2013, the months before Izzy's death. That was the period when Jessica and Will had given up hope of conceiving their second child, when Will had complained of feeling like a 'mobile sperm farm'. Their love life had dwindled to almost nothing. Had he sought out an affair because of that? It was such a cliché. And anyway, it wasn't true that their sex life had completely died, because otherwise how had she got pregnant?

Jessica sat up straighter, the sheet of paper trembling in her hand. Had it all started when Will was helping Izzy with her website? She could imagine a chain of events. She wrote it down:

Will and Izzy start affair (Dec 2012).

Izzy ends it.

Will won't leave her alone.

Izzy threatens to tell me.

Will, afraid of losing everything, including baby, kills her (Mar 2013).

Jessica went over the sentences, seeing it all play out like a TV drama. It was possible. It was plausible, even, a straightforward, logical narrative. She could imagine them both, racked with guilt but unable to stop themselves. It would all have happened rapidly. Jessica had found out she was pregnant in January 2013. She had told Izzy straight away. And Izzy died six weeks later. Could the affair have played itself out that quickly? It was possible . . . Or maybe it wasn't an affair. Maybe Will had made a move on Izzy, she'd rejected him and threatened to tell Jessica, so he'd killed her. Although both scenarios were dreadful, this one was slightly preferable. In this one, only one person had betrayed her.

Could he have done that, even if he'd been desperate enough? It was hard to imagine, but she tried to think clearly, to push past the havoc all this was causing inside her heart. What would the police look at? She thought back to all those crime novels she'd read, the many episodes of *Columbo* and *Murder, She Wrote* she'd watched when she was young.

Jessica had been so swept up in her own grief after Izzy's death that she had hardly thought about Will's feelings. He had been there, by Jessica's side, throughout. He had seemed stoic, strong. She vaguely remembered that she had described him as her rock. Darpak had organised the funeral, but Jessica had helped where she could, although she'd hardly been able to do anything without bursting into tears, a mess of bereavement and pregnancy hormones. The funeral itself was a dark blur in her memory, like driving through heavy rain at night. She didn't think Will had cried, though. He'd been pale and quiet. Serious. He'd spent most of the day minding Felix.

She raked her memory, trying to find a clue that Will had seemed guilty or grief-stricken, but there was nothing. She simply couldn't remember.

Caspar nudged her hand, reminding her that she hadn't stroked his ears for a while. Caspar had been much more energetic back in 2013 and that was one thing Jessica did remember: Will had taken the dog out for a lot of long walks when she was pregnant with Olivia. She had questioned him about it, asking him if he was trying to get away from her. His very reasonable answer had been that the dog needed exercise and he didn't want Jessica to exert herself too much. But what if that had been a cover story? What if he'd actually been out there working through his emotions, the guilt and grief he hadn't shown anyone?

'Did he confess to you?' she asked the dog, who responded by lying on his back and waiting for his belly to be tickled. 'You're no help,' she said.

Where had Will been when Izzy was killed? It had happened on a Thursday afternoon; Jessica would never forget receiving the call that evening, while she was trying to persuade Felix to eat his dinner. Will had got home from work ten minutes later, finding his wife in a hysterical state on the kitchen floor. So Will had been at work that afternoon – that was his story, anyway. It was something that would have to be checked out.

But by whom?

She ripped up the sheet of paper and dropped the shreds in the recycling bin.

A yawn stretched her jaw. She couldn't think straight any more. Maybe if she could sleep, her unconscious mind would work through the knots and she'd wake up with a clear idea of what to do.

She couldn't bear the thought of sleeping in her damp bed so she found a blanket and went through to the living room. Her brain switched itself off the moment she lay on the sofa.

ꙍ

She woke with Olivia standing over her. Light flooded the room and Caspar was asleep in the armchair. Olivia held out Jessica's iPhone.

'Nanny wants to talk to you,' she said.

Jessica took the phone and was greeted by the strident blast of her mother's voice. 'Is it true? What Simon says?'

She sat up, trying to get her thoughts in order. For a blissful moment she had forgotten what had happened last night. Then it all came rushing back.

'You mean, is it true that I told him to leave? Yes, it is.'

She held the phone away from her ear while Mum ranted.

'Have you calmed down now?' Jessica asked.

There was a sigh at the other end of the line, a sigh that Jessica recognised from her teenage years. *What am I going to do with you?* That's what Mum always used to say.

'So, tell me, what happened?' Mum asked. 'Did you . . . communicate with Isabel?'

Jess didn't realise she was going to say 'No' until the word left her mouth. She would have to deal with Olivia, tell her not to say anything to Nanny, but it would be a mistake to let her mother get involved at this point. Jessica needed to investigate first, to gather more information before she accused Will.

'Nothing happened,' she said.

'What, nothing at all?'

'No. Listen, I can't talk now but I'll come by later to drop off Simon's equipment.'

She hung up before Mum had a chance to argue or ask more questions. Then she noticed a text from Will.

Morning. Heading to ferry now. Can't wait to see you later. Love you xx

She hesitated. He would worry if she didn't text back.
But she couldn't bring herself to do it.

Chapter 27

'That was weird,' Will said, coming into the kitchen after reading Olivia her bedtime stories. He and Felix had got home just as Olivia was finishing her tea and now he was with Jessica, two hours later, both of them pausing for breath after the whirl of activity that filled every Sunday evening: homework, baths for both kids, getting the school uniform ready for Monday morning, bedtime for Olivia, 'chill-out' time for Felix.

Jessica knew she ought to act as if everything was normal, but she wasn't going to be able to go through with it. Not tonight.

'What was weird?' she asked as Will grabbed a bottle from the wine rack and searched for the corkscrew.

'Olivia. Halfway through *The Gruffalo* she sat up, flung her arms around my neck and said, "You're on Santa's naughty list, Daddy."'

Jessica, who had been stacking the dishwasher, froze. 'Really?'

He pulled the cork out. 'Yes. Not sure what I'm supposed to have done. Maybe going away for the weekend without her?'

Jessica faked a laugh. 'That's probably it.'

'Also, some of her teddies seem to be missing. She always has Stretch in bed with her but I couldn't find him . . . She said something about him having an accident.'

Jessica was amazed Will had noticed. 'Oh, Caspar got hold of him and made him all mucky. He's in the wash.'

In fact, the giraffe and the other eyeless toys were still in the cupboard where she'd stashed them, and she mentally added 'Order replacements' to her To-Do List, though it was hardly high-priority at the moment.

Will wagged a finger at Caspar. 'Naughty dog.' Caspar looked perplexed.

Thank God he can't speak, Jessica thought.

She had her back to Will, cleaning scraps of food out of the sink. She felt him approaching but before she could turn and ward him off he put his arms around her waist and kissed the back of her head. His body was warm against her spine. She went rigid.

'You feel very tense,' he said. 'What's the matter?'

She wriggled from his grasp. 'It's been a hard couple of days. Olivia's been . . . difficult.'

'Well, I'm back now.'

He took her damp hands and tried to kiss her. He had that look in his eyes, the shadow of desire. He was always like this when he'd been away for a night, absence having made his heart – or some other part of his anatomy – grow fonder.

'I thought maybe we could have an early night,' he said.

'Good idea. I'm exhausted.'

He tried to kiss her again but she turned her face so his lips only met her cheek. He looked at her, trying to read her thoughts, and she stepped away from him. 'I can't have sex tonight,' she said.

'Oh.' He looked like a little boy who'd been told he couldn't have any ice cream.

'I'm too tired and wouldn't be able to relax.'

'All right. Sorry. But can I have a hug?'

She let him put his arms around her, though she knew she must feel as stiff as a piece of wood. After a few seconds he gave up.

She watched him go over to the fridge, open it and peer inside. Could he really have murdered Izzy? The words, the question, bubbled up from inside her, trying to force their way out of her throat.

She would know if he was lying. But if she was wrong, if he was innocent, their marriage might never recover from the accusation. So she swallowed the words back down.

'Did something happen while I was away?' he asked, closing the fridge door.

She picked up the wine bottle, hoping that her hand wasn't trembling. 'No. Why are you asking?'

'I don't know.' He tilted his head, the way he did when he was watching a movie he didn't quite understand. 'You're acting strange.'

'What? Because I won't have sex with you?'

'No. Don't be . . .' He trailed off. 'You seem nervous or something.'

The fridge hummed in the silence. 'Actually, there is something.'

She studied his face, searching for fear or at least anxiety. Because if she were carrying a dark secret, she knew she would always be on edge, waiting to get found out. Even now, five years on, thinking he'd got away with it, it would surely still be something he'd worry about. But he didn't seem worried, just confused.

'What?' he asked.

'The other day I was looking for a radiator key and found some cigarettes in your drawer. Have you been smoking?'

He smiled sheepishly. 'Shit. Busted. Sorry, Jess – I bought them when I went out with Gary for a drink. I only had a few.'

'Did you take them to the Isle of Wight?'

'What? No. I chucked them away the other day. Do you really think I'd smoke around Felix?'

'I don't know.'

'For fuck's sake. Really? I bet you were drinking while you were looking after Olivia on your own.'

They stared at each other. They could have a fight now. A 'domestic'. Jessica would almost welcome it, the chance to unbottle the simmering rage that was always there, lurking inside her, ready to show itself. But she fought it, breathed, knowing that if she lost her temper now she would say too much.

'I don't want to argue,' she said. 'I'm going to bed, all right? I really am exhausted.'

She left the room, continuing to focus on her breathing. She had to stop at the top of the stairs, to grip the banister. Because she had seen something in his eyes. Anger reflected back at her.

She hadn't thought of it before. But now it hit her like a fist in the guts.

If Will was capable of murdering Izzy because he was afraid of being exposed, that meant he was capable of killing her too.

Chapter 28

Jessica ran through the school gate, almost tripping over another parent's buggy. Rain was lashing down and everyone else had umbrellas, a shifting forest of them coming down the hill towards her. She didn't even have a hood and greasy rain slid down beneath her collar. A perfect end to a terrible day.

She had spent the morning combing through Will's computer and the drawers where he kept his paperwork, looking for evidence. Something that proved he had been screwing Izzy. Anything that would expose his guilt. The bill for a meal for two. A receipt for flowers or underwear that he hadn't given to Jessica (come to think of it, when *had* he last bought flowers for her?) or even a scribbled note, a card, a declaration of love and passion. Maybe a possession of Izzy's, some keepsake of their affair. She ransacked drawers, searched through the cupboards in his room, emptied cardboard boxes, even pulled up the edges of the carpet to make sure he hadn't hidden anything under there.

She found nothing. At the end of it she was surrounded by mess and had to put everything back together, hoping he wouldn't notice. Or maybe she wanted him to notice. Wanted him to worry and make some kind of move to reveal himself. Except that was dangerous, wasn't it? She had a vision of waking up with his hands around her throat, whispering something about how she knew too much. The vision shook her. He wouldn't really harm her, would he?

Not unless he was desperate. Like a fox chewing off its leg to escape a trap.

It was all so confusing and difficult and it left her feeling even more exhausted.

'Won't you give me a clue?' she found herself saying out loud. 'Come on, Izzy. Why won't you talk to me?'

Silence.

Was she going to have to get Olivia to communicate with Izzy again? To get the Scrabble pieces out? No. She wasn't going to put her daughter through that stress again. It wouldn't be fair on her. She just wished Izzy would talk to *her*, especially now she had shown that she was willing to listen.

'Please, Izzy,' she said aloud, straining to hear something in return. God, what would people think if they saw her now, covered in dust and talking to her dead sister? *Poor Jess, she still hasn't got over it. It's made her lose her mind.*

She had just finished tidying up when she heard the chime of church bells, ringing in the distance. Three o'clock.

Oh shit – she was going to be late picking up Olivia.

She had raced down the stairs, out to the car, and here she was now, running up the path to the early-years block, dodging brollies and parents who, she was sure, were judging her. *Look, it's Olivia's mum. Always late.*

And her husband was shagging her sister, you know? Her husband, the murderer. But she's too pathetic to do anything about it.

The voices were so real that she was convinced someone had actually said the words aloud. She stared at a woman in a purple cagoule. Ruby's mum. Was it her? Or had it been Jackson's nanny? Or Reuben's dad? She wanted to grab them all, tell them she wasn't a bad mother, a terrible sister, a deluded wife.

Really, she wasn't.

She reached the classroom door and found herself face to face with Ryan. Swiftly, she rearranged her face, smiled, tried not to look like she was completely insane.

'Do we have an appointment?' he asked.

She looked at him blankly. 'What? I'm here to collect Olivia.'

'Oh. It's just that your mum's already picked her up. She said you'd asked her to. I hope that was all right.'

She gawped at him. Oh my God, he was right. She had asked Mum to pick up Olivia today. She had been so swept up in everything that she'd forgotten.

She laughed, hoping she didn't sound like a crazy person. There was no way she could cover this up. She put a hand on her wet head and said, 'I can't believe I forgot. I'm losing it. I'm completely bloody losing it.'

She expected laughter but got a look of concern. 'Are you all right?'

'I . . . Yes . . . I . . .'

He glanced over her shoulder. All the other parents had gone and there were no children left to be collected.

'Do you want to come in for a minute? Dry off a bit? Mrs Rose isn't well today so it's been me and a supply teacher who had to shoot off the moment the bell went.'

She was going to say 'No' and slink away, but found herself saying, 'Thank you.'

She entered the classroom, rain sliding down her face, dripping on to the floor and creating a small puddle. She hugged herself, shivering.

'Oh dear,' Ryan said, as if he was talking to one of his four-year-old charges. 'Wait there.'

He disappeared into an anteroom and came back with a towel, which he handed to her.

'Thank you.' She rubbed at her hair and face with the towel, feeling pathetically grateful. He was watching her intently, as if seeing a woman dry her hair was novel and fascinating.

'I'm actually pleased you're here,' he said.

'Oh?'

'Yeah.' He cleared his throat. 'This whole thing about Olivia being . . . interested in death. She said something strange today. Something about talking to her Auntie Izzy.'

Jessica hung her head. She should have known Olivia wouldn't be able to keep quiet about it. 'What did she say, exactly?'

He closed the classroom door. 'Do you want to sit down?'

She perched on a desk rather than sit in one of the tiny chairs, and put the wet towel aside. He sat down too, facing her. She could smell the cheap deodorant he wore.

'She said that she played a game with you – something to do with spelling out words? We were practising her words at the time. She was writing *Mummy* and *Daddy* and she asked if I had any "Scabble" pieces. The rest of what she said didn't make much sense, to be honest, but it was kind of disturbing.'

This was it. He was going to report her for being an unfit mother. Get social services involved. Olivia would be taken away. And as Ryan looked across the table, something burst inside. She felt a tear run down her cheek and realised she was crying.

She picked up the towel and buried her face in it, unable to stop sobbing. All the drama and worry of the past few weeks, especially the last few days . . . She couldn't keep it bottled up any more. She fought against it, embarrassed – no, mortified – to be letting go like this in Ryan's presence. But then she felt a hand on her shoulder, resting there lightly, and she stopped caring. She let it come.

She wasn't sure exactly how long she cried for. Maybe only a minute; maybe two. When she got hold of herself, she rubbed her face with the damp towel, aware as she took it away that she must look a mess. But Ryan was smiling sympathetically at her.

'I guess you're used to dealing with tears,' she said, her voice thick.

'Yeah. Usually not the parents, though.'

She laughed. 'Oh Jesus. What must you think of me?'

'It sounds like you're going through a tough time.'

'Yeah. You could say that.'

Neither of them spoke for a few seconds. 'So,' he said, 'this thing with the Scrabble tiles. I wasn't sure if Olivia was making it all up . . . but it sounded like some kind of seance.'

'Are you going to report me to social services?'

'What? Of course not. I mean, assuming you don't have Olivia involved with devil-worship or something.' He smiled to show he was joking, but Jessica couldn't make herself smile back.

'I take it you don't believe in all that stuff?' she said. 'Ghosts. Being able to talk to spirits.'

'No, of course not. Why, do you?'

'I used to. Then I stopped believing. Now I'm not sure any more.'

Ryan got up, took a few paces away from her. 'You believe Olivia's actually being haunted by your sister?'

Yes. 'Maybe.'

'And you think you made contact, during this . . . seance?'

I do. 'Again, maybe.'

'Wow.'

'It's crazy, isn't it?'

'And what does Olivia's dad say about it?'

'Will? I haven't told him.'

He raised an eyebrow, as if he was thinking, *But you're telling me?* 'Why not?'

'Ha. Because of what she said.'

Again there was a silence.

'Have you talked to your mother about this?' he asked.

'No way!'

A little smile. 'Jessica, I'm not a counsellor or anything. But I think you should talk to Will about all this. Tell him whatever it was Olivia said.'

'I don't know . . .'

'I'm not an expert, Jessica. I'm not even married and you can tell me to mind my own business, but it seems like the kind of thing you and he should talk about.'

'Maybe.'

It was fully dark outside now, the winter night rendering the windows opaque, and Jessica could see her own reflection in the glass. She looked tired and bedraggled, all her eye make-up rubbed away. And she needed to get going, to pick up Olivia, even though she was dreading seeing her mother and having to deflect all her questions again.

'I have to go. But thank you. And please, forget everything Olivia told you about the . . . seance.'

'As long as you promise you're not a devil-worshipper.'

She laughed. 'I promise.'

'And you should talk to Will,' he said, closing the door behind her.

Chapter 29

Isabel crunched across the gravel to Nina's car. The trees around their house were bare, making her feel exposed. She preferred the house in the warmer seasons, when thick leaves protected it from view.

'You look amazing,' Nina said as Isabel got into the car. She was wearing the Burberry trench coat that Darpak had given her for Christmas and she'd had her hair cut that morning.

'Hmm.'

Nina gave her a curious look, then glanced down at her own clothes. Nina, who was a decade younger than Isabel, was wearing a biker jacket and a short skirt with black tights.

'Do you think I look too scruffy?' she asked. 'I was in a rush and didn't have time to get changed.'

'Shut up. You always look gorgeous.' Isabel reached for her seat belt. 'I'm not even sure of the point of this meeting. Why can't I just turn up and have my photo taken? It's a photo shoot for a newspaper. He's not painting the bloody *Mona Lisa*.'

Nina started the engine. 'But it's Gavin Lawson!'

Isabel laughed. 'So you keep saying. I'd never even heard of him before he started coming to my classes.'

Nina did a 'shock-horror' face. 'That's like saying you've never heard of, I don't know, David Bailey.'

'Who?'

'You're joking, right?'

'Yes, I'm joking. And I get it. Gavin Lawson is a big deal.'

'Yeah. He is. I would love to be photographed by him.'

'He just seems like a typically entitled middle-aged bloke to me. One with a girlfriend half his age.' She remembered how he'd half-swaggered, half-staggered out of his final session.

'Carmen? You know she's a model? I don't think she's actually his girlfriend.' They pulled up at a red light. 'I really wish I'd got to meet him before he stopped going to your classes.'

'Well, don't worry. You'll get to meet him today.'

They drove in silence for a minute, allowing Isabel to gather her thoughts and reflect on what had led to today and what might happen next.

The article about Mind+Body in the local paper, combined with what Isabel imagined to be a swell of chatter among her clients, a number of whom worked in the media, had led to an approach from one of the biggest national newspapers, *The Herald*. They wanted to write a feature about Mind+Body, and Blissful Massage, for their Sunday magazine. It would be the main feature in that issue and there was a good chance her picture would appear on the cover.

'This is huge,' Darpak had said when she told him.

'I'm not sure if I should do it.'

'What? Are you crazy? It's incredible exposure. Think about all the new business it will bring in. We'll be able to open that centre in Manchester. We could even go international.'

We. That was interesting. So he wasn't planning on leaving her. Not yet, anyway.

'But what if they take the piss?' Isabel had asked. 'You know what the press can be like when it comes to sex. Especially anything that has a vaguely New Age air about it. Remember what happened to Sting when he told the world he was into tantric sex? People still go on about it twenty years later!'

In the end, though, she had allowed herself to be persuaded. It would be good for the business, and she would just have to make sure she didn't say anything that could be misinterpreted or used against her. Her biggest worry was that they would bring up Uncle Larry and use that to make her look foolish. The journalist from the *Bromley Gazette* hadn't mentioned the poltergeist in her article in the end, but that was because Darpak knew the head of advertising – they occasionally played squash together – and had had a word with him.

When *The Herald* told her Gavin Lawson was going to do the photo shoot, he had already stopped coming to Mind+Body. And when Isabel told Nina the news, Nina had insisted on showing her Gavin's work.

'It's so sexy,' she'd enthused, showing Isabel a selection of his photos on her iPad. Sexy was right. Or maybe the word should be *explicit*. There was a lot of nudity, tons of young women with their boobs and bums on display, most of them with messy, just-been-fucked hair; couples in clinches, tongues touching; models perched on toilets in grimy bathrooms, or lying on threadbare sofas.

'He'd better not ask me to pose like that,' Isabel had said. 'I don't understand how it's fashion photography when half these women aren't wearing any clothes.'

Nina had laughed. 'All right, Grandma. Look, he does a lot of respectable portraits too.' She navigated to another section of the site, where lots of famous faces – their bodies fully clad – stared out, all of them appearing effortlessly cool, the kind of people who looked like they owned the world. 'Please can I come along?' she'd asked. 'I'd love to meet him.'

'Sure.'

Gavin Lawson's studio was based on the edge of an industrial estate on the outskirts of Croydon. Isabel and Nina pulled up outside and looked up at the building. It was a Victorian red-brick warehouse with arched windows, the brickwork blackened in places as if it had succumbed to a fungal disease.

'Not what I was expecting,' Isabel said.

Nina was more impressed. 'It's gritty. Authentic. That's his style.'

They got out of the car. It was freezing and Isabel hugged herself, shivering. Nina, apparently impervious to the cold, gave her a concerned look.

Isabel had told Nina about Darpak's confession. Nina was furious with her brother and had wanted to have it out with him, but Isabel had stopped her. It would only make things more complicated, and she hadn't yet decided what she was going to do. She and Darpak were in a strange, emotionally raw place. She wanted to both cling to him and push him off a high building. They were drinking a lot, fighting and having angry sex – the kind of sex that went against everything she taught. There was no slow build-up of pleasure here. It was fast, intense, destructive. Sex as a weapon that damaged both parties. Last night she had bitten him so hard she'd drawn blood.

And after the sex, which left her high but fractious, she would carry on drinking. On top of that, she couldn't remember when she'd last managed to sleep without a pill. In the mornings, when she needed to go to work, the only thing that got her out of the house was a bump of speed, or a little pink pill that got her moving. Downers and uppers. She knew how insane it was but she didn't have the strength right now to fight it.

'Come on,' Isabel said. 'Let's get this over with.'

Stepping into the building was like going through a door that connected the Arctic to the Sahara. Vast iron radiators pumped out heat, and she felt herself perspiring beneath her trench coat. Going up the stairs to the studio, which was on the fourth floor, footsteps echoing around her, Isabel had to stop for a moment. She was out of breath and all she wanted to do was go home, crawl back into bed. But she had to get through this. If only she'd brought some of the little pink pills with her.

They knocked on the door of the studio and it was opened by a skinny man with peroxide hair. One of Gavin's assistants, Isabel presumed. He held it open a crack and peered out at them, like a butler opening the door of a creepy old mansion.

'We're here for a photo shoot,' Izzy said.

'Isabel Shah?' He squinted at Nina. 'Who's this? Gavin doesn't like hangers-on.'

How rude. Isabel was about to tell him to piss off when a booming voice from behind the skinny man said, 'What the fuck is going on?'

It was Gavin. He barged past his assistant, pushed the door open and stood there, looking them both up and down. Isabel noticed how his eyes lingered on Nina's body: a second on her legs, then her breasts, before he grinned broadly.

'Ignore this little tosspot,' he said in a loud voice. 'Come in, come in.'

He hustled them into the studio and, to Isabel's surprise, pulled her into a hug.

'So good to see you,' he said. 'How's it all going? Sorry I had to stop coming to your sessions. Been so busy, you know? It was bloody great, though. You're a fucking guru.'

He was wearing a vintage Blondie T-shirt and ripped jeans, and had an odd smell: sweat and something else, a sour odour she couldn't identify. He let Isabel go and threw his arms around Nina, squeezing her as if she were a long-lost friend. He wasn't like this when he came to Mind+Body. But he was on his own turf here. Or maybe he felt that he had to be in character. The edgy, gregarious artist.

He turned from them to address the room. As well as the skinny blonde guy, there were three other people, two men and a woman. They were all young, hip, sullen.

'Everyone,' Gavin announced in that booming voice, his South London accent far more pronounced than it had been when she'd heard him talk before. 'Everyone, this is Isabel. The Queen of Pleasure.'

She cringed, which made him laugh.

'Don't be embarrassed. What you do is amazing. Fucking amazing.' He turned to his audience and said it again, loudly. Was he on something? She noticed a vein throbbing in his temple and wondered what he was taking and whether he'd offer her any.

Instead he said, 'Martin, get these women a drink.'

Martin, a skinny man with cheekbones to die for, hurried over. 'What can I get you? Vodka? Gin? Just a beer?'

It was midday. Isabel laughed, was about to ask for a cup of tea or a water, but heard herself saying, 'I'd love a beer.'

Nina frowned and Gavin noticed. 'What's the matter?'

'I'm driving. Can I have a coffee?'

'Fuck that,' Gavin said. 'Leave your car here, get a cab. The newspaper will pay. Martin, give this gorgeous woman a beer. And one for me.'

Martin came back with three bottles of export lager and handed them out. Gavin held his bottle aloft. 'To pleasure,' he said.

They clinked bottlenecks and Isabel said, 'To pleasure.'

Gavin winked at her. 'Making you rich, eh?'

'How's Carmen?' Isabel asked, ignoring what he'd said.

'Who?'

'Your girlfriend?'

'Oh. Her.' He laughed. 'That wasn't my girlfriend, just a model. I fancied seeing what it was all about and she was up for it so we came along. I have to say, it's genius what you do.'

'Thanks.'

'I bet you get a lot of blokes wanting to come along on their own, don't you? I mean, what a place to meet women who are into sex and don't have loads of boring hang-ups.' He guffawed. 'Anyway, let me start setting up and we can show the world how beautiful you are. You're going to have them queuing up and down the street after this.'

She smiled. 'That's the plan.'

'Hey,' he said, 'I really want to ask you something – about your poltergeist.'

She was speechless.

'Yeah, I found an old article about you online that said you had a haunting when you were a kid. Fucking scary stuff. Maybe when the shoot's over you can tell me all about it.'

'Oh, please, no.'

'She doesn't like talking about it,' Nina said. 'I don't know why. I think it's fascinating. It gives me goose bumps hearing about it all. The phone calls and the flying cups . . .'

'Nina, please!' Isabel needed to shut this conversation down. 'Could we get on, please? I have to go to work after this.'

'Yeah, sure.' Gavin took a couple of strides away then stopped. He turned back and gave Nina the once-over again. 'So you're a model, yeah?'

Isabel expected Nina to roll her eyes, but she looked like this was the best thing anyone had ever said to her. 'No, I'm just Izzy's assistant.'

'Yeah, yeah, I know you're her assistant. But you must have done a bit of modelling, looking like that.'

'No.'

He seemed genuinely shocked. 'Not interested in showing the world what you've got, eh? Shame.'

Then he strode off, grabbing a camera and going into a huddle with two of his assistants. Nina watched him go, apparently contemplating what he had said about her being a model.

'This place is pretty impressive on the inside,' Isabel said.

It was a large, open space, with exposed brick walls. A plain white backdrop was set up at the far end of the room, with huge lights on wheels positioned on either side. There were a couple of battered leather couches, piles of equipment all over the place – cameras and wires and light meters – and, on the walls, a dozen or so massive canvases. These canvases mostly featured pictures of Gavin with models, or women on their own, most of them semi-naked. The photos were familiar from Gavin's website. There were also more sober, fully dressed photos of celebrities, plus a close-up of an elderly woman's face. Isabel approached it, admiring the way he had captured the woman's beauty, the lines in her face like a map of her experience. It was such a contrast to the other works, where all the women appeared to be under twenty-five. She had thought it when she'd looked at his site: if Gavin's work was so gritty, why did all his subjects have such smooth skin? This one picture made her respect him as a photographer; as an artist.

'That's Gavin's mum,' Martin said, coming up behind her.

'It's an incredible picture.'

'Yeah. He dotes on her. He says she's the one woman in the world he truly respects.'

He drifted away before she could respond – *the one woman?* – and she went over to Nina, who had snapped out of her trance.

'Gavin's amazing, isn't he?' Nina said.

'I don't know about that.' Isabel took a swig of her beer. The heat in the room was making her feel faint. This was not her natural environment. Again she thought of her bed back home, the smooth sheets, her soft duvet. She had an unopened bottle of Bathtub gin too. She sipped her beer, wishing she'd asked for something stronger.

Gavin came jogging over to them, rubbing his palms together. His only female assistant – who he presumably didn't respect – stood beside him. She had auburn hair, similar to Jessica's, and was wearing a tight T-shirt and ripped jeans. There was a red dragon tattoo on her forearm, breathing fire that licked at the back of her hand.

'Right. Izzy. Do you want to go with Amber here to choose some clothes for the shoot?' As he spoke, Gavin put his hand on the small of Amber's back and leaned in to her, so close she must have been able to feel his breath on her bare arms. She didn't respond in any way.

'What's wrong with what I've got on?' Isabel asked. She was wearing a black cashmere top and loose-fitting trousers.

'It's a tad boring,' Gavin said. 'Come on, you're all about sex and pleasure. We want the pictures to reflect that. We should show a bit of skin.'

Isabel gestured to a nearby canvas, showing a young woman on all fours on one of the leather couches, her legs apart, with Gavin kneeling behind her, fully clothed. In the photo he was grinning, his tongue protruding, like a grotesque horny gargoyle.

'You want me more like that, do you?'

He snorted. 'Nah, you're too classy. But you can still be classy *and* sexy.'

'I'm a businesswoman. Just because my business involves sexual pleasure, that doesn't mean I need to flash the flesh.'

'Yeah, but—'

'I'm not going to show any skin, Gavin.'

He sighed. 'All right, all right. But can we at least do something with your hair and make-up? Mess it up a bit.'

'Like I've just been fucked over the boardroom table?'

His eyes lit up. 'Exactly! Amber, you can do that, can't you?'

He patted Amber's backside as she walked away, leading Isabel to a small room at the back of the studio. Isabel sat down in front of a mirror and Amber began to rifle through trays of mascara and lipstick.

'I don't really want to look like I've just been fucked,' Isabel said.

Amber paused. 'You'll piss him off.'

'I really don't care. In fact, I want to look more corporate in these pictures, not less. A professional woman. Can you do that?'

A shrug. 'Sure. If that's what you really want.'

As Amber worked on her hair, Isabel said, 'Are you and Gavin in a relationship?'

'What, you mean like boyfriend and girlfriend?' She laughed. 'Gavin doesn't do relationships.'

'But . . . don't you mind him touching you? I saw what he did.'

'What, patting my arse? That's nothing.'

'What do you mean?'

Amber didn't reply, but Isabel pressed.

'It's just something you have to put up with if you want to work with him. He's a genius. It goes with the territory.'

'Oh, you're kidding.'

Amber stepped back, letting go of Isabel's hair. 'I'm a photographer too. And I want to get on, be as successful as him. When I came to work with him he told me that he couldn't work with prudes or people who aren't comfortable with physical contact. It's fine. I can deal with it.'

Her tone was flat.

'What about the models he works with?' Isabel asked. 'Does he touch them too?'

'I can't talk about it.'

Isabel shuddered, thinking about Gavin at Mind+Body, the way he used to glance around the room, what he'd said about it being a great place to meet women. Her flesh crawled. She had made a mistake allowing him into that environment. And she'd made another mistake coming here today. Because she'd suspected he was a creep, hadn't she? And she'd ignored her instincts.

Nine times out of ten she might have stayed – because of the need to be polite, professional. But she wasn't going to do that today. Maybe it was because of the crap she was going through with her cheating husband, but she wasn't going to tolerate any more bullshit from scumbag men.

She got out of the chair and headed for the door, turning around at the last moment. She expected Amber to look shocked, or at least surprised, but she stood there with a raised eyebrow, clearly amused.

'You shouldn't have to deal with it,' Isabel said. 'You should tell him where to stick his job. Go out on your own. You don't need him.'

Amber blinked at her like a cat.

'Oh, sod this,' Isabel said, heading out into the studio. Martin stood nearby, examining the screen on a camera. She marched up to him. 'Where's Nina?' she demanded.

'Your assistant? She's in Gavin's office.' He pointed across the room.

The door was shut. Isabel rapped on it and yanked it open without waiting for an answer.

Nina stood in the centre of the room, which was plastered with Gavin's work, while the famous photographer walked around her, nodding, a lascivious grin on his stupid face.

'Nina, we're going,' Isabel announced.

Both Nina and Gavin said 'What?' at the same time.

Isabel addressed Nina, refusing to look at Gavin. 'I'm not working with a creep like this. Come on.' Nina didn't move. 'Come *on*.'

Finally Nina followed her out of the office, with Gavin a step behind. 'What the fuck are you playing at?' he said. 'This is all arranged.'

'Consider it unarranged.'

His grin had well and truly slipped. 'I was going to make you famous,' he said.

'Whatever.'

It felt so good storming out of there. Standing up for herself, standing up for something she believed in. Refusing to work with a man who represented everything she despised. *The only woman he respects is his mother.* Well, screw him. She finally felt like herself again, after weeks of being in a drama with no script. Things were going to change. And she'd just taken the first step.

Chapter 30

Jessica sat in front of Will's computer. Olivia was in bed, Felix was in his room watching his iPad and Will had called her to say he needed to work late. And here Jessica was, a day after her conversation with Ryan, scrolling through the photos of Izzy, preparing for her conversation with her husband. After talking to Ryan she had made up her mind. She was going to tell Will what had happened while he was away. She was going to look into his eyes as she told him. She was confident that she would be able to read his reaction, to see if he looked scared or guilty. And if he did, then she would go to the police.

She didn't savour the prospect of telling them a story involving ghosts and seances, so she was searching through the computer for some scrap of evidence. What did they call it? A smoking gun. Something she could take to the police, that might prevent her having to mention all the woo-woo stuff that would get her laughed out of the station.

Will had worked on Izzy's site throughout December, but it had dragged on into the new year, even into February. Jessica had a vague recollection of Will telling her they needed some photos of Izzy for the site, as well as a video on which Izzy was, according to Will, 'going to demonstrate the power of Blissful Massage'. Izzy had originally planned to use some pictures that were going to be taken by that fashion guy,

Gavin Lawson, but she'd fallen out with him. Jessica had asked her why and she'd said only that he was a creep.

So, anyway, Will had decided he was going to take the photos rather than wait any longer. He wanted to get the website done and off his desk. She remembered he seemed stroppy about it, like he was only doing it as a favour. Did that mean he and Izzy had fallen out around then? Had their affair turned sour? Or was it an act? A way to throw Jessica off the scent?

Had Jessica been an idiot for not seeing it back then?

It was impossible to look at these pictures of her sister in the same way as before, but she couldn't stop flicking through them. There was one photo in particular that transfixed her. It was a close-up of Izzy, showing her in profile. She had her eyes closed. How could anyone take a picture of a face that serene and beautiful and not fall in love with it? Not desire to kiss those lips?

There was another photo, equally transfixing, in which Izzy was gazing into the camera, her pixie haircut exposing her neck, and she was wearing a low-cut T-shirt so her collarbone was on display. She was standing on the balcony, the one from which she'd fallen – or rather, been pushed. Izzy was in sharp focus while the background was blurred and, despite everything, Jessica couldn't help but admire Will's technical skill.

But there was no evidence here. No smoking gun.

She heard the door open and close downstairs. Will was home.

She put the computer to sleep and went down. He was already in the kitchen, opening a bottle of wine. He smelled faintly of cigarettes and chewing gum, the latter intended to disguise the former.

'Have I missed dinner?' he asked.

'I'm not hungry. I can make you something, though . . .' *Act normal*, she told herself.

He held up his wine glass. 'It's fine. This will do. Jesus, what a day.'

'Can I talk to you about something?' she asked, keeping her distance from him. 'You know Izzy's website . . .'

'Sure. But I need to sit down.'

He trudged through into the living room. Before Jessica could enter the room, Felix ran downstairs and nipped in front of her, talking animatedly about some football match or other. Jessica watched them from the doorway, not really listening to the words. Felix worshipped his dad. What would he do if he found out he was a murderer? If Will was sent to prison? In her rush to discover the truth, to follow up on what Olivia had said, she had barely considered the aftermath.

Felix ran back upstairs and Jessica went into the living room and sat next to Will. He was leaning back now, face turned towards the ceiling. His hair was sticking up and there were bags under his eyes.

'I hate computers,' he said. 'I hate the internet, I hate all our clients, I hate my boss and I hate everyone I work with.'

'That bad, eh?'

'Yeah. But I love you.'

She couldn't bring herself to say it back.

He sat up. 'Anyway, what did you want to talk about? Something about Izzy's website? It's not still up, is it?'

He took out his phone to look but she stopped him. 'No. I wanted to talk about the photos you took of her.'

He put the phone down. 'For the site?'

'Yes. Except you took a lot more, didn't you? I found them on your iMac.'

He frowned. 'Yeah. Well, I had to take a lot so we could choose a few to use. They were good photos, actually. Maybe I should give up this web development lark and become a pro photographer.'

Will stood up.

'Where are you going?' Jessica asked.

'Upstairs. I want to take a look at them.' He left the room and was halfway up the stairs before she could react. This wasn't going how she'd anticipated.

In his office he woke the computer and sat at the desk. The picture of Izzy on the balcony was on the screen.

'Wow,' he said. 'I'd forgotten about this one.'

Jessica stood behind him. 'She was beautiful, wasn't she?'

'Yeah.' A pause. 'I mean, not as beautiful as you.'

'You don't need to lie,' Jessica said. 'I know she was more attractive than me. It was always the same. The boys always wanted to go out with her. And now here she is, frozen in time, forever young, while I get older and uglier.' She could feel the conversation slipping from her control. She hadn't meant to say that. She was meant to be nudging him towards saying something incriminating.

Will turned on his chair. 'Seriously, Jess, Izzy wasn't my type and you are *not* getting ugly. I hate it when you say things like that. To me, you're the most gorgeous, sexy woman on the planet. There was this night . . .' He looked away, not finishing the sentence.

'What?'

He grimaced. Oh God, what was he going to say?

But then he smiled. 'I feel awkward talking about it. But I went round to talk to Izzy about her site and she started telling me all about – what was it called – Blissful Massage. She had this plastic model of a vagina and she started touching it, showing me what they did in her classes. That was . . . well, that was the night Olivia was conceived.'

The rest of it rushed out. 'I don't think we'd . . . done it for a while, because of the whole trying-to-conceive thing, and watching Izzy do that, hearing her talk about sex and pleasure, it struck me – what you and I used to have, how great it used to be between us. I rushed home, praying you wouldn't already be asleep, desperate to take you to bed. To make you feel how Izzy described. To feel that passion again.' He grinned sheepishly. 'And it worked, didn't it? That was the best sex we ever had.'

Jessica stared at him, the memory coming back to her: how he had kissed her with a hunger he hadn't displayed since the early days of their marriage. He had spent a lot of time, an unusual amount – especially in those days when it was all about sperm meeting egg – on foreplay, making her come twice. A few weeks later she'd discovered she was pregnant and the joy of it, the fear that the pregnancy wouldn't 'stick', had blown away the memory of the sex that had led to it.

'I can't believe you think you're less attractive than Isabel was,' he said.

'I was always less attractive than her.'

He shook his head, exasperated. 'You're wrong, Jess. You're gorgeous. You always have been. And I really don't want to say anything negative about Izzy but you're funnier than she ever was. Warmer. More . . . I don't know how to put it. More rounded. More real. Don't get me wrong, Izzy was lovely once you got to know her, but she didn't shine as brightly as you. Not to me, anyway.'

She was thrown into confusion. Was she completely wrong about him and Izzy? Now was the time to ask him, to tell him about the seance. But before she could speak he leaned forward and kissed her on the mouth.

'You always acted like you were in her shadow. And you're still doing it. It's time you stopped.'

She was speechless. Because he was right. She did always feel that she was in Izzy's shadow. Izzy had always been older and cooler, and when they grew up Izzy had been wealthier and more professionally successful. Izzy had always known what she wanted and gone out and got it, while Jessica had just kind of drifted along, ticking off all life's predictable milestones – cohabitation, career, marriage, kids – without even thinking about it. Jessica had always compared herself to her big sister and found herself wanting.

Will had said the words that she had always longed to hear. But was he being genuine or was it all an act?

Before she could think about how to figure this out, he turned back to the computer and looked at the photo again.

'I took another one like this, but the other way round,' he said. 'She was blurred but the background was clear. It was meant to be arty. Where is it?'

He clicked through the photos. Jessica got up and stood behind him, still trying to find a way to broach the subject of what Olivia had done.

'Here it is,' he said. The picture showed Izzy on her balcony, as before, but with her features blurred. The background was crisp and clear, depicting a bright winter's day, the garden and street beyond in sharp focus.

'Will,' she began, 'I need to ask you . . .'

And then she saw it and the words – and the need to speak them – vanished.

'Oh my God,' she said, stepping around him and touching the screen with a fingertip.

'What is it?' he asked, but he saw it at the same time.

There was a figure standing in the cul-de-sac, just beyond the fence at the bottom of Izzy's garden. A man. There was something black obscuring his face. She zoomed in, and could just about make out that one of his arms was raised.

'He's holding something,' she said. 'What is it? Binoculars?'

Will peered closer. 'No. I think it might be a camera.'

Chapter 31

'Are you certain?' Jessica asked.

'I'm not a hundred per cent, but it looks like a camera. Quite a chunky one. I think that's a telescopic lens.'

'Oh . . .' Jessica put her hand on her forehead. 'Someone was watching Izzy's house. Spying on her.'

Jessica looked at her husband, suddenly doubting everything, a sick sensation creeping into her belly.

She was so confused. Hearing the way he'd talked about Isabel – and her – and now this, seeing a man watching Izzy, taking photographs . . . She could feel the house of cards she'd built in her head, the conviction that he had cheated on her and murdered her sister, begin to topple.

'What if Izzy had a stalker?' Jessica said. 'Surely that would make him the number-one suspect.'

'Suspect? But the police said it was an accident.'

'Only because they didn't have any evidence to suggest otherwise.'

He swore. He looked genuinely shocked, in a way that he would never have been able to fake. And the house of cards collapsed.

She watched Will, who had turned back to the photo of Isabel. She had made a mistake. A terrible mistake. She had believed some stupid *game*. Izzy's spirit hadn't told Olivia to spell out *Daddy*. Olivia had done it herself, eager to please, going along with the game. *Daddy*, the first word she had ever spoken, was one of the only words she could spell.

Will hadn't killed Isabel. He was innocent.

'Jessica?' he said. 'What is it?'

How could she tell him she'd thought he'd cheated on her and murdered her sister? Her cheeks burned and tears pricked her eyes. Maybe later, when she was closer to the truth, when she understood more, she would tell him. But not now.

Now, all she said was, 'I'm freaked out, that's all.'

'We should go to the police, show them this picture, tell them someone was watching Izzy. Maybe they'll reopen the case.'

'I'll do it tomorrow.'

She put her arms around him and held him tight. Beneath her breath she whispered, 'I'm sorry.'

ω

'How is she?' Mrs Rose asked the next morning, as Olivia scurried into the classroom to hang up her bag and coat.

Jessica made a noncommittal noise. Ryan was over the other side of the classroom. During the night it had struck her that he might say something to Will about the seance when he next saw him. She needed to ask him not to do that, to tell him it had all been sorted. But not now. It could wait.

Jessica waved goodbye to Olivia. In the car on the way to school Jessica had talked to Olivia about Saturday night, and what she had spelled out with the Scrabble tiles.

'Olivia, you know when you spelled out *Daddy*?'

A nod.

'I want you to know that Daddy didn't do anything to Auntie Isabel.'

Olivia had stared at her.

'I think you wrote *Daddy* because it's one of the words that's easy to spell. Is that right?'

Olivia had continued to stare at her, not answering.

'And of course you know Nanny's name. Mo.'

This time, Olivia had nodded.

'But what about Fred, the car? How did you know that? Did Nanny tell you?'

But Olivia had clammed up, looking like she was about to cry. Jessica had backed off. For now. But she was convinced, now, in the cold light of day, that she should ignore everything she thought she'd learned during the seance.

It had led Jessica down the wrong path, but there were still unanswered questions. Like: how had Olivia got hold of the necklace? And what about all the other stuff Olivia knew and her strange behaviour? Jessica had gone back to wavering between two opposing poles of belief: the part of her that longed for there to be a rational explanation for everything, and the childish part that clung to a belief in the supernatural.

She sat in her car, going through it all in her head, just as she had all night. She had told Will she would take the photograph to the police, but she was reluctant to do so. She couldn't see how they would take it seriously. A picture of a man standing, apparently photographing Izzy, wasn't proof that she had been murdered. It was very far from proof. And she couldn't tell them why she was convinced something sinister had happened to Izzy without talking about the supernatural, something she wasn't prepared to do.

She needed more.

Had Izzy spotted the man herself? Had she suspected she was being watched? No one had ever mentioned it and, as far as Jessica knew, it wasn't something the police had investigated. But maybe this photo would ring a bell with the person who had spent most time with Izzy.

She called Darpak.

ω

He was at home with 'the flu', but his ability to get out of bed and wander around in his dressing gown made Jessica think it was nothing worse than a bad cold. Still, she was pleased he was taking a sick day.

They made small talk in the kitchen while Darpak fixed himself a Lemsip and made a herbal tea for Jessica. He led her up to the living room.

'So, this is a nice surprise,' Darpak said.

'You might not think it's such a nice surprise when I tell you what it's about.'

'It's not something to do with the children, is it?' He looked worried.

'No. Well, not directly . . .'

'Don't tell me Olivia's said more strange stuff about Isabel?'

Jessica hadn't spoken to Darpak about everything that had been going on since the incident on Bonfire Night, mainly because she thought it might upset him. She cringed as she remembered how she had been sure Olivia was going to spell his name out during the seance.

'I'll come back to that,' she said.

'Oh dear.'

'I've got something to show you first.' She took the photograph out of her bag and placed it on the coffee table. 'Will took this a few weeks before Izzy died.'

'She was beautiful,' Darpak said, gazing at the photo of his dead wife. He took a tissue out of his pocket and for a moment she thought he was going to cry again, but he blew his nose. 'And this is a beautiful picture. But I don't understand.'

'Look here,' Jessica said, pointing to the spot where the man with the camera was visible.

Darpak squinted at it. 'What am I looking at?'

'It's harder to see when you can't enlarge it on the computer screen, but it's a man. Will and I are pretty sure he's pointing a camera at your house.'

'What?' He snatched the photo up and held it close to his face. 'Who the hell is this?'

'I was hoping you might have an idea. That she might have said something to you about someone following her.'

He shook his head, still scrutinising the picture. 'No. She never said anything about that. The police asked me the same question back then, but Izzy definitely would have told me if she'd thought someone was watching her.'

'You're absolutely sure? And you never noticed anything?'

'Never.'

Jessica sighed. Was this a dead end? Maybe she would never know who the man with the camera was.

Darpak had put the photo down but was still leaning forward in his chair, his face in his hands. He sniffed.

'Oh God, I'm sorry. I've upset you.'

'No. It's not you. It's . . .' He stared again at the picture of Isabel. 'I was such a fool. Such a stupid bloody fool.'

'What do you mean?'

'I almost lost her. And when she died I don't think she'd fully forgiven me.'

'Forgiven you?' Jessica sat up. 'Darpak, I have no idea what you're talking about.'

He got up and crossed over to the window, gazing out at the garden. Jessica waited, and just as she was about to prompt him he turned and said, 'I did something very stupid.'

ᴡ

Jessica was in shock. Darpak had cheated on Izzy. As he told her the sordid tale of his 'mistake', as he called it, she wondered if she had always been naïve to have faith in human nature. She had always believed Darpak was a doting husband, had defended him to Mum when she had accused him of terrible things. And although she still didn't believe he had done *the* most terrible thing, he wasn't the man she'd thought he was. Okay, maybe it was just a one-night stand, a stupid, drunken fumble as he claimed, but Jessica could imagine how much it must have hurt Izzy. All of a sudden Izzy's drug use made sense. She had been self-medicating. Darpak had driven her to it.

He must have read her mind because he said, 'Maybe if she hadn't been high, she wouldn't have sat on the railing. She wouldn't have lost her balance.' He swallowed. 'I knew she was drinking a lot, but I didn't know about the drugs. I didn't even know she was taking sleeping pills.'

'I wish she'd told me,' Jess said, only half-listening to him.

'About the pills?'

'About all of it.' She was aware that she'd snapped at him but he deserved it.

'I regret it so much,' he said. 'It was a stupid one-off. A moment of weakness.'

'Just one moment?'

'One moment when I decided to do it, yes. The second it was over I knew what a terrible mistake I'd made. How I risked losing everything.'

'Hmm.'

'We were getting back on track, though, Jess. Working it out. We had a good time, our last night together. I left that morning thinking everything was going to be okay, that I wasn't going to lose her after all, even if I deserved to. I was going to book a holiday for us, take her to Hawaii, get Nina to look after the business for a couple of weeks. I had plans. Ha! And God laughed at them.'

Once again Jessica sighed. 'Oh, Darpak.'

'I suppose you hate me now. I understand.'

'I don't hate you. I'm just . . . disappointed.'

'There's nothing worse than a woman's disappointment.'

She smiled, then got to her feet. 'I'd better go.'

'Wait. I just want to know . . . Why are you asking all these questions about Izzy's death now? What made you dig out that photo? Is it something Olivia said? You told me you were going to come back to that subject.'

'I really don't want to get into it now.'

'Please, Jess. I'm going to be worrying about it all night if you don't tell me. Can you pretend you're not disappointed with me for a minute?'

He was turning on the charm. The same charm Izzy had fallen for in the first place. And partly because she was feeling too weak, too punch-drunk, to resist, Jessica told him the whole thing, starting with Halloween, skipping the parts he already knew, and going all the way through to the seance and what had happened since. Darpak listened with growing incredulity. Of course, she didn't tell him she had suspected him at one point.

'So that,' Jessica said, 'is why I'm looking into Izzy's death.'

He pulled his dressing gown tighter around his body. 'Are you serious about all this?'

'Yes, I—'

'But Jessica, it's mad! Ghosts and spirits and seances . . . I can't believe that you could think any of this is real.'

'I know, that's what I thought at first, that there had to be a rational explanation. But there's so much that seems impossible. The song, the necklace . . . Things Olivia knows . . .'

Darpak let out a short, harsh laugh. 'I'm sorry. It's not funny. But Jess, ghosts don't exist. People do not get trapped in this realm, unable to move on to the afterlife until justice is done. There has to be a logical explanation for everything. Maybe . . . I don't know . . . maybe you gave Olivia the necklace back but forgot. Maybe she heard you humming that song. I mean, I sing to myself all the time without realising it. You must have told her about the name of your old car but forgot. Maybe your mum told her. Olivia's behavioural issues . . . well, there could be multiple reasons for them.'

'So you think I'm crazy.'

'No.' His face said otherwise. 'But you've clearly been under a lot of stress.'

'But this photo. It shows that someone was watching Izzy. And she's been trying to reach out to me, to tell me . . .'

'No, Jess. It doesn't prove anything. The person in the photo could be a fan of modern architecture, for all we know, taking a picture of this house. And this ghost thing – it's crazy and, forgive me, but it's stupid. You need to forget the whole thing, Jess, and for God's sake don't tell anyone else.'

'But . . .'

'But what, Jess?'

'It's not the first time it's happened in my life, is it?'

'Oh, Jess,' Darpak said. 'Are you talking about Larry? Your poltergeist?' He tried to suppress a smile but failed, and anger flared hot in Jessica's belly.

'Why are you grinning like that? It's not funny.'

'I know. I'm sorry. But . . . Izzy told me something.'

'What?'

His face twisted with regret. 'I can't tell you. She made me promise never to say anything to you or your mum.'

'Darpak!' She stood up. 'You can't do that. Come on, you broke your vows to her while she was still alive.'

He winced. 'That's a low blow.'

'Not as low as what you did to her. Now, come on, tell me.'

He exhaled. 'Okay. But you're not going to like it.'

Chapter 32

'It was a hoax, Jess. Larry wasn't real. Izzy did it all.'

Jessica opened her mouth but nothing came out.

'The broken picture frame. The cups that had fallen from their place on the shelf. All the objects that apparently moved on their own – Izzy did it, either during the night or when you and your mum were out of the room. She told me that on a couple of occasions she positioned things on the edge of the mantelpiece so they would fall down when you and your mum were watching.'

Jessica closed her eyes for a moment, picturing it. The Toby jug Mum loved, suddenly dropping from its spot above the fireplace, smashing to pieces in front of them.

'All the noises you heard in the night, the banging and scraping sounds. That was Izzy. She didn't explain exactly how she did it, but the way she said it . . . I believed her. She made a tape recording too, she said, which she played down the phone. It was her putting on a voice – she said she managed to distort it so it sounded evil.'

Jessica would never forget Mum's face the day she'd answered the phone and a high-pitched, 'demonic' voice had spoken to her, telling her to get out of the house, swearing and cursing and making threats. Mum had begged the demon to stop.

'*I will never leave you, and you three ugly bitches will never stop me,*' the voice had said, before unleashing a volley of words that Mum wouldn't repeat.

'She did it from the phone box on the corner of your street,' Darpak said.

Jessica sank on to the sofa, remembering. Izzy had run into the room shortly after the call ended, asking what was wrong, allowing Mum to sob against her shoulder. Jessica had been crying too, convinced they really had been phoned by a demon.

'Izzy knew old songs,' Jessica said, her voice shaky. 'She told us she'd heard them at night – someone singing them to her.'

'Yes. She mentioned that too. She'd just gone through your mum's old vinyl collection.' He shrugged. 'Nothing very mysterious there.' Darpak sat down beside her, his expression sympathetic, but tinged with guilt. 'I didn't think you ever really believed in it. Even when Izzy told me and made me promise to keep quiet, I thought she was being silly, that you must have suspected it was her.'

'No. I never did. I mean, of course I tried to come up with a rational explanation. But I was never sure. I was torn. And Izzy . . . I never thought it was her, even later, when she insisted Larry hadn't been real. I guess . . . I guess I never thought she would lie to me like that.'

Jessica had been ten years old. She had been easy to fool, even though she shared a room with Izzy. She wondered if Izzy had ever considered letting her in on it. They had spent so much time together, been so close. But she must have thought Jessica would tell Mum – and, to be fair, she probably would have.

And Mum – she had still been recovering from her husband walking out. She was vulnerable, credulous, and she had always been superstitious anyway. She kept a lucky rabbit's foot; wouldn't walk under ladders; believed in the afterlife.

Jessica narrowed her eyes at Darpak. Could he be lying about this? She studied his face, but though she wanted to believe he was making it up, she couldn't.

Maybe, deep down, she had always known.

'Why did she do it?' Jessica asked. 'Did she tell you?'

'Yes. I mean, she was quite drunk when she told me, but she was embarrassed about it. She said it started as a game. She'd seen that old film, *Poltergeist*, at a friend's house and got the idea from that, plus she said something about a kids' book you both used to read. It all happened just after your dad left, didn't it?'

'That's right.'

Dad walking out had hit Izzy harder than Jessica, who had always been more of a mummy's girl. To her, their dad was almost a stranger, a man who got up early to go to work and came home after dark. On Saturday he went to football and he spent Sunday in the pub with his mates. When he left, it barely made a difference to Jessica. Izzy, though, had been distraught. Jessica would hear her crying from the top bunk. A memory came hurtling out of the past: Izzy shouting at Mum, blaming her for driving him away.

'I'm going to run away and live with him!' Izzy had yelled.

'Go on, then,' Mum had snapped back. 'See if he and that tart want you in their love nest. He never loved you, Izzy. He never loved any of us.'

That had led to slamming doors, hurled objects, sobbing. It hit Jessica in the chest now, a memory so raw it could have happened yesterday.

'Did she think he'd come back if he heard our house was haunted?' she asked Darpak.

'I don't know. I don't think Izzy knew herself. The way she told it, it started out as a "laugh". She thought it would be funny. But when she saw the reaction it provoked, she kept going. Maybe she wanted to punish your mum, initially at least. And then your mum got the newspaper and those investigators involved and it was too late to confess, even when she was bullied at school over it. And then, when the social workers turned up to check your welfare, she realised she needed to stop. It had all got out of hand. But she was too scared to confess. She said she hoped everyone would just forget about it.'

Jessica rubbed at her eyes, where tears were threatening to form. She should have been angry at her sister, but she couldn't find it inside herself. All she could see was a desperate little girl who felt abandoned by her dad.

'She was worried you'd never forgive her if you found out,' Darpak said.

'Oh, Izzy. Of course I would have forgiven her. I'd have forgiven her almost anything.' She raised her eyes to the ceiling, sighing deeply. 'I wish you had told me this before. Because if I'd known . . .'

If she'd known, she wouldn't have been so open to believing in Isabel's ghost.

ω

Jessica drove across town, fizzing with an energy she hadn't felt in weeks. At the traffic lights she thumped the steering wheel with both hands.

'You fucking stupid idiot,' she said, cursing herself. 'You grade-A idiot.'

For most of her life, since leaving school, she had tried to convince herself there must be a logical explanation for everything that had happened at home. But she had never fully let go of the belief that ghosts might exist, and when Olivia first started doing strange things she had allowed doubt to creep in, to creep in so far she had lost the ability to think rationally. Everything that had happened over the last week seemed like madness. Allowing Simon Parker into her home. Conducting that seance. Yes, madness.

None of it would have happened if she'd known Izzy had hoaxed them; if the little girl inside her hadn't still clung to the belief that Larry had been real.

But now she could see clearly. At last.

'A hoax,' she said to herself. 'Another hoax.'

Somebody had set it all up. Somebody had been feeding information to Olivia. It was the only explanation, and she would have seen it earlier if she hadn't been so desperate to believe.

And the person who did it must have known about her childhood 'poltergeist'. They must have known that, because of her experiences, she was susceptible to that kind of thing; that it wouldn't be too hard to make her believe her house was, once again, being visited by a spirit. Somebody had exploited her weakness.

Somebody who had never believed Izzy had killed herself or died because of an accident. Somebody who knew that Izzy had a cat called Oscar and a car called Fred. Somebody who knew Olivia.

There was only one person it could be.

ᙡ

She hammered on the door, heard a voice from inside saying, 'All right, keep your hair on.'

Mum opened the door. 'Jessica! Is everything—'

Jessica stormed past her, checking the living room then the kitchen. 'Are you on your own?'

Mum followed her into the kitchen. The room smelled of freshly baked cakes and there was a tray of cooling buns on the side. Jessica's stomach growled. She hadn't eaten anything yet today. She was thrown back in time to when she was a kid and Mum would make cakes, and she and Izzy would fight over who could scrape the mixture out of the bowl. The memory tempered her anger, which frustrated her. She wanted to feel it, to use it.

'Yes, Pete's gone Christmas shopping. What's going on, Jess?'

'I know what you did,' she said.

'Come again?'

'There's no point denying it. I know.'

Jessica had worked it all through in her head on the way over. Mum had never believed the police had done a thorough job investigating Izzy's death. She had believed for years that Darpak had something to do with it, which was why she always refused to go to his house or have anything to do with him. So she had set about trying to make Jessica believe it too. She knew Mum found it hugely frustrating that Jessica wouldn't listen to her, so she must have decided to use Olivia to deliver a message.

Why had she waited until now? Perhaps it was that magazine story about the woman whose husband killed her that had set Mum off, awakened her need to do something. Mum was a firm believer in the afterlife. Perhaps she wanted to think she'd be able to look Izzy in the eye when they were reunited in heaven, tell her she'd done everything she could to persuade the world that Izzy had been murdered.

'I have no idea what you're talking about,' Mum said. 'Do you want a cup of tea?'

'No, I don't want a fucking cup of tea!'

Mum's mouth opened in shock. Jessica never swore in front of her. She had an automatic filter that meant the strongest words she ever used in her mother's company were *bloody* and *damn*.

Mum recovered quickly. She folded her arms. 'Do you want to tell me what's got you all riled up? What I'm supposed to have done?'

'You know. Come on, I want to hear you say it. To admit it. All the ideas you planted in Olivia's head . . . Do you know what you've done? How disturbed she's been? She bit a child at school. She's been having nightmares, waking up in the night and throwing things around. She got a pair of scissors and cut her teddies' eyes out. She could be messed up forever. How could you do that to your own granddaughter?'

Mum was flustered, open-mouthed. Finally she said, 'Jess, I still don't know what you're talking about.'

Jessica didn't hear her. 'I should have seen it before. You must have taught Olivia that Nirvana song. You know how to use YouTube – it's probably on there. Everything else Livvy knew – it all came from you. The stuff about how she had a secret. You wanted me to think Izzy was visiting her, telling her things, all this stuff that Livvy couldn't possibly know. And all along you were planting the seed in her head, the whole point of what you were doing.'

Mum was silent, watching Jessica from across the kitchen.

'It didn't work,' Jessica said, 'but you wanted Olivia to tell me that Darpak killed Isabel. Because that's what you've always believed, isn't it? That he pushed her.'

'That is what I believe, yes. That bastard should swing for what he did to our Izzy.'

'But he had an alibi, Mum! We've always known that.'

'Like I've always said, he could have got his mates to lie—'

Jessica cut her off. 'I don't get it. Why are you so convinced it was Darpak?'

'Because that bastard cheated on her.'

Jessica reeled. 'You knew about that? How?'

'Izzy told me. I went round there, found her drunk in the middle of the day and forced her to tell me what the hell was going on. I wanted to stay, to give him a piece of my mind, but Izzy insisted it was over, that it was a one-off. I tried to set her straight. Once a cheater, always a cheater.'

'Like Dad?'

'Exactly. I told her she should leave him. Get a good lawyer and clean the bastard out. But Izzy was never as strong as you and me, despite appearances. Two weeks after that, she was dead.'

'But why didn't you tell me?'

'She made me promise not to, and I don't break promises I make to my daughters.' Mum pulled out a kitchen chair and almost fell into it. 'I promise you this, Jess. I haven't done anything. None of the things you're accusing me of, anyway. I hadn't heard that bloody song for years until Olivia started singing it. It was Izzy who taught it to her. Izzy's back – you know that. Simon said . . .'

'Simon's full of shit. He recorded all sorts of activity when we were kids, and guess what? Izzy did it. She hoaxed us.'

Mum stared at her.

'Izzy hoaxed us, Mum. She told Darpak.'

'What?' Mum looked like she'd been punched. 'No, that can't be right. You can't trust anything he says.'

'Mum, listen to me. Izzy tricked us. Uncle Larry didn't come back and haunt us, and Izzy is not haunting Olivia now. There's no such thing as spirits or poltergeists or any of that. Maybe you knew all along, but you're still trying to hide behind those lies, still trying to make me believe in your bullshit. You made me believe Olivia was communicating with Izzy. And your plan didn't even work. Olivia didn't tell me Darpak killed Izzy. She said Will did it!'

'Will? That's ridiculous.'

'I know.' She felt her cheeks colour and hoped Mum didn't notice.

For a few seconds all Jessica could hear was the rush of blood in her ears. That and the slow ticking of the kitchen clock.

'I swear I had nothing to do with this,' Mum said. 'I swear on Olivia's life.'

'Take that back.'

'No. I won't. Do you want me to fetch a Bible and swear on that too? I promise you, it wasn't me. Izzy really is back.'

Jessica let out a howl of rage. 'Mum! Stop! Let me spell it out to you. Ghosts. Don't. Exist. Izzy is not back.'

She felt herself deflate; all the anger rushing out of her. Mum would never swear on Olivia's life if she was lying. She was too superstitious.

The kitchen clock ticked.

'If Izzy isn't back, how do you explain all the stuff Olivia knows?' Mum asked after a minute.

Jessica raked her hands through her hair, unable to answer. She had a headache now, a vein throbbing in her temple. She tried to pull her thoughts together, everything she'd learned that day. She knew that someone had been feeding information to Olivia.

'If it wasn't you,' Jessica said to her mother, 'who the hell was it?'

Chapter 33

January 2013

'What? You went back to see that creep?' Isabel was astounded. If they had not been in Beckenham's swankiest wine bar, surrounded by potential clients, she might have shouted at Nina, asked her what the hell she was thinking.

'Yes,' Nina replied evenly. 'I went back to see Gavin.'

'So, what? He called you?'

'Yeah.' Nina couldn't suppress a grin. 'He asked for my number. That's what we were talking about when you burst in and told me we had to leave.'

Isabel took a big gulp of wine. She had already drunk two-thirds of a bottle and was beginning to feel the buzz.

'Let me guess,' she said. 'Actually, I don't need to guess. I heard him say you should be a model. My God, Nina, it's the oldest line in the book.'

'I know. Believe me, I know what men are like.'

'Do you?' Isabel interrupted. 'You're only twenty-one. You don't really—'

But the look on Nina's face told Isabel to ease off. She was well and truly pissing on her parade.

'He called me three times,' Nina said. 'I told him I wasn't interested, because I was sure it was just a line. But then his assistant Martin called and said Gavin was serious. He really thought I had something. He said Gavin wasn't going to beg and would give up soon if I didn't go along to talk to them.'

Glasses rattled in the dishwasher and a woman on the other side of the bar let loose a high-pitched laugh. Isabel refilled her glass. The wine was thick, like blood, and earthy. She could feel herself tipping over into drunkenness but she didn't care.

Since his confession, and especially since Christmas, things with Darpak had improved. They'd talked a lot, been honest with each other, and she really felt now that it was going to work out. Their marriage might even be better for it. He seemed genuinely terrified of losing her. They had both pictured a future without the other and hadn't liked it. That didn't stop black clouds enveloping her at least once a day, though, the memory of what had happened knocking her off her stride. It had happened on the way over here, making her crave a drink to numb the pain.

'So what happened?' Isabel asked.

'I went along and he was . . . well, he was completely different to how he was last time. He actually apologised, said that he'd been out of order that day. He asked me to pass on his apology to you as well.'

'Hmm. And what about his other assistant, Amber? Did he explain why he was so touchy-feely with her?'

'He said he was aware how it looked, and that he knew he could be overly tactile sometimes. He said it went with the territory, that they worked in a sexually charged atmosphere. She was there. She agreed with him and said it was no big deal.'

'What? They're saying I overreacted?'

'I don't know. All I can say is that I didn't see any sign that Amber was unhappy and uncomfortable, and he was a perfect gentleman with me. He didn't make any inappropriate comments, didn't touch me, didn't try to make me take any clothes off. He told me to keep on exactly what I was wearing: jeans, a T-shirt and my leather jacket. He spent half an hour taking my photo, another half an hour chatting about the industry, giving me advice, and that was it.'

Isabel bit her tongue, stopping herself from saying that he shouldn't be congratulated for not being a sleaze on this one occasion. But maybe she had been wrong about him. Whatever, she had never seen Nina so excited. She had the same energy about her that Jess had had the other day, when she announced her pregnancy.

'So what happens next?' Isabel asked.

'He sent the photos over to this modelling agency he works with. It's one of the big ones. Anyway, they called Gavin straight away and now they want me to go in and meet them, and get Gavin to take some more pictures so I can put together a portfolio. I'm going back to his studio next week.'

'And do you . . . want to be a model?'

'It's not something I've ever thought about, but why not?'

'Well.' Izzy beckoned the waiter over. 'We'd better have champagne, hadn't we? Even if it does mean I'm going to have to find a new assistant.'

'Oh, Izzy, I'm sorry. It might not lead to anything . . .'

'Don't be silly. I'll find someone.' The waiter appeared and took their order, and when the champagne came Isabel raised her glass and said, 'To dreams coming true.'

But as they clinked glasses she felt an itch of foreboding. She wished she'd never had anything to do with Gavin Lawson. She had witnessed his inappropriate behaviour, the way he abused his power. But she had a feeling that it was just the tip of the iceberg. That there was something dangerous about him, beyond what she had already witnessed.

Chapter 34

Jessica made her mother a cup of tea with two heaped sugars and left her at the kitchen table. As Jessica left, Pete came in with armfuls of shopping bags, and Jessica wondered what Mum would tell him. The revelation that Izzy had hoaxed them, and never admitted it, had hit her hard. She was glad Mum had someone else she could talk to.

Jessica went out to her car. Something Mum had said while Jessica was making the tea echoed in her head: 'If this person, whoever's been manipulating Olivia, wanted us to believe Izzy was murdered, why play all the games? Why not just get her to come out and say it? Why does Olivia keep saying "It's a secret"?'

Jessica couldn't answer that, but it didn't sway her conviction. She would demand the answer when she found out who it was.

Because she was going to find them. Somebody had messed with her little girl's head. Somebody had fucked with her family. When she found out who it was . . .

It was two o'clock. Jessica had a little over an hour before she needed to pick up Olivia. She sat in the car with the heating running, waiting for the condensation that fogged the windscreen to clear, wishing it was as easy to clear the confusion inside her head. She closed her eyes and fought to stay calm, to stop the murderous thoughts, the revenge movie that was playing inside her mind. Now was not the time to lose control.

She allowed herself one thump of the steering wheel, and it made her feel a tiny bit better. But only a tiny bit.

She made a decision: it was time to tell Will everything. They were going to have to talk it through with Olivia together, try to get her to tell them who had been telling her all this stuff. Frustratingly, he had already warned her he was going to be working late tonight because they were launching a new website. Despite this she texted him asking if there was any way he could get home before Olivia's bedtime and he replied immediately, saying, I'll do my best.

Trying to work out a strategy for how they could get the information out of their reticent four-year-old, Jessica started the engine and drove out of the quiet cul-de-sac towards the main road. She needed to turn right but there was no break in traffic flowing in the opposite direction. She tapped her hand impatiently on the wheel, trying to creep forward, indicator blinking.

There, pulled up by the kerb on the other side of the road, was the grey car.

Her heart jumped. The car was idling, with somebody in the driver's seat. The traffic was still flowing from the right. She froze for a second, tempted to jump out and run across the road to the Hyundai.

It pulled away.

She screamed with frustration and leaned on the horn, desperate to get on to the main road so she could follow. Nobody stopped, and the Hyundai was almost out of sight now, heading east, though it was being slowed down by the traffic too. Did the driver know Jessica had spotted him or her?

She wound down her window, tried to make eye contact with the drivers flowing from the right, aching with frustration. Let me out, you bastards. *Let me out.*

Fuck it. She stabbed at the horn and pulled out into the traffic. A black Volkswagen hurtled towards her, a middle-aged man behind the wheel. She saw his mouth open with alarm a second before he stamped on the brake. He screeched to a halt just two feet from her door and stared at her with shock that quickly turned to anger. But she didn't care. A gap opened in the traffic on the far side of the road and she put her foot down and swung into it, ignoring the furious beeps from the vehicles she'd forced to stop.

By driving close to the centre of the road and leaning her head out of the window, she could see the grey car, four vehicles ahead. A gap appeared on the opposite side of the road and she swerved into it, leaning on the horn again. The driver in front stared at her with horror as she pulled alongside him, but he slowed and allowed her to overtake, just as a truck came roaring towards her.

Now she was three cars behind the one she was pursuing.

She had never done anything like this. Never driven recklessly. She barely ever entered the fast lane on the motorway. But this was what desperation and anger did. And it felt good. Terrifying but exhilarating.

She was going to catch them. She was going to get answers.

The traffic lights ahead turned red. For a horrible moment she thought the Hyundai was going to sail through and get away, but the car in front of it stopped. She contemplated getting out and running through the traffic to beat on the Hyundai's window, to finally see who had been following her. But the lights changed quickly and they were off again.

Almost immediately, the grey car turned left into a quieter side road. Jessica followed, but as she entered this new street she couldn't see them. There were side streets leading both left and right. She slowed down, craning her neck. The road to the left led into a maze of residential streets. The right turn would take her towards the centre of Beckenham.

She took a gamble. If she were trying to get away from someone she would head towards the centre, where it was easier to get lost. She turned right, putting her foot down, not caring that she was breaking the speed limit. A white van reversed out of a driveway and she sped around it, almost clipping its rear corner, eliciting another long, angry beep. But there was the grey car, about fifty metres ahead. Surprisingly, they appeared to be sticking to the thirty-mile-per-hour limit. They must have thought they'd shaken her.

She increased her speed to fifty. It was a long straight road with little traffic and even fewer pedestrians. Run-down businesses lined the street, overflowing bins left out for the next morning's collection. She was gaining ground. There was a junction ahead, and the grey car was almost there, so Jessica pressed down the accelerator, hitting sixty, knowing at the back of her mind that this was lunacy, but unable to stop herself. She was almost on the Hyundai now. It was still going at thirty. The junction was fifteen seconds away.

The Hyundai's brake lights came on as the driver slowed down and prepared to turn left at the junction. This was Jessica's chance. She pulled level with her quarry, thumped the horn and, in what she would later think of as a suicidal move, swung in front of the Hyundai just before the junction and slammed on the brake.

If the grey car had been going any faster than twenty it would have smashed into her. But it juddered to a halt, six inches away from her rear bumper.

Jessica threw herself out of the car. There was a buzzing in her ears, white noise, and she could smell rubber, could see dots in her vision. It seemed that she was watching herself do this, floating above her car, and it crossed her mind that she had crashed, that she was dead. She looked around wildly, expecting to see Izzy welcoming her to the afterlife.

The door of the grey car opened and a man got out. He was young, with short, prematurely thinning hair and glasses, unremarkable apart from the stunned expression he wore. This was him? The man who had been following her? She didn't recognise him.

'Who are you?' she screamed, jabbing him in the chest.

He stared at her, open-mouthed.

She wanted to punch him, to slap the faux-stupidity off his face.

'Tell me!'

'I don't know who you are,' he said. He had an accent. Eastern European, she thought. Polish or Romanian. 'Why are you—'

'Shut up!' She stepped closer, her face inches from his. The buzzing in her ears grew louder, like a kettle boiling on a stove. 'Why have you been following me?'

He blinked. 'I haven't.'

'Don't lie! I've seen you. And my sister too? How did you know her?' She could hear her voice getting louder but couldn't do anything to control it. 'Was it you? Did you kill her?'

He took a step back, sheltering behind his open car door. 'You are crazy. I don't know you. What are you talking about?'

She stepped around the door, ready to grab hold of him and demand that he admit it, and then she saw her reflection in his side mirror. She didn't recognise herself at first. Her face was red and sweaty, her eyes bulging. She looked like a madwoman. A creature from a horror film. The young guy cowered against his car, looking over her shoulder, searching out help. But there was no one around except an elderly woman walking her dog who called across the road, 'Is everything all right?'

And it broke the spell. Jessica felt like Snow White, coughing up the poisoned apple, coming back to life and reality. The Eastern European man came into focus and the truth hit her. This was the wrong grey car.

She backed away, whispering, 'I'm sorry. I'm so sorry.'

The man continued to stare at her as she sank down and sat on the kerb. He got back into his car, winding down the window. As he pulled away, he leaned out.

'You need help,' he called. 'A doctor.'

Chapter 35

The elderly woman crossed the road tentatively.

'Do you want me to call someone for you?' the woman said.

All the adrenalin had drained from Jessica's body. All she wanted to do was lie here, on the side of the road, and sleep. She could hardly feel the bitter wind that swept litter along the pavement. She didn't want to move or have to deal with anything, with any of the shitstorm that swirled around her. She would just close her eyes and stay here until the bin men came and took her away.

The dog barked, shaking her out of her mortified stupor.

'What time is it?' Jessica asked, raising her face towards the woman. Her own voice sounded like it was coming from far away.

'It's half past two.'

Jessica pushed herself to her feet. Olivia and Felix. The school run. She was going to be so late.

She stumbled back to her car, leaving the woman and her dog staring after her, executed a three-point turn and sped away. She cringed, thinking about what she'd just done. She turned the radio on and up loud so it would block out the screaming in her head.

ω

She collected Felix first. 'Where were you?' he demanded. 'The school were about to call you. All the other children were picked up *ages* ago.'

She said sorry and led him up the slope to the early-years block. Olivia was, once again, the last child in the classroom. *Maybe it would be a blessing for Olivia if social services came and took her away*, Jessica thought. *They can take her to a nice new family while I'm carted off to a padded cell.*

Mrs Rose called Olivia's name the moment she saw Jessica staggering up the path. The teacher looked almost as exhausted as Jessica felt. Ryan was clearing up the mess in the classroom. He looked in Jessica's direction but she avoided his eye, embarrassed about being so late. Another thing that made her look like a bad parent.

Jessica took Olivia's hand, leading her to the car.

'How was your day, Livvy?'

'Fine.'

'What did you do? Wait, don't tell me. You can't remember.'

'Mum,' Felix said, 'can I play a game on your phone?'

Felix got in the front seat with her mobile, immediately losing himself in Super Mario Run. As Jessica was fastening her daughter's seat belt, Olivia said, 'Mummy, do you want to play Scabble again when we get home?'

Felix snorted. He was in one of those annoying moods. '*Scabble?* It's Scrabble, stupid.'

'Felix! Don't call your sister stupid.' She lowered her voice to address Olivia. 'Why do you want to do that?'

'Because . . . Auntie Izzy wants to talk to you again.'

Jessica recoiled. She needed Olivia to stop believing she was being visited by a ghost.

She tried hard to keep the tremble out of her voice. 'Sweetheart, if there's something you want to tell me, you know you can do it anyway.'

Olivia frowned.

'Like, if someone has been talking to you about Auntie Izzy, you can tell me. In fact, you should tell me.'

The frown deepened. 'I can't.'

'Why not, Livvy?'

'Because . . .'

Jessica waited, glancing at Felix to see if he was listening. The phone blasted out loud tinny music from the game and he seemed too absorbed to care about what his sister was saying.

Olivia shuffled in her seat. 'Because if I do, Caspar will get sick and die.'

Jessica leaned further into the car. 'Did someone say that to you? That if you told on them, Caspar would die?'

Olivia's lower lip trembled.

'Sweetheart, Caspar isn't going to get sick or die. I promise. Hand on heart. Who told you that? Please, you have to tell me.'

But Olivia had gone pink, her eyes filling with water. At the same time, a white van came along the road and the driver sounded his horn, forcing Jessica to close the door. She got into the driver's seat and was about to ask Olivia again, but the pinkness of her daughter's face told her it would be better to wait till they got home.

As soon as they got into the house, Felix and Olivia dumped their shoes and coats on the floor. Felix headed to the kitchen to raid the cupboard and Olivia ran up the stairs to her bedroom. *She knows I want to talk to her*, Jessica thought. She was torn. She knew she had to go easy with Olivia, that if she pushed too hard her daughter would go mute. But she needed to know who'd told her Caspar would get sick.

She called up the stairs, 'Would you like some ice cream?' That would usually tempt Olivia down, but there was no response.

She went into the kitchen and found Felix eating a bag of crisps. Caspar sat at his feet, eyes fixed on the snacks, hoping one or two would drop.

'Has Olivia said anything to you?' she asked.

'About what?' Felix said through a mouthful of crisps.

'About somebody talking to her about Auntie Izzy?'

He shook his head. 'She never says anything that makes any sense.'

Jessica tutted. Sometimes she wished she'd had her children closer together, so they could be friends, but then remembered the age gap wasn't by choice.

'She's only four, remember. You were her age once.'

He rolled his eyes. 'Yeah, but I'm sure I never talked as much nonsense as her. Like, the other day she was going on about that necklace with the bat on it, saying she really needed it but you'd taken it away. She was, like, begging me to get it down for her.'

He hopped down from the stool he was sitting on and headed towards the fridge. Jessica blocked his path.

'And did you?'

'Yeah.'

So that explained how she'd got the necklace. Except . . .

'Hang on. You told us you hadn't got it down for her. I texted your dad when you were away on the Isle of Wight and you denied it.'

'That's right. I hadn't done it then. This was the day before yesterday.'

After Jessica had taken the necklace back and returned it to the box.

Felix opened the fridge door and groaned with disgust. 'There's absolutely nothing to eat.'

'Why don't you have an apple? Or a banana?'

'It's all right,' he said, like the world's biggest martyr. 'I'll wait till dinner.'

He went to leave the kitchen, then stopped.

'The thing with that bat necklace . . . I didn't know which one to give her. They both looked the same. And then, by the time I made a decision, she'd got bored and gone back to her room. She's *so* annoying. I'd had to drag a chair all the way out of my room to reach it.'

And then he was gone, running off to his bedroom to play a video game or Skype one of his friends.

They both looked the same? What was he talking about? She went upstairs. Standing on tiptoe, she stretched and took down the box containing Isabel's costume jewellery. She sat with it on the bed and rifled through, chucking old bracelets and trinkets behind her, not caring where they fell. All she cared about was finding the bat necklace.

It was near the bottom of the box. She took it out, let it hang between her fingers, picturing it around Izzy's neck, nestling in that space between her clavicles. She thought about how Izzy had lied to her about Larry; had lied to her for years. If Izzy was still alive, no doubt Jessica would confront her about it, demand to know why she had kept quiet all these years. But it was hard to get angry with the dead.

She continued to search through the box, emptying the rest of its contents on to the bed, and there it was. Another bat necklace.

Felix had been right. There were two. She laid them side by side on the duvet, looking from one to the other, left to right and back again. They were identical, though one was slightly shinier than the other, newer-looking.

Holding both necklaces, she went down the hallway to Olivia's room. She found her daughter sitting on the floor, playing with her Sylvanian Family house. As Jessica entered the room one of the little creatures, a cat, dropped from a window of the house on to the floor. Olivia looked up, startled.

Jessica sat beside her on the carpet.

'Hi, Olivia,' she said, keeping her voice as bright and 'normal' as possible. She held out the shinier bat necklace. 'Would you like this back?'

'Yes please.' She grabbed it.

'Do you want me to put it on you?'

Olivia narrowed her eyes, suddenly suspicious. 'No thanks.'

Jessica affected a smile. 'It's a lovely necklace, isn't it?' She held out the other one, which she was convinced was the original, the one that had belonged to Izzy. 'But it's not the one that used to be Auntie Izzy's. Where did you get it?' she asked.

Olivia picked up the Sylvanian Family cat and walked it up the side of the house, ignoring the question.

Jessica counted to five then said, 'I promise nothing is going to happen to Caspar, Olivia. Cross my heart and hope to die.'

Olivia gave her a sharp look. 'You mustn't say that.'

'You're right. But I do cross my heart.'

Olivia stared at her toy house, then at the necklace in her palm. 'If I tell you who gived it to me, can I keep it?'

'Of course. You can have them both if you like.'

A long pause, Olivia's young brain ticking away in the silence. Her desire for the necklace competing with her lingering fear that something would happen to Caspar.

'Do I have to spell it out with the Scabble things?' she asked.

'No, sweetheart. Just tell me. You can whisper if you like.'

'Okay.'

Olivia leaned close. Her breath was warm and smelled sweet.

She whispered a name in Jessica's ear.

Chapter 36

September 1993

Isabel ran through the doors of the school, the taunts of the other girls ringing in her ears. *I must not cry, I will not cry,* she told herself. And another voice: *It's all your fault. You brought it on yourself.*

Maybe it was time to tell the truth, to confess that the ghost did not exist, that it was all her. But it was too late now. Mum would be furious and it would be so embarrassing. If she'd confessed months ago, before Simon Parker and Madam Grimm got involved, before the whole stupid story was in the newspaper, it wouldn't have been so bad. But now . . . She knew exactly what Mum would say. 'You've made me a laughing stock.'

Jess would be pissed off too. There had been several times when Izzy had almost told her little sister, late at night when they'd been giggling in their bedrooms, taking the mickey out of Madam Grimm. But the words always got stuck in Isabel's throat. Jess would want to know why Isabel hadn't included her in it from the start. She'd probably cry. Worst of all, Isabel didn't think Jess would ever trust her again.

She passed her locker and headed towards the stairwell. There were no teachers around; she guessed they were all in the staff room. Luckily, the bullies hadn't followed her inside. Sharon and Julie and Parminder.

She hated them. They called her Velma, after the girl from *Scooby-Doo*, and had been spreading rumours that she liked to sleep naked and invite the ghost into her bed. 'Touch me with your phantom fingers,' Sharon screeched, and the other girls would make stupid *woooooh* noises, dancing around Isabel in a circle. There was an even worse rumour: that Isabel's mum had murdered Isabel's dad and it was his ghost haunting them.

But even the taunting couldn't make her tell the truth, because then she would be a *liar*. It would be even worse.

There was a space under the stairs where Isabel liked to sit. It was quiet and hidden and she could be alone there, away from the other kids. She wished Dad was here, to give her a cuddle and make it all better. She missed him so much. When she was little she'd thought he was a hero. Big and strong and brave. He would sweep her up in his arms and hold her above his head. 'Can you see the whole world from there?' he'd ask. He smelled of cigarettes and sawdust and he had a bald spot on his head that looked like a full moon.

When he went away he took her heart with him.

It was shortly after he'd left that she got the idea. Her friend Sam lived round the corner from a video shop that would rent out any movie to anybody. Sam always had the latest video nasties and her parents didn't care. One afternoon they'd rented an old film called *Poltergeist*. It was terrifying but brilliant. On the way home from seeing *Poltergeist* Isabel had thought, *What if our house was haunted? Surely Dad would have to come back and rescue us then.* She thought about that story she and Jess used to read too.

But despite everything she'd done, Dad hadn't come back. That's when the awful truth had hit her. He didn't love them any more. He'd moved away to be with that tart and Sam said he was probably too busy having it off with her to think about his kids any more.

From that point, it wasn't about trying to get Dad to come back. It was anger that drove her. Anger with Mum. Dad wouldn't have needed to run off with a tart if he and Mum were happy, and Dad had said Mum was always nagging him about going to the pub and football and all the things he liked doing. So it was her fault, and Isabel had liked seeing how scared she was, convinced that Uncle Larry had come back to haunt her.

Now she was thirteen, she felt ashamed. It wasn't Mum's fault that Dad had run off. It was his. And Izzy had only made things worse.

But it was too late to admit it now. All she could do was stop and hope everyone forgot about it.

She sat with her back pressed against the wall, refusing to let the tears come. She would stay here for ten minutes and then she would go back, with her head held high, and she would ignore the bullies. Sticks and stones, that's what she needed to remind herself. Sticks and . . .

'Are you all right?'

She jumped. 'Jesus, you scared me half to death.'

'Sorry.'

The boy ducked beneath the stairwell, casting a shadow over her. It was that kid, the spotty one with the bowl haircut who had found her crying that time by her locker. God, he had a talent for creeping up on her when she was upset.

He crouched beside her.

'Are you following me?' she asked.

He seemed horrified. 'No! I was . . . heading here myself. I like to come here sometimes to get away from the other kids. It looks like you found my hiding place.'

He spoke haltingly. She was getting used to boys looking at her chest when they spoke to her but this one looked over her left shoulder, unable to meet her eye.

'Why don't you sit down?' she said.

'No, it's fine. I'll go . . .'

'Sit. Please.'

So he sat. And they chatted. She told him all about the girls who had bullied her, and he made sympathetic noises. He didn't tell her anything about himself, just that he didn't have any brothers or sisters and that he hated bullies too. Later, she realised she hadn't asked him about himself because she had been too busy talking about Mum and Jess and even Dad, and the boy seemed happy to listen. He was sweet, and though she didn't find him that fanciable she liked the way he looked at her, kind of like a puppy. He told her how much he hated school dinners, and that one of the dinner ladies had been horrible to him, telling him he needed to eat his greens if he didn't always want to be 'a skinny wimp'.

At one point, he spotted the button badge that was pinned to her coat. 'You're a Kurt Cobain fan.'

'Yeah. I love him.'

'Me too. I mean, I really like Nirvana. What's your favourite song on the new album?' he asked.

'I like all of them. At the moment it's "Dumb".' She sang a couple of lines and he smiled.

'Yeah, I love that one too.'

The bell rang.

She groaned. 'Better go. I've got double science. How about you?'

'Home economics.'

They got up and Isabel brushed the dust off the back of her skirt, noticing how the boy's eyes followed her hand. He caught her looking and his face went red.

'Hey, I didn't ask your name,' she said.

His face faded from red to pink. 'It's Ryan,' he said.

She put out her hand. 'Nice to meet you, Ryan.'

Chapter 37

Jessica could hardly catch her breath. She got off the floor and sat on Olivia's bed, wishing she had a paper bag to breathe into.

'Olivia,' Jessica said, reminding herself to stay calm, 'are you absolutely sure, sweetheart? Mr Cameron gave you the necklace?'

A nod. Olivia was on the verge of tears again, like she was regretting telling the truth, putting Caspar at risk.

She kept her voice soft. 'Why did he give it to you?'

'Because . . . Because I told him you tooked the other one.'

'And did he know it belonged to Auntie Izzy?'

Another nod.

Jessica pressed her palm against her chest. Where had he found a copy of the necklace? Surely Claire's Accessories didn't still sell them? She guessed he must have found it on eBay.

'Has Mr Cameron been talking to you a lot about Izzy?' she asked.

Olivia squirmed, concentrating on her toys and not meeting her mum's eye. 'We played a game. Like when me and you played with the Scabble.'

Jessica shook her head. 'You played with Scrabble letters with him too?'

'No, Mummy. A different game.'

Jessica leaned forward off the edge of the bed. 'What kind of game?'

'I don't know.'

Jessica's entire body had gone cold. *A game.* The very worst images raced through her head. But surely that was impossible. Classroom assistants and teachers weren't allowed to take children off behind closed doors. They had to remain visible at all times. But that didn't mean they had to remain audible. Once again Jessica wished Olivia was a little older, that getting her to impart information wasn't so bloody difficult.

'Can you show me? You be Mr Cameron and I'll be you.'

'Okay.' Olivia smiled, like this was great fun. 'But we need to sit like this.' She got up and sat on the bed, gesturing for Jessica to sit opposite her, with their knees almost touching. 'And we need to hold a book.'

'What book?'

'Any. I have a reading book when we play the game. And so does Mr Cameron.'

'Okay.'

Now Jessica understood when this had happened. She grabbed a couple of storybooks and handed one to Olivia, who opened it in her lap.

Olivia bent her neck. She put on a deep voice, her impression of an adult male. 'We're going to talk to Izzy. Can you hear us, Izzy? Can you say hello to Olivia?'

Jessica stared in horror at her daughter. The anger was swirling inside her again. Red ribbons of fury, like drops of blood falling into a glass of water.

'Mummy!'

She snapped her attention to Olivia.

'You're not playing properly.'

'Sorry . . .'

'You have to close your eyes and say, "Hello, Izzy." You're me, remember!'

'Of course. "Hello, Izzy."'

'That's good. Now I'm going to be Mr Cameron again.'

This time she put on a strange voice, which Jessica figured was her way of impersonating an adult male putting on a woman's voice. *'You're a very good girl, Olivia. I wish I was there so I could meet you in the flesh. But I'm watching over you, Livvy. I'm there with you, always, looking down from heaven.'*

Jessica stared at her daughter. There was no way Olivia was making this up. *In the flesh.* Olivia would never say that unless she was parroting a grown-up. And she was astonished by Olivia's powers of recall.

'What should I say now?' Jessica asked.

But Olivia seemed to be in a trance; a kind of hypnotic state. She went on in the Izzy voice. *'I'm sad, Olivia. Do you want to know why I'm sad?'*

'Yes,' Jessica said.

'Because a man did something bad to me. He made me die. Do you know the balcony at my house? The black balcony?'

Jessica could hardly breathe. 'Yes. I know it.' She tried to imagine what Olivia would have said. 'It's very dangerous.'

'Oh no, it's safe. It's only dangerous if someone pushes you.'

Jessica felt dizzy, the room spinning around her, sucking her into the game. Again she said what she thought Olivia might have said. 'Did someone push you, Auntie Izzy?'

'Yes. A bad man pushed me and made me die.'

'Who?'

'Your daddy.'

Jessica opened her eyes, staring at Olivia, whose voice had dropped to a whisper.

'Your daddy pushed me.'

Suddenly Olivia's eyes snapped open and she threw herself into Jessica's arms. Hot tears soaked through the front of Jessica's top as Olivia sobbed in her embrace. She had worked herself up into such a state that she was almost hyperventilating. Jessica stroked her hair, told her it was all okay, feeling sick and overwhelmed herself. Ryan Cameron. A teaching assistant. A person in a position of trust, looking after children, had done this.

Finally Olivia calmed down enough to speak. 'I wanted to tell you, Mummy, but he said it was a secret. He said that Caspar would die if I told you about the game.'

'I promise you, nothing is going to happen to Caspar.'

But now Olivia had told her mum the secret, she couldn't be comforted until she had seen with her own eyes that Caspar was okay. Jessica lifted her and carried her downstairs to the kitchen. Olivia threw herself on the dog, arms around his neck, burying her face in his fur. He looked up, tongue lolling, clearly enjoying the attention.

'Did he say anyone else would . . . get hurt? Like Mrs Shelton, the dinner lady?'

'I can't remember.'

Jessica sat at the kitchen table, feeling like she'd just stepped off a fairground ride. She needed a minute to recover, to make sense of it.

Olivia hadn't just spelled out *Daddy* because it was one of the few words she knew. She had done it because – and this was at the root of everything that had happened – *Ryan Cameron had made Olivia believe that her dad had killed her auntie.* He must have wanted Olivia to pass that on to Jessica – but without telling anyone about the game, so his involvement wouldn't be revealed. She remembered how keen he had been for Jessica to talk to Will, probably hoping she would see guilt in his eyes. She could imagine how excited he must have felt when it seemed like his plan was working, when Olivia had gone into school and he'd got her to tell him about the 'Scrabble seance'.

To achieve all this, he had made Olivia believe that her Auntie Izzy was with her, watching her. He must have sung her that Nirvana song, told her facts about Izzy that she wouldn't otherwise know, all because he wanted Jessica to believe Izzy really was communicating with Olivia.

And he must have thought she would be susceptible because, as far as he knew, Jessica believed in ghosts. He knew about Larry because he had grown up around here. Maybe he had first-hand knowledge. Had he known them when they were kids? Jessica didn't remember him but maybe Izzy had known him.

Her mind leapt forward. Was he the owner of the grey car? She had seen Ryan get into a red Volkswagen in the school car park, but that didn't mean he didn't have access to another car too.

Was it him in the photo, watching Izzy's house?

Did he see someone push her off the balcony?

Did he see Will?

To set all this up, Ryan must be convinced Will had killed Izzy. But why? And why, if he had seen something, had he not come forward five years ago?

Nausea swirled in Jessica's gut. Had Will fooled her with all his talk about how special she was compared to Izzy? Had he been sleeping with her sister?

Was Will guilty after all?

Olivia was still cuddling Caspar, stroking his ears and whispering to him. Jessica stood up.

There were other questions too, like: wasn't it a coincidence that he happened to be the teaching assistant in Olivia's class?

Was the whole thing some kind of weird, insane prank?

There was no point sitting around trying to figure it out.

She had to talk to him.

ᗡ

Operating on a kind of parenting autopilot, Jessica put the TV on for Olivia, gave her a snack and allowed Caspar to sit next to her on the sofa. Pacing the kitchen, she tried to call Will. It was almost six now, and she hadn't heard from him since she texted him just before she chased that grey Hyundai.

She knew he would be busy, probably in the full grip of work stress as he and his team rushed to launch this new website, but some things were more important. She left a message, asking him to call her urgently. She emailed him too. She didn't want to ring the office landline because Will's boss, who was an arsehole, could be weird about people receiving personal calls unless it was life-or-death. Jessica didn't think this quite qualified. Not yet, anyway.

She wondered if she should call the police, but she wasn't even sure if Ryan had committed a crime. He had certainly broken school rules – smashed them to pieces with a big hammer – but the law? She wasn't certain. She couldn't prove it was him in the photo, watching Izzy's house, and she certainly couldn't prove that he'd killed her.

She pictured herself storming into the classroom tomorrow morning, shoving him up against the wall and demanding answers. Right now, she didn't care about making a scene, and although he was bigger and taller than her, undoubtedly physically stronger, she wasn't scared of him.

Except there was no way she could wait till tomorrow morning to confront him. The frustration and anger were burning her up from the inside. She had to talk to him now. And she wanted to do it face to face.

She grabbed her laptop and typed his name into Google, but got no results. She checked Facebook but couldn't find him on there either. She couldn't exactly phone the school and ask them for his address, and the school office would be shut anyway. She racked her brain, trying to think if he was friends with any of the other parents, but came up blank.

Then she remembered that there was someone who knew everyone in Beckenham. The fount of local knowledge.

Jessica called her mother. 'Are you okay?' she asked. 'Is Pete looking after you?'

'He was, but he went out shortly after you got here to go to the RAFA Club. They always have a meat raffle on Wednesday afternoons.' She blew air into the phone. 'Oh, Jess, I can't stop thinking about everything—'

'You know Olivia's classroom assistant, Ryan Cameron? I don't suppose you know his parents, do you?'

'Ryan? Yes, I've known his mum, Irene, for years. Lives on The Ravens. I met her at Gingerbread. Her husband ran off and left her in the lurch too.' Gingerbread, Jessica recalled, had been an organisation for single parents. 'I used to see her around quite often, but Ryan said she hasn't been well lately.'

'Hang on, you talked to Ryan about his mum? When you picked Olivia up from school?'

'Yes. Or maybe he told Pete at the RAFA.'

'What?'

'Ryan. He helps out at the RAFA sometimes, behind the bar or in the kitchen.'

'You never told me that!'

'Didn't I? I suppose it never came up. What's this all about? Something to do with Isabel?'

Jessica didn't want to go into the details, not right now. 'Will Ryan be at the RAFA now? Can you call Pete and ask him if he's there?'

Mum grumbled but agreed. 'I'll call you back in a moment.'

She hung up and Jessica sat for a couple of minutes, trying to remain calm. After what felt like forever, Mum called back. 'Pete said he was there and they had a chat, but then he had to leave.'

'Shit.'

'Your language has got appalling lately.'

'I know. I really need to track Ryan down. Can you give me Irene's address?'

'Are you not going to tell me what this is about?' She sighed then went quiet for a minute. Jessica could picture her flicking through the address book she'd had for years, the book she referred to every year when she was sending Christmas cards. 'Here you go.' She read out the address.

'Thank you.' Jessica paused, thinking through her plan. Will still hadn't called back or texted. She had no other option. 'Mum, can you do me a favour? I need you to watch Olivia and Felix for me for a couple of hours. I'll bring them round.'

She put the phone down before Mum could protest and opened the kitchen drawer. She took out the sharpest knife and slipped it into her bag.

Chapter 38

After dropping the children off, Jessica drove to the address her mother had given her. The Ravens was a long street lined with expensive detached houses. Jessica had forgotten that there used to be a martial arts club along here, which she and Izzy had attended when they were ten and thirteen because they thought it would be fun and useful to learn judo. Isabel had got bored and given up quickly but Jessica had enjoyed it and worked her way up to a purple belt. She had happy memories of Mum picking her up after lessons and taking her for cake and a milkshake. Izzy would usually stay at home.

Jessica parked and got out of the car. Mrs Cameron resided in one of the biggest houses on the street, a Victorian Gothic place with an oak tree dominating the front garden, its bare branches hanging low over the lawn. It was almost seven, dark already, and the house had that horror movie vibe, an abandoned air about it. A single light burned in a downstairs window.

Despite its creepiness Jessica knew from her addiction to property websites that this place would be worth upwards of £1 million. *This* was where Ryan had grown up? He worked as a teaching assistant, earning a low salary. It didn't fit – unless his mother had cut him off for some reason.

Yeah, Jessica thought. *Being a fucking stalker creep. How's that for a reason?*

She walked up the front path, which was strewn with damp leaves. No security lights came on.

The doorbell rasped when she pressed it, and she stepped back, looking up at the ivy that crept across the house's facade. She tried to mentally rehearse what she was going to say, but nothing came. There was a little voice whispering in her ear, telling her this was dangerous, that she should go, call the police.

But then the door was opening and it was too late.

A woman poked her head out. Jessica had been expecting someone around Mum's age but the woman peering out at her was in her thirties. Did Ryan have a sister? Suddenly Jessica had forgotten what she wanted to say.

The woman, who had strawberry-blonde ringlets and an explosion of freckles across her face, said, 'I'm afraid we're not interested—'

'I'm not selling anything,' Jessica interrupted. 'Is Irene Cameron home?'

'I'm afraid Mrs Cameron is indisposed at the moment.'

From somewhere in the house Jessica heard an older woman's voice. 'Who is it, Becky?'

'Just a salesperson.'

'I'm not a salesperson! I'm . . . I'm a friend of Ryan's.'

Becky looked at her properly this time, and opened the door wider. Now Jessica could see Becky was wearing a uniform. A nurse's uniform.

Becky saw her noticing. 'I'm Mrs Cameron's carer.'

'Oh. Yes.' She cleared her throat. 'Ryan told me. Can I come in a minute?'

Out of sight, Mrs Cameron called again. 'Is it Ryan? Has he come home?'

Becky sighed. 'She's not going to rest now until she knows you're not him.' She leaned closer and whispered. 'She'll accuse me of lying, saying I've driven him away. You'd better come in.'

Jessica found herself in a beautiful hallway. There was an antique grandfather clock in one corner, pictures of fox-hunting scenes hanging on the walls. The floor was tiled with a beautiful fleur-de-lis pattern, though Jessica could see that some of the tiles had come loose in places and others were cracked. The whole house smelled dusty and the flowers in the vase on the sideboard were dead.

'The cleaner comes tomorrow,' Becky said. 'It's not my job.' Again she lowered her voice. 'Ryan could do a lot more to help, including giving that cleaner a good bollocking. Maybe if you're a friend of his . . .'

'I'll have a word,' Jessica said.

'Good.' Becky led Jessica to the door of a sitting room. 'She's in here. I assume Ryan's told you about Mrs C's condition?' She touched the side of her head.

'Dementia?' Jessica guessed.

A sad nod. 'I'm never getting old. I'm going to ask my kids to drive down to Beachy Head and chuck me off if I ever show a hint of getting like that.' Then she smiled and stepped into the room, speaking loudly. 'Mrs Cameron, this is . . .'

'Jessica. I'm a friend of Ryan's.'

From what Mum had said, Irene Cameron was about the same age as her, but she looked at least ten years older. Ravaged from the inside. She sat in a threadbare armchair in front of an enormous TV. There was a photo of a little boy on the mantelpiece, at various stages of childhood. A babe in arms. A toddler. A gap-toothed nine-year-old who was recognisably Ryan. And there he was as a teenager. He was wearing the same William Peacocke school uniform Jessica and Izzy had once worn. He was attempting a smile but it didn't reach his eyes. He looked sad. Haunted.

Irene studied Jessica, gesturing for her to come closer. 'I know you.'

'I don't think . . .'

'Oh my goodness, you've come back.' Irene clasped Jessica's hand. There was still strength there. 'Does Ryan know?'

Gently, Jessica extracted her hand. 'Sorry, I don't . . .' She looked to Becky for help, but she shrugged.

'He'll be so happy,' Irene said. 'So happy to see you, Isabel.'

Jessica opened her mouth to say she wasn't Isabel, then thought better of it. She glanced meaningfully at Becky, willing her to keep quiet. 'I need to find him, Mrs Cameron. Can you tell me his address?'

But now the old woman was staring at her with suspicion. 'You look different. Have you dyed your hair? Grown it out?' She addressed Becky. 'She doesn't look like her pictures, does she?'

Jessica turned to Becky, who clearly had no idea what Irene was talking about. 'Pictures?'

'In his room,' Irene said impatiently. 'Such a pretty girl. Ryan was so lucky to find such a lovely girlfriend.'

Girlfriend?

Had Isabel dated Ryan at some point? Surely not . . . Jessica combed her memory. She hadn't met all of Izzy's boyfriends but she had heard about every one of them, often in excruciating detail. She didn't remember Izzy ever mentioning a Ryan, even as a friend. But now she knew they had gone to school together . . .

'How old is Ryan?' she asked Irene.

'How old? He's thirty-seven.'

The same age Izzy would be now. So they would have been in the same year, maybe the same class.

'Mrs Cameron,' she said, 'do you mind if I pop up to Ryan's room? I lent him a book and I need it back.'

Irene gave her a warm smile. 'Of course. You know where it is. I've heard you both in there.' Her expression changed to what could only be described as a leer. 'Doing it.'

Jessica hurried from the room, with Becky following.

'I'll show you where it is,' Becky said, leading her back through to the hallway. She stopped. 'Didn't you say your name was Jessica?'

'Yes . . . I— Listen, Isabel was my sister.'

'Was?'

'She died, five years ago.' Before Becky could speak, Jessica said, 'I realise you don't know me, but I'm asking you to trust me. I need to find Ryan.'

'Okay . . .'

'What do you think of him?' Jessica asked. 'Do you like him?'

Becky glanced towards the sitting room. 'He's all right.'

'Just all right?'

Becky made a chewing motion, like she was tasting the words she wanted to say. She made a decision. 'All right. To be honest, I don't like the way he treats his mum. He hardly ever comes round, so when I'm not here she's all on her own. I've talked to him about putting her in a care home, where she'll have company, but he refuses to talk about it.' She went on in this vein for a while before saying, 'To be honest, I wonder if he's on drugs. He seems so . . . vacant. It's like talking to someone on another planet. I was shocked when Mrs C said he had a girlfriend.'

Jessica was beginning to realise that the rumours at the school gates, about Ryan having a hairdresser girlfriend, were completely made up. Maybe he'd even started the rumour himself.

'Can you show me his room now?'

They went up a wide staircase, past the first floor to the second.

'Here we are,' Becky said. 'When I first came here I thought Mrs C must have a grandson living here.'

The door had a ceramic plaque attached to it, with a picture of a Beatrix Potter character next to the words RYAN'S ROOM. Above that a teenager had stuck a yellow-and-black sign featuring the nuclear symbol. DANGER! KEEP OUT!

'He comes up here whenever he pops by,' Becky said. 'Like I told you, he hardly talks to poor Mrs C. He just comes up here and locks himself away.' She opened the door.

Jessica stepped into the darkness. Before hitting the light switch she registered that it smelled like a teenage boy's room. Damp and salty, conjuring up images Jessica didn't want to let into her head.

She turned on the light.

'Oh my God.'

As she took in the room, Jessica experienced a surge of nausea so strong that she had to sit down. She pulled a chair quickly towards herself and closed her eyes, waiting for the dizziness to pass. She could taste bile. The seedy smell in the air didn't help, and she asked Becky if she could open the window. Then, with the late-November chill entering her lungs, she was able to look around and make sense of what she was seeing.

There was a bunk bed pushed up against the wall. The bedspreads were pink and purple. Posters of Kurt Cobain were tacked to the plain white walls, along with photos of horses and a Snoopy poster with the slogan *I'm allergic to mornings*. A stack of Stephen King books stood on the bedside table. Cheap costume jewellery hung from a stand on the chest of drawers, next to a boom box. Jessica pressed the eject button and a CD slid out. It was *In Utero* by Nirvana, the album which included the track Olivia had sung.

Becky, who couldn't understand the significance of what she was seeing, said, 'Okay, this is weird. It's like a teenage girl's room.'

'It's my old bedroom,' Jessica whispered. 'A facsimile of it.'

'What?'

'This room. It's my and Isabel's childhood bedroom.'

Chapter 39

'Will you go out with me?'

Ryan stood in front of the mirror, practising the words he longed to say to Isabel. He had never asked a girl out before, mainly because he was convinced they would not only say no, but would mock him and tell all their friends. He could picture it: a group of girls pointing and laughing at him in the playground. This fear had always been enough to put him off asking.

But although there had been other girls he'd fancied, Isabel Brooks was the first one he really *liked*. There was a connection between them. They saw the world in the same way. They were into the same music. They were both outsiders, mocked by the other, less intelligent kids, the common herd who made his life a misery. He could see himself and Isabel forming a unit, them against the world. Nobody would laugh at them any more – and if they did, he wouldn't care.

Also, Isabel was pretty. No – more than that. She was beautiful. She smelled lovely too. It was a smell that made him want to press his face against her skin and inhale. He wanted to consume her, devour her. Ever since he'd seen her in the paper talking about her poltergeist – which was so cool – and even more so after their special conversation beneath the stairs, he hadn't been able to get her out of his head. Suddenly he looked forward to going to school every day. He made sure he washed properly every morning and that he didn't have any dirt on his clothes. Mum kept wondering aloud what had got into him. He dreaded the weekends, when he would mope around the house fantasising that Isabel had looked up his number in the phone book and was going to call him. He had so many things he wanted to say to her. All his theories about the world. She would find them fascinating and laugh at all his jokes.

Then they would meet up and she would kiss him.

He stared into the mirror. 'Will you go out with me?'

But in real life, he was too scared to ask her.

ω

And then, one afternoon, he was coming out of the newsagent's near school, eating a bag of crisps, when he looked up and saw Isabel coming towards him. She was on her own. He went hot and cold at the same time, and his legs stopped working. He stood there, rooted like a lamp post.

'Can I have one?' she asked.

'Huh?'

She laughed. 'A crisp? Can I have one?'

'Oh. Oh, yeah.' He held out the bag and she took one. He noticed that her nails were bitten. Another thing they had in common.

'What are you up to?' she asked.

'Not much.' Suddenly all the witty conversation he'd practised in his head had deserted him. He groped for something to say. 'How about you?'

'I'm trying to get away from those slags.' She looked over her shoulder, as if they might be watching. He assumed she meant the girls who had been mean to her before. 'They've been bugging me all day, following me around singing the *Scooby-Doo* theme. I hate them. I really fucking hate them.'

Her eyes flashed and he fell in love with her even more. She was so cool. So fierce. It took all his strength to prevent himself from reaching out to touch her.

'Do you want to come back to my house?' she asked.

He wasn't sure if he'd heard her correctly. The blood pounded in his ears.

'My mum's taken my little sister to her stupid judo lesson, so the house is empty. I've got *Incesticide* on CD. Have you heard it?'

That was an older Nirvana compilation album. 'No, is it good?'

'Yeah, it's amazing. Come on, I live just round the corner.'

And she took his arm and turned him around, grabbing another crisp as they began to walk.

It was the greatest moment of his life so far.

ᚹ

Thirty minutes later they were in her bedroom, listening to Kurt Cobain singing 'Dumb'. She had bunk beds and they were sitting on the bottom bunk, only a few inches apart. Isabel had poured them both a glass of Coke and he held his with trembling hands, gazing around him, taking it all in. The clothes draped across chairs, the posters on the wall – Kurt next to Take That, who Isabel's younger sister was a fan of – along with all the signs that Isabel was not a little girl any more. Make-up. Bottles of perfume. Grown-up books by Stephen King. There was a chest of drawers that would be, he knew, full of her underwear. He could see the strap of her bra now, peeking out from beneath her blouse. It was white and he longed to touch it.

Her cat, Oscar, came into the room and jumped on to Ryan's lap, purring.

'He likes you,' Isabel said.

Ryan could hardly speak, he was so overwhelmed to be here.

'What time is your mum due back?' he managed.

'Not for a while. She always takes Jess for a cake after her judo lesson. I'm staying away from cake. I'm on a diet.'

'What? Why?'

'Because I'm getting fat. Look.' To his astonishment she pulled her blouse up to reveal her flat belly. She grabbed the flesh between finger and thumb. 'If you can pinch more than an inch . . .'

He stared until she pulled the blouse back down.

'I think you're . . . not fat.' He had gone pink again. 'I mean . . .'

She cut him off. 'Hey, have you seen the new *Smash Hits*? It's Jess's – I wouldn't normally read it – but there's a funny interview with Lenny Kravitz.'

They spent the next twenty minutes leafing through the magazine, shoulder to shoulder on the bottom bunk. He could hardly breathe and the words on the pages swirled and danced before his eyes. He longed to put his arm around her. Maybe he should do that thing where you yawn and stretch . . . He fantasised that she was going to kiss him. He kept trying to think of clever or funny things to say, but he was mostly mute, letting her do all the talking. He wanted to ask her about the poltergeist but was worried she'd think he was taking the piss out of her.

He was just about to say something witty about East 17 when Isabel looked at her watch and said, 'Oh shit, my mum and Jess are going to be home in a minute. You'd better go.'

She stood up and hurried him out of the room and down the stairs, opening the front door. She ushered him out.

'See you at school tomorrow,' she said.

She was about to shut the door when he blurted it out. 'Will you go out with me?'

Her eyes widened and she looked him up and down. 'I don't know.'
'Please?'

Isabel laughed. 'Oh, go on, then.' She leaned forward and pecked
him on the cheek, then shut the door in his face.

He touched his cheek where her kiss glowed. Isabel was his girlfriend. He had been brave and she was actually his girlfriend.

This was the greatest moment of his life so far.

ω

But the next day, when he saw her in the playground at first break,
Isabel ignored him. She was talking to those three girls, the ones she
had called slags the day before, acting like they were great friends. He
approached the little group, hovering at the edge, until one of them,
Sharon, noticed him.

'What are you looking at?' she asked.

Isabel turned around, saw Ryan and, to his horror, looked away
again, as if she didn't recognise him.

'Go on, piss off,' Sharon said.

He stumbled away, mortified. Why had Isabel ignored him? Well,
he knew the answer. She didn't want her friends to know about them.
She wanted it to be a secret. That was fine. That was cool, in fact; made
it even more exciting. His smile returned. He would talk to her later
when she was on her own.

But he didn't see her again that day, not on her own. She was always
with at least one of those other girls. He walked home feeling crest-
fallen, but had a good idea. He would call her! He found her number in
the phone directory and dialled it, heart pounding, terrified she might
not want to talk to him – but she answered the phone and, after a brief
chat, agreed to meet him in Bromley on Saturday.

It was a wonderful day. They went to Our Price and he bought her
the new Smashing Pumpkins CD, and then they went to McDonald's

and had milkshakes and burgers. Finally they went to the cinema and watched *Hocus Pocus*, which was rubbish, but it didn't matter because Isabel reached over halfway through and held his hand, and then – after they got the bus home – she kissed him in a little alley near her house.

It was a proper kiss, not a peck. She even used her tongue. It lasted for several minutes, but it felt like much longer and he would have kissed her for hours if he could. But then she broke away and said, 'I need to get home.'

She was looking at him funny. Frowning.

'Is everything all right?'

'Yeah, fine.'

'Was the kiss okay?'

She rolled her eyes. 'Ryan, don't be so needy.'

'Sorry.'

'And don't apologise all the time.'

She hurried away and he called after her. 'I'll phone you.'

He tried to call her that evening, but her mum answered and, after a long wait, she told him Isabel was in the bath and was then going straight to bed. He wondered if she would dream about him, and about their kiss. He certainly would. He kept touching his lips, until his mum asked him if he was getting a cold sore.

He tried to call Isabel again the next day, but her mum said she wasn't home.

And then on Monday it happened. The terrible thing.

He waited by the school gates, getting there early so he could catch Isabel on her way in. He watched her approaching, walking on her own, and it struck him again how gorgeous she was. She was an angel. And she was his girlfriend.

He was never going to let her go. They would be boyfriend and girlfriend all through school, and then they would probably go to university together. After that they could move in with each other, get married, have children. She would probably be a famous pop star or actress and he would be her manager. They would be rich and happy and he would get to see her naked every day.

Her face fell when she saw him. He knew something was wrong but tried to ignore the sick feeling in his belly.

'Hi, Isabel.'

'All right.' Her voice was flat. The cold, sick sensation spread through his body.

'Are you okay?'

'Yeah. I need to get to registration.'

'We've got ages.'

'I know, but I'm cold. I want to get indoors.'

He wondered if she had her period. If that was the problem. He should try to be sympathetic. To be a good boyfriend. Deciding it almost certainly was her period making her act weird, he relaxed a little. 'Do you want to meet up after school?'

'I can't. I'm busy.'

'Oh. What are you doing?'

She sighed. She kept glancing over his shoulder and he looked back to see Sharon and the other girls just inside the gate. They were all smirking at Isabel.

'Listen, Ryan,' she said, and he knew what she was going to say. He wanted to turn back time like Superman did in the first movie, to go back to Saturday afternoon, when he was happy, when the world was a perfect and just place. But he was no Superman.

'I don't think we should go out any more,' she said.

'But why?' His voice sounded very small in his ears.

'Just because . . .' She looked like she was about to say something else, but she stopped and softened her tone. 'I'm sorry, Ryan. I'm just not ready for a relationship right now.'

'So . . .' He swallowed. 'Maybe you will be, one day?'

'Yeah. Maybe. I've really got to go.'

She put her head down and walked towards the gates and her friends. Leaving him with a broken heart.

But leaving him too with hope.

One day. Maybe one day they could be together again.

Chapter 40

Jessica got to her feet, examining the furniture, the posters, picking up items of jewellery that were exactly the same as the ones Izzy used to wear when she was at school. Ryan must have seen her wearing them and gone out to buy identical pieces.

Now that she was able to take it all in properly, Jessica could see that most of it was slightly wrong. The bedspreads were the right pattern, but the colours were different. The poster of Kurt Cobain was not the same one Izzy had put on their wall. The boom box was a different brand. But the layout was the same. How had he known? Had he been to their house?

She opened the top drawer of the desk and found a thick Manila envelope, which she took out and opened.

It was full of long-range photos, like paparazzi shots. Photos of Izzy. There were pictures of her coming out of work, photos taken on the street, and of Izzy getting into her car. There were shots of her house too, taken from beyond the boundary wall. In a lot of the pictures Izzy was with someone else: Darpak, Nina, a couple of women Jessica didn't recognise. Clients, presumably. Although it sickened her, Jessica wasn't shocked. Now she knew Ryan had been stalking her sister. It made sense that he'd been photographing her too. She shuffled the photos until she came to one taken with a zoom lens, a close-up of Izzy's head and shoulders. She was wearing the bat necklace.

My God, she thought. How much effort had it taken to find out where she'd bought it so that he could buy one too? That, more than anything else, was proof of his obsession.

'Hang on,' Becky said. Jessica had almost forgotten she was in the room. Becky was holding a framed photo that had been on the chest of drawers.

'Take a look at this.'

Jessica took the frame from her. In the photo, Ryan and Izzy were sitting side by side, gazing into each other's eyes.

Izzy was in her wedding dress and Ryan was wearing a smart suit.

'Holy . . .' Jessica couldn't help but laugh. 'It's Photoshopped. This is one of Izzy's wedding pictures. Ryan's put himself in the photo in Darpak's place.'

'Wow. That's messed up.' Seeing Jessica's expression, Becky said, 'Sorry. Understatement of the century.'

Jessica took one more look around and thought about calling the police. She had evidence now that Ryan had committed a crime. Making your bedroom look like that of the object of your obsession was not illegal. But he had stalked Izzy. He had taken photos of her without her knowing. Surely the police would be interested in that. Surely they would reopen the case, look again at the coroner's verdict of accidental death.

But she still wanted to confront him. She wanted to look into his eyes and hear him tell her why he had done it. She needed answers to the rest of her questions. She still didn't think Ryan had murdered Izzy – because, if he had, why would he set up such an elaborate scheme to put the blame on Will, when the case had been closed half a decade ago? She had to know, and she didn't want the police to scare him off.

She would talk to him, demand answers, and only then would she call the cops.

'I need that address now,' she said to Becky. 'And I need to get out of this room.'

She took the Manila envelope with her. As they went down the staircase she checked her phone again. Still no word from Will.

Back in the entrance hall Becky searched through the contacts on her phone and found Ryan's address. She scribbled it down and handed it to Jessica. It was on a street about twenty minutes' drive away.

'Oh, one more thing,' Jessica said. 'Does Mrs Cameron have a car?'

'Er, yeah. But she can't drive any more, obviously. It's in the garage.'

'Is it grey?'

'Yeah, I think so.'

'A Hyundai?'

Becky looked blank. 'Sorry, I don't know much about cars.'

Jessica nodded. She knew Ryan was behind everything now. It didn't really matter if the grey Hyundai he used belonged to his mother or if he simply had two cars.

'Be careful,' Becky said as Jessica left the house.

Jessica nodded. Walking down the path, she dropped her phone in her bag, then reached inside to touch the handle of the knife.

ω

As she was parking outside the address Becky had given her, Jessica's phone rang inside her bag. By the time she'd parked and was able to reach the phone, it had rung off and the screen showed a missed call from Will. At last! She immediately tried to call him back but he was busy. Leaving her a voicemail, no doubt, wanting to know what was going on, hopefully telling her he'd finished for the day. It was getting on for eight now, so he might be on his way home.

She waited, intending to listen to the message before trying him again, and leaned across to peer through the darkness at Ryan's house.

It was much smaller than his childhood home, semi-detached with a small front garden, but this was still an expensive street, full of commuters who were willing to pay a fortune for a place close to the station. Ryan's red Volkswagen was parked outside. He was home. And as she watched, a light went on in an upstairs room and she saw a figure silhouetted in the window.

She forgot all about calling Will back. She heard the chime to indicate she'd received a voicemail as she got out of the car. She stood there, beneath a street light, bathed in its sodium-orange glow, and looked up at the window, at the silhouette there. Although she couldn't see his face, she was certain he was looking at her too. Watching her.

It was as if her feet were glued to her own shadow. Was she doing the right thing, coming here? She tried to work out what she was going to say to him, but her brain was as useless as her feet. Again she reached into her bag to check the knife was still there.

Ryan moved away from the window, breaking the spell. She hurried up the path to his front door.

It opened before she had a chance to knock and Ryan stood before her. His hair was messy and there was a ripe smell coming off him, the stink of sweat mixed with that nasty deodorant he always wore. He seemed frightened, agitated, jigging from foot to foot, and his skin looked streaky, like he'd been wearing fake tan that had rubbed off. Jessica was hit by an unexpected emotion. Not fear. Not hatred or anger. No, seeing him now, she felt something else.

Pity.

Until she remembered what he'd done to Olivia, and the anger came rushing back.

'How did you get here so quickly?' he asked.

'I—'

He jerked his head, trying to see over her shoulder. 'Are the police coming?'

She was confused. Had his mother or Becky called him and told him she'd been round? Surely not. 'No, I haven't called them.'

'But you're going to?' He was acting like someone was sending electric jolts through his body, unable to keep still.

'You *want* me to call the police?'

He stepped forward, as if to grab hold of her, and she jumped back.

'You have to,' he said. 'You have to tell them. It's time to be brave, Jess.'

What the fuck was going on?

'We can do it together,' he said, gesturing for her to come inside. She hesitated. The voice in her head was screaming at her now, telling her to get away. But why was he telling her to call the police?

'Please,' he said, and his voice was so pleading, so pathetic, that she felt sorry for him again. She entered the house, but kept her distance from him.

This hallway was very different to the one at his mother's house. It was narrow, with nothing on the walls. There were two doors to the right, both shut, and a flight of stairs at the end. The carpet, she couldn't help but notice, was threadbare and needed replacing. The stink of Ryan's sweat was much stronger in here. The smell of fear.

He had his back to the door, his head down, still making strange jerky motions, shifting from foot to foot. Then he looked at her. 'Wait. You *have* listened to it, haven't you?'

She kept her voice calm. 'Listened to what?'

'The voicemail. On your phone. Oh my God, you haven't. You haven't had time.'

'Ryan. You're really—'

He took a sudden step towards her, sending her further back towards the stairs. 'Where is it?' he demanded. His eyes were wild and Jessica thought, *Oh shit, I have made a terrible mistake.* 'Where's your phone?'

'It's here,' she said quickly, holding up her bag. 'Let me . . .'

273

He snatched the bag from her grasp. She tried to grab it back but he was stronger and faster. He stared at her. 'You need to hear it, Jess! I know you didn't believe it before, but now you will. You'll see. You'll finally see.' He stuck his hand inside the bag, and yelped with pain. 'What the fuck?'

He withdrew his hand. Blood dripped from his middle finger. He stared at her, shocked and accusatory, then reached back into the bag, slowly this time. He took out the knife, examining it like he'd never seen one before.

He dropped the bag by his feet and jabbed the tip of the knife towards her. His voice rose an octave. 'What's this? Why did you bring this?'

She was too scared to reply. She had been an idiot to come here alone, to bring the knife. She was soon going to be as dead as Isabel, and Olivia and Felix would be left without a mother, and she would never see them grow up. He was standing between her and the door. There was no way out.

'I lied about the police,' she said. 'They're on their way right now. I've seen your bedroom at your mum's house, Ryan. I know what you've been doing with Olivia, talking to her about Izzy. I know you were stalking Izzy. I know everything.'

He stared at her, then broke into a grin. 'You don't know everything, actually. Not until you've heard this.'

Crouching, with the knife still in his right hand, he fished in her bag once more and found her phone. It was locked. 'What's the code?'

She had no choice but to tell him. He unlocked it, navigated to her voicemails and laid the phone on the floor between them.

Will's voice came out of the speaker. It took a moment for her to recognise it, because this was not the confident, laid-back voice she knew. This was a tremulous, terrified version, something cracking in his throat, the words emerging hesitantly, like an actor being forced to recite lines at gunpoint.

'Jessica,' Will said on the recording, 'I have something important to tell you. It was me. I murdered Isabel. I was . . .' He broke off and muttered something, and she heard another harsh voice in the background. 'I was sleeping with her and . . . I pushed her off that balcony.'

Ryan pointed at the phone as Will's confession continued. There was triumph in his eyes. Spittle flew from his lips as he spoke. 'Are you listening to this?'

Jessica had slowly backed up until her heels touched the bottom stair. Again she tried to ensure her voice was calm, though there was a tremor there, echoing the distress in Will's voice as he continued to talk on the voicemail. 'Will didn't kill Isabel. That's not a real confession. I can hear you in the background, forcing him to say it.'

Ryan pressed stop on the voicemail and laughed. 'You stupid, trusting bitch. You don't know. You don't know what I saw. What I *heard*.'

'Where is he?' Jessica asked. 'Where is Will?'

Ryan pointed the blade of Jessica's knife towards the ceiling. He grinned, his unnaturally white teeth glowing in the gloom. 'He's here,' he said. 'Do you want to hear him confess to your face?'

Chapter 41

Ryan forced Jessica upstairs, the knife at her back.

'Along here,' he said when they reached the landing.

It was dark and Jessica had to feel her way along the wall. She could hear Ryan breathing heavily behind her as she made her way towards a door which was edged with light.

'Open it,' Ryan said.

She did as he told her, grasping the handle and pushing the door open. Bright light from within momentarily dazzled her. Ryan put a hand on her back and pushed her inside, following her in and shutting the door behind him.

'Oh . . . Oh, Will!'

He was lying on his side on the floor, in a foetal position, with his eyes closed. Asleep – or unconscious. Jessica stepped closer. His T-shirt was rucked up to expose his belly and one shoe was missing. There was blood on the one hand she could see. It appeared one of his fingernails was missing. His face was even worse, covered with fresh bruises, and there was a gash across his upturned cheek. His lip was split too and, with horror, Jessica saw a small white object lying in a puddle of blood not far from his face. A tooth.

A baseball bat was propped against the wall on the far side of the room. Next to it, a pair of pliers. Apart from these objects, and Will, the room was completely empty.

Jessica threw herself on to the floor beside her husband, whispering his name and gently stroking the side of his head. He made a low moaning sound but didn't open his eyes.

She looked up at Ryan, who was standing in the doorway, holding the knife by his side.

'You animal,' she spat. 'This was how you got him to leave me that message? You beat him? Tortured him? You really think his confession means anything?'

Ryan gazed down at her. He was no longer bouncing around. He was still, but there was a flicker of doubt on his face.

'Will didn't push Izzy,' she said. 'Olivia spelled out *Daddy* because she doesn't know how to spell anything else. You're her teaching assistant. You should know that.'

He shook his head. 'It was him. I know it was him. Olivia passed the message on, but you didn't do anything about it. You were supposed to get him to admit it, Jess. But you backed away . . . Too cowardly, too blinkered and stupid to accept the truth.'

There was something missing here. A piece of the puzzle.

'How did you know what I was thinking?' she asked, but the realisation hit her as soon as the words left her mouth. 'It was Pete, wasn't it? You talked to him at the RAFA Club?' Mum must have recounted their conversation, when Jessica had accused her of everything, to Pete.

'Oh yes. We've become good friends, Pete and me. He loves a good gossip.'

Jessica cursed silently. She guessed Pete had been feeding information back to Ryan all along, unaware of the damage he was doing.

She stroked Will's head softly and tried to keep her voice even. 'You're wrong about Will. You're the one who was following Izzy around. You were stalking her. Do you know what I think? I think *you* killed her.'

'*Me?* I loved her! I would never have harmed her!'

He took a step towards her, waving the knife in front of him, and she flinched away.

'Okay.' She held up both palms, trying to pacify him. From the corner of her eye she could see the baseball bat. Could she reach it and strike Ryan with it before he stabbed her? He was pacing the floor now, lips moving like he was arguing with himself.

He stopped and pointed a finger at her.

'I *wasn't* stalking her.'

'Okay . . .'

'I just wanted to be close to her.'

She breathed deeply, refusing to allow herself to say what she longed to say. Instead she said, 'I understand.'

'And if I hadn't been watching out for her, no one would know what happened to her.'

Jessica's heart skipped. The way he was talking, the whining tone, reminded her of a little boy, agitated and confused. A boy who had never grown up. She used the same voice when Felix was upset. 'What was that, Ryan?'

He had started pacing again. 'I loved her from the moment I met her at school. She was so sad and lonely and the other girls, those bitches, they were bullying her. I was there for her! I told her I believed her when she claimed to have a ghost. I made her smile, Jess. I made her *smile.*'

Jessica took a deep breath. 'That's . . . I'm sure she appreciated it.'

'No!' he yelled. Beside her, Will stirred, but still didn't open his eyes. 'We had a wonderful time together, the best day of my life, but something . . . something made her go off me. I think it was those slags, Parminder and Sharon and Julie. They told her I wasn't good enough for her. Told her I was a loser. She dumped me!' He clenched his teeth together, jaw muscles flexing.

'So you hated her?' Jessica asked.

Were there tears in his eyes? He rubbed at them with the back of his hand. When he spoke, his voice was croaky. 'No. I still loved her.' He pushed his palm against his chest. 'Always. And I went through years of agony, seeing her at school. My heart never had a chance to heal because she tore the wound open every day.'

'I loved her too,' Jessica said.

He didn't seem to hear. 'When we left school I didn't see her for a long time. I didn't go to university, but I went away. Mum gave me some money and I went travelling. I lived in Thailand for a while. I had a girlfriend out there, a local girl. She was sweet. Compliant. She helped me forget all about your sister. But then, well, we broke up and I came back to this shithole. That was in 2012.'

Jessica nodded for him to go on.

'Almost the first thing I saw when I returned to Beckenham was a story about Izzy in the local paper. A sex therapist! I always knew she'd do something remarkable. And seeing her in the paper, it was like – like a sign that we were meant to be together. I found out she was going to a business networking event, and I went up to talk to her afterwards. She didn't recognise me.'

'That must have been hard.'

He sneered. 'Hard? *Hard?* It felt like she'd stabbed me, right here.' He pointed the tip of the knife at his heart.

'So you wanted to get back at her?' Jessica suggested, trying to sound matter-of-fact. 'I can understand that.'

Ryan turned the knife around, pointing it back at Jessica. She glanced over at the baseball bat again. Beside her, Will moaned softly.

'No. You *don't* understand,' Ryan said.

'So tell me, Ryan.'

He opened his mouth. Shut it. Let out a humourless laugh. Then he met Jessica's eye. 'All I wanted was to be near her, to be in her orbit. And yes, I wanted her to notice me. To acknowledge my fucking existence. That's why I followed her and took photos of her. I was trying to learn everything about her, the woman she had become. I was trying to work out a strategy . . .'

He fell quiet and Jessica said, 'A strategy to make her notice you?'

'To make her *love* me.' His voice had become high-pitched and desperate. 'And I was getting there, Jess. I was figuring it out. Getting into her head.' He stared at the carpet. 'But then it was too late. She was dead.'

Jess snuck another look at the baseball bat. If only she were a metre closer, she was confident she could leap over there and grab it before Ryan stopped her. Maybe if she shuffled towards it, inch by inch . . .

Ryan sniffed loudly, drawing her attention back to him. His shoulders shook. He was crying.

He took a shuddering breath and raised his tear-streaked face. 'We lost her, Jess. Not just you. I lost her as well.'

For a moment her pity almost returned, came close to becoming empathy. The shared grief of losing someone they both loved. But she caught herself. How dare he equate his feelings with hers? She was Izzy's sister. Ryan . . . He was her fucking stalker.

She was about to tell him this when Will spoke.

'You're pathetic,' he said.

Startled, Jessica scooted closer to him. He had one eye open; the other was sealed shut by his injuries. His voice was thick with pain. He tried to roll on to his back, gasping as he did so, revealing the gap where his lost tooth had been. Jessica held his shoulders gently, urged him to lie still.

'I didn't kill her,' he whispered.

'I know.'

A shadow stretched across the floor. Ryan was there, looming over them. He had wiped away his tears but he still looked wretched. 'Liar! I saw you!' he yelled at Will. 'The day she died . . . You were there.'

Chapter 42

The sky was crowded with fat, grey clouds but Ryan was sweating. He had parked his mum's car in its usual spot in the cul-de-sac behind The Heights. From here, when the trees were bare, he had a perfect view of Isabel's house. The balcony on which she often stood, his very own Juliet. Sometimes he imagined himself below, calling up to her, and then he would imagine them both dying, poison rushing through their veins, a beautiful suicide pact, the only way they could be together. Star-crossed lovers, together forever in the afterlife.

It was funny. After leaving school, Ryan had done everything he could to forget about Isabel. He had moved away, first into central London and then, after a few years doing dead-end jobs, he'd trained as an EFL teacher and gone abroad. He went to Japan first, and then to Thailand, where he'd lived for the best part of a decade. He'd had a girlfriend over there, Phaelin, and they were happy for a while, but she never made him feel like Izzy had. When he got into one of his black moods he would take it out on her.

When he eventually pushed her too far, she left him and told her older brothers what Ryan had done to her. Suddenly Thailand wasn't a safe place to be. Plus his mum was getting old and less healthy, and he thought he'd better remind her of his existence before she signed his inheritance over to someone else, so he came home. Back to Beckenham.

And who had he spotted just a few days after he got back? Isabel. And, just like that, all the old feelings – the obsessive love, the pain, the longing to be close to her – came rushing back.

She was the one who got away. And the more he thought about it, the more he came to believe that his life so far had been shit because of her absence from it.

Thankfully, it wasn't too late to change that.

He gazed up at the house for a little while, watching for signs of life. He'd got here a little later than usual, so had missed seeing Isabel drinking her morning coffee. The house seemed quiet, empty. Just as he had hoped.

He got out of the car and, checking there were no nosy neighbours spying on him, he walked around the fence that ringed Isabel and Darpak's house. On one of his previous recces he had discovered a loose fence panel, hidden by trees. Over the weeks, he had worked at it, wriggling and tugging at it like a child working at a loose tooth, until it could now be easily pulled aside.

Sucking in his belly, he was just about able to squeeze through.

More trees stood around the edge of the garden, and he used these to conceal himself – though he was confident no one was home – as he approached the house and slipped down the side passage to the front courtyard.

Darpak's car was here but that wasn't a surprise. He often took a cab or walked to the station if he had a meeting in town. It was extremely rare for the man Ryan thought of as his love rival to be at home after 9.30 on a weekday morning. Isabel often hung around a little longer, but her car wasn't here. She must have gone out.

He went back round to the garden and, trying to ignore the spasms of excitement and fear in his chest, reached into the stone planter that stood to the left of the patio. A couple of months ago he had watched Darpak and Isabel arrive home and, after a short while, fish something out of this planter. Shortly afterwards, Darpak had come back and dropped a small object back into it.

The object Ryan now held in his hand. Their spare front door key.

He went back round and stood on the doorstep. This was the most nerve-wracking part. The emblem of a security company was attached to the wall above where he stood, but he wasn't sure if his beloved regularly armed the burglar alarm before going out. His mum had a burglar alarm and she almost always forgot to arm it, believing that the security logo outside was enough of a deterrent. Ryan had recently watched a documentary in which a cop had explained that a high percentage of people were just like his mother.

He had decided to risk it. If an alarm went off, he would run. No harm would be done. He would just have to figure out another way of getting into Isabel's home.

He slid the key into the lock, counted to three and turned it.

No alarm sounded.

He pushed the door open. Still no alarm.

He was in. For the second time in his life he was inside Isabel's home. Okay, the first time he had been invited, but this occasion was almost as thrilling. He had to take a moment to compose himself, to stop his heart exploding out of his chest.

He headed towards the stairs. He didn't want to be in here long, even though he would love to spend hours exploring Isabel's domain. Sitting on her sofa. Putting his lips to the cup from which she drank her morning coffee. Pressing her clothes against his skin.

A delicious notion came to him. She would have a laundry basket somewhere. In her bedroom, probably. And in that basket he would be sure to find some items of her underwear . . .

His heart was pounding again now as he pictured himself pressing a pair of her panties to his face, inhaling her sweet scent. They would surely be lacy, expensive. But it wouldn't matter if they were tatty and cheap. If they were hers, he would treasure them forever.

That was all he wanted: some new mementoes. A few items that she wouldn't miss, that she would think she had misplaced. While he was here he also planned to take some photos of her bedroom, so he could update the shrine at his mum's place. Isabel wasn't a girl any more. She was a grown woman, and he wanted his shrine to reflect that. He was sure he could source whatever art hung on her bedroom walls, could find the bedding, replicate the technology . . .

Oh God . . . Would she have a vibrator in her bedside drawer? He wouldn't dare to take that – she would miss it – but the idea of touching it was exquisite, making him so turned on that he was finding it difficult to walk up the stairs. He had to stop for a moment, forcing himself to think of something repulsive – he imagined pulling Darpak's dirty boxer shorts from the laundry basket – so he was able to carry on.

He reached the top of the stairs, and the doorbell rang.

He froze.

He was able, once his pulse had slowed, to convince himself it was nothing to worry about. Probably just the postman. He began to creep slowly along the hallway, wondering which of the doors led to the master bedroom, when the bell sounded again.

And he heard movement from within one of the rooms along the hallway. A splashing sound, then a soft thump.

Someone was home!

The doorbell sounded again and he heard Isabel call out, 'Hold your horses!'

Oh shit. Oh fuck. Isabel was here! Just beyond that door. And he could hear her coming towards him.

Panicking, he looked around wildly. There was a door behind him. He pulled it open and found himself staring into a closet. Quickly, he ducked inside and closed the door. There was no handle on the inside and he wasn't able to pull it fully shut, so it remained ajar an inch. He heard Isabel's quiet footsteps coming towards him and he sucked down a breath, convinced she was going to find him and that he was going to have a terrible time explaining himself. But she ran down the stairs and said something to someone. *Please*, he prayed, *let it be the postman.* But then, a few seconds later, he heard the front door shut and the bass rumble of a man's voice.

They were coming up the stairs.

He strained, trying to work out who it was. He had watched videos on YouTube of Darpak giving dull business presentations, and he didn't think it was him. Then he heard Isabel laugh and say, 'Oh, Will.'

Huddled in the dark closet, dust tickling his nose, Ryan gritted his teeth. Will! What the fuck was he doing here? Over the last few weeks, he'd watched Jessica's husband come and go several times. Were they having an affair? He hadn't dared believe it – the thought that Isabel could be sleeping with two other men was unbearable – and Will hadn't been here for a week or two, so he had stopped worrying about it.

But here he was, coming up the stairs.

'No, in here,' Isabel said. 'It's better in here.'

What did she mean? Unable to resist, Ryan peeked out through the gap and saw the two of them disappear into a room on the right. The bedroom?

He held his breath. Had Isabel really just taken her brother-in-law into the bedroom? He couldn't hear anything for a minute, and he was preparing to leave the closet, to get out of the house, when he heard something unmistakable.

The sound of a woman's pleasure.

Soft moans. Sharp breaths. And as Ryan listened in abject horror, the moans grew louder, approaching orgasm. Oh God, they were doing it, right now, metres from where he stood. He clamped his hands over his ears, unable to bear it. His love, his perfect Isabel, was fucking her sister's husband and clearly enjoying it immensely. Ryan tried not to weep. It should have been him. It should have been him!

Ryan knew that when they were teenagers he hadn't been good enough for Isabel. Too weedy. Too nerdy. But since encountering her again he had done everything he could to counter that. He spent a lot of time at the gym. He had a fake tan, a trendy haircut. He had made himself attractive so she would notice him, but she still didn't know he existed. Oh, how ironic – she was screwing her computer-nerd brother-in-law!

The noises stopped and he could hear them talking, though he couldn't make out the words, just the low rumble of Will's voice and the sweeter pitch of Isabel's.

But then Will's voice began to grow louder. He sounded exasperated. Angry? Ryan tensed.

Will shouted, 'Oh, for fuck's sake!'

He was angry. What had happened? Had Isabel told him it had to end? Had she criticised his sexual performance? She was, after all, an expert. Will yelled something else, and Ryan could hear Isabel trying to defend herself. They were still in the bedroom, and Ryan realised this was his chance to escape. The best chance he'd get.

He peered out through the crack, then pushed the door open. They were still arguing, their voices loud, though he couldn't make out what they were rowing about. He took a deep breath and exited the closet. He paused for a second – full of regret that he hadn't managed to take any photos or find any souvenirs – then padded down the stairs and out the front door. He ran back around the garden, out through the gap in the fence, and threw himself into his car. He was sweating again, but he could finally breathe.

ᛒ

Later that day he heard the terrible news on the radio. *Sex therapist found dead at her Beckenham home.*

There was no mention of Will. And later still, when the coroner ruled it an accident, Ryan was left feeling powerless and furious, with Will and himself.

He knew that Will – angry, possibly desperate to keep their affair a secret – must have pushed Isabel off that balcony. But there was nothing he could do about it. No one he could tell.

Chapter 43

'You were there,' Ryan repeated, stabbing a finger at Will. 'I know because I was in the house . . .'

'What?' Will and Jessica said it simultaneously. Now Jessica knew why Ryan hadn't gone to the police; why he had felt the need to get across what he thought he knew in such an elaborate way. He couldn't let anyone know he had been inside Isabel's house. It would immediately have made him the prime suspect.

'Isabel invited me in,' he said.

'Liar!' Will exclaimed, raising his head. When he spoke, the bloody gap where his front tooth had been was exposed. 'She never said . . .'

He stopped, his words killed by Jessica's glare.

'So *you* were there too?' she said, hardly able to believe what she was hearing. 'The day Izzy died, you were at her house?'

Will laid his head back down on the floor. 'Yes, okay. I popped round to talk about her website . . .'

'To fuck her,' spat Ryan.

'No, Ryan. Don't be ridiculous. I didn't do anything like that.'

'I heard you! I heard you make her come.'

Will's shoulders shook and, for a second, Jessica thought he was crying. But it wasn't tears, it was laughter. 'I was showing her a video,' he said when he managed to get his breath back.

'What, porn? To get you in the mood?'

'No, you idiot. A video for her website. A short clip to advertise Blissful Massage.' He raised his head again. 'Jess, you've seen it.'

She nodded. She remembered the video, which Will had made shortly before Izzy's death. It was an arty video, using flowers to represent female genitalia. Male fingers touching shiny, dewy flowers, as she remembered. The soundtrack was a woman making orgasmic panting sounds. Isabel making orgasmic panting sounds, to be precise. Watching it, hearing those noises, had made Jessica cringe and she'd told Will to turn it off.

'I went round because the video was the last thing I needed to do for her bloody site and I wanted to get it off my desk. We went up to her bedroom to watch it . . .'

'Her *bedroom?*'

'Yes. Her iMac was in there. She and Darpak used it like a TV, to watch Netflix in bed. She said she wanted to see the video on the big screen.' He winced with pain as he spoke, his voice distorted by his swollen lips and missing tooth. 'Ryan, that's what you heard. The bloody video. And she still wasn't happy with it and . . . well, Jess, I'm afraid I lost my temper with her. I'd spent so long working on it, on the whole stupid site, and she was so fussy. I shouted at her, told her I was sick of it, that she should find someone else to work on it. We argued about it for a few minutes, and then I left.'

Jessica wanted to know why Will hadn't told her he'd been at Isabel's the day she died. But now was not the time to quiz him. She had to deal with Ryan first, who was pacing around them, clearly trying to process what he was hearing.

Ryan moved to the furthest point from the baseball bat and Jessica saw her chance. She sprung to her feet and dashed across the room. She felt Ryan move behind her, leaping over Will, coming after her, but she was too fast. She snatched up the bat and grasped it with both hands, holding it level with her shoulder as she whirled around to face Ryan.

He stopped. He was two metres away from her, still holding the knife. She had one chance. If she swung and missed, it would unbalance her and give him the upper hand.

She took half a step towards him. 'Drop the knife!'

He didn't move. She adjusted the bat, becoming accustomed to its weight. One hard strike to his head and this would be over. She shifted her feet, gritted her teeth and tried to look confident.

He took a tiny step back, the knife trembling in his hand.

'Drop it,' she repeated.

He shook his head, glanced over his shoulder at Will, who had pushed himself up into a half-sitting position. 'Do what she says,' Will said.

Jessica moved a little closer, within striking distance. 'Just drop the fucking knife, Ryan.'

But he wasn't looking at her any more. He had gone inside himself, frowning with confusion. Then he looked up at her.

'It was you' he said.

'What?'

His lip curled. 'You were always jealous of her, and when you found out Will was fucking her, it was the last straw, wasn't it?'

'Will wasn't fucking her.' As she said the words, she asked herself if she believed them even though Will hadn't told her he'd been there that day. She found that she did. The story about the video was too plausible and she had been watching Will's face as he told it. He hadn't been lying.

But Ryan was in denial. 'No. I bet . . . I bet you found out and, after I left, you went round there. Confronted her. You pushed her!'

'Ryan . . . Drop the knife.'

But he wasn't listening. He pointed at Jessica with his free hand. '*You* did it.'

She had no time to speak. He charged at her, the knife in his fist, screaming with rage. Jessica didn't think. She swung the bat.

It connected with his skull. He crashed to the floor and lay still.

ಹ

Jessica sat next to Will, waiting for the ambulance to arrive. The crack that had rung out when the bat made contact with Ryan's skull would, she knew, reverberate in her dreams for months to come. She had dropped to her knees after he fell, crawling across to him, fighting back the urge to vomit.

He was still breathing.

Will was sitting up now, holding the tooth he had lost between thumb and forefinger.

'How did he get you here?' she asked.

'He called me at work. He must have got my number from school records, or maybe from Pete. He called me and told me he had Olivia, that if I called the police or contacted you, he would hurt her, then kill her.'

In the distance, Jessica heard a siren.

'Why didn't you tell me?' she asked. 'That you were at Isabel's that morning.'

He closed his eyes. 'Because I was scared people would suspect me of killing her. You. Darpak. The police. I knew if they interviewed me and asked me to recount what happened I wouldn't be able to lie. I'd have to tell them I got angry with her. I thought they'd accuse me of killing her. But you have to believe me, Jess. She was alive and well when I left. And she was nowhere near that balcony.'

'I do,' she said. 'I do believe you.'

They were both quiet for a while before Will said, 'Do you think it was him? Ryan?'

She shook her head. 'No. He's demented. He was obsessed with her. I mean, Jesus, he was in her house. But I think he genuinely believes you did it. There's no way he would have stirred all this up, nearly five years after the police closed the case, if he was guilty.'

She looked across the room at Ryan. His phone was lying close to him and Jessica crawled over and picked it up. She lifted Ryan's hand and used his thumb to unlock it, then scrolled through the photos. There were numerous pictures of their house, their cars, photos of Jessica coming out of their front door. There was even a picture of Caspar in the back garden, which must have been taken over the fence. This was proof, on top of everything else, that Ryan had been following them. He must have been doing it because he was desperate to see what was going on, if there were signs of stress or conflict between them. He wanted to know if his plan was working.

Disgusted, she tossed the phone aside.

A blue light flickered outside the window. The ambulance was here. Probably the police too.

'So it was an accident after all?' Will asked.

Jessica didn't answer immediately. She was thinking about the photos in the Manila envelope in her car. A record of Izzy's life in the months leading up to her death.

'I don't know,' she said. 'But I'm going to find out.'

Chapter 44

Jessica sat beside Will's bed. They had kept him in overnight for observation, in case he had concussion, and wanted him to stay for another twenty-four hours. Olivia and Felix were with Mum and Pete. Jessica had decided to keep them off school because, right now, she couldn't bear the thought of them going back to that place, where Ryan had so badly abused his position. She had also decided to forgive Pete for his indiscretion. He'd had no idea what his loose lips would lead to.

The head teacher, the rest of the early-years staff, the governors – they were going to have serious questions to answer about how they had allowed it to happen. The head teacher had already phoned Jessica to apologise, promising an inquiry, but it seemed that Ryan had taken Olivia into an empty classroom for what Mrs Rose thought was one-on-one literacy practice. It was something they did occasionally, especially with children who'd had behavioural issues. Apparently it was allowed as long as other staff could see into the room and, as there was a large window that gave a full view of what was happening inside, Ryan hadn't broken that rule. Unfortunately no one had been able to hear what he was telling Olivia. The words he had used to make her believe she was being visited by her dead aunt. As far as Jessica was concerned, the school had failed in its duty to look after her daughter, and it was something she was going to have to deal with later.

'You were amazing,' Will said, squeezing her hand. He looked strange with a missing front tooth, but the swelling around his lips had diminished a little. 'When you hit him with the baseball bat.'

She cringed. 'Don't.'

'But it was impressive. Did you play a lot of rounders when you were a kid?'

She laughed, before a silence fell between them.

'You should have told me you went to see Isabel that day,' she said.

'I know. I'm so sorry. The day she died I made a gut decision not to say anything, and then it was too late.'

'Will you make me a promise?' she said. 'From now on, no more secrets.'

'That's easy. Of course I promise.'

She hugged him, but he flinched away.

'Sorry,' he said. 'The bruises. It still hurts.'

She stood up. 'I'll see you later, okay?'

'Where are you going?'

She hesitated.

'Come on, no more secrets.'

'All right. Don't try to dissuade me. I'm going to try to talk to Ryan.'

ᛒ

Ryan was in a private room on the next floor up. As Jessica approached, DS Michelle Ward came out. DS Ward had been involved in the investigation into Izzy's death back in 2013. She was a brunette in her late thirties who gave off a capable but impatient air. She was with another plain-clothes cop, a young man. Ward saw Jessica and stopped.

'You know, you shouldn't have gone to his house,' she said. 'It was a foolish thing to do.'

Jessica brushed off the comment. 'Has he told you anything about what he saw the day Izzy died? About breaking into her house?'

'We can't interview him properly until he's been discharged and we can get him to the station. But he keeps going on about your husband.'

'I thought he might.'

'And how he thinks you killed Isabel because you were jealous of her.'

'You don't believe him, do you? I can prove I wasn't anywhere near her house that day.'

DS Ward waved a hand. 'It's fine. I know it wasn't you. I am going to need to talk to Will, though.'

'He didn't do anything! I'm certain—'

Ward cut her off. 'I still need to have a chat with him.'

Jessica sighed. 'All right. I understand.'

'And I'm going to have to talk to you again too. This whole case is . . .' Ward pulled a face like she'd tasted something sour. The story Jessica had told them last night, about Ryan faking a haunting, was unlike anything they'd encountered before. Jessica had seen the scepticism on their faces. 'But we'll do that later.'

During this exchange the other detective had been on the phone. He ended the call and said, 'The uniform's been delayed. He's not going to get here for another ten minutes.'

'Oh, for pity's sake.'

Jessica listened to their conversation. It became apparent that they were waiting for a police officer to arrive to stand guard. Ward looked at the door of Ryan's room, clearly eager to get moving.

The other detective said, 'It'll be okay for ten minutes. He's not going anywhere.'

Ward turned to Jessica. 'Do you think Will's up to a quick chat now? Is he awake?'

'He was five minutes ago. Do you need me there? I, er, need to get back to my children.'

'No, you go ahead.'

The two cops headed towards the lift, Jessica a step behind them. They all got in together and descended one floor, where the detectives exited.

'I'll call you later,' Ward said. 'I have some more questions for you.'

'Sure.'

Jessica rode down one more floor, got out, then pressed the button to go back up. From what Ward and the other detective had said, she had ten minutes. She hurried along the corridor and went straight into Ryan's room.

Chapter 45

Ryan was in the bed, his head wrapped in a bandage. The TV was on, tuned to some antiques show. Jessica was gratified to see fear appear on Ryan's face when he noticed her. He immediately went for the assistance cord beside his bed, but she was too fast. She grabbed his wrist. She was strong, unafraid. She pushed his arm down until he gave up and went limp.

'I just want to talk to you for a minute,' she said.

He stared at her. His eyes were bloodshot and puffy.

'We both want the same thing, Ryan. We want to find out what happened to Izzy. Are you going to help me?'

'I know what happened to her. Will killed her. Or you did. Maybe you were in it together.'

'Oh, for God's sake. Listen to yourself. Insisting that it was Will or me isn't doing anyone, including Izzy, any favours. Do you want to find out what really happened?'

He fell silent. He had the air of a beaten man. His words emerged in a whisper. 'More than anything.'

'Then help me.'

Finally she seemed to have got through to him. He gave her a sly look. 'Maybe if you do something for me . . . Tell the police I didn't mean any harm . . . I thought I was doing the right thing, Jessica. For Izzy.'

She wanted to slap him. But she kept hold of her temper. She was learning to control it, to use it to her advantage. And she wasn't afraid to lie to him if it helped her get what she wanted.

'I understand now why you did what you did with Olivia. You couldn't tell me or the police what you'd seen, not directly, because you didn't want anyone to know you were stalking Izzy.'

'I wasn't stalking her! I was . . . watching her. Watching out for her.'

'You broke into her house!'

'Only because . . . I wanted to be close to her.'

Jessica shuddered and took an involuntary step away from him. It filled her with shame to think she had been so friendly with him. If she was truly honest with herself, she had found him attractive. But now he made her skin crawl.

'I loved her, Jess,' he said, his eyes brimming with tears. 'I always loved her. If she hadn't dumped me . . .'

Jessica still couldn't remember Izzy ever mentioning Ryan. She'd had several boyfriends between the ages of thirteen and sixteen, and although Jessica could remember some of them coming round, and Isabel telling her to go away so they could have some privacy, she was sure her sister had never mentioned Ryan. Clearly, he hadn't been important to her.

'After she died I was stuck with this knowledge that I couldn't do anything with,' Ryan said. 'Knowing that . . . someone had killed Izzy . . . It tormented me. I kept an eye on Will for a while . . .'

'Wait. You stalked Will? Back in 2013?'

'Not stalked. Kept an eye on.'

It wasn't, she decided, worth arguing with him about the definition.

He went on. 'I wanted to see if he would do anything I could use against him, some way I could get him to confess without revealing I'd been in the house that day. But I didn't get anywhere. And then the weeks and months flew by and I started to believe Will had got away with it. I was so angry. It was so unfair! But there was nothing I could do except let it go. I had a shrine to Izzy at my mum's house . . .'

She nodded slowly, not wanting to distract him by letting him know she'd seen it.

'It was my way of keeping her alive. Of remembering her. And it reminded me of that beautiful time I spent in her bedroom, listening to music with her. I think . . .' His eyes glistened. 'I think she would have liked it.'

Jessica was astonished that he couldn't see that what he'd done was about as creepy as it got. It made her feel like there were bugs on her skin; made her want to get out of this room. But there was still so much she needed him to tell her, and the police 'guard' would be here any minute.

'Were you working at Foxgrove at this point?' she asked. 'In 2013? I don't remember seeing you.'

He wiped his eyes with the back of his hand. 'No. Not until a year ago. I was at St John's Primary before then. And I didn't know your kids went to Foxgrove. I remember seeing you in the playground a few days after I started. It was such a shock. Felix was – what – year four then, so I didn't have any contact with him, but it still freaked me out, knowing you were there. And . . .' He swallowed. 'I knew you had a three-year-old, that she would be starting at Foxgrove soon, and there was a good chance she'd be in my class. I'd seen her with you. She looks so much like Izzy . . . I thought it would be nice to be close to her.'

'Jesus Christ.'

Ryan didn't seem to hear her. 'She's so like Izzy. I mean, she has your red hair, but it's her face and smile. Her frown too. She has this way of looking at people as if they're ridiculous. As soon as Olivia came into my class it was as if I had a piece of Izzy near me every day.'

He looked up, saw the way she was staring at him.

'Oh. No. I don't mean . . . There was nothing weird about it . . .'

Jessica blinked in disbelief. *Nothing weird?*

There was a glass of water next to his bed. He took a sip. 'I didn't know how much Olivia knew about Izzy; whether you talked about her at home. So I asked her if she had any aunts or uncles and she said, "I had an Auntie Izzy, but she's dead." She didn't seem to know much about her. I swore her to secrecy, and I started to tell her little things, stuff I knew from when Izzy and I were together. About how she had a cat called Oscar, and that you used to call your car Fred. I found that Nirvana song that Izzy and I liked on Spotify and played it to her on my phone. And I told her about your poltergeist.'

Jessica didn't respond. Ryan was on a roll now.

'She was fascinated by that. She wanted to know all about Larry. And that . . . that's when the idea came to me. How I could get a message to you. Because I knew you and your mum believed in that kind of thing. I thought you might be able to persuade the police to look at the case again. I thought if you confronted Will he would confess.'

This all chimed with what she had already figured out. 'What made you think I believed in ghosts? That I'd be susceptible?'

'Pete told me. We had a chat about it one night at the RAFA. He told me that, according to your mum, Izzy was always sceptical but you were a believer. That was back in September, just after Olivia started in my class.'

Bloody Pete.

'And you had to do everything slowly? So I'd be ready to believe her when she finally told me what had happened?'

Finally he had the good grace to look ashamed. 'Yes. Except . . . I hadn't realised how hard it would be, even though I work with four-year-olds every day. I forgot how unpredictable and illogical they can be.'

Jessica glanced at the door. There was still no sign of the uniformed cop. He or she must have got held up further.

'Olivia seemed to enjoy the game, to think that she was communicating with Auntie Izzy. I told her that she couldn't tell anyone that I was helping her talk to Auntie Izzy, not yet . . . I said it was very important to keep it a secret, that it was a game that other people wouldn't understand. I don't know how much she understood but at first it didn't seem to be doing her any harm.'

'Except you convinced her that our dog would die if she told anyone.'

He winced. 'I'm not proud of that. But I was scared. Her behaviour started to change and I realised she was getting freaked out by what was going on.'

'Not freaked out, Ryan. Disturbed.'

'Yeah. And I stopped straight away, as soon as there was that incident when she was bitten. When Mrs Rose said Olivia was obsessed with death. I thought maybe I'd gone too far. But it was too late then . . . She really believed Auntie Izzy was visiting her, even though I tried to tell her it was just a game. It got out of control . . . but then she did it. She told you Izzy had been pushed. She told you it was Will.'

Jessica was thrown back to that night. It felt like a fever dream now. A brief period of madness.

'After all my hard work I thought justice was finally going to be done. And when nothing happened, when Pete told me what you'd said to your mum, how you didn't believe Will was guilty, I snapped. I realised I was going to have to take a more direct approach to get Will to confess.'

'So, what? You were going to expose yourself, admit to being in Isabel's house?'

He took another sip of water. 'That wasn't part of the plan. I was going to sit Will down, tell him what I'd heard, persuade him that he needed to hand himself in to the police. I was going to tell him how much better he'd feel if he confessed. But he wouldn't cooperate. He kept denying it and I guess my frustration boiled over. Things got . . . physical.'

Jessica had to restrain herself from smacking him around the head.

She glanced at the door again. 'What about the predictions Olivia made? About Pete getting sick and Pat Shelton dying? The fire at the school?'

He gave her a blank look. 'I don't know what you're talking about.'

'Don't lie, Ryan.'

'I'm not lying!'

There was a noise out in the corridor. The cop must be coming. She had to hurry.

'Did you see anyone else with Izzy in the days leading to her death? Apart from Will? Anyone she might have fought with? Who might have meant her harm?'

'No . . . I don't remember . . .'

'Think!'

'I don't know.' He rubbed his forehead, trying to dislodge any memories that might be lurking there. Jessica wanted to shake him. She took a step towards him.

'What the hell's going on?'

Jessica whirled around. A uniformed policeman stood in the doorway.

'You're not supposed to be in here.'

He entered the room, tried to grab hold of Jessica's arm, but she slipped around him and headed for the door.

'Wait!' Ryan called. 'The night before. Izzy was talking to a woman outside where she worked. She looked nervous. I don't know who she was, but there might be a photo. There's an envelope . . .'

The cop came towards her again, but she was too fast. Jessica ran out of the room, ignoring the shouts that followed her down the corridor.

ω

Mark Edwards

She hurried out to her car, pulled the Manila envelope out of her bag and started searching through Ryan's photos. He had written the dates they were taken on the backs and kept them roughly in chronological order. As she sorted through them she saw several pictures of Will going into and coming out of Izzy's house. Jessica saw herself numerous times too.

And then she found them – the last photos Ryan had taken of Izzy. She was coming out of Mind+Body, locking the door, with her back to the camera. She was turning her head, as if she'd heard someone.

Jessica looked at the final photo. There was another woman in the frame, approaching from the right, her arm raised, clearly showing the back of her hand.

A woman Jessica recognised.

Chapter 46

February 2013

Isabel was locking up after the final session of the evening. All she wanted was to go home, where she would resist having a drink. Since things had got better with Darpak, and as the pain of his betrayal slowly receded, she could get through the evenings without alcohol. Well, most evenings. She had lapsed once or twice. Maybe three times. Possibly four. And not drinking hadn't helped ease her reliance on sleeping pills, or uppers to get her going in the morning. But that was fine – she could only tackle one addiction at a time.

She remembered this morning. Darpak had been dressing for work while she blow-dried her hair. He had stopped suddenly, shirt half-buttoned, and sat on the bed with his face in his hands.

She had turned off the hairdryer. 'What is it?'

'I nearly screwed it all up, didn't I?'

And he had wept. She didn't go over to him, didn't try to comfort him. She wanted him to be sorry. She needed to know he appreciated what he had, and what he could have lost. Seeing his contrition, the evidence that he still loved her, gave her hope. People recovered from affairs. They would survive this. *She* would survive.

She finished locking the door. Her car was in the garage being serviced, so she was going to have to get a cab home. She was about to call one when someone behind her said, 'Isabel?'

She spun round, clutching her chest, and a woman stepped out of the darkness. It was Amber. Gavin Lawson's assistant.

'Jesus, you made me jump.'

'Sorry.'

Amber wasn't wearing any make-up and looked paler than when Isabel had last seen her, almost ghostly.

'Could I . . . have a word?' she said. She seemed nervous. No, more than that. Scared.

'What about?'

Amber glanced around. 'I need to talk to you in private.'

'Okay . . . There's a pub down the road.'

'No. We might be overheard there.' She nodded at the door. 'Can we go in here?'

Curiosity, and the instinctive desire to help someone who was clearly in distress, overrode Isabel's desire to get home. She led Amber through to the back office.

'I don't suppose you have anything to drink, do you?' Amber asked as she sat down.

Isabel laughed. 'I . . . Oh, sod it.' There was a bottle of gin in her desk drawer, which she'd been meaning to tip away all week. She found a couple of plastic cups and poured a drink for both of them. She'd give up boozing tomorrow.

'So . . . is it Gavin?' Isabel asked. 'Did he finally push you too far?'

Amber's worried silence seemed to confirm this.

'What did he do to you?'

'Not me. He didn't do anything to me. Well, nothing new . . .'

Isabel clenched her fists. She had a horrible feeling she knew what Amber was going to say.

Amber swallowed a mouthful of gin. 'Nina came back again so Gavin could take the shots for her portfolio. Did she tell you about that?'

'She told me she'd been back to see him. So this was another visit? The second time without me?'

'That's right. And it was fine at first. I mean, he was his usual self, an overexcited schoolboy, but professional. He didn't touch her, didn't try to get her to do anything she didn't want to do. Not at first. But then—'

'Hang on, when was this?'

'Two nights ago. I've been trying to decide what to do about it since. Going over and over it in my head. Thinking about all the stuff I've seen him do. The times he's touched me. And I finally decided . . . enough is enough.'

Isabel breathed deeply, afraid of what Amber was going to tell her. 'You said two *nights* ago.'

'Yeah. It was late. Gavin couldn't fit her in during the day, and he says he does a lot of his best work after dark anyway.'

'That figures.'

'Yeah. Ha. Anyway, he sent everyone else home but I had some work to catch up on so I hung around. I guess . . . well, I wanted to keep an eye on him. Since our conversation, since you refused to take any of Gavin's shit, I've been thinking about it. About his behaviour. All the times I've turned a blind eye. You made me feel guilty. Like I was complicit.'

'You shouldn't think like that, Amber. He's the one with the power. I understand . . .'

Amber waved a hand. 'Let me tell you what happened.'

'Okay.'

'I was in the back office, editing some photos, and Gavin came in looking for a bottle of champagne. They were celebrating, he said.'

'Celebrating what?'

She shrugged. 'He never needs a reason. He had some coke too. I mean, he does coke every day, so it's not like I even raised an eyebrow at that. He went back out and put some music on, turned it up loud. And then I guess I got sucked into my work.'

Amber stared into her empty glass.

Isabel refilled it.

Amber sighed. 'There was a lull in the music, between tracks, and I heard Nina laugh. Except it sounded like a nervous laugh, you know? And then she said his name. She sounded . . . distressed.' She met Isabel's eye. 'I knew exactly what was going on. It's happened so many times. Normally I would just put my head down and pretend there was nothing going on. And even though I'd stayed behind to keep an eye on him, I froze. I was afraid of what would happen if I went out. Afraid of what it would lead to.'

She pushed her hair out of her face. 'When I went out they were both standing on the platform, against the screen. Nina was in just her underwear and Gavin was naked. He was . . . excited.'

'He had an erection?'

'Yeah.' She swallowed. 'He had his Polaroid camera in one hand, held above his head, and he kept pointing at his dick. She was shaking her head, trying to get away from him, but he wouldn't let her. I saw him grab her wrist, try to pull her hand towards his dick.' Amber was talking in a rush now, needing to get the words out. 'Gavin must have heard me coming because he turned round, his fucking dick pointing at me, and he asked me if I wanted to join them. He said something like, "Come on, babe, show her what to do." I told him to fuck off.'

Amber told the rest of it. How Gavin had said he and Nina were 'just having fun'. How they'd taken some 'smoking-hot' pictures. How Nina was going to be a star, but she needed to loosen up a bit if she wanted to make it in this industry. He pointed at his penis again and asked Nina if she wanted to help him out with 'a big problem'. He touched her lips. And then he laughed like it was all a huge joke. He found his trousers, pulled them on, told Nina – who looked terrified and confused – that she should get dressed. Once they had their clothes on he calmed down, acted like nothing had happened. He told Nina that he would sort out her portfolio and send her the pictures for her approval.

'And then we left. I walked Nina down to the exit. She was pretty fucking shaken. Like, actually in shock. I thought she was going to throw up. She kept saying she needed a taxi and she was trying to order one on her phone but her hands were shaking so much she couldn't do it. It was horrible. In the end I had to take the phone from her and do it myself.'

'That bastard,' Isabel said.

Amber nodded. 'I told her she should report it, go to the police. I said I'd go with her and confirm I'd witnessed it. I was shaking too because it felt like such a huge decision. Like it could end my career. But I'd seen him do it to too many women.' She met Isabel's eye. 'I should have spoken out sooner.'

Isabel didn't say anything. She liked to think she would have acted sooner if she were Amber, but would she really? It took guts to blow the whistle on someone like Gavin. She could hear his mealy-mouthed defence. *He hadn't raped anyone, had he? He hadn't forced Nina or anyone else to do anything they didn't want to do. The women knew exactly what kind of bargain they were striking, didn't they? It was all consensual.*

Men like him had been getting away with this shit since the dawn of time.

'What did Nina say?' Isabel asked.

'That she was exhausted, that she didn't want to talk about it. She was freaking out so I thought I'd better leave it. Then the taxi turned up and she went home.'

Amber took another sip of gin. 'I've tried to call her since but she never picks up. I don't know what to do. I've called in sick the last couple of days and Gavin clearly knows something's up because *he* keeps calling *me*. But I've made up my mind. I'm not going back. I'm finally going to strike out on my own.'

'Good for you.'

'But I don't know what to do about Nina. That's why I came here. I thought you could—'

'Leave it with me,' Isabel said. 'I'll talk to her.'

Chapter 47

Although Jessica had met Amber at the Bonfire Night gathering she didn't have her contact details, and she knew if she asked Nina for them she would have to deflect a barrage of questions. Luckily, Amber was easy to track down. She was on Instagram, Twitter, Facebook and Tumblr. She had her own website too, where she showcased her work, and there was an address for her studio in Shoreditch.

Earlier that morning Amber had tweeted that she was going to be working in her studio all day. *If you see me on here, throw things!* she wrote. She hadn't updated since.

Before heading there, Jessica read Amber's official bio. She was originally from Swansea and had set up her own business in 2013 after spending several years as Gavin Lawson's assistant. She was known for her edgy fashion work and portraits of women. On her site she described herself as 'a sex-positive feminist whose mission is to capture the natural strength and complexity of women, free from the male gaze'. There was a link to an interview in which she talked about creating a comfortable, empowering environment for the models and subjects she worked with.

There were numerous self-portraits among the photos but the woman who featured in most of her pictures was Nina. Jessica had encountered photos of Nina in magazines and on the occasional poster.

She knew how photogenic she was. But in Amber's photos, which tended to feature in arty style magazines or just on Amber's Instagram feed, Nina looked like a warrior: fierce and wise and powerful.

ϖ

The studio was on a cul-de-sac near Silicon Roundabout, close to where she'd first met Will. It was in a converted warehouse with a flat roof. Jessica found the front door open and went inside.

Amber was sitting at a desk by the far wall, in front of an enormous monitor on which she appeared to be editing a photo of a naked woman with red hair. It was a self-portrait, Jessica realised.

Amber looked up from the screen, startled. 'Jessica?'

'I was hoping to have a word with you.'

Amber looked confused, but nodded towards a spare chair and said, 'Sure. Is everything all right?'

Jessica didn't sit. She didn't know how safe she was here.

'Why are you looking at me like that?' Amber asked.

Jessica rested one hand on the back of the chair Amber had offered. The other hand hovered over her phone, which sat just inside her shoulder bag. She had pressed record before coming into the studio. She might have brought the knife with her too if the police hadn't taken it away.

'You went to see Isabel the day before she died,' Jessica said.

Amber sat up a little straighter. 'How did you know that?'

'Someone told me.'

A frown. 'And you're coming to ask me about it now, four years on?'

'Nearly five years.'

'Um, okay . . . Will you please sit down? You're making me nervous.' Amber attempted a laugh but it came out strangled. When she realised Jessica wasn't going to move she said, 'Yeah, I went to talk to her about Nina. This was when I was still Gavin's assistant. You know,

Gavin Lawson?' She pulled a face when she said his name, like she'd smelled something foul.

Now Jessica was confused. 'Why did you need to talk to Izzy about Nina?'

Amber took a deep breath. 'It's a long story. I'm going to get myself a glass of water. Do you want one?'

She went over to a water cooler and filled two plastic cups before returning to her seat.

'Okay,' she said.

Halfway through the story, Jessica decided to take that seat after all. Her legs had gone weak, and her insides churned with a mixture of anger and hatred and despair. She had never met Gavin, but she could see the scene at his studio playing out, could imagine the distress and fear Nina must have experienced. There had been a lot of stories in the press recently in which a whole swathe of sexual predators – actors and movie producers and musicians – had been exposed for similar behaviour. Like nearly every woman she knew, Jessica had her own 'me too' stories: unwanted, unwelcome advances, lewd suggestions, men who thought women existed for them to touch and openly lust over. So-called 'bad dates' when the man had pushed and pressured her, failing or refusing to read the signals she was giving. When she'd worked for the PR agency she'd had a boss who was always asking his female employees for a hug, hugs that lasted an uncomfortable length of time. But that didn't make this story any less horrific.

'What do you think would have happened?' she asked. 'If you hadn't come in?'

'I don't know. His usual method was to keep pressing, over and over, cajoling until the woman either ran away or gave in. And a lot of them did what he wanted. They were frightened. Pressured. He made it clear their careers would be damaged if they said no. Not only that but he fed them this bullshit that fashion was supposed to be wild and dangerous, that if you didn't go along with it, if you didn't join in, you were in the wrong game. Worse than that, you weren't fun. You were uncool. Frigid.' Jessica could see the muscles in Amber's jaw clenching and unclenching. 'He's been getting away with it for years.'

'So what happened? After you spoke to Izzy?'

Amber shook her head. 'Nothing.'

'What do you mean?'

'Izzy said she was going to talk to Nina and try to persuade her to go to the police. I was waiting to hear from her – and then . . . the next I heard, Izzy was dead. I didn't see Nina again for a couple of months – until after I quit my job with Gavin and set up on my own – but she told me Izzy hadn't said anything to her. Nina had started modelling by that point. She actually got taken on by the agency Gavin introduced her to, though she told them she wouldn't work with him again.'

'And they were okay with that?'

'Yeah. They know what he's like. There are quite a few models who won't work with him. That doesn't stop the agency from sending others to him, though.'

'Jesus.'

'Yeah. Anyway, that's when Nina sort of became my special project. We helped each other become successful.'

Jessica tried to take it all in. She got up again, pacing in front of the desk while Amber watched her, trying to process it all.

Then suddenly Jessica stopped pacing and stared at Amber.

'Didn't you think it was weird that Izzy died the day after you spoke to her?'

Amber looked exhausted. 'What do you mean?'

'Well, it seems like too much of a coincidence, doesn't it?'

'Why? It said in the paper that she'd been drinking and taking drugs. They had a photo of her balcony in the paper and . . . well, I've been to the house since, of course, seen it with my own eyes.' She paused, and Jessica assumed Amber was remembering that horrible

314

moment when Olivia had appeared on the balcony. 'But even back then I could see how it must have happened. Izzy getting drunk and falling.'

Listening to Amber's story, Jessica had almost forgotten she'd come here suspecting Amber of pushing Izzy to her death.

'Did you tell Gavin that Izzy was going to talk to Nina about exposing him?'

'No. Of course not.'

'But there has to be a connection. If she was going to talk to Nina, persuade her to tell the police, and he found out . . . he'd try to stop her, wouldn't he?'

Amber gawped at her. 'You think Gavin pushed her?'

But Jessica was already on her way to the exit.

Chapter 48

'Wait!' Amber shouted as Jessica reached the door.

Jessica paused. She could feel her phone vibrating in her pocket. Probably Mum, asking when she was going to pick up the kids, or Will, wanting to know if she was coming back to the hospital. But she couldn't worry about them right now. The truth was within touching distance.

Amber had grabbed a laptop and was on the sofa, bashing at the keys, her sleeve pulled up so her tattoo was fully visible, the orange-and-red flames licking over her wrist. She gestured for Jessica to come over.

'I used to look after Gavin's diary, all his appointments and travel and so on,' Amber said. 'It was a pain in the arse because he was so difficult and was always cancelling on people and needing hotel rooms at the last minute . . . Anyway, I used the Calendar app on my Mac to keep track of everything and when I bought my new one it all synced across. When did Isabel die?'

'March the first.'

'Two thousand and thirteen?' She tapped at the keys. 'Gavin was in Berlin. I know because I booked the flights and his hotel. He flew out on the twenty-eighth and stayed for two nights.'

'But . . .' Jessica floundered. 'Are you sure he went? Maybe he just wanted you to think he was in Germany so he'd have an alibi.'

Amber thought about it. 'No. He definitely went. The hotel sent him a bill afterwards for smoking in his room and burning a hole in the carpet. Gavin denied it but the hotel said he'd be banned from the whole chain . . . In the end I arranged the payment.'

'Are you sure it was that trip?'

'Hang on.' Amber's fingers flew over the keyboard. 'Yes. I've still got the emails.'

'But . . . maybe he hired someone to do it.'

'Jessica . . .'

'Like a hitman, or . . .'

'Jessica,' Amber said softly. 'It wasn't him. Believe me, I would love to see him in jail for the things he's done. But he didn't do this.'

Jessica wanted to scream. Every time she thought she was getting close to finding out the truth, it slipped away. Darpak, Will, Ryan, Amber, Gavin. She had suspected all of them, but none of them ~~were~~ *was* guilty.

Maybe the coroner had been right all along. No one was guilty. Nobody had pushed her sister off that balcony and Jessica had allowed herself to be swept up in Ryan's mad game. He had believed someone killed Izzy, had set about trying to convince her of that, and she'd fallen for it. She was still falling for it even after finding out what he'd done.

She was as crazy as he was.

Feeling weak, she sank into a chair and closed her eyes. She was in a wood, mist hanging between the branches. Izzy was walking towards the trees. She stopped and looked back, just for a moment, before she was swallowed by shadows.

A bell was ringing somewhere in the distance. A church bell, tolling for Izzy. Telling Jessica it was time to say goodbye.

Jessica sat there for a long time, lost in the same shadows that had swallowed Izzy whole. She was so tired. She wanted to lie down, surrender to oblivion. A voice whispered in her head, telling her to give in, let it happen, let it go.

Let her go.

'Jessica?' Amber was leaning over her. 'Jessica, are you all right?'

Jessica kept her eyes shut. She could see Isabel, coming back towards her through the trees. She was mouthing something. *'Don't give up.'*

But it felt like the end of a long, torturous journey. She had been round in a loop, travelled through the woods, gone into the dark, and here she was, back where she had started.

'I need to go,' she said, getting shakily to her feet. 'I have to go and collect the children.'

The idea of that, of embracing Olivia and Felix, made her feel a little better. Yes, she had been round in a circle, but at least now they could all move forward, get on with their lives. Her family shaken, with an Isabel-sized hole, but together. No longer haunted.

'I'll see you out,' Amber said. They went down the stairs, Amber leading. She opened the outside door which led to the back of the building, where Jessica had parked.

As they stepped out on to the pavement – the sun bright and low in the sky, dazzling her – Jessica heard an engine, and a car came around the corner into the cul-de-sac.

A grey car.

The grey car.

Jessica stared, the blood rushing and pounding in her ears, and she could hear Isabel talking to her again, her words inaudible because Amber spoke at the same time.

'Ah, here she is,' Amber said as the driver of the car tried to manoeuvre into a tight parking space, and as the car reversed Jessica got a clear view of the woman behind the wheel.

Jessica moved her lips but couldn't get the words to form. Finally she was able to say, 'Why . . . why is she driving that car?'

'Huh? Oh, it's mine. She borrows it all the time.' She said something else, something about a Mazda. 'She needs to sort it out, get the battery replaced, but she hasn't got round to it . . .'

The grey Hyundai stopped moving and the driver looked up at Jessica. Their eyes met.

Nina.

Nina was driving the grey car.

Chapter 49

March 2013

Isabel couldn't sleep, despite the alcohol sloshing about her system. She couldn't get the scene Amber had described out of her head; couldn't make her heart slow down. She had called Nina as soon as she got home and asked her to come round in the morning, and she kept rehearsing what she would say. At the same time she was trying to resist the call of the little bottle of sleeping pills that was hidden in a drawer in the bathroom.

Darpak stirred beside her. 'Do you want to talk about it?' he asked, grabbing his phone and squinting at it. 'It's two a.m.'

She considered telling him, unsure how he would react. Part of her worried he might blame Nina for 'getting herself into that situation'. He had been less than keen when he'd heard about Nina's newfound desire to be a model; he seemed to think it was demeaning, that she should use her brains. He'd said that Isabel's growing business needed her, that they would try to find her a more demanding role in the company. But Izzy was more worried about what Darpak might do to Gavin. He knew people, scary people. The kind of men who would take great pleasure in kicking Gavin's head in. And although that was an image that gave her great pleasure, she was afraid of the repercussions.

So she decided not to tell him. Not until after she'd spoken to Nina, anyway.

'My brain's full of work stuff,' she said. 'I can't relax.'

He propped himself up on one elbow, reaching over to touch her, laying a warm hand on her hip. He shuffled closer. 'Maybe we could . . .'

She smiled and edged closer to him, but an image of him with that intern flashed in her head. She sat up.

'Izzy . . .'

'It's okay. I'm okay. I just need to go to the bathroom.'

In the en suite she dug out the sleeping pills and took one, putting them back into their hiding place. She went back and Darpak reached out for her, and suddenly it felt like something she needed. Something that would help.

Halfway through, the pill began to kick in, and she closed her eyes, felt herself floating away as he held her. In that moment, in the arms of the only man she had ever loved, she was happy. It was the first day of March, the month when winter turned to spring. It would be a new start.

ᴡ

Darpak had a meeting in town and, knowing it would be difficult to get a parking spot at the train station, he had ordered a taxi.

'What are you doing today?' he asked.

'I'm going to work from home.'

'I don't blame you. Oh, the garage should call later to let you know when they're going to bring the car back.'

'Okay, cool.'

'Love you,' he said, kissing her goodbye. 'Call me later?'

'Will do.'

He paused at the door. 'I love you.'

'You said that already.'

'Oh yeah. But I do.' He stepped towards her and pulled her into an embrace. 'I'm so sorry, Izzy.'

'Go on, you're going to be late.' She kissed him again and, finally, he left.

She made herself a cup of tea and took it upstairs to the en suite, where she ran herself a bath. She added just a little cold so the water was almost unbearably hot, and slid into it, gasping at the heat. She closed her eyes and lay back, trying to relax, to push away all the thoughts about work and Darpak and the conversation she needed to have later with Nina.

She had only been in the bath for ten minutes when the doorbell rang. She wanted to ignore it and was going to put her head under the water when it rang again. Damn. Was it those idiots from the garage bringing the car back without calling first to warn her?

She got out of the bath and grabbed her dressing gown. The doorbell sounded again and she shouted, 'Hold your horses!'

She exited the bedroom and ran down the stairs. It was Will.

'Oh. Sorry,' he said, looking at her pink, damp face. 'Did I get you out of the bath? I wanted to show you that video.'

ω

Two hours later Isabel was pacing the house. She probably shouldn't have criticised Will's video, although she couldn't help being a perfectionist. It was her business and it was important to get it right, but Will had messed up the soundtrack. It was supposed to be subtle; she wanted the sounds of pleasure she had recorded to be in the background, almost like a heartbeat. Instead it sounded like she was the star of a bad porno. And she understood that he wanted to get the project off his desk but he had, she thought, overreacted somewhat, shouting at her like that. She sighed. People were right when they said you shouldn't get family involved in business – speaking of which, it was noon and Nina should be here by now.

Isabel could still feel the effects of last night's pill clinging to her, like she was draped in cobwebs. She had run out of uppers and the temptation to call the man who procured them for her was almost overwhelming. Fighting it, she heated a bowl of tomato soup and took it into the living room, which was stuffy and too hot. Either she or Darpak needed to talk to the heating guy about the faulty thermostat. There was a strange smell in the air too, a faint whiff of cheap deodorant.

Maybe it was the temperature in the room but she couldn't stomach the soup. As she was pouring it away, her phone rang. It was Nina.

'I'm outside,' she said. 'By the back door. Can you let me in?'

At the door Isabel said, 'Did you walk?'

A nod. 'I was trying to clear my head.'

'I know the feeling. Did it work?'

Nina didn't answer. She went into the kitchen and nodded at the fridge. 'Do you think it's too early for a drink?'

Isabel licked her lips. Maybe a small glass of white wine would blow the clinging cobwebs away and make this conversation easier. 'Yes, it's too early,' she said, taking a corkscrew from the drawer. 'But fuck it, right?'

She poured the wine. It was cold and a little tart. She meant to take just a few sips but, within seconds, she'd downed half the glass.

'Let's go and have that chat,' she said.

Nina pulled a face. 'Do we have to?'

'Yes, Nina. We do.'

They carried their glasses up the stairs and into the living room. Even though she had lived here for two years, Isabel sometimes still caught her breath when she entered this space, with its floor-to-ceiling glass. Rain was coming but the last of the morning sunshine strained through the clouds, filling the room with watery, shifting light.

'My God, it's hot in here,' Nina said, shrugging off her jacket.

'I know.' She explained about the thermostat.

'Let me guess, Darpak doesn't want to pay anyone to fix it.' She met Isabel's eye. 'So how is everything with my brother?'

'It's fine. But we're not here to talk about me.'

Nina sighed.

'Amber told me about what happened,' Isabel said. 'With Gavin.'

Nina wrapped her arms around herself. 'I don't know what you're talking about.'

So that was the way she was going to play it. Denial.

'He assaulted you,' Isabel said, raising her voice a fraction and taking a step towards her sister-in-law. 'You need to report it.'

Nina went over to the window, facing the view. Tower blocks and church steeples. The Crystal Palace TV transmitter standing tall in the distance. 'I can't,' she said.

Isabel put her wine down and approached Nina, who immediately tried to move away. Isabel grabbed her arm. 'Stop trying to get away from me! You have to report him, Nina. Amber told me what he did. Thrusting his dick at you. Trying to—'

Nina winced. 'Don't.' She moved away from Isabel again. 'Please, can we open a window? It's so hot I think I'm going to collapse.'

'Fine.' Isabel slid open the doors to the balcony. Winter air flooded into the room. 'Better?'

'Much.' There was a sheen of sweat on Nina's forehead, which she wiped away. 'Thank you. But Izzy, I'm not going to the police. I can't face it.'

'Why? Because it'll ruin your budding modelling career?'

Nina looked appalled. 'How can you say that? Do you think I'm that shallow?'

'No.'

'You don't get it, Izzy. You're talking like it's always been a dream of mine to be a model. I hadn't even thought about modelling until I met Gavin.'

'But you want to do it, don't you?'

Nina shrugged. 'Yeah, if it happens, great. I'd be pretty stupid to pass up on this opportunity, wouldn't I? But it's not my desperate desire to parade catwalks and be in magazines that's stopping me from reporting Gavin.'

'Then what is it?'

Nina was still sweating, despite the chill that was now entering the room. She dragged a hand across her brow again. 'Izzy, can we leave it, please? I need to go to the toilet.'

She left the room and Isabel swore aloud. Should she stop pushing Nina? She was clearly distressed. It might be best to leave it . . . but on the other hand Isabel felt very strongly that Gavin needed to be stopped. Somebody had to speak up. Perhaps Amber, who had apparently suffered harassment at his hands for years, could do it. But it would be much stronger coming from Nina, with Amber backing her up as a witness.

Isabel understood why women so often didn't report incidents like this. She had recently watched a documentary that detailed what it was like for a victim of rape to go through the whole legal process, and the pitifully low percentage of reported rapes that ended with a conviction. It was the same with assault. Yes, Nina had a witness, but that didn't diminish the trauma of making statements to the police, of standing up in court, of having to relive the encounter over and over again. Isabel liked to think that she wouldn't hesitate to come forward if it happened to her – until she remembered all the times she had been touched, all the suggestive 'jokes' and unwelcome approaches she'd suffered. She had never reported any of those men. She had pretended not to care, pretended to absorb each affront as if it hadn't hurt. Persuaded herself that they hadn't meant any harm. They were just men. It was the way of the world.

Maybe if she was Nina she would want to forget about it too.

She wished she could think straight, that the cobwebs of sleep weren't still clogging her brain.

Nina returned, and Isabel was shocked to see a smear of white powder beneath her left nostril. Isabel knew Nina smoked weed quite regularly but she had never mentioned taking cocaine before.

'You're doing coke?'

Nina rubbed at her nose. 'Please don't tell me off, Izzy. I can't bear it. All you do is judge, judge, judge!'

Isabel held up her hands. 'Hey, I'm not judging you.'

'You are. I don't need to stay here and listen to you lecturing me.' She strode towards the door.

Isabel stepped into her path.

Nina screamed in her face. 'Leave me alone!'

Chapter 50

Nina's expression – the look of a child caught stealing, the hot flush of shame and fear – told Jessica everything. And Nina must have seen the shocked realisation reflected back by Jessica because suddenly the car was moving again, backing out of the parking space, her hands frantically moving the wheel back and forth, engine growling as she stamped on the clutch.

'What the hell is she doing?' Amber asked, stepping forward.

Jessica shouted, 'No!' but it was too late. Head down, Nina reversed at speed out of the parking spot.

Straight into Amber.

She went down, the sickening smack of bone hitting asphalt, and Nina gawped out through the car window, mouth wide open, unable to reverse further, to get away.

Jessica rushed over and knelt by Amber. She wasn't moving and Jessica grabbed her wrist to feel for a pulse, but there was no need – the contact made Amber open her eyes. She tried to move and let out a cry of agony.

'Stay still!' Jessica said, groping in her pocket for her phone. Still crouching on the road, Jessica dialled 999. From the corner of her eye she was aware of Nina getting out of the car, standing a few feet away with her hands in her hair, clearly horrified by what she'd done. Jessica shouted into the phone: 'I need an ambulance.'

She met Nina's eye. 'Police too.'

And Nina ran.

Jessica hesitated. She didn't want to leave Amber here on her own, but she couldn't let Nina get away.

Amber saw her indecision. 'Go. Stop her. I'll be . . . fine.' She grimaced with pain.

'Here. Take this.' Jessica pushed her phone into Amber's hand and sprang to her feet.

Nina was by the door to the building, looking left and right, panicking like a rabbit chased by dogs. To the right was a dead end. Jessica was to Nina's left.

'Don't move!' Jessica shouted, and that broke the spell. Nina turned, yanked open the door and vanished into the building.

With one last look back at Amber, who had closed her eyes, beads of sweat popping on her forehead, Jessica followed.

As she entered the building she heard Nina's footsteps echoing down the stairwell. She called, 'Wait!' but there was no response, only the sound of a door slamming above. Jessica increased her pace until she reached the door of Amber's studio. She peered inside but there was no sign of Nina. She must have gone up further.

Jessica climbed the remaining steps until she reached a heavy grey door with FIRE EXIT stamped in block capitals on its surface. She pushed it open and stepped out on to the flat roof of the building.

Nina stood at the centre of the empty space, shoulders slumped, panting. The rooftops of London stretched out behind her. Up here, the wind was strong and the sun had disappeared behind a thick bank of clouds. Once again Nina met Jessica's eye and Jessica could see the shame and fear there. She was sweating despite the cold, hair whipping into her face. She looked very far from her usual sleek self.

'Tell me,' Jessica said, taking a step towards Nina. She had to shout to make her voice heard through the wind.

Nina said something but her words were blown away, and Jessica had to take another step towards her, so they were now just six feet apart.

'You killed Izzy,' Jessica said.

It had all come to her when she'd seen Nina in that grey car. Because it wasn't just shame and fear she'd seen in Nina's eyes. It was guilt. All at once the pieces slid into place:

Amber had told Izzy about what she'd seen at Gavin's studio. Izzy would have called Nina, told her she wanted to talk to her about it. And after Will and that creep Ryan had left, Nina must have come round. Jessica could picture it. A fight had broken out between them, Nina refusing to back down and Izzy – always so strong-willed, so sure about what was right and wrong – would have kept on at her, trying to persuade her.

And Nina, desperate and afraid, had lashed out. A split second that changed everything.

But Nina was shaking her head. 'No . . . No, I didn't . . .'

'Liar! You killed Izzy because she tried to make you report Gavin for assaulting you. That's right, isn't it? You didn't want to wreck your new modelling career.' Jessica spat out the words with disgust.

Nina looked stricken, but she shook her head again. 'That's not right. I didn't even care about being a model, not that much. Not enough to kill someone. To kill *Izzy*. She was my friend, Jess. Please, you have to believe me.'

'No! You're lying. You murdered her! Oh my God, Nina, how could you live with yourself for all these years? Coming to family lunches? Hanging out with me and my children? Enjoying all the fruits of your fucking modelling career?'

She took another couple of steps towards Nina, and Nina scurried backwards until she was only a few feet from the edge of the rooftop.

Jessica moved closer still, Nina peering back over her own shoulder, aware of the fatal drop behind her, eyes darting left and right, again reminding Jessica of a hunted animal.

'How do you sleep at night, huh?' Jessica yelled. 'How the hell can you live with yourself?'

Nina sobbed. 'I swear, Jess. It was an accident.'

'Then why have you been following me around?'

'I . . .' She made an attempt to stand straight. 'It was only twice. It was because I wanted to talk to you, to tell you . . . But I lost my nerve.'

'You were going to confess? Tell me you killed her?'

'No!' Nina pushed her hair out of her eyes, but the wind whipped it straight back. 'I was going to tell you I was there. Before Izzy did.'

'What?'

Nina hung her head. 'I wanted to tell you before Izzy did.'

It took a second for the meaning to sink in. 'Wait. You think Izzy has actually come back? That her ghost has been talking to Olivia?'

'I didn't know. I saw your mum and she told me how everything had escalated. All the stuff Olivia knew, and how you'd got some expert involved, the same one who helped you with your poltergeist.'

'Oh my God.' Jessica remembered how Nina had always been fascinated by stories about Larry. And she remembered Mum telling her she'd bumped into Nina and had a chat with her.

'You don't know what I've been through the past five years,' Nina said, her voice cracked and pathetic. 'My brother, you, your mum . . . Seeing your pain but not being able to tell you what I saw. And she was my friend too. I loved her too, Jess.'

'Bullshit.'

'It's not . . . I've been on pills ever since it happened. Anti-anxiety pills. Sleeping tablets. Whatever I could get my hands on. You ask how I can sleep – well, that's how. And even then I dream about her. Every night. She's haunted me, Jess, ever since it happened.'

Nina was crying again, but Jessica refused to allow herself to feel sympathy. They were crocodile tears. She jabbed a finger at Nina. 'You feel guilty because you pushed her.'

'No! Guilty because I *saw* her fall. And I hid it. I didn't know if anyone would believe me when I told them it was an accident. I panicked, Jess. There was the cocaine too. I thought if people knew I'd given her the coke they would say it was all my fault, even if they believed I hadn't pushed her. Or they would say I was so high I wouldn't know what I'd done. I couldn't bear the thought of it . . . The shame. I have aunties and uncles, a grandmother . . . What would they think? And worst of all, what would Darpak think? Even if he believed me, he would still hate me. I'd caused the accident. I'd given Izzy drugs.'

Nina took a shuddering breath. 'I rationalised it. Isabel was already dead. What good would it do, telling people I was there?' She looked at Jessica with red eyes. 'I sneaked out the back door. I ran.'

This speech appeared to take away the last of Nina's strength. Her shoulders drooped, her head slumped. The tears dried up, as if she didn't even have the energy to cry.

While she was speaking, the wind had dropped so the air on the rooftop was almost still and calm. Jessica took a half-step forward, clenching her fists, her mind torn in two. Nina sounded sincere. She looked so young, so broken, the beauty that she used to glide through life stripped away to expose the weakness at her core. She looked like a lost little girl, and half of Jessica wanted to comfort her, to take her in her arms and soothe her.

But the other half of her was screaming, her anger gauge swinging so far and fast it had caught fire. This half of her didn't believe a word Nina was saying. Nina's tears were tears of self-pity. She had been caught, exposed. She was terrified of what was going to happen to her and she was spewing lies in a desperate attempt to save her own skin.

It was as if grief and despair and frustration – everything Jessica had felt since she'd lost her sister – were chemical elements, combining in her veins to create an inferno. A red mist enveloped her. She looked at the woman before her and saw a murderer, a thief of life. A liar.

One good shove. That was all it had taken to snuff out Isabel's life. And it would only take one good shove now to get revenge.

To get justice.

Nina must have seen the rage burning in Jessica's eyes because she took a couple of steps away from her, to the very edge of the building.

Jessica moved towards her.

Chapter 51

March 2013

'Leave me alone!' Nina shouted.

Isabel put her hands up in a gesture of surrender. This was getting out of control. She needed to do something to get Nina back onside, to stop her from storming off. She thought for a moment, then said, 'I was going to ask if I could have some of your coke.'

'What?'

'Just a little. I need something to wake me up. If that's okay.'

Nina paused, suddenly unsure.

'Please.'

'Yeah. Okay.' Nina produced a wrap of coke from her bag and knelt by the coffee table, chopping out a couple of lines. 'Help yourself.'

Isabel knelt beside her. It had been a long time since she had done coke. She had forgotten how it made her feel instantly more alert and awake. The sense of certainty came back and she remembered why she had asked Nina to come here.

She sprang to her feet and grabbed hold of Nina's arm.

'You have to report that creep.'

'Oh God. I thought you were going to stop bugging me.'

Nina broke free and escaped through the open doors on to the balcony. Isabel followed, more determined than ever to persuade Nina to do the right thing. It was bitterly cold outside and the air was heavy with the promise of rain.

Isabel went over to the railing, standing with her back to it. Nina remained by the door. She was still sweating. Exactly how much coke had she taken this morning?

'Listen,' Isabel began to say, 'I know why you might not want to report him. I know why you're scared. But you have to do it. And if *you* won't, *I* will.'

She took out her phone and pushed herself up until she was perched on the edge of the railing, legs bent so her feet were flat against the wrought iron. She had done this many times before.

Nina paced in front of her like a crazed polar bear in an enclosure. 'No!' she said. 'You can't.'

'It's not just for you,' Isabel said, the cocaine buzzing in her blood, making her feel absolutely certain she was doing the right thing. 'It's for all the women he's going to do it to in the future. How would you feel if you heard he'd raped someone? Could you live with that? I know I couldn't. That's why I have to do it, Nina. And you're going to talk to the police.'

She unlocked her phone and began to thumb the screen, looking for the number of the local police station.

'Stop it.' Nina stepped closer to her. Her eyes were wide, arms waving, sweat popping on her skin. 'You don't understand.'

But Isabel wasn't listening. She was going to do this, do the right thing. That arsehole Gavin wasn't going to get away with it, not this time.

She was so busy searching for the local police number that she didn't notice Nina step closer to her, not until she looked up and saw Nina right there in her face.

'No,' Nina said. 'I won't let you.' She lunged for the phone.

Instinctively, Isabel recoiled.

There was a moment when she felt herself suspended, teetering. She tried to grab the railing, but it was too late, she had lost her balance, and she heard Nina cry out, and then she was falling. Her life didn't flash before her eyes. All she felt was a screaming blast of panic. Terror.

And then she was gone.

Chapter 52

Jessica stared at Nina through the red mist, arms out before her, not thinking of the consequences, not thinking about anything.

'Please. Jess. What are you doing?' Nina was frozen to the spot, the precipice just a foot behind her.

Now the air was still, Jessica no longer had to raise her voice. 'This is for Izzy,' she said, taking another step forward.

'No, Jess, please.' Nina's words accelerated, tumbling over each other. 'I swear I promise it was an accident, an accident. I tried to grab the phone and she fell and . . . and . . . Jessica please I'm not lying, I'm not!'

'Shut up.'

Nina cowered and looked left and right. She was poised, ready to run, to try to escape. But it was too late. Jessica was too close.

She grabbed hold of Nina's arms, tried to push her, and Nina must have found strength from somewhere – her survival instinct kicking in – because she pushed back, surprisingly strong. Jessica staggered, but still had hold of Nina's arms, and she pulled her towards her, until their faces were almost touching, noses an inch apart. Jessica could smell the sour stench of alcohol on Nina's breath, was so close she could see the red blood vessels in her eyes.

Nina pushed but Jessica pushed back. And though Nina was fighting for her life, Jessica was stronger. Locked together in an embrace, they stumbled towards the edge of the building. From somewhere below, Jessica became aware of a siren, the wail of an ambulance, coming closer. She got hold of the front of Nina's coat and, grunting with effort, pushed her towards the precipice. It loomed up behind her, the drop, the plummet into certain death, into oblivion. Nina cried out, a final wordless plea, and Jessica tensed her muscles, poised to give that final shove, to let go, to send Nina flying towards her end.

Something cold passed through Jessica's body.

It felt like someone stepping through her, like ice dragging across her guts, her lungs, her heart. She froze. At the same time, Nina's eyes went wide and she gasped in shock, like she'd felt it too.

Jessica let go of her.

Nina remained still for a second, mouth open, then she scrambled away from the lip of the building, falling to her hands and knees, panting and retching. Jessica sank to her haunches. The wind had picked up again, and a blast of cold air made her fall forward on to her knees.

Nina lifted her head. 'Did you feel it too?'

Jessica felt like she was emerging from a deep sleep. From a nightmare. She blinked at Nina.

'Did you?' Nina asked. '*Did you feel it?*'

Jessica nodded. 'It was the wind. Just . . .' She broke off, unable to speak. She thought she might vomit and had to fight to hold it back.

Below them, down at street level, the sirens grew closer, then stopped. The ambulance was here. Maybe the police too.

Nina hugged her knees, trembling with shock, opening and closing her mouth several times before she could find any words. She started to talk and it took a second for Jessica to tune in.

'. . . swear it was an accident. I tried to grab the phone because I couldn't let Izzy call the police. But it wasn't because I was worried about not being a model. I did it for Izzy.'

Jessica was trembling too. She could still feel it. That cold that had passed through her. A tiny shard of ice lingered inside, embedded in her heart.

'Gavin threatened me,' Nina went on. 'After what happened at his studio, when Amber dragged me out of there, he called me. I thought he was going to try to justify what he'd done. Maybe even apologise. But he threatened me.'

Jessica still couldn't speak. She could hear voices below, men. The paramedics, she guessed, come to help Amber.

'You know Gavin went to one of Izzy's classes with this girl he was seeing? Carmen?'

Jessica was just about able to nod.

'Well, Gavin said that if I told anyone what had happened, he would ruin Izzy's business. He knows a lot of journalists. He's mates with the editors of most of the tabloids. He said they'd love a juicy story about sex in the suburbs, and that he had already sounded out one of his editor mates. He was going to get Carmen to say she was sexually assaulted at one of the classes, that Izzy had touched her down there. And Carmen was only, like, sixteen at the time. She was still at school.'

Jessica finally spoke. 'What?'

'She looked a lot older – I thought she was in her early twenties. And, of course, it was legal for him to sleep with a sixteen-year-old, but Izzy's classes were meant to be for over-eighteens only. There's no way her business could have survived the scandal.'

Jessica heard a door slam below them.

Nina must have heard it too, as she spoke faster. 'That's why I couldn't do it. I couldn't risk letting Gavin destroy Izzy's business. She'd just been through loads of crap with my brother and she was fragile, Jess. And I couldn't tell Izzy about the threat because I knew she'd go mental, that she wouldn't be able to resist storming round to his studio and making everything worse.'

Jessica closed her eyes. She could see it. Izzy giving Gavin a piece of her mind.

Nina crawled closer to Jessica.

'I can't describe it. What it was like, seeing her fall. The shock of it. I looked down, saw the blood, the way her neck was . . . twisted. I knew she was dead. She had . . . Her phone was lying on top of her body, her hand half-covering it. Oh God, if I hadn't tried to grab it.'

She let out a terrible keening noise.

'I'm so, so sorry,' Nina said, wiping her face with her sleeve and composing herself. 'I don't know how to express how sorry I am. But do you believe me? That it was an accident?'

Did she? Jessica was finding it hard to think. She stared at Nina, who had her arms wrapped round herself, crying again. Jessica forced herself to process what Nina had said. The detail about Gavin threatening Izzy's business, the terrible irony of it, seemed too elaborate for Nina to have invented. And Jessica could see it happening exactly as Nina had described. She'd seen Isabel sit on that balcony railing before, lifting her feet off the ground, completely unafraid.

The door to the rooftop opened and a uniformed policewoman came through.

'Yes,' Jessica said. 'I believe you.'

Nina held her breath.

'But that doesn't mean I can forgive you.'

'I understand.' Nina hung her head. 'I wouldn't forgive me either.'

Nina got to her feet and took a staggering step towards the policewoman, who said, 'Are you Nina Shah? I need you to come with me.'

Before leading Nina away, the cop looked over at Jessica. 'Are you all right?'

Jessica nodded. But it was a lie. She had almost killed someone. Almost done what she had accused Nina of. And something had happened, something that Jessica would never speak of, something she couldn't explain. That feeling, like someone had walked through her body. It had saved Nina. And it had saved Jessica from her worst self.

'But we still have something to do, don't we?' she whispered.

The policewoman said, 'Pardon?'

Jessica smiled. 'I wasn't talking to you.'

Chapter 53

The photo shoot was taking place in Brockwell Park in Herne Hill. Jessica knew this because at lunchtime Gavin had posted a photo of himself on Instagram, sipping from a paper cup outside the cafe in the middle of the park. *Totally stoked for today's shoot!* Jessica recognised Brockwell Hall, where the cafe was located. She'd been there many times with the kids.

It was three o'clock now. The sun would be going down soon and Jessica didn't know if Gavin would still be there. She parked in a side road then walked across the park from its south-east corner, heading to the stately hall in the centre. The sky was ice-blue, clear and bright and cold. White Christmas lights were strung in the trees.

There was no sign of Gavin near the cafe, which was also decked out with festive lights. Jessica asked a young woman who was clearing tables outside if she had seen him, showing her the Instagram snap on her phone. The woman nodded and said, 'I think they went to the lake.'

Jessica knew where she meant. Just past the little community garden and the paddling pool, which was closed for winter, were a number of small duck ponds. Jessica walked around the first pond and saw them, just beyond the spiky bare trees. A young model, posing by the edge of the lake. She was dressed in summer clothes: a T-shirt and short skirt exposing her long brown limbs.

Gavin Lawson was crouching on the ground before the model, the camera obscuring his face. A young man and woman in their early twenties, all cheekbones and boredom, stood behind him.

Gavin stood up and lowered the camera. He saw Jessica coming towards him but it was clear that he didn't know who she was, which wasn't surprising. He had only encountered her once, back in 2012, coming out of Izzy's class with his sixteen-year-old girlfriend.

He had no idea of the impact he'd had on Jessica's life. He probably slept like a baby, conscience clear, unaware of all the damage he had done. Not just to Izzy, but to all the other women he had taken advantage of, and to Jessica and her family too. When Gavin had assaulted Nina it was like he'd dropped a rock into a pond, and the ripples were still spreading. Darpak, Will, Felix, Jessica, Olivia, Amber, Jessica's mum. Nina too. They were all affected. They had all been hurt, contaminated by his actions.

And now she had a plan for Gavin. But she knew she would never be able to rest until she let him know what he had done. She wanted him to know exactly why his life was about to be destroyed. She wanted him to think about it and to remember Isabel until his dying day.

Gavin lit a cigarette as the model put on a coat and approached him. He laughed at something the model said and touched her arm, his hand lingering on the fabric of her sleeve. The model wore an uncomfortable smile. It slipped as she saw Jessica approaching, storming up the path towards them. Gavin must have seen her expression change because he turned to see what the model was staring at, just as Jessica reached him.

His mouth fell open. 'What—?'

Jessica punched him in the face. Her fist connected with his nose – there was a satisfying crunch – and she pulled back her arm to strike him again but he scuttled backwards, out of reach.

She hadn't been planning to do that. But as she'd approached him, seen the smile on his face, evidence that he was happy, she hadn't been able to hold back.

He wasn't smiling any more.

He lifted a hand to his nose then gawped at his bloody fingers. The cigarette still smouldered in his other hand. The model and the two assistants stared at Jessica, but none of them rushed to help.

'Who the fuck are you?' Gavin wiped at his face, smearing his sleeve with blood. The male assistant rooted in his bag and produced a pack of tissues. Gavin snatched it from him.

Jessica had her arm pulled back, fist hovering beside her ear, like a cobra ready to strike once more.

'If you've broken my nose I'm going to fucking sue you, you bitch. Whoever you are.'

'I'm Isabel Shah's sister. Remember her?'

'What? The sex therapist? Didn't she die?'

'Yes, Gavin. She did.'

'And what the fuck's that got to do with me?'

She took a step towards him and he moved back. He was a coward. A joke. His eyes darted sideways, appealing for help, and Jessica was gratified to see how scared of her he was.

'You don't remember what you did to Nina? Nina Shah?'

His eyes darted across to the model and his two assistants, who were all gawping at the scene.

'Piss off,' Gavin said, trying to pull himself up to his full height. He had dropped the cigarette now. It lay burning at his feet. 'Why don't you go and jump off a fucking balcony.'

She hadn't been planning to hit him again. Not until he said that. She leapt at him. One of the judo moves she had learned when she was a kid must have come back to her, because she reached around and grasped the back of his coat, turned sideways and pulled him into her, lifting him and throwing him to the ground. He lay flat on his back, staring up with shock, and she threw herself down, knees on his chest, and grabbed his throat. He tried to push her off but, right now, with the anger coursing through her, she was too strong. He was too weak. She squeezed, pressing against his Adam's apple. He tried to speak but could only hiss, his eyes bulging.

She spotted the half-smoked cigarette lying on the path beside Gavin's head, and snatched it up with her left hand.

She held the tip an inch from his face.

'Which eye?' she said, loosening the grip on his throat a little. He made a retching sound. 'Which eye do you want to keep?'

He tried to thrash his head, but she pushed it against the concrete path. She lowered the burning cigarette a fraction. She was going to do it. Maybe she should do both, ruin him. No more photographs. No more staring at women. He fought against her, but it was as if her fury made her twice as heavy.

'Don't do it.'

The voice came from above her. It was the model, looking down at Jessica.

'I can guess what he did to you or those women you mention, but he's not worth it.' She sneered at Gavin. 'He's *really* not worth it.'

The model took the cigarette from Jessica's hand and flicked it away towards the lake.

Gavin opened his eyes. He tried to look defiant but it didn't work. All Jessica could see was fear.

Slowly, she shifted off him and got to her feet. Gavin's assistants hurried to his aid, and the model gave Jessica a smile, lighting her own cigarette and settling down on a bench as the scene played out before her.

Jessica gave Gavin one final look, dusted herself down, then walked back up the path towards the exit of the park.

She looked up at the Christmas lights, twinkling into life among the bare branches of the trees, and as Gavin yelled and swore behind her, Jessica was sure that she could feel Isabel walking beside her.

Isabel was smiling. 'Nice one, Jess,' she said.

Epilogue

Nine months later

'Are you having a good time?'

'It's the best *ever*,' Olivia said, reaching up and flinging her arms around Jessica's neck. 'Thanks, Mummy.'

Jessica hadn't really needed to ask the question. Olivia had been running around with a huge grin on her face since the moment she'd woken up and bounced on to their bed, yelling for presents. She'd been spoiled this year, more than ever, with a new scooter, a hugely overpriced Shopkins playset and lots of cuddly toys to replace those whose eyes had been cut out back in the winter. Jessica had attempted to sew the eyes back on but her efforts had made the toys look crazed and malevolent, like taxidermy gone horribly wrong. In the end she'd taken them to the rubbish dump, whispering an apology to the stuffed animals as she chucked them into the burnables bin. But as she got back into her car she had felt a tremble of relief, as if the toys had retained a trace of the madness that had invaded their household back in November, and by having them burned she was finally exorcising that demon.

Saying goodbye to the ghost, once and for all.

It was a glorious August afternoon, the sky as rich and blue as it ever got in England, the kind of heat that made Jessica feel the need to constantly check the children were covered up or suitably smeared with sunblock. Olivia's fifth birthday party was taking place at a city farm near Wimbledon and she and a dozen of her friends were running around, out of their minds on Fruit Shoots and pick 'n' mix, cooing over the ducks and chickens and rabbits, clambering on the tractor. There had even been a pony ride for some of the kids, though Olivia hadn't wanted to do it, declaring that she didn't like 'real' ponies, only the plastic, brightly coloured ones she collected. The feeling appeared to be mutual, as the horses seemed a little spooked when Olivia went near them, backing up, ears flattening and nostrils flaring.

'Izzy never liked horses either,' Mum said to Jessica. 'It was only you who wanted a pony. Izzy was always happier on a bike.'

'Yeah. And Izzy got her bike. I never got my pony.'

'You had a bike too!' Mum said, and was about to launch into a defence of her parenting record when Jessica laughed and pulled her into an embrace. 'What was that for?' Mum asked when Jessica let her go. 'Are you feeling all right?'

'I'm great, Mum. I just wanted to give you a hug. Is that wrong?'

'Don't complain,' said Pete, squeezing Mum's arm. 'Come on, Mo, I want to have a look at the goats.' They wandered away. Jessica could hear Pete telling Mum what amazing animals they are. As Jessica watched, Olivia ran over to join them, and Mum took her hand, leading her into the goat pen.

Jessica sat back down at the trestle table on the lawn near the cafe and watched the children playing. Will was standing by the fence with Felix, pointing at the cows, and he must have sensed Jessica watching because he turned his head and smiled at her, showing his new tooth. He had had a dental implant to replace the tooth Ryan had knocked out.

She blew him a kiss.

Somehow, the events of the winter had reinvigorated their marriage. She still felt a little guilty for suspecting him of murdering Izzy, and also a little angry with him for not telling her he'd seen Izzy that day. But they had talked about it to the point where they were both sick of the subject. Now they were going on more regular date nights. Even their sex life had improved, though Jessica had balked at Will's suggestion that they try out Blissful Massage.

'I think regular married sex is fine, if that's okay with you,' she had said, laughing at his look of relief.

She was about to open the newspaper again, for the tenth time that day, when Darpak came over and sat down opposite her.

'Great party,' he said. 'The kids seem to be having an amazing time.'

'Yeah.' She smiled at him. There was a tiny part of her that still bristled at the thought of him cheating on Izzy. She had talked to Will about it and made a decision. If Izzy had been prepared to forgive him and move on, then she would too. They hadn't been round quite so often for Sunday lunch recently, but they still saw Darpak monthly. He would always be part of their lives.

'I miss Nina, though,' Darpak said. 'Despite everything.'

Nina had been arrested for careless driving after reversing into Amber. Luckily, Amber hadn't broken anything. She was left with nothing but bruises and a head injury from where she'd hit the road, from which she'd recovered after a few days. Nina appeared in court, was fined and given points on her licence. She'd also moved down to Brighton. Not too far, but far enough that Jessica didn't have to see her.

The police had also interviewed Nina about what had happened the day Izzy died. DS Ward had called Jessica afterwards to explain that, without any evidence to contradict Nina's account, they were not going to charge her. The CPS had looked at it and decided there wasn't a realistic prospect of proving that Nina's actions were unlawful, especially as she claimed she was trying to protect Izzy when she attempted to grab her phone. The coroner's ruling of accidental death would stand.

'I know,' Jessica said to Darpak. 'But . . . I can't have her around. Maybe one day, but not yet.'

'I understand. I feel the same. Except . . . well, we're blood, aren't we? And if she'd told me everything from the start, I would have forgiven her.'

'Would you, though?'

He stared into his glass of Coke, as if the answer was among the bubbles. 'Probably. Maybe. I miss having her around, though.' Another pause. 'But not as much as I miss Izzy.'

'Me too.'

'It's like . . . I know you probably don't want to hear this after everything that happened, but I can't help but feel Izzy's with us on days like this. Joining in with the fun. Secretly trying to persuade Olivia's friends' mums and dads to come along to her classes.' Darpak laughed. 'I keep expecting to turn a corner and see her.'

She reached across and squeezed his hand. 'I feel the same.'

'I miss her,' he said after a beat.

'We all do. But Darpak, listen. Next time you come, you can bring Sunita.' That was his new girlfriend. Finally, after five long years, he was moving on. 'She'd be very welcome.'

'Thank you, Jess.'

He got up from the table and muttered something about needing to find the loo, leaving Jessica thinking about Nina. She was happy that Nina hadn't been charged with manslaughter, not least because it meant she'd been able to help with what happened next.

Jessica pulled the copy of *The Herald* towards her and opened it to pages four and five, drinking in the headline again.

GAVIN LAWSON: MORE WOMEN COME FORWARD.

Nina had been the first to accuse Gavin of sexual assault, back in the spring. Amber was her witness. They went to one of the more liberal newspapers, one where Gavin didn't have any friends. Amber had already called a number of other women who she had seen suffer at Gavin's hands, and several of them were willing to back up Nina's story. A few years earlier they might have been reluctant, but now, after a series of high-profile revelations against numerous movie producers, actors and other public figures, they were emboldened.

The story was huge. Over the following week, every magazine publisher and brand Gavin worked with broke ties with him, each of them expressing great disappointment and disgust. The company that was meant to be publishing his next book cancelled his contract. Suddenly everyone was scrambling to disassociate themselves from him. Of course, they had all known what he was like. A lot of people had turned a blind eye over the years. But now his name was toxic.

And then a nineteen-year-old model had come forward, given courage by Gavin's new pariah status, and reported that he had raped her a year earlier, on a photo shoot at his studio. And then more women came forward. Six in all. Two of them accused him of rape.

Yesterday, the day before Olivia's birthday, Gavin had been arrested.

It didn't make Jessica happy knowing how many women he had assaulted. Nor was she shocked to learn he had gone further, committing rape. He would deny it, of course. It would be his word against the women's. Maybe he wouldn't be found guilty of that crime, because rape was so sickeningly hard to prove. But his career was ruined, along with his reputation and his legacy.

It wouldn't bring Izzy back, nor undo the damage he had done to all those women, and to Jessica and her family. But it was a form of justice. It was the best she could hope for.

ϖ

Jessica got up from the table just as Olivia came running over. Mum and Pete came out of the goat pen behind her.

'Mummy, can we get a goat?'

'I don't think so, sweetheart. You know goats eat everything?'

'They'll eat all the washing off the line,' Mum said as she arrived.

She seemed faintly troubled, and Jessica asked her what was wrong.

'I'll tell you in a minute. Olivia, why don't you go and play with your friends? Look, isn't that Grace?' Olivia whirled round, spotted her friend over by the fence, and skipped away to join her.

'What is it?' Jessica asked.

'Just . . . something weird happened.'

Jessica rolled her eyes. 'Don't tell me. Izzy appeared in the goat shed. Or was it Larry?'

'Don't make fun of me, Jess.'

Pete had sat down at the trestle table and was mopping his head with a handkerchief. 'Yes, listen to what your mother has to say.'

'All right, now you're scaring me. What is it?'

Mum sat down too. 'Well, we were feeding the goats and Pete was talking to Livvy all about man's relationship with them, and the long history of domestic animals . . .'

'I don't think she was really listening,' Pete interjected.

Jessica smiled. Who could blame her?

Mum went on. 'And Livvy was stroking this white nanny goat, feeding it out of her palm, really enjoying it. One of the attendants was in there, keeping an eye on things. A young woman. Anyway, Olivia put her hand on the goat's head and said, "Poor thing." Then she turned to me and said, "Do goats go to heaven?" And then she got tears in her eyes and started trying to hug this animal and she kept saying, "Poor old goat."'

Pete spoke up. 'Tell her what the attendant said, Mo.'

'I'm coming to that.' She tutted. 'Olivia went off to the corner and the attendant came up to me and said, "Your granddaughter must be psychic." Because guess what? That goat looked absolutely fine, the picture of health, but apparently it's really sick. It's got something wrong with its heart and they're expecting it to die any day.'

'Weird, isn't it?' said Pete.

Jessica stared at him, then at Mum. 'Are you sure it didn't look sick?'

'Yes. Like I said, it looked completely healthy.'

A silence fell between them for a minute. In the distance, Jessica could hear Olivia shrieking with laughter. Over by the fence, Will was chatting with one of the other dads. The sky was just as blue and cloud-free as it had been ten minutes earlier. But now Jessica was cold.

'You never got to the bottom of it, did you?' Mum said, dropping her voice to a stage whisper.

She meant the predictions Olivia had made. Pete getting sick. The school catching fire. And the dinner lady, Pat Shelton, falling and dying at home.

'No. Ryan still denies it. But he would, wouldn't he? He'd be charged with murder and arson otherwise.'

'It had to be him,' Pete said. He was certain Ryan had slipped something into the food at the RAFA Club, making him ill. And Ryan didn't have an alibi for when Pat had died, or when the school had caught fire. He said he'd been at home on his own.

Olivia refused to talk about it. Whenever anyone asked her if Mr Cameron had told her about Pat Shelton dying, along with the other things she had 'predicted', Olivia said she couldn't remember. It was frustrating because Jessica knew the answer was in her daughter's head somewhere. She had demonstrated almost total recall of her conversations with Ryan, after all. But Olivia had clearly decided she didn't want to talk about it any more. She was done. And, really, Jessica couldn't blame her.

Right now, Ryan was in prison for abducting and attacking Will, because the CPS had decided they were the only charges that would stick. He had pleaded guilty to them, in fact, and the police had told Jessica, and Pat's family, that this was the best they could hope for. Plus, of course, he would never work with children again.

Jessica was sure Ryan was guilty of everything, even if they couldn't prove it. Mum, on the other hand, wasn't so sure. Because even though she now knew Izzy had hoaxed them when she was a child, Mum still couldn't let go of her long-held beliefs.

'So how did Olivia know about the goat?' she asked.

'She couldn't really know,' Jessica replied. 'It doesn't mean anything.'

'But what if Ryan unleashed something with all his antics? What if Izzy did actually come back and tell Olivia things that were going to happen? Or maybe it's nothing to do with Izzy. Olivia could have a gift. Simon said—'

'Mum. Stop it!' Jessica couldn't help but snap. 'I don't want to hear any more about it. It's time we put all that nonsense behind us forever. Olivia's moved on. We should too. Okay?'

'But what—?'

'*Okay?*'

Mum pressed her lips together. 'Fine.'

Jessica nodded. 'Good. Now I'm going to spend some time with my daughter on her birthday.'

But as she walked over to Olivia, shielding her eyes from the sun, she couldn't shake it. The fear. No matter how much she told herself that Ryan was guilty of everything, and that it didn't matter what Olivia had said about some silly goat, a niggling doubt remained. Because she had felt something up on that rooftop, when that chill, that unforgettable chill, had passed through her body. Sometimes she would wake up in the small hours, convinced it had been Isabel, stopping her from doing something she would regret forever.

It was only on days like this, when the sun was high in the sky, and ghosts and spirits and the idea of an afterlife seemed like nothing more than make-believe, that she was able to persuade herself otherwise.

It had been the wind, that was all. Just the wind.

Acknowledgments

First and foremost, thank you to my editors, Laura Deacon and Ian Pindar, for asking all those difficult questions and forcing me to raise my game. Where would we writers be without good editors?

Thanks too to my agent, Sam Copeland, and to everyone at Thomas & Mercer, including Hatty, Eoin, Nicole, Gracie and Sana.

For answering my questions and helping with research, thank you to Neil White, Nick Thompson and Elliott Finch.

Several readers volunteered their names for characters in this book: Suzanna Salter, Michelle Ward and Nichola Rose. I hope you like meeting your namesakes!

A couple of books were helpful when researching this novel: *Paranormal Intruder* by Caroline Mitchell (an account of a poltergeist visitation which I highly recommend); and *This House is Haunted* by Guy Lyon Playfair.

Thank you as always to my family, especially my wife, Sara, who helped me brainstorm ideas and who was, as always, my first reader. Thanks too to Ellie and Poppy, and my sons, Archie and Harry, who helped inspire this book in multiple ways!

I want to thank some members of the crime-writing community who do great things to bring writers and readers together: Tracy Mearns of Tequila Mockingbird; Tracy Fenton of THE Book Club; Wendy

Clarke of The Fiction Café; Shell Baker of the Crime Book Club; and Anne Cater of Book Connectors.

Finally, a huge thank you to all my loyal readers, including the members of my Facebook page and all the readers on Twitter and Instagram. You make being an author a far from lonely occupation, and I love hearing from you. And if this is your first Mark Edwards book, thanks for giving it a go!

Free *Short Sharp Shockers* Box Set

Join Mark Edwards Readers Club and immediately get a free box set of stories: 'Kissing Games', 'Consenting Adults' and 'Guardian Angel'. You will also receive regular news and access to exclusive giveaways. Join here: www.markedwardsauthor.com/free

About the Author

Mark Edwards writes psychological thrillers in which scary things happen to ordinary people.

He has sold over 2 million books since his first novel, *The Magpies*, was published in 2013, and has topped the bestseller lists seven times. His other novels include *Follow You Home*, *The Retreat*, *Because She Loves Me*, *The Devil's Work* and *The Lucky Ones*. He has also co-authored six books with Louise Voss.

Originally from Hastings in East Sussex, Mark now lives in Wolverhampton with his wife, their three children, two cats and a golden retriever.

Mark loves hearing from readers and can be contacted through his website, www.markedwardsauthor.com, or you can find him on Facebook (@markedwardsbooks), Twitter (@mredwards) and Instagram (@markedwardsauthor).